BREAKING DOWN

THE BREAKING SERIES BOOK 4

JULIANA HAYGERT

COPYRIGHT

AUTHOR'S NOTE

I hope you enjoy reading *Breaking Down*!

Don't forget to sign up for my Newsletter to find out about new releases, cover reveals, giveaways, and more!

If you want to see exclusive teasers, help me decide on covers, read excerpts, talk about books, etc, join my reader group on Facebook: Juliana's Club!

English - Portuguese

For a complete list of words used in the series <u>click here</u>!

Note that some words and expression don't have a perfect literal translation. The translation you see here is the one that fits the context of my novels.

Abobaba – fool, idiot

Ai – ouch

Ainda bem – thank goodness

Até depois – see you later

Beijinho – a sweet made with condensed sweetened milk

Bem – fine, good, well

Boa noite – good night

Boa sorte – good luck

Boa tarde – good afternoon

Bom – well

Bom dia – good morning

Bomba – item to drink chimarrão with

Bombacha – typical pants used by gaúchos

Branquinho – same as Beijinho

Brigadeiro – a sweet made with condensed sweetened milk and cocoa powder

Café colonial – continental breakfast

Calma – calm down

Carreteiro – typical dish made of leftover steaks from barbecues

Chato – a name for someone who annoys you

Chimarrão – herb-based drink from the south of Brazil

Churrasco – Brazilian barbecue

Churrasqueira – a type of a grill where Brazilian barbecue is made

Claro – of course

Credo – jeez/damn

Cuia – kind of cup to drink chimarrão with

Dança folclórica gaúcha – typical dance from the south of Brazil

De nada – you're welcome

De novo – again

Delícia – delicious

Desculpa – sorry

Deus do céu – Lord above/Oh my God

Droga – crap

E aí – what's up?

É assim – this way

Eita – whoa

Então – so?

Eu não vou me atrasar – I won't be late

Eu te amo – I love you

Eu vou te matar – I'll kill you

Feijoada – dish made with black beans

Feliz Páscoa – Happy Easter

Filha da puta (daughter of a bitch), mimada (spoiled), china (it's like *prenda*, but in a bad way), rapariga sem vergonha (girl without shame), invejosa (jealous) – insulting names for women/girls

Filho duma puta – son of a bitch

Gaúcho(a) – people from the south of Brazil

Graças a Deus – thank God, thank goodness

Grande coisa – whatever

Guria – girl

Idiota – idiot

Irmã – sister

Irmãzinha – little sister

Mãe – mother

Me dá – give it to me

Me deixa em paz – leave me alone

Merda – shit

Meu Deus – my God

Morena – brunette, but in Brazil this term is used in a caring way, like darling or sweetie

Não – no

Negrinho – same as Brigadeiro

Nossa – wow/whoa

O que – what?

O que é isso – what is this?

Obrigado (a) – thanks

Oi – hi/hello

Ótimo – great

Pai – father

Pão de queijo – cheese bread

Parabéns - congratulations

Peão/Peões –cowboys in Brazil

Perfeita(o) – perfect

Pois então – well/you see

Por favor – please

Por que/por quê – why

Porque – because

Porcaria – crap/jeez/damn/shit/bad stuff

Porra – fuck/shit

Prazer – Pleasure, a short way of saying "nice to meet you"

Prenda – just like a gaúcha

Presta atenção – pay attention

Preta – black

Puta merda – fuck/shit/bullshit

Puta que pariu – goddamn it, holy shit, fuck

Que droga – crap/jeez/damn/this sucks

Que foi – what?

Que mentira – what a lie

Que nada – nonsense

Que porcaria é essa – what the hell is this?

Querida – dear

Rio Grande do Sul – southernmost state in Brazil

Sem rodeios – without rodeos, means without dillydallying

Senhorita – miss

Sério – really

Sete de Setembro – Brazil's Independence Day

Sim – yes

Tá bom/bem – okay

Tá tudo bem – it's okay

Também – too/also

Tchau – bye

Tche – common expression used by gaúchos – it can mean many things. A salutation, an exasperated exclamation, or even addressing someone

Te amo – I love you

Te comporta – behave

Tia – aunt

Tio – uncle

Tudo bem/Tudo bom – how are you?

Um minuto – one minute

Vai com – go with

Veado – deer. In Brazil, it's a nickname for homosexuals. Between friends, it's used as a friendly, teasing name.

Vestibular – an extensive and hard test Brazilians take to enter college – each college has its own vestibular test and if the student doesn't pass it, he/she doesn't enter that particular college.

Você – you

 Created with Vellum

1

GABI

"Hey, pretty boy." I reached over the stall door and rested my hand on Tostado's muzzle. "Did you have a good night sleep?"

My horse neighed, bobbing his head up and down. I smiled. If only he could really communicate with me. But maybe he could. I had had him for more than three years now. If he did understand, he would be the only one lately. Horse or human.

My phone beeped. I fished it from my jeans' back pocket and checked the message.

Priscila: *Practice is canceled.*

Merda.

Me: *Why?*

Priscila: *The other girls are not coming. It would be just you and me.*

Me: *But the tournament is coming up.*

And I would be away for the next ten days. We had to practice now, and then hard once I was back, or we would lose the tournament. Badly.

Priscila: *That's the other thing. The club is canceling the women's tournament. They didn't get enough registrations, so they are only going to have the men's tournament.*

A wave of rage swept through me.

Me: *That's bullshit.*

Priscila: *I'm with you, but unless we come up with at least three other teams before next weekend, there will be no tournament for us.*

Man, this sucked. We had barely four permanent girls to play on our team. We actually had six because one or more never could meet up for practice or games. Time and time again, there were two or three of us who showed up, and we had to forfeit games because of it.

Women's polo was the worst, especially in Brazil.

I sighed.

If only I had someone to help me. Someone who had some influence and could talk to the club and ask them to keep the women's category, even with only two or three teams signed up.

The person in my mind walked into the stable and a conspiring grin spread across my lips.

Me: *All right. I'll talk to you later.*

I stashed my phone back into my pocket and turned my smile to the man approaching me.

"*Oi pai.*" I greeted my father. Like all Fernandeses, my father was tall with broad shoulders and bright green-blue eyes. Although, now in his mid-fifties, he didn't have as much hair as my brother and my cousins.

"*Bom dia*, Gabi." He glanced at my horse, then at me. "Going out for a ride this early?"

"No. I have to finish packing."

His brows furrowed. "Oh, yes. You're going to visit your brother. You're leaving tonight, right?"

"*Sim.*"

"Don't your classes start soon?"

I groaned. "*Sim.* In two weeks." All I wanted was to forget about that for now. I wanted to go to Santa Barbara, have a great time with my brother, cousins, and friends, and enjoy my freedom before college life tied me down. I shuddered. "I'll be back in ten days. Four days should be enough to get ready for college."

There was nothing else to do, really. I was signed up for my classes, I had all the material I needed, and my accommodations and transportation were all set up—I would stay in our townhouse in the city during the weekdays and come back to the ranch on the weekends.

"That's good." He reached over and rested a big hand on my shoulder. "Finally starting college. It'll be a big day."

"*Sim* ..." I pressed my lips into a thin line, trying to come up with the right words. "*Pai*, hm, you know the country club has a polo tournament coming up, right?"

"Yes, we're sponsoring it, as always."

"So ... they said they don't have enough women's teams signed up so they are thinking about canceling the women's category. I was thinking that maybe you could—"

"That's good," he interrupted me.

I gaped. "W-what?"

"Isn't the tournament right when your classes start?"

It would actually be a week later. "Yes ..."

"It would be hard to play the games and attend classes. This way, you can focus on college. Besides, we both know that there's no future in polo for you. You're a great player, Gabi, almost as good as your brother and cousins, but you know that women's polo isn't going anywhere. You can fight for it, but you'll only be wasting your time. Better to focus on college, which is a more concrete path."

I clamped my mouth so the words of outrage and frustration didn't spill past my lips, and clenched my fist. I knew he wasn't trying to be harsh. He was just stating the facts—and he was right. I knew he was right. But that didn't mean I had to accept it.

If I had to go to college to satisfy my parents while I worked toward my dream, so be it. One way or another, I would play polo for a living. I would live my dream. Someday.

WITH A HAPPY SIGH, I plopped down on the couch and propped my legs on the coffee table. Now, here was exactly where I wanted to be.

"Hey, if you're gonna put your paws there, take off your shoes."

The company, though.

I rolled my eyes and lifted my hand, giving my brother the finger.

He groaned, and beside him, Hilary chuckled. "Gui, let her be," she said.

"But her boots are dirty," he complained. I glanced over my shoulder and witnessed as my brother, my big, strong brother, pouted at his girlfriend.

Hilary chuckled again and waved him off. "You do that all the time."

"That's different," he snapped, glaring at me.

Shaking her head, Hilary whirled around and grabbed a tub of ice cream from the fridge.

"Oh, I want some too," I said.

"One scoop? Two scoops? Three scoops?" she asked, grabbing bowls from the cabinets.

Gui took the tub from her and began serving the ice cream— our Friday afternoon snack. Looking at them moving around the kitchen like they had been doing that for years, no one would have guessed they had only been dating for six months. And, last week on Valentine's Day, Gui invited Hilary to move in with him. And she had accepted. They were moving her stuff in this weekend, and I would probably help, since I was here visiting.

We had a big party with lots of food coming up tonight, so I just said, "One scoop is fine. For now."

"Aren't you going to ask how many scoops I want?" Gui asked her sarcastically. She rolled her eyes and handed him a chocolate bar. He wasn't a fan of ice cream, but he always made some kind of joke when we were all eating it.

I picked up the remote from the coffee table and turned on the TV. Even Netflix here was different from in Brazil—there were more movies and series options here. And I wanted to find a new obsession to binge during the remaining nine days I had here. Not that I wanted to spend my time watching TV, but everyone else was busy. Gui, Leo, Ri, and Pedro had practice, Bia and Garrett went to vet school, Hilary would go back to L.A. on Sunday night for her classes, Hannah had the ranch, and Iris was in college. They would all be busy during the day and I would be alone. Sometimes, I wondered why I even bothered visiting them outside of holidays.

A soft shuffling sound came from the hallway leading to the bedrooms and Pedro came into the room, dragging his flip-flops across the hardwood floor. He looked like shit—apparently he and Iris had had a big fight and hadn't spoken in four days. And Pedro refused to tell anyone about it.

"I heard the word scoops." Even his voice sounded like shit. He glanced at Hilary, then shifted his gaze to the bowls of ice cream. "Can I have some too, please?"

"Sure," Hil said. She reached behind them and grabbed another bowl, and Gui served him.

Pedro plopped down on the couch beside me and started devouring his ice cream.

I couldn't take his miserable looks. "Want to talk about it?"

"No," he grumbled.

"Okay." I scooted a little away from him, pretending I was afraid of him. "Sorry for asking."

He sighed and looked at me. "No, sorry. I'm just …" He sighed again. "I don't want to talk about it."

Hil and Gui joined us in the living room. They sat on the other couch and Gui put his feet up the coffee table—but he had on socks.

Trying to break the awkward silence, Hil glanced at me. "Gui told me your classes start in March. Vet school without pre-vet. So cool."

In Brazil, there was no pre-vet, pre-med, or pre-law. A person wanting to become a veterinarian only needed to apply for it and take a test called *vestibular*. If the person passed it, she was in. Those majors took one or two years longer than other degrees.

"Not that cool, when you don't really want to do it," I muttered, shoving my spoon in my ice cream.

"Give it a chance," Gui said. He had already finished his chocolate bar. "Maybe you'll love it and won't want to do anything else."

"I doubt it."

"You'll see," my brother said. "I bet it'll change everything."

Hilary scrunched her nose. "March. What an odd time to start the semester."

"You have to remember that it's still summer there right now," Pedro said, surprising us. I thought he was lost in thought, but apparently he had been paying attention to our conversation. "The school year goes from March to early December, with a two- or three-week break between semesters in July, when it's winter."

Hil nodded. "Right. I keep forgetting that." She turned her eyes to me again. "Just two more weeks, then. I don't get it. It's impossible that you aren't at least a little excited."

I groaned. "At first, I thought I would be, but now that it's getting close … ugh, I'm so not ready for this." And, even though I had just turned twenty, most of my classmates would be eighteen or nineteen. I know. One or two years didn't really make a huge difference, but since I was trying to run away from college, any excuse was a good excuse. "I want to play polo."

Pedro frowned. "I thought you were playing. Don't you have a tournament coming up?"

"I wish. I have six *gurias* on my team, and if I can get two together to practice, it's a miracle. As for the tournament ..." Frustration filled my chest as I remembered it. "The club isn't having it. There will be no women's category. Again."

My brother tsked. "That sucks."

"It does," I whispered. "If only there was a women's team at the club here. They could hire me and give me a visa, like they did with you guys."

"I don't think there are any women's teams around here," Gui said.

"Yeah, never heard of any," Pedro said. "Only private groups, I think, but those won't get you a visa."

My chest deflated some more. "I know they won't."

Hil reached across the couches and held my hand in hers. "Don't worry too much, Gabi. I'm sure things will work out the way they are supposed to."

I squeezed her hand and offered her a small smile, glad this beautiful, amazing girl was my brother's girlfriend and my dear friend.

Although, as much as I would love to believe her, I wasn't so sure.

I SHOULD HAVE GIVEN Bia some credit. My cousin wouldn't do anything halfway, so when she mentioned having Garrett's surprise birthday party at a restaurant, I thought it was odd. At a restaurant? So it would be only us—and "only us" was already a lot of people. I had expected more from her.

We stopped at the restaurant's hostess. She led us to a back room and I knew I had been right. Bia didn't do anything halfway.

The back room was a large event room with tables and chairs lining the place, a bar along the back wall, a small dance floor in the middle, and double glass doors that led directly to the restaurant's bar.

When we arrived, the place was already half full.

"I thought Garrett was from out of town," I said as we walked into the back room.

"He is, but you know Bia," Gui said. He held Hil's hand tightly in his. It was cute. "She's friends with everyone, so everyone is friends with Garrett too."

Beside me, Pedro groaned. "I think I'm gonna just ..." He gestured toward the bar, and without saying hi to anyone, he sidestepped and made a beeline to the bar.

Before we left the apartment, Pedro had complained about having to come to a party. We almost left him there, but Gui insisted Bia would be upset with him, and Garrett was his friend, so Pedro agreed to come. I guess he'd be drowning his sorrows with alcohol all night long.

"I wish there was something we could do to make him feel better," Hil said.

"Have any of you talked to Iris?" I asked.

"Bia said she tried, but Iris shut her out," Gui said.

That didn't make sense.

We reached the sea of people and found the rest of our family. A big table had been set up for us. *Tio* João Pedro and *tia* Agnes sat in the center, while Ri, Leo, and Hannah stood a few steps behind them, talking and laughing. In the small crowd, I also recognized Reese, Malcolm, Lucas, Megan, Blaire, and Andrea, and more people from the club. But there were a lot of twenty-something girls and guys here who I didn't know.

After greeting a few people we knew, Gui, Hil, and I joined *tio* João Pedro and *tia* Agnes at our table. Tia Agnes pulled me into a hug. I had arrived yesterday afternoon, so I hadn't seen most of my family yet.

"Glad to have you around for a few days," *tia* Agnes said. "When the guys are practicing and you don't have much to do, come have a *chimarrão* with me."

I smiled at her. "I sure will."

I greeted Leo, Hannah, and Ri—I embraced them like I hadn't seen them in an entire year.

"I heard you're starting college soon," Hannah said with a smile. "Decided to settle down, hm?"

"Decided? More like was obligated."

"I know it's not what you wanted, but you should give it a chance," Ri said. "College is a good thing."

I scrunched my nose. I knew what they were trying to do—sounding all cheerful and happy, like college was a great thing, to make me feel better—but it wasn't working.

"Not good, apparently," Hannah said.

"Sorry, guys. I know college is a good thing and there are a lot of people who would do anything to be accepted and can't, but ... it's not exactly what I want." I felt and sounded like a broken record. They all knew what I wanted.

Gui changed subjects and asked Ri about his latest girlfriend. Or whatever he was calling the girls he spent time with. He had been Gui's wingman when both of them were single and my brother was the one with all the girlfriends, but since Gui started dating Hil, that had changed. Ri now was out all the time and with a different girl every weekend.

At least that was probably the only topic that didn't involve horses or riding or ranching or polo. Living with this family wasn't easy.

Hannah's phoned beeped and she glanced at the screen.

"They're coming," she said to us. Then, she turned around. "Everyone, Bia is bringing Garrett now. Get ready."

Excitement made its way through my chest. I loved a good party, and even though I didn't know Garrett well, he seemed like a good guy.

Someone turned off a couple of lights, making the room darker than it already was, and we all stayed out of the main door's line of sight.

"Just a second. I need to check on something," Bia's voice was low. The sound of boot heels clicked across the tile flooring.

"What is it?" Garrett asked, his voice just outside.

Bia stepped into the room, pulling Garrett by his hand.

"Surprise!" we yelled together.

The lights came back on, casting the place into its previous dim mood.

With wide eyes, Garrett stared at Bia, then at the guests, then at Bia again. "You're sneaky." He smiled at her. "You did all this?"

Bia shrugged. "Not alone."

Still stunned, Garrett went around, greeting the guests.

Our group was the last.

After I embraced Garrett and congratulated him, Bia wound her arms tight around me. "*Guria*, so glad you're here!"

"Me too," I whispered in her ear.

Our circle grew with Bia and Garrett added to the mix. Then, Malcolm joined us and suddenly the subject switched back to polo. The practices, the next tournaments, their rankings ... It was all too much for me.

"I'm gonna go get a drink," I muttered to no one before weaving through the crowd to the bar.

"Here." A hand closed around my arm and pulled me to the side. "Gabi will decide for us," Megan said.

I stared at her, then at the smiling faces of Blaire and Andrea. "What did I do?"

Megan chuckled. "Nothing, silly. We just need another opinion."

I frowned. I couldn't say Megan and the others were friends of mine, but they were people from the polo world. Their families belonged to the club where the guys played. Despite myself, I felt a little jealous they had been born amid it all. I had, too, but in another country.

I straightened. "Okay."

Blaire hooked her arm on mine and leaned in close. "See that couple standing with Reese and Lucas over there?" She jutted her chin out and I followed the line until my eyes landed on a couple talking to Reese and Lucas. I was used to overhearing Megan, Blaire, and Andrea gossiping about guys like they were on the runway, and most of the time, they were model material, but this guy wasn't. The young man was tall and looked regal in slacks and a dress shirt. What the guy was lacking in looks, the girl had in spades. She was stunning, and she wore a red dress that had been molded to her body.

"*Sim*. What about them?"

"Their names are Bryce and Alyssa, and they are new members at the club," Andrea said. "Since they joined a couple of weeks ago, a rumor has been going around."

Megan showed a sly smile. "They say that Alyssa is poor, like almost the homeless kind, and only married Bryce for his money."

I glanced at girls. They smiled widely, and even though they probably didn't even notice it, their bodies were turned to each other, their arms always touching—that when they weren't absently touching each other on the arm or waist.

"I don't know," I finally said.

"Come on," Blaire said, tugging on our hooked arms. "She is obviously trying too hard."

Maybe I was seeing things, but the girl's smile did look too wide, and she did smile at her husband way too often. But that could simply be love. Passion. She was in love with her husband and that was a good thing.

"I honestly don't know."

"Ugh, you're no help." Andrea rolled her eyes. "We have to find out."

"It's not like I can glance at them and read their minds."

"We know that," Megan said, only missing a duh at the end of her sentence. "But we thought maybe you could see something we were missing. A telltale gesture or something."

"It's okay," Blaire said. "We can continue investigating."

The three of them chuckled, and they suddenly reminded me of three witches plotting to take over the town. Or the club, in this situation.

I stepped back from their circle, afraid they would notice me sneaking off, but they were already too engrossed in the next rumor. Those three were all about the rumors.

To my luck, Pedro sat in the middle of the bar, and there were two vacant stools to his left.

I took one and glanced at him. "You all right over here?"

He didn't take his eyes from his whiskey glass. "Never been better."

"Pedro ..." I started, but shut my mouth because I really didn't have any idea of what I should say to him. We still didn't know what had happened with Iris, and I wouldn't push the subject now.

The bartender showed up across the counter a few seconds later. "What can I get for you, miss?"

"A dirty Jack, please."

He nodded and turned around to fix my drink.

"If you're here to keep me company, don't bother," Pedro said. "Go back to the others and have fun."

"I'm avoiding them at the moment."

Pedro lifted an eyebrow at me. "Avoiding them? And here I

thought you wanted to move here and live near us, because you can't get enough of us."

I rolled my eyes. "You know I do, but they are talking about polo and that kind of makes me frustrated at the moment, you know."

He gave one sharp nod. "I know. Sorry this is so hard for you. I wish I could help you. If there was any way, I would do it." His eyes lit up. "I know. We can force Ri to retire, then you can take his place."

I gaped at him. "Now you're making jokes?"

He shrugged. "I couldn't let that one pass."

"You're terrible." The bartender returned with my drink and I thanked him. I wrapped my hands around the cold glass. "Even if Ri retired, mixed teams are just for fun. The kind of tournaments you guys play don't accept mixed teams."

"I'll keep an eye out for a women's team. If I find one that is hiring, I'll let you know."

I shook my head. "That won't work."

"Why?"

"Because ..." I lifted my index finger. "One, women's teams aren't big and famous like men's teams. They don't pay well and they certainly won't invest in paying for a visa for one of their players. Two, there are no teams in the area. I know. I've looked. The nearest team is in San Francisco and that's too far away. I want to live here not just so I can play polo, but so I can be with you guys."

"You're asking too much."

"Probably, but if I can't have it all, then I prefer to tuck my tail between my legs and go to college in Brazil."

He narrowed his eyes at me. "No, you don't."

No, I didn't. But what other option did I have? Apply for college here and get a student visa? International students had to be full-time students, and needed to get good grades in order to keep their visas, which meant I would need to go to classes and study—and not search for a polo team or go to practice. That didn't work either.

Pedro fell silent, nursing his whiskey and his wounds.

And I did the same before Bia or Hil came looking for me and dragged me to the dance floor. And, even though I didn't feel like dancing, I knew that if they came and dragged me, it would be good. I would probably be able to shed my worries and enjoy the company of my family and friends. I loved them so much.

I wished my father wasn't the one in charge of the ranch in Brazil. If he left it to a trusted employee, he could come to the U.S. too and be a partner of *tio* João Pedro here. That would get him a visa—and I would get one too. At least, until I was twenty-one. After that, even if my parents decided to move, I wouldn't be able to get a visa through them. However, I understood my father's position. The Montenegro name was big in Brazil and our ranch was known all over the world for our great polo horses and our polo school. *Tio* João Pedro had already abandoned ship because of his sons and my brother. My father couldn't leave all their hard work behind like that.

I sighed.

There had to be a solution to my problems—all of them.

Maybe I would find it at the end of this glass of whiskey.

2

TYLER

I REALLY DIDN'T KNOW why I had come.

Scratch that. I knew why. I needed a break from all the fucking problems in my life and when Bia told me it was Garrett's birthday party ... well, he had been a good friend from the moment I met him a couple of years ago. I should be at his party.

But now that I was here, I wasn't so sure I had done the right thing.

I sat around a long table with my ex-classmates, and they all talked about classes and internships and graduation. A couple of them had already graduated last semester and told us about their jobs and aspirations—one was working with a big time veterinarian, one was working at the university animal hospital and was going to start teaching, and one was planning on opening his own clinic.

I groaned internally, trying not to show how much it hurt me. I tipped my beer bottle and dried it in a second.

"I'm gonna get another beer," I muttered to no one in particular, and then stood from our table and took a step toward the bar.

"Hey, Ty."

I turned toward the voice and grinned. "Hey, Garrett." I had already told him happy birthday at the beginning of the party, but he was moving fast, going from guest to guest. "How have you been, man?"

We clasped hands and bumped shoulders.

"I'm good, good. How about you? Haven't seen you in a while."

"Yeah ..." I sighed.

Garrett's brows furrowed. "How ... are things? How are you holding up?"

I suppressed a groan. Garrett was one of the few people who knew the real extent of my problems. He wasn't being nosy, I told my defensive side. He was asking out of sympathy. "It's ... okay, I guess. As well as it can be in this situation."

Garrett nodded. "And you?"

"What about me?"

"How are you doing?"

I shrugged and repeated, "As well I as I can in this situation."

Garrett clasped my shoulder. "Hey, man, I said it before and I'll say it again. If you need anything, don't hesitate. I'm here, okay?"

I nodded as a lump choked my throat. "Thanks," I forced out.

Garrett glanced around, smiling. "No plus one?"

"You mean a girl?" I snorted. "With all the shit in my life, do you really think I've been worried about girls?"

Garrett's smile faded. "Probably not. Sorry about giving you a hard time."

"It's okay." I was getting used to it. "I'm gonna ..." I pointed to my empty bottle.

"Sure, sure, go ahead." He stepped to the side to let me pass. "Talk to you later."

I nodded as I walked past him, aiming for the bar. I took the only vacant stool at the bar counter, beside a girl with pretty, long dark hair. The bartender was right there and took my order.

I showed him my empty bottle. "Another, please."

Nodding, the bartender took the bottle from me. As he turned around to get me a beer, I glanced to the side and found the girl staring at me.

I straightened. "Hi," I said, my voice harder than usual.

"Hm, hi," she said, turning her stool a little more toward me. "Here for Garrett's party, huh?" She had an accent, almost like Bia's.

"Yeah, I guess so."

She chuckled. "Sorry. That was quite obvious, wasn't it?" She tilted her head and the light coming from the pendant fixtures over the counter hit her face exactly right. I was shocked by the intensity of her blue eyes. They were incredible, almost unreal. "How do you know Garrett?"

"We used to go to vet school together," I said as the bartender placed my beer in front of me. "Thanks," I muttered to him before he went to take someone else's order.

"Used to?" the girl asked.

Frustration knotted my shoulders. That was one topic I hated talking about. "Yeah. Long story. How about you?"

"I'm Bia's cousin."

"Oh, so you're from Brazil too?"

"*Sim,*" she said. That explained the accent. She smiled, and I realized that not only were her eyes pretty, but her entire face was. Her dark hair and bright eyes and red lips went really well with her fair skin and delicate features. "Where are my manners?" She stuck her hand between us, bringing me back from my thoughts. "Hi, I'm Gabriela. Though, call me Gabi. I prefer Gabi."

I took her soft hand in my calloused one. "Hi, I'm Tyler. Nice to meet you."

"You too." She pulled her hand away.

I took a sip of my beer, trying to think of what to say next. I hadn't talked to a girl, other than dog and cat owners who stopped by the clinic, in months. I used to be good at this, at flirting and earning easy smiles. Now, I felt like everyone was watching me, waiting for me to fuck up my life a little more.

Shit, I was overthinking this. *Just talk to her.*

It didn't have to mean anything or lead anywhere. Just a conversation with someone other than my noisy neighbors, or with Lena, the clinic's secretary.

I opened my mouth to ask her what she thought of the U.S. when my cell phone rang. With a frown, I fished my phone from my jeans, and without looking at the screen, answered the call.

"Hello?"

"May I speak with Tyler Reid, please?"

"This is Tyler."

"Tyler, my name is Will Boris and I'm with the collector's office."

Oh, shit.

I turned my stool so my back was to Gabi. "How can I help you?"

"Well, sir, I'm calling you because I have here four of your unpaid bills, and I would like to negotiate a payment."

"Mr. Boris, I know about the bills." And the many others stacked in a neat pile in my apartment. "However, I've got a lot on my plate right now, okay? And a lot of bills to pay. I'll get to all of them. Eventually." I hoped. The situation wasn't looking pretty, and to be honest, I didn't think I would get to all the bills even if I lived to be a hundred—and worked until my last breath.

"Sir, I understand you may be in a hard position right now, but—"

"Listen," I said, raising my voice. Before Gabi heard me, I stood and walked out of the room, into the restaurant's entrance hallway. "I'm doing what I can, okay? Send the damn bills to me. I'll pay them when I can."

I turned off the call and let out a deep, shaky breath. This was my damn life now. I had to learn to deal with these calls and the bills I couldn't pay, or I would die of an ulcer or heart attack before I made it to thirty. At least if I did, all the debt would die with me. That was one solution.

I shook my head, ashamed for thinking such things.

Coming to this party had been a bad idea. First, I felt irritated seeing my ex-classmates happy. Then, I got this damn call, further souring my mood. Besides, I was here wasting precious minutes, hours, when I could be working and earning some money. I knew it wouldn't be enough—it would never be enough—but every little bit helped.

By the time I reached my truck in the parking lot behind the restaurant, I had already arranged to take a few hours of the overnight shift at the vet clinic.

3

GABI

"Hello," Tyler answered his phone. "This is Tyler." He angled his body away from me. "How can I help you?"

I took that as a hint and straightened my stool, facing the bar. On my other side, Pedro was messing with his phone—probably stalking Iris on social media. However, I hadn't seen her post anything lately.

"Mr. Boris, I know about the bills," Tyler said into the phone, his voice tighter. "However, I've got a lot on my plate right now, okay? And a lot of bills to pay. I'll get to all of them. Eventually." There was a tense pause. "Listen," he hissed before standing up and walking away from the bar. With hurried steps, he exited the room and went to the front of the restaurant. Was he leaving the party? Without saying goodbye to Garrett? And what was that about having a lot of bills to pay? Was he in debt or something?

Well, none of my business.

I took a long swallow from my drink, then pulled out my phone to check on my emails and social media. Priscila posted pictures of her with her horse, then right below, pictures with one of her cousins at a club. Mateus posted about getting ready to start the new semester in college, studying hard, and being more focused. Silvia, another girl from my polo team, posted about her aunt who needed some prayers for a surgery. Reading the comments, I found out it was nothing serious, just routine stuff. Even so, I shot some positive thoughts her way. Raquel, a girl who had played with us a couple of times then gave up polo, posted about her last days at her summer internship and, like Mateus, getting ready for a new semester in college.

Scrolling down, a picture of Mateus with his arm draped over a pretty girl's shoulder showed up in my feed. Apparently, she—Helena—had posted the picture and tagged him. There was no caption on the picture, but from the people dressed up around them, I assumed they were out clubbing. She had a big smile on her face and he seemed happy too, or too drunk.

My stomach sank.

It had been quite some time since we broke up. He even had tried to get back together with me a few times, but I guess he wouldn't wait forever for me. I mean, I didn't want him back. He was free to go out and *ficar* with other girls—*ficar* was a common thing in Brazil. It was when a girl and a guy met at the club and kissed and made out while there, then left and went back home alone as if nothing had happened. There was no obligation to call or get in touch the next day or whenever. A little cold and slutty in my opinion, but almost everyone did it once in a while.

Still, I couldn't shake the heavy feeling that settled in my stomach, making me a little jealous. I told myself it was normal. After all, we had been together for almost four years. I had thought we would be together forever.

I sighed.

It was time to stop this pity party. Determined, I turned back to Pedro, to bother him until he at least tried to tell another joke, but Bia stepped between us and hooked her arm through mine.

"You're coming with me," she said with a big smile.

Just like I had predicted, she dragged me to the dance floor, where the rest of the gang—minus Pedro and Iris—danced and chatted and laughed.

After two songs, I decided something was not right. Actually, someone was missing.

"Be right back," I yelled over the loud music.

I raced back to the bar, and this time, I hooked my arm through Pedro's.

"*Tche*," he started.

"Don't *tche* me. I don't care if you just stand there with your drink, but you gotta be with us." I tugged on his arm. "Now."

He rolled his eyes, but didn't fight me as I pulled him away from the bar and onto the dance floor.

Our group cheered when Pedro joined us, and he rolled his eyes once more. I remained by his side, bumping my hip against his, grabbing his arms and trying to move them, until finally, he started dancing—which was only swaying pathetically, but I would take it.

We all danced together—Gui, Hil, Leo, Hannah, Bia, Garrett, Pedro, Ri, *tio* João Pedro, *tia* Agnes, and me. Happiness filled my chest and a huge smile spread across my lips. I glanced around at my family. It didn't matter if I was living in Brazil and they were here. It didn't matter if they were living the dream and I wasn't. We were still family. We still loved each other. We would still celebrate every little or big thing together—even if that meant I would have to find a way to come visit them more often.

It didn't matter, as long as we had each other.

BEFORE LEAVING for a practice game on Monday morning, Gui and Pedro had invited me to go with them—which was nice because they always let me practice with them. But I wasn't feeling well.

Not physically, just emotionally, so I passed and stayed holed up in the apartment, plopped on the couch wrapped in a thin blanket, and munched on popcorn while watching reruns of *The Bachelor*.

Reality shows were terrible, but they always made me feel less pathetic about my own life. Come on, as if I would ever expose all of my flaws and odd customs for the whole world to see? At least these people looked like they had way more problems than me. And were less mature and plain stupid.

At the moment, a young woman yelled at the guy about how he was giving hope to four of them, instead of actually choosing one and going for it. A few minutes later, another girl yelled at the same guy, saying that a third girl was trying to be chosen just for the status it would give her.

The words engaged and status stuck in my mind, creating a cascade of images. The couple from Saturday night, the one Megan, Blaire, and Andrea had pointed out to me came to mind, and it made me think of my current visitor visa status.

A marriage to get a green card.

That had crossed my mind several times actually. To offer money to an American guy to marry me so I could get a green card, but who the hell would do that? Nobody we knew needed money. At least I didn't think so. Maybe if I went to the vet school with Bia and Garrett, I would find a guy who needed money and would agree to marry me.

I laughed on the inside. *Meu Deus*, as if I would ever have the courage to do that. Thinking about it was one thing. Doing it was another. Well, if maybe he was Liam Hemsworth, then maybe I would get over it and ask him to marry me. Maybe.

Then, another image popped into my mind and my breath caught.

That guy on the phone, Tyler, complaining about unpaid bills. Maybe ... maybe he needed money. A lot of money. Maybe if I offered him the amount he needed, he would marry me.

A humorless laugh bubbled up from my throat, but it didn't come out. It was a ridiculous idea and yet I couldn't shake it off.

I tried turning my attention back to *The Bachelor*, but even though my eyes were on the screen, I was seeing and hearing nothing. My mind raced, thinking, planning something I knew I wouldn't have the courage to do.

Would I?

It was my only option. If I wanted to stay here, if I wanted to stay with my family and friends, if I wanted to join a polo team or even to get a team together without worrying about sponsors for visas, this was it.

Besides, asking couldn't hurt, right? The worst that could happen was Tyler saying no, and then I would leave and probably never see him again. No harm, no foul.

But even with all the planning and all the certainty that there was no other way, I couldn't find the strength, the courage, to get up from the couch and do something about it. I wasn't that brave.

But I could be.

I had to be.

I reached for my iPad on the coffee table and opened my social media app. I went to Garrett's profile and searched for Tyler on his friends' list. I was almost sure he wouldn't have an account—he struck me that way—but I was mistaken. There he was. Tyler Reid. I clicked on his link and his profile filled the screen. Apparently, he didn't check his social media often because his last post was dated six months ago—that or most of his posts were private. I scrolled through his few posts and all of them were about new methods of treating horses, and horse racing, and a lot about horses. By the look of it, he was into horses too.

But it didn't mention anything else I could use, like where he worked or studied, and where I could find him.

So, I took a long breath and called Garrett. He answered after two rings.

"Hey, Gabi, everything okay?"

"Yeah, I think so." I paused. "Bia isn't with you, is she?"

"No, she's in class right now."

"Okay, cool." I sighed, already feeling embarrassed by what I was planning. "Garrett, I need to find Tyler Reid. Can you tell me his number or where he studies or works?"

He didn't answer right away. "Why?"

"It's kind of a long story ..."

"I have thirty minutes before my next class."

Droga. "*Então,* here's the thing ..."

And then I told him everything.

I PARKED Gui's Jeep in the parking lot and killed the engine.

All right. This was it.

Let's do it.

Ten minutes later, I was still inside the Jeep and holding the steering wheel so tight, my knuckles were white. *Meu Deus,* this was crazy. This was absolutely crazy. Someone should stop me.

But nobody came. And in five days I had to go back to Brazil. Go back to my parents' house and start college. I cringed. I would have to give up my dream. I would have to give up polo.

I sucked in a long breath and exited the Jeep.

I can do this, I told myself as I walked from my parking space to the sidewalk that led to an old but cute white house. A big wooden sign hung from a post on the lawn: B+D Veterinary Clinic.

I stepped onto the sidewalk and stared at the house.

Não, droga, I couldn't do it.

With a deflating sigh, I turned around and started walking back to the Jeep. As I opened the driver's side door, someone called me.

"Gabriela?"

A cold wave rushed through me and I froze. *Droga.*

I glanced over my shoulder. "Hi, Tyler."

A frown creased his forehead as he walked toward the parking lot, toward me. "Hey. Hm, what are you doing here?"

I whirled, shutting the car door, and leaned against the side of the Jeep. "I … hm." *Droga,* what was I supposed to say now?

"Is … is everything all right?"

"Yes, sure, it's just …" I took a long breath. I could do this. I had come here to do this. I had to do this. It was now or never. "I need you to marry me," I blurted out.

He took a step back. "W-what?"

"Sorry, that came out wrong. It's just … *Meu Deus,* do you have a girlfriend? Shit, you aren't already married, are you?"

"Whoa, slow down. What the hell are you talking about?"

I sucked in a sharp breath and decided to be honest. "I overheard you the other night, about the bills. Sorry, I didn't mean to, but I'm glad that I did. I thought maybe, we could make a deal."

He crossed his arms. "Let me guess. To marry you? What kind of deal is that?"

"One that gets me a green card."

He stared at me like I was crazy. "You're asking me to marry you for a green card?"

"Yes. We would need to stay married for two years. In exchange, I'll give you the money you need to pay whatever bills you have." I frowned, suddenly worried his bills were in the millions.

He paused and narrowed his eyes at me. "How did you find me?"

"Garrett." Right after I had told Garrett my plan, he had called me crazy. But then he agreed that we wouldn't be hurting anyone. I needed to stay here and Tyler needed money. As long as we didn't break any other law, it should be fine.

"Garrett knows you're here right now?" he asked incredulously. I nodded. "Shit, this is crazy ..."

"It's my only option."

"Are you that desperate to leave your country?"

Merda, this was going worse than I had planned. "It's not about the country; it's about my dreams. And yes, I am."

He shook his head once. "Even if I considered it, I need a lot of money. You couldn't offer me what I need."

"You don't know that."

"Trust me, I know." He tilted his head, watching me. "Besides, you don't sound or look so sure about this."

I paused. "To be honest, I'm not. But it's my only choice."

"You know this sounds crazy."

I sucked in a sharp breath. "I know."

"I'm ... I'm sorry, Gabriela. You're a beautiful girl, but I can't do that. I won't marry anyone for money."

The little line of hope in my chest shriveled. "What can I offer you, then? More money? How much do you need?"

"It's not the money," he said, his voice hard. "We're talking about our lives here. Marriage is a big thing and, when or if I ever do get married, it won't be a pretense."

"I see." I gulped, trying to swallow my shame, my embarrassment. "Please, forget I ever asked. Sorry to have bothered you."

With my pride in the dirt, I threw open the door to the Jeep, jumped in, slammed the door, and turned the key, my heart hammering in my chest and tears burning my eyes. I peeled out of the clinic's parking lot before I broke down in front of him.

I wasn't sad he had refused me. I kind of expected it. I mean, it was crazy. Some chick comes over and asks him to marry her, just like that? Too crazy. No, his response was understandable. No, I felt sad and frustrated, because now I had no options. I was returning to Brazil, to a life I didn't want.

4

TYLER

THE GIRL WAS CRAZY.

And yet I couldn't get her out of my mind.

I had left the clinic for a quick lunch break—at almost three in the afternoon—when I found her outside. At first, I thought she was lost, then I thought she had a pet and was bringing it in for an appointment. Not in a million years had I expected what she had proposed.

Marry her? For money?

Granted, the money would be a life saver. I seriously needed the money, but this was my life too. I was already sacrificing too much of myself. I had never really considered marriage before, much less in the last couple of years, and I certainly wouldn't marry some random girl, no matter how rich she was.

I barely ate during my lunch break. And hours later, when I dragged my feet inside my apartment and threw my jacket over the back of the couch, I was still thinking about her. It was absolutely crazy. That was why I was still thinking about it. I had never had something like that happen to me before and I was still shocked. I was still amused.

I looked around my apartment. So pathetic. We had never been rich, far from it, but we had always had a nice townhouse in a nice neighborhood with a nice backyard. Now, I lived in a crappy two-bedroom apartment with cracking walls, rotting carpet, and a heady stench of mold. The appliances in the kitchen looked thirty years old, as did the bathtub in the bathroom.

Tired, I grabbed a frozen dinner from the freezer and threw it in the microwave. Once more, I would sit alone at the dining table and pretend it was a steak with loaded mashed potatoes. Or a four-cheese fettuccine. Or some chicken marsala. Anything other than a frozen dinner that tasted of cardboard. But it was the best I could manage with the little money I had, and with how tired I was. I hadn't cooked in ... I didn't even know when the last time was.

As I inhaled my dinner, my eyes found the stack of letters on top of the side table in the living room—the same stack I had been trying to avoid for the last month, and the one that grew each time I opened the mailbox. A mistake, of course, but the thing was always overflowing. I had no choice but to pick the letters up. Then, I ignored them when they were in here.

But I couldn't sweep the mess under the rug forever. One day or another, I would have to face it all.

With a sigh, I stood and took my plate to the sink. After washing it and setting it on the drying rack, I grabbed a beer and sat on the couch beside the stack. I stared at it, took a swig of my beer, and instead of doing the responsible thing, I swiped the remote control from the coffee table and turned on the TV. There was nothing I wanted to watch, really, but it was better than staring at the walls. Besides, I had to go to bed soon because I had an early shift tomorrow.

I turned on *The Walking Dead*—other than being about zombies, I had no idea what the show was about and didn't really care—and pretended that, just for a few hours, everything was normal. Everything was okay.

I would leave the worry, the tension, the deep hole in my gut for tomorrow.

5

GABI

I SAT on my bed and looked around.

Droga. This wasn't even my bed. It was just a regular bed in the guest bedroom. It could have been my bed, though. I wanted it to be my bed. Well, if Tyler had taken my deal, this probably wouldn't have been my bed.

Heat crept up my cheeks and I buried my face in my hands, wishing I could crawl under the bed and never come out again. *Droga,* how embarrassing that had been. I was still shocked I had been brave enough, that I had actually proposed to him. To be honest, I thought I would chicken out and not do it.

And he said no.

Apparently, he wasn't as desperate for money as I first believed.

I lifted my head and let out a long breath. It didn't matter anymore. It was done. Tyler said no and I had no other choice. I had to go back to Brazil in less than five days and start college next week.

I reached for one of the sweaters spread out on the bed. I slid a hanger through the neckline and put it inside the small closet that also wasn't mine. And it would never be mine.

The next time I could come to visit would be July, during my winter vacation. It was only February ... July seemed so far away.

A little more sadness and frustration filled me, and I fought the urge to curl into myself and cry.

A knock on the half-open door stopped me from doing it.

"*E aí, guria*?" Bia stepped in, but stayed by the door. "What are you up to?"

"*Nada*," I grumbled.

With a sympathetic smile, she walked to me and wrapped her arms around me. "Gabi, I know that face. Don't worry. I bet you'll love college and make lots of friends and soon you won't even want to come visit us anymore."

I snorted, seriously doubting that. Didn't she know me at all? Or had she forgotten about me in the three and a half years she had been living here?

Jealousy mixed with sadness and frustration.

"So, what are you making for dinner?" I asked, changing the topic. And food was high on my list.

She smiled at me and grabbed my hand. "Come help me."

Together, we went to the kitchen. Garrett, who was already playing video games with Gui, waved at me. I waved back at him. His eyes held mine for a second too long, but other than that, he didn't say anything. I was glad he was keeping quiet. I didn't need to feel more embarrassed about it than I already did.

Sighing, I glanced around. Pedro lay on one of the couches, his eyes still downcast, and Hil was on the balcony, talking on the phone.

"Are the others coming?"

Bia handed me an apron. "I think so. At least, everyone was invited."

I took the apron and wrapped it around my waist. I leaned close to her and whispered, "And Iris?"

Bia pressed her lips together and shook her head. "She's not answering any of our calls."

So odd. And Pedro wouldn't talk about it either. We all had theories. The one that everyone mentioned was cheating. One of them cheated on the other. But no one could be sure unless one of them said something, which didn't seem would be any time soon.

Bia pulled out pans and boxes of pasta and cans of red sauce from the cabinets, then she grabbed tomatoes and onions and cheese and heavy milk and some green stuff from the fridge.

"I can only assume you're making us pasta."

She smiled at me and handed me two onions. "Chop those."

She knew I hated chopping. "Excuse me?"

Laughing, she took a cutting board and a sharp knife from under the counter and handed them to me. "Chop the onions."

With a smile, Hil came in from the balcony and joined us. "What do we have here?"

I handed her the onions and the knife. "Bia wants you to chop these."

Hil raised an eyebrow, but said nothing as she took them from me and stood in front of the cutting board.

"Cheater," Bia whispered.

I lifted one shoulder. "A girl's gotta do what a girl's gotta do."

While Bia and Hil handled the kitchen, I reached across the kitchen's island where a wooden bar stood against a wall and grabbed a bottle of whiskey. Then, I snagged a Coke from the fridge and filled a few glasses with ice.

"Who wants a Jack and Coke?"

"Me," Bia said. Pedro raised his hand. At least one action from him today.

"I want plain," Gui said, his eyes on the TV.

"Me too," Garrett said, nodding at me before returning his attention to the video game.

I had finished preparing the drinks when the front door opened and the rest of the gang arrived. Hannah, Leo, and Ri.

"Drinks?" I asked as they entered, throwing their jackets and purses on the couches.

"The usual," Ri said. He sat down beside Garrett and started commenting on the game.

"I'll grab mine," Leo said, coming to the kitchen. He took a Coke from the fridge and promptly went back to the living room to join the video game crew.

Hannah joined us in the kitchen for a second, then she started setting the table.

I watched as everyone moved, talked, shouted at the TV, laughed, and chatted. A well-oiled machine. A group of not only family, but friends.

The conversation between the girls flowed easily. Hannah's ranch, Hil's school and her move to this apartment, Bia's party for Garrett's graduation in May.

A new wave of sadness washed over me.

I came to visit as often as I could, and they welcomed me with open arms, but it wasn't the same. As much as it hurt to admit it, I knew I would never be a part of it. Not really. I wrapped my fingers around my glass and slipped away to the balcony. As much as I wanted to stay with them, to be a part of it all, right now it hurt too much. I needed a little fresh air before joining them again. I leaned over, resting my elbows on the rail, and looked up at the beautiful starry sky. Here, in the middle of town, the lights muted the soft starlight, but it was still pretty, and the moon was almost full, chasing the shadows away.

I sucked in a long breath, trying to rein in my emotions. I wasn't a crier. Quite the opposite. I was always the optimist, the one who always had a smile on her face and a hand to help. Most days, I could rival Bia's chipper and sassy spirit.

Not today.

I took a long sip of my drink and sent a prayer to the sky.

Please, please. Send me a sign. Anything. What should I do?

Faint footsteps approached and I glanced over my shoulder. With his hands tucked inside the pockets of his jeans, Garrett joined me at the rail. A long minute passed before he finally said, "Do I need to ask, or are you going to tell me?"

I sighed. "He refused. Simple as that." I stared at him. "I thought he was desperate for money."

"He is, I swear. I ..." He shook his head. "This idea was crazy, I told you that before, but I actually thought he would accept."

"*Bom*, he didn't." I frowned, wondering about something. "Why does he need money?"

He tsked. "I've already said too much, Gabi. He doesn't like anyone knowing he's in a bad situation. If you want to find out more, you'll have to ask him."

I snorted. "I'll probably never see him again."

Garrett nodded.

We watched the sky in silence for one more minute, then Garrett poked me with his elbow. "Come on. They all came tonight to spend time with you before you leave in a few days. Enjoy your time with them."

So cheesy, but so true.

I did love them. I loved each one of them. I loved the group. I loved how I felt when among them, when here with them.

I plastered a smile, even if forced, on my lips and followed Garrett back into the apartment.

"There you are!" Hannah said with a wide smile.

"What happened?" I asked, walking up to the girls, still huddled around the kitchen's island.

"Hil is telling us about her big showcase in May," Bia said. She had a small grin on her lips.

I had heard about the showcase. "Oh, yeah." I turned to Hil. "I bet you have it all planned already?"

Hil tilted her head, staring at me. "Well, almost. I know what clothing designs I'm going to use. I just need models."

She kept staring at me.

Then, it dawned on me. "Wait. *O que?*" I glanced at all the girls, then to Hilary again. "Why me?"

"Actually, I'm inviting all of you," Hil said. "I want you all to be my models."

I gaped at her. "No way!"

"Yes, way," she said, smiling wide.

Bia almost jumped up and down. "Come on, say yes. I already accepted it."

I chuckled. "Of course you did." I turned to Hannah. "What about you?"

Hannah let out a long breath. "I'll do it if we all do it." She pointed at Hil. "Even you. You have to go down the runway at least once, or no deal."

Hilary groaned. "Really?"

Hannah nodded vehemently. "Oh yeah."

Hil lifted her eyebrows at me. "Now say you'll do it."

"Wait ... your showcase is in May. It'll be the middle of my semester."

"Well, the showcase is on the weekend. You can miss classes on Friday and Monday for us, right?"

Merda. She had thought of it all. I sighed, defeated. "I'll do it."

"Yes!" she yelped before embracing me tight.

It seemed I would be visiting my family a little earlier than I had expected, and it made me happy.

6

TYLER

I YAWNED as I parked my car in its reserved space. After checking to see if I had grabbed everything, I hopped out and walked into my building. The postman was right there in the lobby, distributing the letters into their appropriate boxes.

"Good morning," the man said with a chipper smile. "What's your number?"

"302."

He looked over the box on the floor, fished out a thick stack and handed it to me. "Here you go."

I took the stack. "Thanks."

Wanting to burn the letters, I raced up the stairs and entered my apartment. First thing I did was to throw the mail with the rest of the unopened letters on the corner table in the living room. The stack fell from the table and letters spread across the floor.

"Shit." Groaning, I let go of my bag and coffee mug, and knelt on the floor. I picked up a few letters and noticed not all were bad news. With another groan, I sat down on the floor and started sorting through the mail. Ads, magazines, credit card applications, and any other shit went directly to the trash. But the stack that remained was still thick.

I knew better, but I couldn't help it. I opened the letter on top. A medical bill. I should have stopped there, but now I was in the thick of it. I opened the letters and found more medical bills, most past due, and several electrical and water and cell phone bills. And another notice on rent. I leaned back on the counter and let my shoulders droop.

As much as I tried to fight the current, I was drowning in bills. Rent was late and soon I would be kicked out. I hadn't bought real groceries in the longest time—other than pop tarts and cheap frozen food, bread, and milk—and the last time I slept for over five hours ... well, I couldn't really remember when that happened. Maybe a year ago? Eighteen months?

And it would never end. Never. I would have all this debt for the rest of my life, and soon I would be homeless because no one would rent me an apartment, even a shitty one. Shittier than this one.

I closed my eyes and let out a long breath.

There was nothing I could do. Nothing more than I already did. I quit school, I worked all the time, I cut all the fluff from my life. No gym, no real food, no internet, no latest model phone, no nice clothes, no movies, no eating out, no dating, no flirting even. Nothing. I was a shell walking around, running around, trying to make ends meet, when I knew, *I knew*, I would never catch up. Never.

There had to be a way. There had to be something that could help me, that could make this burden a little easier to carry.

A beautiful face with dark hair and bright blue eyes appeared behind my eyelids, and I snapped my eyes open.

Shit.

Gabriela had offered to make me a deal, a deal that could change all of this shit. A deal that would make me debt free in a couple of years—if she could cover the amount of money I owed. But even if she couldn't, perhaps she would offer me enough to pay the most pressing bills, to keep me afloat while I figured out what to do next.

But marriage? Would it be so bad to be married to her for two years, just two years, and then be debt free? In two years, we would get a divorce. I could go back to vet school, I could rent a nicer apartment, and I could start my life anew.

Shit. I would be twenty-seven then, and I was talking about starting my life.

I exhaled. Marriage. Damn, marriage. Could I get married? I mean, we could elope and pretend we lived together, right? That wouldn't be too hard, right?

All right, all right. Think.

Fake marriage to a pretty girl and be debt free, hopefully, in two years, or continue with my miserable existence and be homeless and never eat a decent meal again?

There was no option there.

Shit, it seemed I would be getting hitched.

Still reluctant, I picked up my phone and realized I didn't have her number. How would I find her, then? Garrett. She had mentioned Garrett knew about this.

Holding my breath, I called Garrett.

He answered on the third ring. "Hey, Ty. Everything all right?"

"Actually, no," I confessed. "But maybe it'll be. I need to talk to Gabriela. Can you give me her number?"

ALL WEEK, I had gone to practice with the guys early in the morning, had a late lunch with them, then Gui, Pedro, and I came back to the apartment. Pedro sulked, while Gui played video games and texted with Hilary.

Usually after a snack in the middle of the afternoon, Gui and Pedro went to the gym to work out. And I usually went with them.

Friday morning was no different.

"Ready?" Gui asked as he filled his water bottle from the fridge's water dispenser.

"Ready," I said, picking up my backpack. I had all the clothing I could need there, but my mood was going south. "Though I'm not sure I'll practice today."

He turned to me, screwing the cap back onto his bottle. "*Por quê?*"

"Feeling a little off, is all." I shrugged, taking a seat on one of the kitchen stools, in no rush. We still had to wait for Pedro who had ignored his snooze alarm and was now running late.

Gui snorted. "You say that now. I bet when we're there and you see the field and the horses and the mallets, you'll be the first on the field." He knew me well. Damn him. He patted my shoulder. "I'm gonna check on Pedro."

To pass the time, I took my phone out of my bag and found a new message from a number I didn't know.

It's Tyler. Can we talk? What time can I call you?

Tyler had sent me that message about an hour ago. *Droga.*

I quickly replied to him.

You might not want to call me since my number is international.

Not even thirty seconds later, my phone dinged with a new message.

Then tell me your address. And what time I should come by.

I bit the inside of my cheek. *Droga.* What did he want now? To humiliate me some more? But of course, my brain rushed ahead, assuming he wanted to tell me he had reconsidered and wanted to accept my deal.

My heart raced as I typed in the apartment address and told him he could come by in about thirty minutes.

Okay was his reply.

I stared at the phone and barely registered Gui coming back to the kitchen.

"What are you doing?"

I lowered my phone as if he had caught me drooling at pics of shirtless men on the internet. "Nothing, just checking my social media."

Pedro stumbled out of the hallway. "I'm here, I'm here. Let's go."

I scrunched my nose. "Actually, I'm not going."

"What happened?" Gui asked, concern lacing his words.

I smiled at him. "Nothing to be worried about. I just ... I got my period yesterday and things are nasty down here." I gestured toward my lower parts, making both guys cringe. Bingo. "And the cramps are starting. I better stay in bed for a little while more."

"Hm, *sim*, do that." Gui retreated a few steps as if it could be contagious. I bit back a laugh.

"*Isso.* Rest." Pedro waved at me and marched to the door. "See you later."

The guys bolted out of the apartment and I chuckled. Then, I froze.

Meu Deus, Tyler was coming here. Now.

I looked down at myself, to make sure I looked okay. Jeans, a plaid shirt with rolled up sleeves, and cowboy boots. Nothing much. My practice clothes were in my backpack, and I also had a few things in Gui's locker at the club.

For the next thirty minutes, I paced the living room, checked my phone two hundred times, turned on *The Bachelor* but didn't pay any attention to it, and I tried not to bite my nails off.

Forty minutes passed.

Then fifty.

Then sixty.

What was he thinking, that he could toy with me? I had just opened the messaging app and was about to text him when the intercom rang. I raced to the kitchen, almost tripping on my feet in the process, and answered the call.

"Good afternoon, Miss Fernandes," the bellman said. "Tyler Reid is here. Should I send him up?"

"Yes, please." My voice was calm but my hands started shaking.

Even though it would take him a couple of minutes to hop on the elevator and come up, I rushed to the door as if the kitchen was on fire. My heart beat fast against my ribs as I opened the door and waited, wondering, wishing, hoping, he was here for a good reason.

The elevator's soft ding echoed through the hallway, and two seconds later, Tyler stepped out. I held my breath. Instantly, his eyes found mine.

He was more handsome than I remembered, which made my

heart do a flip. And taller too. His shirt hugged his wide shoulders, and his jeans seemed to have been molded to his thick thighs. I tried not to stare at him, but I was too nervous to do anything else.

"Hi," he said, his voice devoid of emotion.

Suddenly on the defensive, I crossed my arms. "Hey."

He ran a hand through his hair. "Can we talk?"

He was here. Did that mean he had reconsidered my offer? He wouldn't have come all this way to tell me no again, right?

I stopped the thoughts hemorrhaging in my brain and stepped back, allowing him to enter the apartment.

He walked in and glanced around. "Nice place."

"It's my brother's, not mine." I closed the front door and walked around him. "I was going to get a Coke for me. Do you want anything?" I started for the kitchen. "There's Coke, *guaraná*, orange and grape juice, water, sparkling water, and also the essentials like beer, whiskey, and wine."

He followed me into the kitchen, but halted on the other side of the island. "What's *guaraná*?"

I couldn't help but smile. "It's a Brazilian soda made from a fruit called *guaraná*. It's rather good. Want to try it?"

A knot knitted his forehead. "Um, no. Not right now. And since it's too early for the essentials, maybe a Coke."

I opened the fridge and grabbed two cans of Coke. "Here you go." I handed him the can and then leaned back on the counter. I took a sip from my Coke and stared at him while he still scanned the apartment. My defensive mode rang louder. "All right, Tyler, I don't have the heart for this, and I'm leaving for Brazil in four days. If you have something to say, say it."

He returned his eyes to me and sighed. "I lied before. I'm desperate for money and I want ... to talk more about your proposition."

"Okay ... hm, but first tell me, how much do you need?"

He paused. "Two hundred and fifty thousand dollars and counting."

It was a lot of money, but not too bad. At least he didn't need millions. "May I ask if you're in trouble, like do you owe money to some mafia boss or something? Sorry, but I don't want to be attached to a criminal. That wouldn't help with the green card process."

He let out a hollow chuckle. "No, I'm not a criminal. Only if having lots of debt is a crime. I mean, it certainly doesn't look good, but I'm not a guy who'll end up in jail—maybe homeless." He inhaled sharply. "How much can you offer me?"

"Don't you want to know the other details first?"

"I know they matter, but right now, I'm more interest about my end of the deal."

I took a deep breath. "Three hundred thousand dollars." His eyes widened and I went on. "If we get married and I apply for a green card, we have to stay married for two years before divorcing. If we divorce before completing two years, I lose the green card. So, here's my deal: I'll give you one third of the money on the night of our wedding, the second third on our first anniversary, and the final third on our second anniversary. Does that sound okay?"

He swallowed hard, his Adam's apple bobbing in his throat. "What else do I need to know about your end of the deal?"

"I would have to research more, but I think the first thing would be to actually get married and move in together."

"Move in together? Can't we just pretend to live together?"

I shook my head. "The immigration officer assigned to our case will find out if we're not living together and then my green card would be denied."

"Okay. What else?"

"After the wedding, I can contact an immigration lawyer, and he'll handle the green card application. As far as I know, the immigration office will then contact us and schedule an interview, about three or four months after the application is received. They will ask questions about us, about our relationship, like how we met, when we found out we were in love, and even about our everyday life. They are hard on these, and if they suspect we're lying, they will interview us separately and ask questions like what's our favorite color, and other small things like that, to make sure we know each other. I found a list of questions online—not sure if it's accurate, but we can study those." I had done extensive research about the green card process in the last few days, simply because I couldn't stop dreaming. "If they still aren't sure about us, I heard they can come to family gatherings to see us together, to see how we behave together. If they conclude we're lying, I'll be deported and I'll never be able to come back, not even to visit my family and you ... you'll end up in jail."

8

I STARED at her with wide eyes, sure I hadn't heard her right. "What? Jail?"

Gabi brushed a loose strand of her hair back and glanced to her feet before returning her gaze to me. "Yeah. Hm, you should be aware of all the consequences of this deal."

Shit, this thing kept getting more and more complicated. "Give me a sec," I muttered as I tried to sort through the thoughts swirling in my head.

"Sure," she said.

Risk going to jail? Was this worth it? I had been convinced that accepting Gabi's deal was a good solution. My only solution, actually, but now I wasn't so sure.

"Just ... let me say this," Gabi said. "If we do our parts well, if we pretend well, if we fool even my family, the immigration officers won't know. They will believe what we tell them. As long as we do this right."

So, when out with witnesses, we had to be kind to each other, sit together, stand side by side, smile at each other—there were plenty of couples who didn't kiss or even touch much in public.

We could be one of those—and we had to nail the answers to the interview questions. I could do that, right? For money? For a debt free life? For vet school?

"All right," I said, still feeling wary about this, but trying to push through. "And after the interview?"

"Nothing much. If the interview goes well, I'm given the green card. After that, we need to stay married for two years. Once the two years are up, we get a divorce, which should be quick, and done. We both go our separate ways."

That did sound too good to be true. Two years and a couple of months until I was debt free. It sounded like a dream, to be honest.

The yes was on the tip of my tongue, but I still had to get some things straight. "What about your family?"

"What about them?"

"You'll just get married and they won't be pissed with you about that?"

She bit her lower lip. "*Sim, bem*, I kind of thought about that and had an idea."

"I'm listening."

"We can elope today. Right now, if you want. The sooner we get married, the faster this thing will go and the sooner we'll be able to get a divorce. But you're right, my family would freak out if I showed up married. So, we can elope today and talk to an immigration lawyer next week and get everything moving, but I think we should lie to my family."

"Lie ..."

"*Sim*, hm, we could tell them that we are engaged and will be moving in together, but we aren't in a rush to get married. They don't need to know we eloped, and they certainly won't find out about the green card process unless we tell them about it."

"Or if an immigration officer thinks it's necessary to interview them. Or come to one of our gatherings."

"Not if we fool them." She cringed, as if she didn't like the idea of fooling anyone. "If we nail the interview questions, if we show them pictures of us together during the next few months leading to the interview, if we post these pictures on social media, they will believe us." She sighed. "It's not the most noble thing. I hate having to lie to people like that. I'll hate lying to the immigration officers, probably not as much as I'll hate lying to my family, but it's for a good cause. We won't be hurting anyone. I'll be able to follow my dreams, and you'll get the money you need. No harm done."

She was right, of course, but a sham marriage was a hard thing to swallow.

"Why can't we tell your family we eloped?"

Her eyes bulged as if that idea hadn't even crossed her mind. "My family would freak out. Really, like a full-blown freak out with lots of yelling and disinheritance threats. My parents would fly here and my father would certainly try to drag me back to Brazil by my hair." She shook her head. "Besides, they know I want to live here. The moment I tell them we are married, they would be onto us. They would know I married you for the green card and ... I don't know what would happen. Just know that it wouldn't be pretty." She snorted. "And trust me, when we tell them we're engaged, they will already freak out. Just not as much."

"But won't your family think you're engaged to me to get married and get a green card?"

"Probably, but I have an idea for that." I stayed quiet and let her continue, "Besides the green card suspicion, they will probably bother us about a wedding date. We can tell them we're not in a hurry. Some couples get engaged and don't get married for years. We can pretend to be one of those couples. At first, we can tell them we're waiting a year or so, so there's no rush to organize a wedding. And when it gets closer, we postpone it a couple more months. Then, we'll postpone again and again, until the two-year mark is up. Once we're divorced, we can tell them we broke up. They will never have to know."

"But what will happen after? How will you explain suddenly having a green card after the divorce?"

Shit ... I hadn't thought about that part. "Maybe ... my job will be going well and I can lie that the company sponsored a green card for me."

Job? She already had a job here? I cocked my head, watching her sad eyes. "You don't look happy about it."

"About the lying part, no, I'm not. I'm close to my family. They mean everything to me, and it'll be hard to lie to them, but I think it'll be worth it. And like I said, we won't be hurting anyone." She gasped. "*Meu Deus*, your family. What about your family? Won't they be pissed at you too?"

A big frown settled between my brows. "There's only one person in my family, and I don't think he'll care."

She mirrored my expression. "Is that a good or bad thing?"

I shrugged. "It's neither. Like I said, don't worry about it."

"Okay," she said, sounding unsure, but she didn't push it. Instead, she changed subjects. "We should talk about living together ..."

"Yeah, I know. I think you'll have to move in with me, but ..." I shut my mouth. I didn't want to tell her why I needed the money and my most-of-the-time-absent roommate. Not yet, at least. "My apartment isn't in the best neighborhood and it's small and old and messy." And I hadn't paid rent in forever and had just received a letter telling me I would be evicted if I didn't pay for it soon. But, with the money I received from her as soon as we got married, I could pay all the rent I owed and even pay a few months in advance. Or ... "What about if we looked for a better apartment in a nicer neighborhood first and then moved in there?"

She smiled at me and my breath caught. Damn, she was pretty. "That sounds good. Though, we can't take too long since we'll already be married." Her voice caught on the last word. Her smile faded. "So, are you ready?"

My mind spun. That was a lot to process. Get married? Meeting her family? Lawyer? New apartment ... It was too much, too fast. Then, I remembered that one hundred thousand dollars would be hitting my account by this evening, and I could make a lot of things work with that. I could pay my rent. I could pay my utility bills before they were cut off. I could buy some fucking real food and go grocery shopping for real, fill up the tank of my truck for the first time in over a year, and work a little less.

I sighed, knowing all too well that there was no decision to be made here.

I stood. "All right. Let's do this."

9

GABI

FOR A MOMENT THERE—WHEN I mentioned jail—I was sure Tyler would back out, and I would have to go pick up my suitcase and head to the airport.

I was surprised when he said yes.

Meu Deus, I had proposed and the guy had said yes! This was crazy.

"Okay, hm." I smoothed my sweaty palms over my jeans. "We need to start moving. We need to dress up and go to the courthouse to get a license and the ceremony done."

"Dress up? Ceremony? Aren't we eloping?"

"Yes, but we need to show the pictures to the immigration officer when it's time for our interview. It needs to look like we planned this, not like we were in a rush. So ..." I got my iPad from the living room and placed it on the kitchen's island. "We should check for stores where we can rent a dress and a tux and also what documents we need to bring to the ceremony." I gasped. "*Meu Deus*, I'll need a ring."

His face paled. "I don't ... I can't ..."

I waved him off. "Don't worry. I won't ask any of that from you. I'll rent our clothes, pay for the ceremony fees and pictures, and I'll buy the ring. We'll just pretend you got the ring for me."

"More pretending," he muttered.

"Tyler, for the next two years, pretending will be part of our lives. Try to come to terms with that now, otherwise this will be harder and harder." I had to come to terms with that too. I had never lied to my family like this, and I still couldn't believe I was going to do it now.

He let out a long breath. "It's okay. I mean, it's a lot to take in and I'll need a moment to adjust, but I'm okay. I'm still in."

I nodded once. "Good. Now let's see where we can find our outfits."

We browsed the internet and made a list of where we needed to go and what we would need.

Tyler left to go find his tux, promising to pick me up here in two hours so we could go to the courthouse together.

Meu Deus, I would be married in two hours!

Panic rushed through me, but I pushed it aside. No time to panic now.

I made a mental list of all the things I needed to do, shut the emotional part of my brain down—I could deal with that part later—and got moving.

First, I sent a message to my family, telling them I had a surprise for them tonight and wanted everyone at the apartment by six. Of course, everyone texted back asking what it was about. And my answer was: wait and see.

Next, I researched a local but good immigration lawyer, called the office, and scheduled an appointment for next Tuesday.

Then, I stopped by a nearby jeweler and looked for an engagement ring.

In Brazil, it wasn't customary to get big rings. When a couple got engaged, they bought matching wedding bands and wore them on their right hands until their wedding, then they changed the bands to the left hand. That was it.

But since my husband-to-be—*Meu Deus*, that sounded so strange, even in my head—was American, I thought he would follow American traditions.

I felt lost while browsing. There were small rings with a tiny diamond and huge rings that could give Hannah's humongous stone a run for its money. But then I remembered Tyler was desperate for money, which meant his financial situation wasn't good and he couldn't afford an expensive ring.

My gaze settled on a ring with two thin white gold bands and one small diamond set between them. The bands connected and turned into one at the bottom. It was modern, simple, and pretty.

The attendant, who had been asking nonstop which ones I wanted to try on, was happy when I finally told her to get a ring from the display. I tried the ring on and it was a little loose on my finger, but I bought it anyway. After all, I needed a ring for the courthouse and for my family tonight. I looked at the ring on my finger and a shiver slid down my spine. Shit was getting real, and as the hours passed, I was getting nervous about facing my family.

Before leaving, I picked a simple white gold band for Tyler—he would probably have to wear one for the ceremony today—and a matching thin band for me, to wear with the ring. I also scheduled with the store to come back to get the rings resized.

Next, I went to the rental store I had found online, The Dress Shop.

"Looking for something specific?" the attendant asked as soon as I stepped into the store. There were party gowns and wedding dresses crammed along the walls and some wire hangers in the middle of the store. It was overwhelming.

"Hm, I'm getting married in a few hours and I need a dress," I said, feeling incredibly shy talking about my upcoming wedding.

She gestured to the back of the store, where the white gowns dominated the area. "Do you have a model in mind?"

I walked alongside her to the back as my eyes rummaged through the displays in the store. "I want something simple and light. No big, fluffy skirts, and no veils. But still elegant."

"We might have something for you."

She took me to a display in the back and started showing me the dresses. I had lost count of how many dresses she had pulled out for me when finally she held one that I liked.

I slipped it on and, even though it was a little big at the waist and hips, I loved it.

The bodice was made of lace with a nude fabric underneath, several thin straps of small white stones covered the shoulders, and the neckline dipped between my breasts. The white skirt was made of a flowing gossamer, but it didn't have any fluff, and it went down past my knees. Lines of small white stones trickled down the skirt, shining bright when the light caught them.

The attendant, Sandra, brought over white stilettos and an elegant tiara made of the same white stones on the dress. I stepped into the shoes and she pulled my hair back, holding it precariously up with three bobby pins, then placed the tiara on my head. I looked at my reflection in the mirror and my eyes filled with tears.

Even though my hair was a mess and I was makeup-less, I looked pretty. The dress and the tiara, it was all pretty.

"We need to adjust this here." She pulled the loose fabric on the waist and placed a few pins around the hem.

"I don't have much time."

She waved me off. "Don't worry about it. Just go to the left." She pointed her index finger to the store's entrance, "and one block away you'll find Vivid Hair Salon. Talia or Carla will get your hair and your makeup ready in no time. Oh, and don't forget to stop by the Pink Flower across the street on your way back. I bet the florists there can have a bouquet prepared for you in minutes. And by the time you're back here, I'll have this ready." She smiled at me through the mirror.

And I smiled back at her.

I GLANCED at my phone again. I still had over thirty minutes before I had to go pick up Gabi, and then we both would do the craziest thing of our entire lives.

Sighing, I leaned my head back against my truck's seat and closed my eyes.

A couple of years ago, I wouldn't have guessed my life could get this screwed up, could turn into an infinite black hole. I couldn't even ask myself where things had gone wrong, because I knew what had happened and it hadn't been my fault. Or anyone else's.

There was a light at the end of that tunnel now, at least. Granted, it was a crazy light and it could get all kinds of complicated, but it was the only damn light I had seen since this mess started and I was going to hold on to it with all I had.

That didn't mean I would enjoy all the pretense, but it was all part of the deal. And I really, really needed this deal.

After leaving Gabi's place, I had gone to the vet clinic and filled out a vacation form for the next week so I could get some things done, like going to the immigration lawyer with Gabi, looking for an apartment, perhaps moving, paying bills ...

Lena was usually nice, but once she saw I was skipping work without any notice, she shot me a glare. I didn't wait until Dr. Bohm acknowledged my request. He could call me if he wanted to argue about it.

Next, I went to a tux and suit rental place and rented a black tux with a white bow—I thought white would be fitting, since I expected Gabi would be wearing white. Right?

And now I was seated in my truck just around the corner from Gabi's place, waiting for the time to pass so we could get the first step of this crazy journey done.

My phone dinged with a new text. I picked it up and checked it.

Gabi: *I'm ready at The Dress Shop. Come pick me up, please.*

I frowned. She had said to pick her up here. What the hell?

Grunting, I started the engine and drove to the place, which was only four blocks from where I had been waiting. There was a no-parking sign in front of the store, but I ignored it. I pulled over and killed the engine right there. With another grunt, I hopped out of the car and walked around to the sidewalk. A short man with graying hair walked by and stared at my tux. Right. I was dressed up, and it would catch anyone's attention. Shit.

I reached for the doorknob and saw her through the glass. Gabi twirled to me and halted, a small smile on her lips. My heart skipped one ... two beats before kicking into overdrive. Shit, she looked stunning. Like a princess.

I forgot what I was about to do. I almost forgot my name as she walked to the door, her eyes still on mine. She reached for the door and I shook the daze out of my mind. I fumbled to open the door from the outside before she could and stepped to the side.

"Hey," I said, feeling so fucking lame.

"*Oi*," she muttered, halting in front of me.

Her sweet perfume tickled my nose and I inhaled deeply. I couldn't identify the scent, but it was floral, beautiful and delicate—just like her.

"You ..." My throat felt dry. "You look beautiful."

Her smile widened and I almost put a hand over my heart to slow it down. "You clean up well too."

I cleared my throat. "Ready to go?"

She took in a deep breath. "I think so."

Trying to play my role, I offered her my arm. She still had a small smile when she hooked her arm on mine and let me guide her to my beat-up truck. Anxiety hit me. My truck was old and rusty and dirty. She would get her dress dirty too.

I opened the passenger door for her and, without thinking, caught her in my arms. She let out a small "oomph" in surprise.

"Sorry, I just ... The truck is dirty and I don't want your dress to get ruined." I gently deposited her on the passenger's seat.

"Thank you," she whispered. Her blue eyes stared back at me, and I found it hard to breathe.

I nodded, then closed the truck's door and jogged to the other side. Once I was seated and had my seat belt fastened, I started the engine and pulled the truck into the streets of Santa Barbara.

Once we were on the road, Gabi said, "Sorry I wasn't at the apartment waiting. I thought ... the bellman would see me dressed like this and tell my brother or cousins."

"Oh, yeah, no, you're right. That makes sense."

It was only a five-minute drive to the courthouse and soon we were both standing in line. Thankfully, we weren't the only ones dressed up for a wedding ceremony, so I felt a little better about that.

Then, it was our turn. We filled out the paperwork, showed them our IDs, and Gabi paid the fees.

"Please, come with me," a short lady who smelled like hairspray said. She also smelled of baby powder and had lipstick smeared outside her lips.

Gabi and I followed her through a door into a hallway and then into a courtyard. There was a small table set up with a white cloth, a man in a dark gray suit behind it, a short woman with yellow-blond hair beside him, and another woman with red hair and a big camera off to the side of the table.

"Hi, I'm Jeffry Osment," the man in the suit said. "I'm going to perform your ceremony. This is Lenna, your witness." He gestured to the blonde and she waved at us. "And this is Carol, the photographer."

We greeted them all. Mr. Osment asked Gabi for the rings, and she handed a black box to him. That caught me by surprise, since I only expected her to have bought her engagement ring, not the wedding bands too.

Then, Mr. Osment started.

"We're gathered here in the presence of this witness for the purpose of uniting in marriage Tyler and Gabriela. I remind you both that love, loyalty, and understanding are the foundations of a happy and enduring home ..." He went on with a small sermon about the duty of a husband and a wife, then he proceeded, "Tyler, do you take Gabi as your lawfully wedded wife?"

I didn't hesitate. "I do."

"Do you promise to have and to hold, in sickness and in health, in good times and woe, for richer or poorer, keeping yourself solely unto her for as long as you both shall live?"

"I do."

"Gabi, do you take Tyler to be your lawfully wedded husband?"

She didn't answer.

11

GABI

It was like my voice wouldn't leave my throat. There was a stone stuck there and it was blocking everything. Even air.

This was it. I was getting married. Even though it was fake, even if we divorced later, I would have married this man, this handsome man standing by my side. If—when—I married some other guy for love later, it would always be my second marriage.

"Gabi?" Tyler whispered, his eyes wide.

But it was this or I wouldn't be able to live in the U.S. I wouldn't have the freedom to pursue my dream, and I would do anything for my dream, even temporarily marrying a stranger.

"I do," I finally said, breathless. "Sorry, I'm ... feeling emotional," I added with a small smile for Mr. Osment. "I do," I repeated, louder and clearer.

Mr. Osment narrowed his eyes, but continued, "Do you promise to have and to hold, in sickness and in health, in good times and woe, for richer or poorer, keeping yourself solely unto him for as long as you both shall live?"

This time I didn't hesitate. "I do."

"Okay, that's great, now face each other and join your hands."

Tyler and I turned to each other. He extended his hands to me. I dropped my bouquet on the table and then rested my hand in them, aware that I was shaking like a leaf in the wind. Gently, Tyler squeezed my hands, as if telling me it was okay. The man opened the black velvet box with the wedding bands and turned it to Tyler. "Now, Tyler, repeat after me while placing the band on her finger. I, Tyler, take you, Gabriela, ..."

The man went on reciting the same sentence he said before, just this time Tyler had to recite it all while holding my shaking hands and looking into my eyes. His hazel eyes were bright and slightly scared. I bet mine were a mirror of his. Despite the fear stamped on our faces, we held on. We stared into each other's eyes and held on tight.

Tyler plucked the thin band from the box and slowly slid the band onto my finger. It fit with the engagement ring perfectly.

Then, I repeated the same words and put the wedding band on Tyler's finger. His band was slightly wider than mine—the attendant at the jewelry store had told me men liked them that way, so I went with that.

"By the authority vested in me by the state of California," Mr. Osment said, "I now pronounce you husband and wife. You may now kiss."

My eyes went wide. Kiss? Who said anything about kissing? *Meu Deus*, of course there would be kissing. *Droga*, why hadn't I thought of that before? I would have prepared myself for this.

Tyler squeezed my hand once more, and I cut the crazy words hemorrhaging in my brain.

This was just a kiss. I had kissed a few guys before. This was no big deal.

He tugged at my hand and I nodded, trying to relax. With his eyes on mine, Tyler took the lead. He stepped in and leaned down to me. He let go of one of my hands and cupped my cheek as his warm lips pressed against mine. He held on for four seconds—I counted—before letting go.

Warmth spread through my cheeks.

"All right, that's done," Mr. Osment said, flipping a paper on the table toward us. This was the man's job. He did this a few dozens of times each day. He didn't really care about our feelings right now. He certainly wouldn't care how I felt like running and hiding under a blanket. "Now, please, Lenna, our witness, sign here." The blonde leaned over the table and signed the paper. "Now, you two sign here."

Composed, Tyler caught the pen from the table and handed it to me. Forcing a small smile, I took the pen from him and poised the pen to sign. My hand still shook, and I had to let out a long breath and try to relax before signing the paper. Then I gave Tyler the pen and he signed.

There. It was done.

"Okay," Mr. Osment said, picking up the paper. "I'm going to go register your license and make your certified copy, and then I'll be back in a moment. Meanwhile, Carol will take some pictures of you two."

"Thank you," Tyler said.

"Thank you so much," I said automatically.

"You're welcome." Mr. Osment nodded and walked away into the courthouse.

Carol stepped in front of us with a big smile. "I already took a few pictures of you two during the ceremony, but now I would like a few posed pictures here in the garden." She gestured to some bushes to our side. "Stand here, facing each other. Gabriela, you're holding the bouquet with one hand, the other hand you give it to Tyler. Tyler I want you to reach for Gabriela's waist." We did as we were told. "Now look at each other. Let me see the love."

What love? This woman was dreaming.

These pictures were part of my golden ticket for my green

card. I had to appear happy, satisfied during these pictures. I smiled wide, thinking of my green card, and more importantly, thinking of polo.

Tyler, on the other hand, had a tight-lipped smile, but it was okay. We could blame nerves.

Carol guided us through a few more pictures around the garden and all of the pictures had us touching each other, sometimes holding hands, other times we were in a half-embrace, or with my back against his chest, and almost all the pictures had us looking at each other lovingly.

Twenty minutes later, Mr. Osment came back with a white envelope. "All right, I have your certificate of marriage ready for you."

"Great," Tyler said, his voice tight. "It's official."

"It is." Mr. Osment handed the envelope to Tyler. "Please check to see if your names are spelled right." Tyler pulled the certificate from the envelope and he held it between us.

Tyler nodded, returning the certificate to the envelope. "It all looks good."

"Then congratulations." Mr. Osment shook our hands. "You guys are all done."

"Great, thanks," Tyler said.

I tried for a smile. "Thanks."

Tyler grabbed my hand and we walked out of the courthouse as a married couple.

Meu Deus, meu Deus, meu Deus, meu Deus.

I was married. I was a married woman.

I couldn't believe I had done it. I had gone through with it.

The silence was thick inside Tyler's truck as he drove me back to the store, where I would return the rented dress and put on my clothes that I had left there.

Like before, Tyler stopped the car in the no-parking spot in front of the store.

He turned slightly to me. "So ..."

I swallowed hard. "So ..."

"We're married now."

"*Sim.*" *Meu Deus*, I was married. I wondered how much time I needed to get my brain wrapped around that. "I'm freaking out," I confessed in a whisper. He let out a low chuckle and I gaped at him. "What's so funny?"

"It's not funny," he said as his chuckle faded. "It's ... I don't know what it is, but I'm freaking out too."

I narrowed my eyes at him. "You don't look like it."

"I'm trying to remain calm so I won't scare you."

A tiny smile took over my lips. "*Bem*, thanks." My half-smile fell and I turned more toward him. "You don't regret it, right?"

"No." He gave one sharp shake of his head. "Not yet, at least."

I snorted. "Wait until I have my stuff all over your apartment. You'll regret then."

One corner of his lips tugged up. "I might."

"*Bem*, even if you do, I want to thank you for taking the deal and going through this crazy thing with me."

"You're welcome," he said simply.

"So, hm, I'll see you later?"

He nodded. "Five at the apartment, right?"

"Right."

"I'll be there."

"Great." I opened the door and got out. The last thing I needed was to ruin the dress. But ... the bouquet. It was so pretty, I didn't want to throw it away, but I couldn't take it home either. "Would you mind taking this with you?" He stared as I deposited the bouquet onto the passenger seat. "Take it to your place and put it in a vase or a glass with water."

"Okay," he said, sounding a little wary.

"Great. Thanks." I closed the truck's door and stepped back, waiting for him to take off, but he stayed there, watching me. Self-consciousness wrapped around me and, after turning around, I bolted into the store.

The same attendant came to greet me. "Back already."

"Yes. We have a flight to catch and we can't waste time," I lied, thinking of my real flight tomorrow night. I had to do something about that.

She guided me to the dressing room where I slipped into a stall. I reached for the zipper on the back, but caught my reflection in the mirror and stopped. It was silly of me, but I liked how this dress made me look, how it accentuated my curves and made me look like a gorgeous, strong woman.

Maybe it was my emotions running high, maybe it was the moment, or maybe it was the craziness in my head, but I slowly took off the dress, folded it on a hanger, put on my clothes from before, and walked to the front of the store to buy my rented wedding dress.

12

GABI

I PACED MY BEDROOM, watching the time on my phone. It was five fifteen and Tyler wasn't here. *Meu Deus.* He wouldn't show up. And my family was on the way. What would I tell them?

Ha, I got you. I just wanted to see you all one more time before I go back to Brazil.

No, that wouldn't work.

Gui and Pedro came back shortly after I had come back from my wedding—*tche*, that was hard to swallow. I hid the dress in the guest bedroom's closet and the ring in my suitcase. The guys stayed most of the afternoon in the living room, playing video games, but I was too nervous to play with them. Instead, I retreated to the guest bedroom, took a long shower, and changed into nicer clothes. Since this would be a celebration, I chose a jean miniskirt and an off-shoulder beige blouse with 3/4 sleeves, and brown cowboy boots. We Fernandeses were big lovers of cowboy boots. I pulled my hair up in a ponytail and applied a little makeup—second time in one day. Since I rarely used any makeup, it had to be a record.

At five thirty, I started panicking. *Meu Deus*, he wouldn't show up.

I was reaching for my phone to call Tyler and ask him why the hell he wasn't here already when a knock came from the door. Two seconds later, Gui stuck his head inside. "Hey, hm, the doorman told me there's a Tyler downstairs asking for you."

My hands started shaking and I hid them behind my back. "Send him up."

Gui crossed his arms. "Who's Tyler?"

"Just send him up, Gui."

With suspicion in his eyes, Gui marched to the kitchen—and I followed him—where he told the doorman to let Tyler up. Pedro was probably holed up in his room, not up for another get-together, and Hilary sat on a high stool at the kitchen's island, drawing on her pad. I spied over her shoulder and saw a beautiful feminine suit with elegant lines and sharp edges.

"Pretty," I said.

She smiled at me. "Thanks."

"I know you had class this afternoon and have class tomorrow morning. Thanks for coming."

She waved me off. "That's why I didn't take any classes early morning or late evening this semester, so I could drive up here to spend the evenings with you guys if I wanted to. Besides, your message made me curious."

From across the kitchen, Gui glared at me. I ignored him and went to the front door. I took a long breath, sent a prayer out, and opened the door. I counted five seconds until the elevator dinged and Tyler walked out. He halted and stared at me.

My cheeks heated up as I realized he looked nice in dark jeans, a white polo shirt, and brown cowboy boots. It was like we had planned our outfits to match.

"Ready?" I asked in a low voice.

His eyes held my stare as he nodded. He resumed walking and was soon standing beside me inside the apartment. By then, Hil had abandoned her drawing pad. She and Gui watched us with curious eyes.

"Come on," I told Tyler, gesturing him to follow me to the kitchen.

I halted near Gui and Hil. "Guys, this is Tyler Reid. Tyler, this is my brother Gui and his girlfriend, Hilary."

"Hey there," Tyler said, extending his hand to Gui.

My brother watched Tyler's outstretched hand for two seconds before taking it. "Nice to meet you."

Tyler shook Hil's hand next, and even though she was kind, I could see the question in her gaze.

Gui stuffed his chest and crossed his arms. "So, hm, Tyler, how do you know Gabi?"

Tyler opened his mouth to answer, but the doorbell rang. Saved by the bell!

Usually, I ran to the door to answer it, but I didn't want to risk leaving Tyler alone with Gui, not even for a second. When the bell rang a second time, Gui finally moved and went to the door.

"You have the damn keys," he complained to Bia as she and Garrett entered the apartment. "Why didn't you use it?"

"I told her to use it," Garrett said, shrugging.

"*Oi pra você também*," Bia said, strutting across the living room. Then, her eyes landed on the guy by my side. "Tyler? What are you doing here?"

With narrowed eyes, Garrett walked by Bia and greeted Tyler, clasping hands like friends usually did. "Hey, Ty, how is it going?"

"Good, good."

Gui looked from Bia to Garrett to Tyler to me. "You all know each other?"

Garrett stared at me for a moment and I averted my eyes, ready to blurt some new lie and then the doorbell rang again. Gui had to go back the three steps he had just advanced. He opened the door for Leo and Hannah. Five minutes later, Ri also showed up.

I let out a long breath. They were all here. *Bom*, apart from Pedro who was in his bedroom, and Iris. I wondered if we could still consider her part of the group. I mean, everyone hoped she and Pedro would make up soon.

Once more, I introduced Tyler to the rest of my family and friends. It was probably a little confusing to understand who was who, but he would get it soon.

For once, the guys stood around the kitchen's island with us instead of sitting in the living room playing video games, and when the drinks were being passed around, Gui continued being a pain in my ass.

"Tyler, you didn't answer my question before," Gui said, his tone a little wary. A little challenging. "How do you know my sister?"

Tyler and I exchanged a brief glance and I nodded. He lifted his chin and held my brother's hard stare with his own. "Well, to tell you the truth, I've known her for a year now. And we've been dating for almost just as long."

Gui's jaw hit the floor. Bia spat out her drink. Ri chuckled as if it was a joke, and the rest of the gang stared at us—at me—as if I had grown an alien head.

"Come again?" Gui finally asked, his voice low.

"That's impossible," Bia said, not more than a gasp. "Gabi would have told us if she had been dating you." She looked at me. "Right?"

I grimaced and the pain that crossed her features hit deep in me. *Droga*, I knew that besides Gui, she would be disappointed in me for the lie, but I hadn't expected it to hurt this bad.

"I'm sorry," I muttered. Then, I cleared my throat and continued, "I'm sorry I didn't tell you all before." I took a step closer to Tyler, brushing my arm against his. A shiver ran up from the spot where we touched to my shoulder and up my neck. "To be honest, our relationship wasn't serious at first."

"What do you mean?" Ri asked, a little amused. "You were in Brazil most of the time."

"That was why I didn't think it was serious. We only saw each other when I visited, and when I was in Brazil, we would talk every day via Skype and phone and text messages. But, we realized we really liked each other."

"And a few days ago I realized she was leaving once more," Tyler took over, "and this time she wouldn't be back until July, and I felt ... I realized I didn't want her to go. So ..."

I gulped, willing the shaking of my hands to go away. Slowly, I fished the ring from my skirt pocket and slipped it into my finger.

Everyone gasped and then the room went quiet.

Nobody moved a muscle or even breathed for a few, long seconds. I thought Gui's eyes would pop from their sockets. Or the tense muscle in his neck would burst open.

"*Que porcaria é essa*?" Gui finally asked, his voice low and laced with something I couldn't decipher. Anger? Frustration? Shock? "That's ... absurd."

At that, the room erupted with loud voices asking, talking, crying, and even laughing.

Overwhelmed, I stared, not sure what to do or who to answer first.

"*Tche*, the apartment better be on fire or I'll think you all went crazy," Pedro shouted from the hallway leading to the bedrooms, his hair disheveled and three-day-old stubble darkening his jawline. That shut everyone up again and we all turned to him. He crossed his arms. "*Então*, what's going on?"

Gui was the first one to answer. "My dear sister is engaged." He gestured to my hand.

Pedro's eyes went wide, then a small smile spread over his lips. He looked from me to Tyler and back to me. "Are you happy?"

"Y-yes," I answered, caught by surprise. I focused on the fact that I would stay here in the U.S. with my family and friends, and I could pursue my dreams. That made me happy. "Yes, I am happy."

Pedro took a step closer and pulled me into a tight hug. "Then, I'm happy for you too. Congratulations."

After embracing me, he shook Tyler's hand and congratulated him too.

"Thanks," Tyler said, his voice rough. I hoped no one saw how disconcerted he was right now.

All the while, everyone watched our exchange.

Pedro frowned at our family. "*O quê*? Aren't you happy for her? You should be. You guys should congratulate her. Them."

Hilary was the first to smile and congratulate us. Next was Hannah. Then the rest of them—except for Bia and Gui. They stayed in the back of the group, glaring at me. At us. They didn't utter another word for a long while.

More questions were asked—how we met, how we managed to sneak around, what Tyler did, where he lived, what our plans were. I answered most of them as honestly as I could—which wasn't honest at all—and to some, like what our plans were, I answered with a "We're still talking about it."

At some point, Garrett pulled Tyler into the living room where they played video games with Leo, Ri, and Pedro. Hil and Hannah finally changed subjects and started talking about Hil's upcoming showcase.

Gui came to my side, leaned against the kitchen's counter like me, and watched over our family and friends. "Have you already told *mãe* and *pai*?"

Droga, I hadn't really considered how I would do that yet. "*Ainda não*. I'll Skype with them tomorrow morning and tell them everything, including that I won't be going to Brazil tomorrow."

His eyes bulged. "You won't be going? What will you do, then? Just quit college?"

"Something like that." I hadn't actually thought that far ahead. Of course, staying here meant I wouldn't be going back to Brazil, to my parents, and I wouldn't be going to college. One more thing to add to my to-do list: call the university and drop my classes for the semester.

"They will kill you."

"I'm hoping they won't."

"*Pai* will." He finally turned his eyes to me. "You know how this looks like, right? What is he getting from all of this? You get the green card and he gets what?"

I blanched. Of course I expected Gui, and everyone else actually, to connect the dots and accuse us of a sham engagement, but hearing it out loud was different.

Gosh, if my brother was this mad because of an engagement, imagine if I had told him I was actually already married to the guy.

Once more, I donned the act I had barely begun but was starting to hate. "How can you think that of me? Don't you know me? As if I would ever get married like that. You're so wrong."

His jaw popped, and after a moment, he continued, "If it's not a pretense, then you should have gone slower. Can you imagine how *pai* will react once you introduce him to a guy and tell him you're already engaged? You're in so much trouble."

I lifted my chin and faced my brother. "I don't need his permission to do anything. I'm already twenty years old. I have my own money, and—"

"His money. Grandpa's money. My money. We gave it to you."

I flinched. "Wow, that's a low blow."

"It's true."

"Fine. You want your money back? I'll make a transfer tonight before I go to bed. Happy?"

I turned my back to him and went to the balcony for some fresh air.

Leaning on the rail, I inhaled a lungful and exhaled slowly. *Tche*, this was going to be harder than I thought.

And Gui had just landed a nice punch to my gut. His money ... It wasn't only his money, or our father's money. It was our family's money. The ranch started with our grandfather, and the money had been passed down to the family. I had money that I had inherited from our grandparents, and more that our father had given to me through the years. Gui had given me some from his polo winnings as birthday and Christmas gifts. If he wanted that back, I was glad to give it to him.

I felt heat simmering in my head as I was about to explode. The fresh air of the balcony wasn't helping.

I had gotten only a few minutes of silence for myself before I heard the balcony glass door sliding open then closed. Steps approached and then Bia leaned on the rail beside me.

She stayed quiet, watching the stars. She was never, ever quiet.

"You're mad at me," I said, breaking the tense silence.

"That's one way to put it." Her voice was terribly calm. Not a good sign. "I just ..." She looked at me and I could see the disappointment and hurt in her sea-green eyes. "We were always so, so close, despite our age difference. And despite the distance."

For some reason, I wanted to defend myself. "We haven't been that close the last three years."

"It isn't easy to maintain a friendship when you're so far away."

"Believe me, I know."

"I should have tried harder, though," she said. Me too. But that was done now. Those three years were gone. "Still ... why didn't you tell me?"

My defensive side was still on. "Why didn't you tell me you were having trouble in Fort Howell? Why didn't you tell me about Garrett? I never found out about all of that until months after."

She flinched. "Touché."

"Sorry, I didn't mean that in a bad way." I sighed and stared at her. Garrett knew the truth about Tyler and me. It would be hard for him to keep this from Bia. But if I told her the truth ... To be honest, I needed someone who knew about it besides Garrett. Someone I could talk to. Someone who, after the first shock, would be there for me. "It's a sham, Bia."

She blinked at me. "*O qué?*"

"The engagement. Actually, Tyler and I got married this afternoon." I let out a hollow chuckled.

Her jaw dropped open. "*O quê?*"

"I found out he needed money, and I needed to stay here. So, I offered him a deal. I would pay him to marry me. Then, we get a divorce in two years." She just stared at me, her sea-green eyes huge. "I know it's not the best solution, but it was the only one I had. And I don't regret it. Not right now at least. We're not hurting anyone. In fact, we're helping each other. Tyler will be debt free and I'll be playing polo here. And I'll be with you guys." I paused. "Hm, one more thing. Garrett knows. He helped me track Tyler down. I asked him not to tell you. I didn't want you to worry if Tyler turned my offer down."

She blinked again. "Garrett knows?"

"Don't be mad at him. I made him promise he wouldn't tell you."

She crossed her arms. "And why are you telling me?"

"Because you've always been my best friend, and even though we grew a little apart, I still consider you that."

She looked out to the dark night. "So, what's your plan? Lie to your brother and my brothers for the next two years?" She gasped, returning her gaze to me. "*Meu Deus*, what about your father?"

I flinched. "Tyler and I will stay engaged for the next two years. When someone asks about the date, we'll just say we aren't in a rush. When the two years are up, we'll get a divorce, and we'll just tell everyone else that we broke up."

Bia shook her head. "You know that's crazy, right?"

"I know." I reached for her, but she took a step back. *Droga*. "I understand you're mad at me, but please, don't tell anyone."

"I won't tell anyone," she said, her tone harsh. "But that doesn't mean I'm okay with it."

"I know," I whispered.

The hurt was still clear on her pretty face. Without another word, Bia retreated into the apartment. I stayed on the balcony, looking up at the stars and doubting everything.

What had I done? I had married a stranger and now had to pretend to be in love with him in front of all the people who mattered to me. Even though I wanted a life here, I hadn't really thought about how I would have to abandon my entire life in Brazil. *Meu Deus*, my horse. What would I do without Tostado?

A deep sadness dug a hole in my chest and tears welled in my eyes.

13

I HANDED the remote control to Garrett. "That was fun," I admitted. I hadn't played video games in so long, I had forgotten how much fun it could be. And, from what I gathered from our conversations so far, the guys here—Garrett, Leo, Pedro, and Ricardo—seemed to be into horses, obviously, video games, monster truck racing, and working out. So far, so good.

"Wait until you reach level twenty," Garrett said. "It gets crazy. Good crazy."

"Don't worry," Ricardo said. "Soon you'll be mastering all these games too."

Pedro snorted. "As if you've mastered them all."

Ricardo sat up straighter. "Is that a challenge?"

Pedro, who had been sulking most of the time, stood up and puffed his chest. "It is!"

Garrett jerked his chin to the two brothers bickering. "They do that a lot," he said with a chuckle.

I just stared, amused.

As Pedro and Ricardo assumed the control of the video game for their challenge, I scanned the place, taking in everything and everyone. The apartment was large—the living room alone was probably the size of my entire shitty two-bedroom apartment—and the furniture and the decorations on the shelves and walls looked expensive. The sofas were large and comfortable, the dining table was heavy and long with big, high chairs, and even the kitchen looked like it cost at least twice more than my former college's annual tuition.

Hilary stood beside Guilherme behind the tall counter-slash-island that separated the kitchen from the living room. She seemed serene while Guilherme emitted harsh vibes, especially when he glared at me every ten seconds.

Then, I saw as Bia entered the apartment from the balcony, her face as harsh as Guilherme's. And Gabi was alone on the balcony.

I took my beer bottle from the side table and went out to her. Even with her back to me, I saw Gabi wipe at her eyes and straighten, as if getting ready for another fight.

I leaned my lower back on the rail beside her. "Hey."

She glanced at me, and I thought I saw something like relief flashing in her eyes. "Hey." She glanced over her shoulder to the inside of the apartment, then returned her gaze to the starry sky. "How was it going in there?"

I watched her family inside the apartment through the glass doors. "It's fine ... Garrett is my friend from vet school, so we always got along fine, and the rest of your family ... well, they are a little wary, but most of them are nice and are trying to make me feel welcome." I felt myself starting to smile. It had been kind of fun in there. "All except for Bia and your brother." The tentative smile was gone and I frowned. "I expected that from your brother, but not from Bia. I mean, I was never as close to her as I am to Garrett, but she knows me. We always got along fine too."

She sighed. "She's mad at me for not telling her about us sooner."

"Oh, I see." I knew she would face a lot of that from her family, and I suddenly felt bad for her. "She'll come around."

"She will, but she'll make me suffer first."

I turned to her. "They are watching us."

She stiffened. "Who?"

"Everyone. Not straight out, but they keep stealing glances this way."

She blushed. "They are probably expecting us to be a couple like, you know …"

"Hold hands, hug, and kiss?"

The blush in her cheeks increased. "Yes."

Before I could stop myself, I reached over and took one of her hands into mine and weaved our fingers together. "Is this okay?"

Her eyes went wide. "*Sim.* Yeah. Sure. We should do more of that. Holding hands is safe, easy."

I lowered my gaze to our hands. Her skin was so smooth, so pale compared to mine, but her hand fit so well into mine. "It is," I said, my voice hoarse.

She looked up the stars again, and I couldn't help it but stare at her pretty face. Her small nose, her high cheekbones, her round jaw, and her naturally pouted lips. And her eyes. Her bright blue eyes were the most amazing shade. Her dark, wavy hair was pulled back into a thick ponytail, and even though I had seen her hair before and liked it down, I also liked it this way. I especially liked the way it showed off her long neck and slender, bare shoulders.

An urge to lean into her and brush my lips on her soft shoulder and neck hit me hard, taking me by surprise. I wasn't stupid. I thought she was beautiful from the first moment I laid eyes on her, and every second spent with her only made me think she was even more beautiful. But I knew this was a fake marriage. There would be nothing between us.

Debt free. This deal meant being debt free. That was all.

Right?

I shook those thoughts from my head. "You were right."

"I'm right most of the time," she teased. "But what are you talking about specifically?"

"About your family. They seem freaked out that we're engaged. I can't imagine how they'd react if we had told them the truth."

She snorted. "They would kill me. Or you. Probably you. And then they would make me suffer."

I groaned. When she said things like that, I almost regretted this damn deal. "That's not very comforting."

"Sorry ... but they are good people. Once we tell them we're not in a rush and will take things slow with the engagement, they will relax and Gui will be more like his normal self, and you'll see they are great. All of them." She turned her pretty eyes to me and tugged at my hand. "We better go inside and socialize. After all, one of the reasons I want to live here is to spend more time with them." She jerked her head toward her family.

I confess, curiosity about what other reasons she had for wanting to live here poked at my gut, but to be honest, it wasn't my business. So, I pushed those thoughts aside and focused on pretending some more.

Still holding hands, we walked back into the apartment.

THE REST of the evening went fine.

Hil was able to control Gui, and he didn't say anything mean again, but he also didn't try to be nice. He just stood there, in the kitchen or at the back of the living room, watching with hard eyes.

And Bia avoided me as much as she could. When all the girls were around the kitchen's island, she talked to Hannah or Hilary, but never with me.

That hurt so damn much.

But I pushed past it. I knew she would forgive me in a few days. I just had to endure it for now. Her and Gui's glare.

"So." Hannah turned to me with a big smile. "We are dying for another wedding in the family. When is the big day?"

I forced a smile. "We don't have a date yet, actually. I'll probably move in with him in a few days, and we'll see how that goes. We're in no rush."

Hil frowned. "So no date? No plans for me to design another dress?"

If only she knew … "*Bem*, the few times we talked about dates, we thought at the beginning of next year."

"That is so far away," Hannah pointed out.

"I know, but like I said, we aren't in a rush. We want to live together first."

"That makes sense," Hannah said. "Leo and I lived together for almost two years before getting married."

"Before he proposed, you mean," Bia said, still sounding hurt. "It usually goes with moving in together, then getting engaged, then marrying."

"Not all love stories are the same, Bia," I protested.

Bia rolled her eyes and went to the bar along the wall to get herself another drink.

I let out a long exhale.

"She'll come around," Hannah said.

"I know ..." I sighed. "I just ... I didn't mean to hurt her feelings." I looked at the girls in front of me. "Anyone's feelings. I'm sorry I kept it from you guys." *I'm sorry I'm still keeping a lot from you guys.*

Hil reached across the island and held my hand in mine. "It's okay, Gabi. We were just a little surprised. But, if you're happy, if this is what you want, then we're happy for you too."

Hannah nodded in agreement.

I offered them a small smile. "Thanks."

Bia joined us a few moments later with a glass filled to the brim with Coke and whiskey. Thankfully, Hannah changed the subject by asking Hilary more about the upcoming showcase at her school. Hilary beamed and launched into a detailed narration of her plans for the show.

I paid attention to the conversation for about ten seconds before my thoughts betrayed me and I turned my eyes to the living room, where Tyler was with the guys. Even Gui was there, though he made a point of sitting on the farthest corner of the couch, so he was far away from Tyler.

Garrett and Ri were the ones playing at the moment, while

Gui, Leo, and Tyler watched, and Pedro messed with his phone. The guys narrated the objectives of the game and the shortcuts on the controller so Tyler would learn how to be as good as them in no time.

I smiled.

Despite this all being a sham, I was glad Tyler seemed to be getting along with my family. After all, he would have to endure them for two years.

Leo made a joke about Ri's video game skills, and as usual, Ri took it more seriously than he should. Ri lunged at Leo and they were play-fighting. I heard Garrett say, "Told you. It happens all the time," to Tyler, who wore a smile.

I sucked in a sharp breath.

Meu Deus, he was handsome, especially when he smiled like that. Even from here, I could see the amused shine in his hazel eyes. He had shaved recently—the sharp lines of his jaw and chin were even more chiseled with a clean face.

My fingers itched and I realized I wanted to run my fingertips down his jaw, his neck, to where his polo shirt dipped to reveal the top of his chest and—

I stopped those thoughts before it was too late.

No, no, no. This was a *sham* wedding, that was all. We would probably become friends with each other during that time since we would be together a lot, but that was it. I wasn't the type of girl to be friends with benefits. At least, I didn't think I was.

I shook my head again.

What was wrong with me?

Tyler's eyes found mine and his smile dimmed a little. His eyes were still lit with amusement. A small smile spread through my lips.

After excusing himself, Tyler stood and came to the kitchen. He halted beside me. "Hey."

"*Oi,*" I whispered, feeling incredibly lame.

"Where's the trash?" he asked.

"Here," I said, taking the empty beer bottle from his hand. I stepped back and opened a cabinet that had the trash hidden inside. I gestured to it, so he would know where it was next time. Tyler nodded. "Want another beer?" I turned to the fridge.

The girls, still chatting around the island, paid us no attention. Except for Bia. I could feel her side glance burning my back.

"No, no more alcohol. I have to drive later. How about a Coke?"

I grabbed a can of *guaraná* from the fridge. "How about this one?"

He shook his head. "No way. Coke, please."

I got the *guaraná* for me and handed him a Coke can. "It seems like you're having fun." I jerked my chin toward the guys in the living room.

Sporting a lopsided grin, Tyler popped his can open. "They are cool."

I nodded and took a long swallow from my soda. Tyler's eyes rummaged around, no apparent destination, but I noticed when he caught Bia spying on us. He tensed beside me, and then, smoothly, he slid a hand around my waist, pulling me slightly closer to him. My shoulder rested against his chest and the right side of my ass touched his thigh. I swallowed hard.

But he didn't stop there. Tyler leaned into me and put his mouth over my ear. His heady, musky scent hit my nose and I stopped breathing for a moment before I leaned into him too. "Relax or she'll notice."

Shit, I had to let him know that I had told everything to Bia too.

But now more people were looking at us, so it was best if we kept pretending. I let out a shallow breath and smiled, as if he had told me something funny, or even kissed me on the cheek. He held my gaze as he backed out, returning to his glued-to-my-side position.

His hand on my waist? It was all over my mind. I could feel the heat from his palm through my blouse and, *Meu Deus*, it was burning.

In the living room, Garrett stood. "Hey, Ty, your turn. Come on."

"K." Tyler took a step out, then halted as if he had remembered something. He turned back to me, planted a soft peck on my cheek, and strolled to the living room, where he got the controller and sat down beside Garrett to play whatever game they had on.

Meanwhile, my cheeks burned. From his kiss and from the heat inside me.

Meu Deus.

"Aw, look at her," I heard Hannah say.

I turned to the girls and found them staring at me. "What?"

"You were looking at Tyler with loving eyes and a smile," Hil added. "So cute."

Hannah batted her eyelashes. "So in love."

Wow, they mistook my shocked gaze for love. That was fine with me.

To play along with the lie, I showed them a demure smile, then changed the subject so I wouldn't have to lie.

Two more hours went on like that—the guys taking turns on the video game, the girls talking around the kitchen island, the food and drink going around—before everyone started leaving.

"It's a weeknight," Ri said, walking to the door. "We gotta wake up early tomorrow morning."

"Same here," Hannah said beside Leo.

"So you're not returning to Brazil Saturday night, right?" Leo asked.

"Not now," I said.

"You should take Tyler there sometime soon," Hannah said. "I've only been there a couple of times so far, but it's so pretty. You're gonna love it," she said to Tyler.

He grinned at her. "I bet I will."

"Dinner tomorrow too?" Ri asked and everyone agreed.

After everyone left, Pedro let out a big yawn. "*Bom*, I'm beat. *Boa noite*." He waved at us and disappeared into the hallway leading to the bedrooms.

"I also have to wake up early to drive to L.A. tomorrow morning, so good night," Hilary said. She tugged Gui's arm, but he didn't budge. "Come on," she whispered.

Finally, after shooting another glare toward Tyler and me, Gui relented. "*Boa noite*," he said, his voice tight. Then, Hilary dragged him to their bedroom.

After they were gone, I counted to thirty, then I plopped down on the couch and let out a long breath. "That was tough."

Tyler sat beside me. "It wasn't so bad."

I stared at him, wondering where he had been all night, because it wasn't here. "How can you say that? Gui and Bia were terrible." And it wasn't only that. It was everything. I hated lying to my family. I hated how my body reacted each time Tyler and I pretended to be a couple, each time he touched me or held my hand or smiled at me.

And I still wasn't at peace with the fact that I had married a stranger.

"That was expected, right?"

I glanced at the door behind us, checking for any movement beyond the corridor. No one seemed to be out of their bedrooms. Even so, I lowered my voice as I said, "Gui knows."

Tyler's body went rigid beside me. "What? How?"

"No, no, I mean, he doesn't know we are married, but he accused me of getting engaged to you so I can get a green card."

He ran a hand through his hair. "Shit. What did you say?"

"I lied, of course!" I hissed. "I asked him how he could think that of me? And I told him we would prove to him we're serious." *Droga*, I still had to transfer his money back to him before I went to bed. I dropped my face in my hands. "*Meu Deus*, how could he think that of me? I am just like that."

"No, you're not," Tyler said, serious. "Look, we knew there would be some resistance, right? With time, they will stop bugging you about it." He frowned. "By the way, is it always like this?"

"Like what?"

"Everyone always together and so close, and doing the same things, and talking at the same time." He shuddered, as if the idea of a tight-knit family was horrifying.

"Hm, *sim*, we are all like this."

He let out a long breath. "That will be hard getting used to."

I felt myself tensing. *Droga*. I had to keep relaxed, even when I didn't agree with him, or didn't like the way he reacted to things. Two years was a long time to be tense and feel awkward about this.

However, he had surprised me tonight. I had expected more opposition from him. I thought he wouldn't play the role of the loving fiancé well. Not that it had been perfect. I was sure I hadn't done a great job of it either, but it seemed we had passed the first test.

"So, are you free tomorrow?" I asked, breaking the tense silence. "I thought we could look for an apartment."

"That should work." He stood. "So, I'll pick you up here tomorrow?"

"Sure."

"What time?"

I stood beside him. "I have some things to take care of in the morning, so how about noon? We can look at apartments all afternoon."

He took a step back. "Sounds good." He turned and walked to the front door.

I followed him and halted beside the open door. "Thank you. I mean it. Thank you for all of this."

He stepped out of the apartment. "No problem."

"*Boa noite.*"

"Night," was all he said as he pressed the button for the eleva-tor. I stayed by the door, watching him as he waited. Too soon, the elevator arrived and, without looking back or saying another word, Tyler disappeared into the car.

When I was sure he was gone, I closed the door of the apartment and let out another long breath.

Meu Deus, what had I done?

I WAS a nervous wreck two mornings later.

I knew Gui and Pedro had practice early morning this Saturday, and Hil would go to her parents' house, so I stayed in bed until I was sure they were all gone.

Then, I made a quick breakfast, sat down on a stool around the kitchen's island, and opened the calculator app from my phone. I made a quick calculation of all the gifts Gui had given me over the years, then rounded them up a little, and made a transfer to his bank account. It was a lot of money, but it didn't really make a huge dent on my end.

I put my iPad up with a stand. My hands shook as I opened the Skype app and called my parents.

My mother answered on the fifth ring.

"*Oi querida,*" she said with a smile. "Sorry I didn't answer right away. I was putting away the grocery shopping."

I glanced at the clock on the corner of the iPad. It was nine thirty in the morning, which meant it was two thirty in the after-noon there. Depending on the time of the year, Brazil could be four to seven hours ahead of here.

"It's okay," I assured her.

"So, wanna tell me why I'm not at the airport picking you up right now?"

"I will, but can you call *pai*? I want to talk to you both about it."

Her smile faltered. "*Claro*," she muttered, before disappearing from the screen. My father was probably in his office, working on something from the Montenegro ranch. He lived and breathed that ranch, for the entire Montenegro name, really, be it the breeding farm or the polo team.

Two minutes, in which I stuffed my face with my toast, passed until my mother was back with my father. As I expected, he didn't look happy to see me from across the screen and not at the airport.

"Are you okay?" was the first thing he asked, his voice full of concern, and a lump rose in my throat. He was worried about me, and I was about to make him very mad at me. "What happened?"

"Hm, *bom*, I didn't tell anyone before ..." I started then pressed my lips together. *Tche*, this was harder than I thought it would be. "Actually Garrett knew, but not the others, and—"

"Gabi, what is it?" my mother asked with urgency. They were probably thinking the worse right now.

I placed my shaking hands and sweaty palms on my thighs under the counter, where they couldn't see it. "I've been dating an American guy for over a year now, and this week, he proposed."

Like the night before, silence met me.

My father burst out laughing. "Gabi, I didn't know you could tell jokes like that. Good one." He chuckled once more, then took a long breath to calm himself down. "Now, tell us, why didn't you come home?"

I bit the inside of my cheek, not sure what to say next.

My mother gasped. "*Meu Deus*, Luis Carlos, she's serious."

My father snorted. "She can't be serious." He leaned closer to the screen as if he could see me better. "You're serious?"

I nodded. "*Sim.*"

His eyes bulged and the look of horror on his face made me cringe.

"How-how did this happen?" my mother asked. "You haven't told us anything about this man. What is his name?"

"Tyler. His name is Tyler Reid." And then I told them what I told the rest of the family last night. That Tyler and I met through Garrett—poor Garrett—and that we began seeing each other, and we spoke even when I was away. And things moved quickly until we realized we didn't want to be so far apart anymore. Lies, lies, and more lies that made me sick to my stomach.

My mother listened with a hand over her mouth, as if she was afraid that she would yell at me. And my father paced behind my mother, his eyes downcast and his shoulders tense.

After a moment of silence, my mother lowered her hand. "W-what now? You're just gonna stay there and get married? What about us?"

"*De jeito nenhum, porra!*" my father shouted and I flinched. He rarely cussed and he rarely shouted. That he did both at the same time ... I was in big trouble. "This is nonsense. You're going to stop this madness and you're coming home right now."

I took a long breath. "I admit I may have handled this situation wrong. I should have come home last night and told you all about this face-to-face, but it's done now. I'm here and I'm staying. Tyler and I still haven't decided—"

"You're not deciding anything!" my father shouted again. "You better be on the next flight home, or so help me—" He pressed his lips together, his jaw ticking. "Just ... come home."

I inhaled sharply. I hated hurting them, but the mess was done now and I had to show I was an adult who could stand behind her decisions. "I'm sorry, *pai*. My home is here now. I wish you tw—"

"The hell it is!" he yelled. He slapped the counter where the laptop was set, making the screen shake a little bit. "You better be here by the weekend, young lady, or I'm going there to get you." Then, he stomped away.

My mother and I watched him until he disappeared from the room. A few seconds later, I heard as the door to his office slammed shut.

My mother grimaced. "Hm, I'm sorry, Gabi. You caught us by surprise." Welcome to the club. She tried to smile but failed. "I'm going to talk to him, okay? Try to calm him down."

"Sure."

"I'll talk to you later."

"Okay. *Tchau*."

"*Tchau*," she said and promptly turned off the call.

I stared at the screen for a couple of minutes, trying to take it all in. *Droga*. When the iPad's screen went black, I turned my gaze to my breakfast. I had barely touched my food, but now my stomach was in knots and I couldn't eat anything.

I stood from the stool and put everything in the trash.

15

TYLER

IN THE END, Gabi and I agreed to meet for lunch at a diner near her brother's apartment. After all, it was lunchtime and we had a lot of details to talk about, and we had to start studying the questions for the interview, even if it was still a couple of months away.

I barely had taken time off for lunch breaks. I usually brought a pop tart or a frozen meal to the office, heated it up, and ate while filling out reports or checking inventory, so as not to waste time.

But now my account was momentarily full—soon all that money would go to paying the bigger bills on my long list—and I could afford to eat better.

She was already seated at a corner booth and looking over the menu when I arrived. A lot of things would be hard to get used to with this deal and one of them was how pretty she always looked. Her hair was loose today, falling like a wave down her back, and she had on a blue blouse.

When I slid into the booth across from her, she lifted her face to me and I sucked in a sharp breath. Shit, the blouse made her blue eyes pop.

"Hey."

She offered me a small smile. "*Oi.*" We stared at each other and the air around us became awkward. "Hm, how was work?"

"I took the day off," I told her. "In fact, I took next week off too, since we'll probably be moving into a new apartment."

"That is a good thing, I guess." She frowned. "You're at vet school with Garrett, right? So working at a clinic must be nice."

I pressed my lips tight, not sure what to say to that. I sighed, remembering I would be living with this girl for the next two years, so I decided to tell her some basic stuff. "I didn't finish vet school, so I'm an assistant. Plus, I work more with dogs and cats. Dr. Bohm knows I want to treat the horses in the area, but he doesn't share those with me too often."

Her frown deepened. "So you're also a horse lover?"

I nodded. "Yup. Always have been."

"Oh," was all she said, and I felt like she wanted me to say more.

And for some reason, I did. "I rode a lot when I was younger, but I wasn't good enough to pursue professional polo or jumping or anything like that. I tried riding on weekends when I was in college, but it was hard to keep up with everything. After a year, I gave up. But my love for horses is still there."

Her forehead smoothed and the half-smile was back. "*Bom*, my family has a big ranch about twenty minutes from town, you know. You're welcome to go there and ride anytime."

This time, I frowned. What was I supposed to say to that?

The waitress saved me as she arrived to get our orders. Surprising me, Gabi asked for a cheeseburger with fries and a chocolate milkshake. From her slender figure, I thought she ate like a bird. I asked for the same, though I switched the milkshake for a soda.

When the waitress was gone, the awkward silence returned.

Gabi folded her hands on the table and I saw the ring glittering on her finger. It wasn't a big diamond, but it was big enough to make me sure I could never afford that. I couldn't exactly explain why, but I hated that ring.

"So, hm, I talked to my parents this morning ..." she started.

My gut clenched. "Uh-oh."

"Uh-oh indeed. They didn't take it well. In fact, my father said that if I'm not home by the weekend, he's coming here to get me."

"Would he do that?"

She nodded. "*Sim*, he would. And I wanted to give you the heads up because it means he'll be here soon and he'll come hard at us. *Bom*, more at you than at me. I think."

Shit. "Are you trying to make me back out of our deal?"

Her eyes widened. "Of course not! But I feel like I should prepare you for the challenges ahead."

"Will there be many?"

"Maybe. Probably." She sighed. "Sorry."

"For?"

"When I offered you this deal, I had the illusion that all the pieces of the puzzle would align and all the bad things that could happen would simply vanish." She shook her head once. "It seems I'm too optimistic."

"Sometimes that's a good thing."

The waitress brought our drinks and instead of drinking her milkshake, Gabi started playing with her straw.

"I was thinking ..." Gabi started.

"About?"

"Maybe we should go to Brazil instead."

I stared at her. "You mean instead of your parents coming here?"

She nodded. "I think it would be easier to control the situation there. We'll be at their place, where they are most comfortable. Here, they will be on edge all the time." One corner of her lips tugged. "Besides, I really could use that trip to bring more of my stuff here."

"Just back up a minute. You're talking about going to Brazil?"

"Hm, *sim.*" She played with her straw again. "Not now. Maybe in a month? I don't know. But we shouldn't wait too long."

I shook my head. "Can I think about this first?"

She shrugged. "Sure. Just consider that, if we don't go, my father will come here. He'll expect to meet you as soon as possible."

Go to Brazil? Even if for a few days? That sounded ludicrous. "Do you do everything your family expects you to?"

She stared at me as if I had thrown my drink at her. "This isn't only about my family, you know. I wouldn't mind going to the immigration office tomorrow or this afternoon, really, to get everything rolling." Her voice rose. "If I could simply hand you the money and you handed me the green card, the situation would be perfect. But it doesn't work that way. My family is from Brazil. It makes sense if we go there to visit and spend time with them. The immigration office will see pictures we can post online from there, and they will see we're having a good time there, that we aren't faking. In fact, we should take pictures of us together all the time and post everywhere. That will make our relationship seem real to the party that matters."

I didn't like it. I didn't like it at all, but ... "It makes sense." It really did and now that I had agreed to this, now that I could see myself debt free in a couple of years, I didn't want to let this deal go. Even if it meant having to go through some seriously uncomfortable situations. "Sorry I'm such a pain in the ass. I guess I'm just having a harder time getting used to all of this than I thought."

"You think I'm not?" She grimaced. "I confess that getting hitched to get a green card had crossed my mind a couple of times, but I had never really considered it. I'm not the most romantic girl out there, but I visualized my future wedding, and let me tell you, it was never, ever like this. So, don't think you're the only one suffering here."

I cringed. That was a strong word. "I'm not suffering. The entire situation makes me uncomfortable, that's all. I guess once we move in together and settle down for the next two years, I'll be able to relax again." I was about to ask her something when the waitress came back with our burgers.

Gabi thanked her then dug in, without even glancing at me again.

She was halfway through her burger and fries when I couldn't hold the question anymore. "Are you suffering?"

She stopped eating and stared at me. "What?"

"You said I'm not the only one suffering, so I'm assuming you're suffering."

Sighing, she leaned back on her booth. "Not suffering, but ... like I said, I never considered this situation. I didn't think things through."

"What do you mean?"

"My horse. Tostado, my beautiful horse, is in Brazil."

"Oh." That sucked. If I had a horse of my own, I wouldn't want to be that far away from him. "There's nothing you can do about that?"

"My brother and my cousins brought some of their horses when they moved here four years ago, but ... it's not a fast or easy process. I won't bring my horse here until I know—" She pressed her lips together.

"Until you know what?"

I thought she wouldn't answer me, but after a moment, she continued, "Until I know this deal will really work out and I have the green card in my hands."

"It makes sense," I said. We both wanted it to work, but we never knew what could happen. The immigration office could be onto us and deny her the green card, or something could happen along the way and she could need to leave.

We finished our burgers surrounded by tense silence and the loud chattering of the other customers.

"So," Gabi started after she was done eating, "after you left last night, I went online and searched for apartments that seemed nice." She pulled out a thick sheet of paper from her purse and spread them over the table between our plates. "These are the ones I liked the most."

I leaned over the table and glanced at the apartments staring back at me. "They seem ... expensive."

She waved me off. "Don't worry about that now. Let's just take a look at them."

I sighed, not in the mood to argue more. I nodded, and once I was done with my lunch, I paid our tab—she wanted to split it—and we left to go apartment hunting.

16

GABI

I COULD FEEL the tension and pain radiating from Tyler's body all afternoon. Right after lunch, we met with a real estate agent who specialized in rentals, and we went around town, looking at the apartments I had pre-selected and some I hadn't seen.

Agent Lucy Bowman took us first to some luxurious apartments in downtown—only one of those were on my list. The others I had selected were less expensive. Tyler cringed the entire time we looked at those. Soon, I was cutting most of the list and sticking to the lower end on pricing. It wouldn't hurt me to live in a smaller, simpler apartment, but apparently, it would hurt Tyler's ego if I chose something out of his price range.

Besides the price, Tyler's only request was an apartment with three bedrooms, which didn't really make sense since we only needed two—one for him and one for me, but I didn't ask about it, since he looked like he would bite my face off if I spoke to him. In the end, I didn't mind. If my parents did come to visit us at some point and wanted to stay with us instead of at Gui's, then we would have plenty of space.

So, by early evening, we had narrowed the list down to four

possibilities. They all looked nice and were a good distance from the vet clinic and my brother's apartment. And the most important point, according to Tyler, was that they weren't too expensive.

I had gotten that money was a sensitive subject, but I didn't get why he turned so sour when I mentioned paying the rent. Didn't it defeat the purpose of me giving him money to pay off his debt if he used it to pay his rent instead?

He was driving me back to Gui's apartment when my phone dinged.

Hil: *We're leaving for Malcolm's party. You're coming, right?*

Droga, I had forgotten about Malcolm's party. I was supposed to be in Brazil, not apartment hunting in Santa Barbara.

"Hm," I started, not sure how to phrase it. Since we were a couple now, we had to go to these parties together, right? "Hilary just reminded me of a party tonight. It's the birthday of a guy from polo, Malcolm. Want to come with me?"

His brows narrowed. Tyler glanced at me, then returned his eyes to the road. "I can't. I already have something scheduled tonight."

My gut twisted. I opened my mouth to say and ask so many things.

We're a couple now. You have to come with me.

Already tired of me?

Do you have a date? With someone else? What if anyone sees you? What if the immigration officer finds out?

Please, please, don't put our deal at risk.

But the afternoon had already been tense and I was tired. What I wanted was a nice hot shower and my pajamas. No more talking, no more walking.

So, I swallowed all my worries, and sent a quick reply to Hilary.

Me: *I had forgotten. Tyler and I already made other plans. Send a happy birthday to Malcolm for me.*

Hil: *Oh, okay. Will do. Have fun!*
Me: *You too.*

A minute later, Tyler pulled over in front of my brother's building.

I turned to him. "Hm, so, if you can, take a look at the apartments online again, and let me know which one you like the most. If we can, we should make a decision by Monday."

He looked out to the street. "Will do."

"All right." I opened the door, feeling like something was off, like many things were off. "Thanks."

"Bye," was all he said.

I hopped out of his truck and walked to the entrance of the building. He didn't even wait for me to reach the front door before he peeled away.

I frowned, watching as his truck turned onto the next street and disappeared from my sight. I really, really wanted a shower and to eat some pizza while watching *The Bachelor*, but that would have to wait a few more minutes.

Hilary had mentioned they were leaving for the party, which meant they could still be here—getting ready to leave or leaving at this second. If they saw me, I would have to lie more, and I was so freaking tired of lying today.

Determined, I turned away from the building and jogged to the nearest coffee shop, where I bought a caramel latte and waited the next thirty minutes. Meanwhile, I texted Priscila, since she was going nuts over the fact I had stayed here and I hadn't told her anything yet.

But now I would have to lie to her—something I had never done before.

Me: *So, I have something to tell you ...*

Then, I spilled the same lie I told my family. I was lying to everyone, and that just wasn't right.

17

TYLER

THIS AFTERNOON HAD BEEN PAINFUL.

All those apartments, and Gabi looking rather excited about it all.

I shuddered.

And what was that about rent? Like hell I would let her pay the entire thing by herself. I was her future roommate for the next two years, not her new toy.

To top it off, she invited me to another freaking party tonight. What did these people do? Party every night? What the hell?

Shit, this was getting complicated.

Groaning, I parked my truck in the hospital's parking lot and sat back.

What the fuck had I done? This entire situation was ridiculous.

Debt free, debt free.

It was all I could do not to turn around and ask Gabi to annul this insane marriage.

Debt free, debt free.

With a sigh, I climbed out of my truck and entered the hospital.

The lady at reception nodded at me as I walked past her. Then, I crossed paths with two nurses I saw often and they nodded at me too.

I knew every doctor and nurse and technician who worked on this floor of the hospital—a fact that I hated. A fact that stated things were going from bad to worse.

I paused at the room's door, trying to find the words I would say, but nothing came. For once, my mind was blank. Maybe that was a good thing. Maybe I wasn't supposed to think too much about this all.

After a soft knock, I stepped into the room.

My father smiled at me from the bed in the middle of the room. "Hey, you. I didn't expect to see you until tomorrow morning." He pointed the remote to the TV and lowered the volume. "Everything okay?"

He looked better than usual—a little less pale, a little less tired—which was a relief.

I walked up to his bed. "I should ask you that. How are you feeling?"

"Today is one of the good days," he replied.

A rare one, then.

"That's good," I said, taking the big armchair beside the bed.

He smiled at me. "So, what's new with you?"

I paused, considering what to tell him. "Hm, I'm planning on moving to a better apartment."

His smile was gone. "But ... why? I mean, our current place stinks, but we can't afford paying rent for a better apartment. Our financial situation is bad, isn't it? We can't afford that, Tyler."

I sighed. Until yesterday, our financial situation was even worse than he imagined. He had no idea I couldn't even afford rent anymore. But now things would change. Come Monday, I would pay a lot of our bills and things would start looking up.

I reached over and rested my hand on his arm. "We can, Dad. This time, we can."

"What do you mean?"

"Just ... trust me, okay."

"Tyler, you're not doing anything illegal, right? You're not ... playing poker or selling drugs or working for some mafia boss or—"

I chuckled. "No, Dad, nothing illegal." Not totally illegal. After all, I *was* married to Gabi. That part wasn't illegal. "Don't worry about it. Just worry about getting better, okay?"

He stared at me as if trying to see through my eyes. I must have looked trustworthy because he nodded. "Okay."

18

———————

GABI

I DIDN'T SEE Tyler on Sunday, though I went out again in the afternoon, lying to my family I was meeting Tyler somewhere. I walked around the neighborhood, feeling as if I was hiding a bomb inside my purse that could explode at any moment.

On Monday, he sent me a text letting me know which apartment he had liked the best. Again, when I left Gui's place to meet with the real estate agent, I lied I was meeting Tyler instead. That afternoon, I signed the papers for the apartment, and to make sure Tyler didn't bother me about rent at all, I paid a full year in advance. There, now he wouldn't be able to argue about it.

Then, on Tuesday, Tyler picked me up at 9:15, as agreed, and drove us to the immigration lawyer's office. There, the secretary told us to sit down in the waiting area until someone came to get us.

I took a spot on a loveseat and Tyler sat in an armchair, not too far, but not close to me either. He stared at the news show on the TV and didn't utter a word the entire twenty minutes we waited. In fact, I realized that besides the "good morning" when I entered his truck earlier, he hadn't spoken a single word to me yet.

I was about to ask him what was going on when a tall woman with black hair pulled in to a tight bun stepped into the waiting area.

"You two must be Tyler Reid and Gabriela Fernandes. I'm Anita Wyatt, nice to meet you."

After greeting her, Tyler and I followed the lawyer back to her elegant office. She stopped at the door and offered us water or coffee. When we declined, she closed the door and took the seat behind her desk.

"So, what can I do for you?" she asked, clasping her hand together over her desk.

"Well," I started. In a couple of minutes, I told her about our wedding last week and when I started telling her about how we met, she interrupted us.

"I can smell a fake wedding a mile away," she said, making me cringe. Tyler, finally, showed some emotion. He straightened in his chair with a big frown between his brows.

Actually, I had no dreams we could trick the lawyer. I was hoping she would help us trick the government, as bad as it sounded.

"I can explain." I told her about our situation, about why we decided to get married and why I wanted a green card—to play polo here. At that, Tyler looked at me from the corner of his eyes. I guess we hadn't talked about that yet, had we?

Like Tyler and I, the attorney didn't think we were harming anyone, though she had one condition. She didn't want us tricking the government any further, which meant, she wouldn't let us fabricate a history with photoshopped pictures of us together from before our wedding date, or fake older messages and emails. She explained to us the consequences if we were found out by the government—deportation for me and jail for Tyler.

"That's an exaggeration, of course," Anita said. "I think I only saw one man go to jail for a marriage-based green card before, but that was because he was marrying the daughter of a powerful international criminal. Her father had plans to smuggle weapons and drugs into the country through her. Most of the time, there's a hefty fine."

Tyler's jaw popped at that. I knew he didn't want to go to jail—no one wanted to—and money was already a problem for him. He couldn't have yet more debt.

I turned to him. "It's okay if you want to give up," I said in a low voice. I knew the lawyer still could hear me, but speaking in hushed tones made me feel a little less awkward. "We can get the marriage annulled and we can forget this ever happened."

He stared at me with those intense hazel eyes, his jaw even harder than before. "No, I'm not giving up now."

I wanted to ask him if he was sure, but the look he gave me, a depthless glare, made me shut my mouth and nod.

The lawyer, after stipulating a hefty retainer, finally agreed to help us with the green card application and the process.

"All right, you two have to move in together right away and take lots of pictures together," Anita said. "All the time. Selfies everywhere. Always smiling, always happy. Oh, and study the interview questions. Know them by heart."

We knew that was a part of the deal, but being close together and pretending to love each other was still our biggest challenge.

The lawyer gave us a few forms to fill out, an invoice to pay, then told us she would have it all sent out before the end of the day. She probably would receive confirmation that the government received our application by Friday or the beginning of next week.

Tyler and I left the lawyer's office a little before noon, and for some reason, I felt heavy. Concerned. Defeated.

And he was still tense and hard like a damn rock.

"Hey, what is it?"

He shrugged. "I don't know, just not a good day, I guess."

I glanced at my phone. It was almost noon. "Are you hungry? There's this sandwich place I like around the corner."

He looked at me with his eternal frown and said, "I have some stuff to do." He ran a hand through his hair.

"Do you want some company?"

"No, it's fine. I can drive you back to your brother's apartment, though."

I shook off the shock. I hadn't truly expected him to say no to both offers. I was trying here, damn it. "No, it's okay. I'll walk."

"Okay, hm. I pick you up Friday morning."

I nodded. "Yes. We'll get the apartment keys and start moving."

He nodded. "Okay. See you, then."

Then, he just turned around and walked to his truck before I could say anything. Because I had plenty to say, but when I tried, he either left in a hurry or the words got stuck in my throat.

I walked back to the guys' apartment, trying not to think too hard about Tyler and our current situation.

19

I HAD RENTED a small U-Haul truck for the move. My pride was too fucking big and I didn't ask for help when trying to load all the things we had in my shitty apartment into the truck, but a neighbor who always greeted me in the hallway saw me and offered some help. I wanted to say no, but I dropped a big chair and broke its leg. Then, I relented and let him help me.

I had already put everything in boxes or bags, so it took only a little over an hour to load the truck—I didn't have much, and all I had was junk. My neighbor offered to help me at my new place, but I told him I was fine. However, I had no idea how I would carry the sofa up the stairs alone.

To my surprise, Gabi was already at the apartment. The living room hardwood shone and a heavy citrus smell hung in the air; she had been cleaning.

"*Oi*," she said from the kitchen. She had a small, white rag in her hands, which didn't match her plaid shirt and jean shorts and cowboy boots. She reached over the fridge, standing on her tiptoes and giving me a full view of her long, lean legs. Damn, she was fine. "I'm just finishing here, and then I can help you bring your stuff up."

I averted my gaze. "No, it's fine. I can do it myself," I said, not sure why I lied to her.

"Don't be silly. I'm almost done cleaning, and all my stuff is already in my room. My new bedroom furniture won't arrive until later, so I have plenty of time to help you."

Groaning, I dropped the bags I had brought and turned around to retrieve more. I had taken three loads of boxes and bags up when Gabi joined me at the truck. Without hesitation, she reached for a large bag.

"That's heavy," I warned her.

She lifted it in her hands, testing it. "It's fine. I work out, you know."

She whirled on her heels and hauled the heavy bag up the stairs, while I caught another glance at her legs. Yes, I did know she worked out.

Sighing, I picked up an end table and took it upstairs. Though most of my furniture was the cheapest stuff from Ikea or thrift stores, some pieces were large and heavy for a single person. Like the TV stand and the couch.

I stared at it from outside the truck, wondering how I would do this.

"Let's give it a try." Gabi climbed up on the bed of the truck.

"I confess I'm impressed with some of the boxes and bags you took inside, but I don't think we can carry these."

She stared at me, her hands on her waist. "What do you want to do, then? Just stare at it and will it upstairs? I'm the only thing you got right now, so just pipe down and let me help."

Damn, girl.

I hated how she was right. She was the only thing I had right now, for better or for worse, and she didn't even know it.

I shook my head but reached for the couch.

It took us a few minutes and two quick rest stops on the stairs, but we did it. We hauled the couch upstairs to our apartment, and then the TV stand and the armchairs. I had to admit, her help was essential.

Soon, my stuff was inside the apartment. Now came the boring part of opening the boxes and bags and organizing everything.

My stomach growled.

Beside me, Gabi chuckled. "Someone is hungry."

I glanced at the time on my phone. "It's almost four in the afternoon and I haven't eaten since seven in the morning."

She gaped at me. "You woke up at seven today? But you didn't even have to go to work this morning."

"I woke up at six thirty, because I had to finish packing all this stuff—" I gestured to the boxes and bags littering the living room. "—out of my apartment by noon." That was the time I had agreed with the landlord.

In the end, he had pitied me and let me pay only half of what I owed him. A little guilt snaked its way into me as I accepted his offer. Now, I had money, because of my deal with Gabi, but it wouldn't last long. And I hadn't even paid all my bills yet. I had to save all I could.

My stomach growled again.

"Why don't you get started here, and I'll get us a pizza?"

I frowned. "That's okay. I'll go out later and grab something." I reached for a box and opened it up.

Gabi came to stand on the other side of the box. "Tyler, stop being stubborn. I'm gonna buy a pizza. What do you like?"

Shit. When she looked at me with those blue marbles, all serious and unrelenting, it was hard saying no. "Plain pepperoni."

She smiled. "Great. I'll be right back."

I couldn't help but watch her, her smile, her silky hair bouncing side to side, and her body and long legs as she sashayed out of the apartment.

I braced the box with my forearms and lowered my forehead. Shit. It had been one week. Only one week of this arrangement and the few times I had been close to her had already started driving me crazy. Mad. Enraged. Jealous. Lusty.

Living with her for two years would be hell. I had to find a way to put more distance between us somehow.

20

GABI

THERE WAS a pizza place right around the corner. I ordered an extra-large pepperoni pizza and also one of their cookie-pizza desserts, and in less than twenty minutes, I was back at my new apartment. In the little time I was gone, Tyler managed to open his boxes and spread his things through the place.

I halted in the door and looked around. He had told me he didn't have much and what he had was simple, but so far it looked like he had a good taste. At least right now he had way more things than me in the apartment. So far, I had only two suitcases in my bedroom. My furniture would arrive—a queen bed and mattress, two nightstands, a dresser, and an armchair. I would have to think about the little walk-in-closet. There was only a couple of wire shelves in there and it wouldn't be enough. But that was for later.

"Pizza is here," I announced, weaving through the open boxes.

Tyler's head poked up from behind a stack of boxes. "Oh, good."

I placed the pizza on the kitchen counter and looked around. No plates, forks, or knifes. I glanced at Tyler. "Do you know where your kitchen stuff is?"

He halted beside the counter. "Hm, I'm not sure. I don't remember seeing it just now, so it must be in one of the boxes I haven't opened yet. Why?"

"So we can eat." I wasn't going to eat pizza at this time of the afternoon, but I was dying to sink my teeth into the cinnamon-scented cookie.

Tyler let out a low chuckle. "We don't need that." Unceremoniously, he opened the pizza box and grabbed a slice with his hand. Then, he bit into it. All the while looking at me.

I scrunched my nose. "I forget you Americans eat pizza like that."

He swallowed. "Is there any other way to eat pizza?"

I rolled my eyes. "*Bem*, if you let us, Brazilians will eat even cheeseburgers with a fork and knife. Or at least holding it with a napkin."

"It seems Brazilians are nuts."

I smiled. "Perhaps."

He stopped chewing and his eyes flicked to my mouth for half a second. I lost my smile and turned to the second box I had brought. "There's this too." I opened the smaller box with the cookie pizza. "I think it's just a giant, thick cookie in a pizza shape, but it looks so good."

He nodded. "I've had it before. It is really good."

I picked up a small slice in my hand, wishing I had a plate and utensils. "It would probably go well with coffee."

Tyler glanced over his shoulder. "The coffee machine isn't in a box. I saw it a few minutes ago."

He took a step back, but I raised my hand. "It's okay. Eat your pizza and I'll look around for the coffee machine."

I dropped my slice of cookie pizza back into the box and made my way through all the things spread around the living room. Looking at it all so messy, I wondered if this small apartment would be enough to house everything. But I knew once Tyler picked it all up and organized his things, I would probably have to go out and buy more furniture and decorations. As far as I knew, guys weren't into details, while I needed them.

I rummaged through the boxes until I saw it, lying on the floor beside an open box. I bent down to pick it up, but the contents of the open box caught my attention. Right on top of the box was a small jewelry box, and right beside it, a picture frame. I picked up the picture frame and smiled at a young Tyler, probably three or four years old, on a horse's back, his smile wide and his entire face alight. Underneath the frame, there was an open shoe box filled with pictures. Curiosity won over, and instead of picking up the coffee machine and bring it over to the kitchen, I grabbed the box.

"Look what I found," I told Tyler as I walked back to the kitchen. I placed the box right beside the pizza on the counter. I reached for the picture on top—a young couple and a baby, who I assumed were Tyler and his parents. "You never told me about your family." The moment my fingers closed around the photo, Tyler snatched it from me. I was about to snap at him, but then I looked up at him. His eyes were rounded, his jaw taut, his shoulders tense. "What happened?"

"You shouldn't have touched this," he said, his voice low and harsh.

"It was just lying there. I didn't mean to—"

"It doesn't matter where it was. It isn't yours."

I stepped back, surprised by his tone. "Hey, I—"

The doorbell rang. We stared at each other for another moment, neither of us ready to give in. The doorbell rang again.

Without a word, Tyler grabbed the box and marched to the hallway leading to the bedrooms.

I let out a sigh and rushed to the door.

"Hi," the man standing at the hallway said as soon as I opened the door. "We're here to deliver some furniture. Are you Gabriela Fernandes?"

"Yes."

Soon, he and his colleague brought my new furniture to my bedroom and they started assembling it. Meanwhile, I didn't know what to do with myself. Tyler appeared in the living room and kitchen every few minutes, to get more of his stuff into his bedroom, but since he had been so sensitive about me touching his stuff, I didn't offer to help.

Instead, I made sure the guys putting my room together had all they needed, then I left the apartment. I needed time and space. I needed fresh air.

I walked aimlessly around the neighborhood, trying to pay attention to the little shops and services nearby. Better than thinking of Tyler and his snappy mood. So that was how our two years living under the same roof would be? I couldn't touch his stuff or he would freak out. Well, I better put a line dividing the kitchen then, so I wouldn't risk losing a finger if I used one of his mugs or plates.

I let out a long breath.

This was ridiculous. We couldn't live like that for long.

No, we had to sit down and talk about this. Establish rules. Otherwise, he would drive me nuts, and we would never be able to have anyone come over.

I walked around for over an hour—with a quick pitstop at the cute, local bookstore, and a small pet shop—then I decided it was enough. It was almost seven in the evening and now I was hungry.

I stopped by a Chinese restaurant and ordered dinner for Tyler and me.

Back at the apartment, the living room looked much better, with the couch and the TV stand in place, and with only a few more boxes pushed to the side, and a few more boxes along the kitchen's counter. The men working on my furniture were gone, and Tyler seemed to be in his bedroom, from the shuffling and rustling and dragging sounds coming from there.

I halted at the end of the hallway, wondering if I should call him for dinner, or simply leave the food on the counter and hope he found it.

In the end, I decided to be the better man. But, as I started walking down the hallway, Tyler crossed by his door and saw me.

He straightened. "Hey."

I lifted the bag in my hands. "I brought dinner. I hope you like Chinese." Then, without hearing if he did like or not, or if he wanted to eat or not, I turned and marched to the kitchen.

There were some plates and knives and forks on the counter now, but with these we wouldn't need them. I picked a box with noodles and leaned against the counter.

A second later, Tyler emerged from the hallway. He came to the kitchen, picked up his box, and leaned against the counter, standing across from me.

He gestured to the box. "Thanks."

"*De nada*." I looked down at my food.

I had eaten almost half of it when Tyler cleared his throat. "Um," he started. I looked up at him. His expression was relaxed and his body wasn't tense. "I want to apologize ... for before. I didn't mean to be a jerk. I just ... my family is a sensitive topic, and I usually shut anyone out before they can ask me about it." He paused. "But that's no excuse for being a jerk. So, I'm sorry."

Not the best apology I had ever heard, but that would do. For now. "It's okay." Then, I frowned. "As long as you don't turn into a psycho who is going to bully me all the time and treat me like dirt, it's okay."

He had noticed my teasing tone, otherwise the corner of one of his lips wouldn't have curled up. "I'll try my best."

I rolled my eyes, then went back to my dinner.

SATURDAY WAS AN AWKWARD DAY.

The apartment was mostly organized, and now that there wasn't much to do with it, Tyler and I didn't know what to do when around each other. He wasn't the warmest person I had met, but thankfully he hadn't been a jerk.

In the morning, I went grocery shopping, while Tyler finished organizing the last of his stuff. In the afternoon, I made a list of things we needed for the apartment—new curtains, more dishes, a good frying pan, some cute mugs, more vases and glass decorations for the living room, and maybe a painting or two to hang on the walls—while Tyler went out for a couple of hours.

Before he left, I had told him about a dinner at my brother's apartment.

"Another one?"

I sighed. "Yes. It's like that almost every Saturday. And many other days of the week too."

He grumbled something about rich people not having anything to do, then left without letting me know if we would have dinner with my family or not. And I wouldn't go alone. I would rather lie again that we had something else planned than show up there alone.

While Tyler was out, I took a shower and got dressed—cropped jeans, an off-the-shoulder blouse, and ballet flats. I brushed my long, wavy hair until it shone, then decided to put it in a ponytail.

Then, I waited.

And waited.

So I wouldn't bite my nails, I texted Pri.

Me: *What are you up to tonight?*

It took her a few minutes to reply.

Pri: *The usual. Going out to dinner with Lucia and Adriana, then we'll probably go to a club. You?*

Me: *The usual. Going to my brother's apt for dinner.*

Pri: *And how are things with your man?*

I almost asked her "what man? I don't have a man" but decided she didn't need to know about that yet. I planned on telling her the truth, but I would rather do that face-to-face.

Me: *It's all good.*

Pri: *When am I gonna meet him?*

Me: *I'm not sure. I have to talk to him about going down there.*

Pri: *Yes! Bring him and let's show him what partying really means.*

I shook my head. Partying in Brazil wasn't that much different than here. It just started later and went into early morning.

I was typing some funny retort when she texted again.

Pri: *I gotta go now. Talk to you later.*

Me: *Okay. Have fun!*

Pri: *Always!*

I smiled at my phone, suddenly missing her and wishing she was here, so she could make my days less awkward. More fun. So I could tell her the truth and she could make the situation less dire. Lighter.

I was still smiling when my phone rang again with a new text. This time though, it wasn't from Pri.

Mateus: *I tried letting it go. I tried not caring. But I can't. I have to know. Is it true?*

I inhaled deeply.

Me: *What's true?*

Mateus: *That you're staying there because you're engaged to some dude.*

Since the beginning of our relationship, Mateus had always been jealous. Even my brother and cousins and best friends weren't as bad. And, even though we had broken up eighteen months ago, he still acted like a jealous jerk.

Me: *Sim.*

Mateus: *I don't believe it. That's not like you.*

I didn't know what to say, so I didn't reply.

But he did.

Mateus: *You're doing that for a green card, right? You're getting married to some punk just to be able to stay there.*

I pressed my lips tight. *Droga.*

Me: *If I tell you it's not like that, you won't believe me, so ... believe whatever you want.*

Mateus: *You sold yourself.*

Me: *If you're gonna insult me, then I'll block your number.*

Mateus: *It's not an insult if it's the truth.*

Grunting, I dropped my phone on the couch and stared daggers at it. Who did he think he was? He hadn't been this much of a jerk when he was my boyfriend.

The front door opened fast, startling me.

My hand flew to my racing heart. "*Meu Deus*," I whispered.

Without looking at me, Tyler strode to the kitchen, opened the fridge, grabbed a beer, and took a long, long sip. He settled it on the counter and finally acknowledged me.

"Are you ready?"

I frowned. "For?"

"To go to your brother's apartment."

I gaped at him. "I ... I didn't think you wanted to go."

"I don't," he snapped. "But it's all part of the facade, right?"

I stood. "Tyler, we don't need to go. I can just—"

"No, it's fine." He finished the beer in another swallow. "Let's go."

21

From the passenger seat, Gabi gave me the eye. That eye, that told me she wanted to say things, but was holding her tongue. What? Did she want to lecture me about drinking and driving? I had had one measly beer. That was nothing.

So far, my Saturday sucked.

Besides the awkward feeling of having to stay around Gabi in the morning, I had gone to visit my father at the hospital in the afternoon. He wasn't doing well. I had hoped to take him home the next week—even though I would have to tell Gabi about my father—but the doctor said that he couldn't make any promises.

Before heading back to the apartment, I stopped by a coffee shop with my laptop so I could do some planning. I didn't know why, but I didn't feel comfortable looking at my bank accounts and my debt with Gabi around.

So, I planned. I made a list of bills that I still hadn't paid and needed to as soon as possible, and the ones that would have to wait. I also calculated what I needed to live a little better than before, taking into consideration my salary at the vet clinic, and set that aside. If nothing crazy happened, the amount should be enough until I got the second part of the payment from Gabi.

I was better than before, but the stress and worry still ate at me. Incredible how the money simply disappeared, and I was sure to accumulate more debt until I got the full payment.

I hoped I would because that meant my father would live longer.

Shit, I should have asked for more when signing off on this deal.

I glanced at Gabi. She was still staring at me from the corner of her eyes, those two blue lasers boring holes on my face.

"What?"

She cringed, averting her eyes. "Nothing," she muttered.

I let out a long sigh. The night at her brother's promised to be bad, making my day even more sucky.

Thankfully, Gabi didn't say anything for the rest of the ride, or when we arrived there, and took the elevator to the apartment.

Only when the elevator doors opened, she extended her hand to me. "We gotta keep pretending, right?"

I groaned on the inside. "Right."

I slipped my hand in hers, and together, we walked out in the hallway. The apartment's door was open, and voices and music drifted from inside.

"Ready?" she asked, squeezing my hand.

I wasn't sure why I didn't answer. Instead, I tugged on her hand and pulled her into the apartment with me.

At first, nobody noticed us.

Garrett, Pedro, Leo, and Guilherme were seated on the big couches, watching a trailer from an upcoming video game.

Bia, Hannah, Hilary, and Ricardo were around the kitchen's island. Ricardo seemed to be getting some drinks ready, while Hilary and Hannah organized appetizers, and Bia, wearing an apron, checked the oven.

"*Boa noite*," Gabi said from beside me.

All eyes turned to us.

"There you are," Leo said, smiling. "I thought you two had gotten lost."

Pedro elbowed him in the ribs. "Maybe not lost, but busy."

Guilherme rolled his eyes. After a pointed look at me and Gabi, he stood and went to the kitchen.

After some more quick hellos and how are yous from everyone, Garrett beckoned me to the couch. "We're gonna start a new game."

Trying to be a sympathetic fiancé, I turned to Gabi first, as if asking her permission to leave her and join the guys.

She smiled at me. And even though the smile didn't reach her eyes, my heart skipped a beat. Those eyes, that smile, that exposed neck and shoulders, and the sweet scent of her perfume wrapped around me ... I shook my head once, erasing all of *those* kinds of thoughts from my mind.

"Go have fun," she said, her tone light, as if we hadn't been ignoring or snapping at each other a few minutes ago.

For the sake of pretending, I leaned into her and pressed my lips to hers. Just a light, brief touch. When I pulled back, her eyes widened in surprise, but she recovered and pushed me away.

I let out a long breath.

Leo and Pedro called dibs, and when the game started, they were seated on the center couch, joysticks in hand. Ricardo and Guilherme came back from the kitchen with drinks for us. With a slight frown, Guilherme handed me a beer bottle.

"Thanks," I said, genuinely surprised. I took it before he changed his mind and dump it on my head.

He nodded, then sat as far away from me as possible.

Progress, then a step back?

Who cared? I wasn't here to make friends. I was here to pretend. To earn my part of the deal.

Laughter came from the kitchen and I looked over. Bia was tending to the range, while Hannah prepared more drinks. Hilary had a sketchpad on the kitchen counter and she drew a little, then talked a little. Gabi took a seat on a stool among them.

Hilary said something else and Gabi smiled at her. A true smile, one that did reach her eyes. My heart skipped another beat. All the women in the kitchen were pretty, but Gabi ... Gabi was something else. She was beautiful. And right now, among her family and happy, she was stunning. Breathtaking.

What the fuck had I done?

"Hey, Gabi," Pedro called from beside me. I stared at him, wondering if he had read my thoughts and would now tell her about it. I hadn't even seen when he switched places with Garrett. Gabi turned a soft smile to him. "Are you coming to practice this week?"

I frowned.

"Probably," she said, taking a few steps closer to the living room. "It depends on my schedule."

"And what schedule is that?" Gui asked, his voice tight.

Her smile faded. "I want to play polo, don't I?" Did she? "I won't find my own team if I keep practicing with you."

"She has a good point," Pedro said, nodding to Gui then to me. I nodded too, even though I was still lost on what they were talking about.

"So, my plan is to go to a few practices so I won't get rusty, but I'll also work on getting my own team together."

"I like that," Ricardo said. "Any idea on how you're gonna do that?"

Her smile stretched, one corner higher than the other. "You'll see ..." Then, she turned back to the other girls.

I kept staring at her.

Pedro let out an amused chuckle. "I like her guts."

"It's a shame the club doesn't sponsor mixed teams," Ricardo said. "We could certainly get three guys to play with her."

A team of three males and one female? Gabi playing alongside three guys? For some reason, that didn't sit well with me.

"I haven't been feeling the game lately," Pedro said, his face serious. Gabi had told me Pedro and his girlfriend had broken up right before Valentine's Day, and nobody knew what happened. "Maybe I'll break an arm. I'll need at least a month, maybe two to recover. She can play in my place."

Guilherme slapped him on the knee. "Don't joke like that. No one wants to see you with broken body parts."

Pedro shrugged. "I'm just saying ..."

The conversation paused as the guys played video games and drank, except for Leo, and my thoughts turned to the new information it had received.

So Gabi played polo too?

That was interesting.

22

GABI

Hɪʟ sʜowᴇᴅ ʜᴇʀ ᴅʀᴀwɪɴɢ ᴘᴀᴅ. "Something like this."

The dress was beautiful. Dark green, summery, and flowy, but a little revealing. It looked like a beautiful piece for Hil's showcase.

Someone touched my elbow. I turned and found Gui, his face taut, standing behind me.

"Can I talk to you for a minute?"

Apprehension pulled in my stomach. "Sure," I muttered.

I followed my brother to the balcony. He rested his elbows on the rail and looked up at the night sky. Clouds drifted in from the ocean, covering the moon and the stars, and supposedly bringing rain tomorrow.

I stood two steps back, waiting. He had barely talked to me since Tyler and I announced our engagement. Even last week, when I was still in this apartment, he only said *bom dia, tudo bem,* and *boa noite.* Although, he had asked me if I needed any help moving. He even offered to leave his Jeep with me for the day, but I told him I had everything handled.

Finally, Gui turned to me and fixed those eyes, mirrors of mine, on me. "I'm sorry."

I frowned. "For?"

"For being a jerk." He sighed. "I didn't mean to freak out last week, and I definitely didn't mean to shut you out. I just … needed time to process it all. But I'm okay now. I mean, I think it'll take me a little while to be totally okay with you getting engaged so suddenly and moving in with a guy I barely know, but … I'll try to be more understanding from now on."

A small smile tugged at my lips. "Thank you. That's all I wanted." I tsked. "That and a little help with *pai*. He's still not answering my texts and phone calls. Even *mãe* seems to be a little upset with me."

Gui hissed. "That is all on you."

I slapped his shoulder. "Coward."

He chuckled. "Come on! Who wants to go head to head with Luis Carlos Fernandes? Oh, yeah, Gabriela wants to."

I rolled my eyes at him. "You're impossible."

He looked at me, his shoulders relaxed. "Give them a little time. They will come around." He shrugged. "After all, you won't change your mind just because they are upset, *certo*? So eventually, they will have to reach out to you."

At least they had stopped threatening to come here and drag me back by my hair. "*Bom*, I don't plan on arguing with them."

"That's a good plan."

I tilted my head at him. "Thank you."

"I'm not done."

"Oh?"

He fished keys from the pocket of his jeans. "This is for you." He grabbed my hand and placed the keys in my open palm. "I know you probably can't buy a car in your name right now, because of all the visa restrictions, so I thought I would give one to you." He ran a hand through his hair. "As an apology present."

I stared at the keys, then at him, then back at the keys. "You didn't have to …"

"I know." He shrugged. "I wanted to. Once you can have it in your name, I'll transfer it to you."

From the logo on the keys, I knew it was one from their sponsor, Jeep. "Which model is it?"

He laughed. "It's parked beside mine in the underground garage. You'll see when you leave."

I gaped at him. "No fair."

Turning, he winked at me. "Of course it's fair." He shuffled his weight. "I also transferred the money back to your account this afternoon."

I gaped at him. "Gui, you shouldn't—"

"Yes, I should. No matter what I said. We already established I was being a major jerk. The fact is that money came from gifts, and gifts aren't made to be taken back."

"But ..."

He shook his head. "No buts. That money is yours. I know you don't need it, but I want you to have it." He stared at me. "Okay?"

I wanted to argue about it, but knew he wouldn't relent, so I nodded. "Deal."

He dipped his chin once, then he walked away and into the apartment.

I stared at the car keys, wanting to ditch the dinner to go check on my new car. That had been so sweet of him. I hoped now he would stop being an ass to Tyler. Not that the two of them would ever be best friends, but Gui could at least treat Tyler like a cool acquaintance.

"Hey."

I snapped my head to the sliding doors. "*Oi*," I said to Tyler. He stood at the door, one of his arms folded behind him.

"Hilary said dinner is ready."

I nodded. "Thanks. I'll be right there."

A small frown marred his forehead as he took three steps out in the balcony. "So ... what was that about you playing polo?"

I let a defensive wall fall over me. "I play polo. So?"

He shrugged. "I found it a little odd, I guess. Not that I haven't seen women playing before, but I don't think I've ever met a girl who played."

I nodded. "Not many people do."

"And you want to put your own team together?"

I sighed. I didn't owe him any explanation, especially not after the snappy, jerky way he had been acting, but since he had brought it up, this was a good time to be clear about that. The more he knew about it, the better it would be. For the green card interview purposes, of course.

"I've been playing since I was little, and if it depended on me, I would have started playing it professionally years ago. But polo isn't a common sport in Brazil. It's exactly the opposite, so even the men's division is, let's say, lacking. That's why the guys came to live here. Because they were too good for Brazil, and to compete with better teams, they had to spend the entire year traveling. Tired of that, they got a deal with the club here. They still travel, of course, but now it's easier to play the tournaments in the U.S."

"And you?"

"I couldn't even put a team together in Brazil. My best friend, Priscila, played with me, but it was a pain in the ass to get the girls together to train. Not to mention to convince the clubs to let us play in tournaments. None of them accepted women's teams. And that's one of the two main reasons I wanted to move here."

He nodded. "To be with your family and to play polo."

"*Sim*. Women's polo isn't great here either, but it's *much* better than in Brazil."

"That's ... cool, I guess."

I felt a smile spreading over my lips. "It's what I love. Truly, truly love."

One corner of his lips tugged up. "I can see that." He gestured to my face. "You're glowing, just speaking about it."

My cheeks heated up and I could bet I was turning red. "*Bom*, there's nothing I can do about that."

He let out a low chuckle. "It's cool." Then, his grin faded. "I'm sorry I was a little cold today. Again." He shook his head. "It seems I'm always apologizing for my behavior. I don't have any excuses other than I had a crappy afternoon, and I let my mood get the better of me. So ... I'm sorry."

"I get it. I mean, everyone has a bad day here and there, right?" I frowned. "Just ... try not to be a jerk to me all the time. I understand this isn't the ideal situation. For you or me. But I gotta live with you for the next two years. I might murder you if you keep acting like a jerk."

The lopsided grin was back. "I'll try."

Silence fell over us while we stared at each other.

"Hey, aren't you two coming?" Hil asked from the balcony's door.

"Hm, *sim*," I answered, glancing at her. While staring at Tyler, while thinking about his cocky smile and his handsome eyes, I had forgotten about dinner. "We're coming."

Hil disappeared inside the apartment.

Tyler offered me his hand. "Come on. Let's put on a show."

I slipped my hand into his and let him take me into the apartment.

THE CLUB WASN'T TOO full at nine in the morning on a Tuesday, which was great. I wasn't in the mood to greet someone every three steps I took.

During the dinner at my brother's apartment on Saturday, I thought Tyler and I had made a breakthrough in our relationship. I thought we would finally find a common ground. Even when Bia started pushing everyone to go clubbing, and one by one, they accepted it, I thought Tyler would say yes. But then he came up with a lie of having to work early Sunday morning, so we left right after that. And since then, we had barely spoken to each other. In fact, I had barely seen him the last two days. Sunday, he was buried in his bedroom for a long time, then he spent a couple of hours out in the evening. And Monday, he left for work early and came back super late. He ate a quick snack for dinner and went to bed.

And this morning, I saw as he left for work, again way too early.

I sighed, pushing thoughts of Tyler back.

I knew the guys would be getting ready for practice at the main field, so before doing what I had come here to do, I went to say hi.

Ri was the first one who saw me approaching. "Look who is here!"

The other guys and *tio* João Pedro turned and waved at me.

"What are you doing here?" my brother asked.

I halted beside them. "Came to talk to Mr. Helms, the polo director. My first step to try and get a women's team running."

"Oh, so that's your plan," Ri said, nodding. "I like it."

"If you need someone to vouch for you, I'm here," *tio* João Pedro said as he tapped on his iPad.

"That's great, thank you." A little more hope snaked into my chest. "I'll let you know if I need any help."

"Did you bring your gear?" Leo asked as he zipped up his boots. Usually, they started practice with stretches then a cardio workout of sorts for an hour before playing, but once a week, they only stretched and did a few exercises, which took no more than twenty minutes, then played the rest of their allotted time.

"It's in my car."

"After your talk, you should come practice with us," Pedro said. He looked a little better than the last times I had seen him. I guess polo would do that to him. To all of us.

I smiled. "I'll see how the conversation goes and how my mood is after that, but I'll certainly come back here, even if it's just to say *tchau*."

Gui put on his helmet and offered me one of his teasing grins. "What? Are you afraid of getting your ass kicked?"

I snorted. "As if! You all know if I had been born a guy, I would be on that team instead of you."

Leo, Ri, and Pedro uttered "ooooh" while *tio* João Pedro chuckled.

"Is that a challenge?" Gui asked, standing tall in front of me.

Because of his height, I had to look up at him. So, I stepped on a bench and looked down at him. "Name the place and time."

"All right, you two," *tio* João Pedro called out, hiding a smile. "We can settle that next time Gabi joins us for practice. For now, guys, on the field."

They said *tchau* to me as they went get their horses, then *tio* João Pedro turned to me. "Good luck in there."

"*Obrigada,*" I whispered.

He nodded then followed the guys.

I watched as the guys jogged across the field to where their horses were secured, *tio* João Pedro on their heels, and sucked in a deep breath. *Droga*, how I wanted to be them, to do what they did, to jog across the field with my own team, my own girls.

I took another long breath, then left the field and walked into the club's administration building.

I stopped by the main reception.

"Good morning," a woman wearing a nice suit said. "How can I help you?"

"Hi." I placed my hands on the tall counter between us. "I'm here to talk with Mr. Helms."

"Do you have an appointment?"

"Hm, no. I called last week and he was out of town. I was told to come by sometime this week. So, here I am."

"Oh-kay." The receptionist glanced at a computer screen. "I'm looking here at his schedule and it seems Mr. Helms isn't coming to the club today."

My shoulders deflated. "Oh."

"Do you want to schedule an appointment with him?"

Did I have another option? "That would be great."

She clicked on the computer mouse a couple of times, and then finally looked up at me. "The first time I have available is on April twentieth."

My jaw hit the floor. "But ... that's over a month away."

"Yes, Mr. Helms is very busy."

Merda. What now? I had no choice here. "Okay, put me down for any time on April twentieth, then."

She glanced at the screen again. "Does ten thirty sound good?"

I groaned. "Yes."

"And do you want to leave a little note saying what this is about?"

"Hm, sure. I'm the sister of Guilherme Fernandes from the Montenegro team, and I have some business I'd like to discuss with Mr. Helms."

She narrowed her eyes at me. "Business."

"Yes." I paused, not sure if I should proceed or not, but what did I have to lose? "I want to talk to him about a women's team."

The receptionist gaped at me. "A women's team?"

"Yes. For polo."

"Oh-kay." She typed a quick note on her computer, and then smiled back at me. "All set. We'll see you then."

"Great."

With my tail between my legs, I walked out of the administration building, feeling down. Damn it.

Maybe playing polo with the guys would lift my spirits, or maybe it would only bring me down more. As much as I loved playing with them, it was a constant reminder that they were living their dreams, while I sat on the bleachers and watched.

I was happy for them and wished them all the best. That they kept winning tournaments, making lots of money, and that they took the first four spots in the world ranking. But I wanted that for me too. Maybe not the money part, since I didn't need money, but the realization of waking up every day knowing I would get up and do what I loved the most. That ... that was what I wanted.

Avoiding the main field, I walked around the building, taking the longer side path, just so the guys wouldn't see me as I dragged my feet back to my car. The last thing I wanted right now was them all over me, trying to comfort me. I would be fine. I just needed a moment to myself.

I slid inside my car and my phone beeped. I picked it up and gaped at the screen.

Mateus: Oi

I sighed. What could he want now? To insult me more?

Me: Oi

Mateus: *How are you?*

Me: *I'm good.*

I saw he was typing something else, but I asked before he could enter his message:

Me: *What do you want?*

Mateus: *I wanted to apologize for the other day.*

A pause.

Mateus: *I was jealous and upset and I drank too much and I said things I shouldn't have and I behaved like a complete jerk. I'm sorry.*

That was unexpected.

Me: *It's okay. I mean, it wasn't okay, but you're forgiven.*

Mateus: *So ... how is the new life treating you?*

I stared at the screen. What did he want? Why was he contacting me again? If he wanted to apologize, he had done that, I had forgiven him. Now, could we move on?

However, after our many years together and our mostly amicable break up, I thought he deserved some consideration. Besides, I was not a bitch. Quite the contrary. I was too nice and usually got into trouble because of it.

Me: *Everything is fine. I like it here.*

Mateus: *I know you like it there. You were always talking about the United States, ever since your brother and cousins started playing there.*

True. I would have done anything to come have fun with them and Bia.

Mateus: *But I want to know if you're happy.*

Was I happy? I guess I was, though my happiness wasn't complete yet.

Me: *I am.*

Mateus: *That was a short answer.*

What else did he want me to say?

Me: *Mateus, not that I mind talking to you, but ... seriously, what do you want?*

A pause.

Mateus: *I miss you. I really, really miss you. And, after finding out you're engaged ... I always knew I still had feelings for you, but I hadn't realized how strong they were until you were snatched from me. Until you were promised to someone else.*

I swallowed hard.

Me: *I don't know what to say to that.*

Mateus: *Well, you could say you realize you still love me too and that you'll break up with that guy and come back to Brasil to be with me.*

I didn't answer because there was nothing to say about that.

Mateus: *I was joking. Sorta.*

Me: *I have some things to do now.*

Mateus: *Okay.*

Me: *Tchau, Mateus. Take care.*

Mateus: *Tchau.*

I put my phone down and stared at the trees lining the parking lot at the club, but I wasn't really seeing them. What the hell had that been? I just hoped Mateus figured out whatever his problem was and moved on, because him hanging on to me because I had someone else—even if fake—wasn't cool.

I let out a sigh, and forced all thoughts of Mateus out of my mind.

THE GUYS INVITED me to go to a horse sale with them on Friday. Since I didn't have anything better to do, I went with them. *Tio* João Pedro drove us to a ranch in Nevada—six hours away—in his Grand Cherokee. I guess with our big family, the third row came in handy.

Ri sat in the passenger seat, Leo and Gui sat in the middle row, and Pedro sat in the back with me.

Criado em Galpão blasted from the speakers— a *tradicionalista* song from Rio Grande do Sul, our home state— and the *chimarrão* was being passed around.

At some point, I leaned into Pedro and rested my head on his shoulders. I had woken up at four in the morning to be ready when they came to pick me up at four thirty. The unusual early morning was catching up to me.

I closed my eyes, hoping to nap, but my traitorous mind drifted to Tyler instead. In the seven days we had been living together, he had been gone most of the days. And nights. Since he went back to work on Monday, he left around seven thirty, and came back around nine, if not later. Then, when he finally got back, he shoved something down his throat, took a shower, and went to bed.

Perhaps this was better than the awkward moments, or the jerky reactions, but so far, I felt like I was living with a ghost.

"How is Tyler?" Pedro asked, catching me by surprise.

I opened my eyes. "Good. I invited him to come, but he has to work." That was another lie. Tyler knew I was going to the sale, but I hadn't invited him.

I felt his head moving against mine as he nodded. "We train hard, but we're blessed we can set our own hours."

"*Sim*, you guys are." In more than just being able to determine their schedules and take impromptu trips to horse sales on Fridays.

"You'll get there too, I know."

I sighed. Good thing he knew it because I wasn't as sure anymore. "I'm not so sure."

He chuckled. "Gabi, you've been here for what, two weeks? That's nothing. These things don't happen that fast. It might be months before you see any progress. Be patient."

"My lack of patience is one of my many flaws."

He mocked gasped at me. "You? Flaws? No! I thought you were perfect."

I punched him in the gut and he let out a half-howl, half-chuckle. "I have many flaws. I can even name a few of them. For example, my lack of patience, my curiosity, my inability to be really rude and say no to people, and my belief that love solves everything." Pedro quieted down. I pulled back and looked at him. "Want to talk about it?"

He shook his head. "Not really." I thought he wouldn't say anything, but he surprised me. "I haven't talked to her since we broke up."

Over a month ago. Poor Pedro. "I'm sorry ..."

He shrugged. "It's okay ..." He forced a smile. "And how are you and the engaged life?"

I rolled my eyes. Engaged. Right. If only they knew ... However, I had to sell the product. They thought we had gotten engaged and moved in together and were having the time of our lives. "It's good.

Great even. It's been easier to get used to living with someone than I thought it would be, but at the same time, sometimes I'm surprised by the fact that I am living with someone else other than my parents or you guys."

He clasped my hand. "Hope he's making you happy."

I smiled at him, at his concern for me. "He is," I lied. *Bom*, Tyler wasn't making me unhappy either, but he certainly wasn't doing anything to make me happy.

Another hour on the road and we finally arrived at the ranch. It was ten forty-five and the place was already packed.

"Are we late?" Ri asked as we all exited the car.

I glanced between us. If we didn't look like a team, wearing jeans of varying tones and black Montenegro polo shirts and cowboy boots, we never would. To complete the visuals, *tio* João Pedro wore a black cowboy hat, and Gui and Pedro had black Montenegro baseball hats.

"No," *tio* João Pedro said. "The preview is at eleven, and the sale starts at one."

"Apparently, they just invited a lot of people," Leo said.

"We better split up for the preview, then," Gui suggested.

"*Boa ideia*," *tio* João Pedro said. "Take notes of horses you like and then we can all go see the top ones before the sale."

"Good plan," Pedro said.

Tio João Pedro and Ri went to the left, while Leo and Gui went to the right, and Pedro and I went to the middle.

The horses were spread through the arena, separated by tall steel fencing on medium size pens, and there were a lot of men walking around, taking notes, petting the horses.

"See anything you like?" Pedro asked, as we walked by the pens, looking to make sure we didn't miss any of the many horses around.

"I see a lot of horses I like," I said, smiling. "I want to buy them all."

Pedro chuckled. "Me too."

We walked for another two minutes before Pedro stopped in front of a tall horse with a light brown coat.

"He's pretty," I said, leaning on the fence to take a better look at his legs.

"*Sim*. I like this one." Pedro pulled out his phone, opened the notes app, and entered the number written on a plaque attached to the fence.

My phone dinged and I glanced at it.

Pri: *Guess who has been asking about you nonstop?*

I rolled my eyes.

Me: *Mateus.*

Pri: *Right. How did you know?*

Me: *He texted me last Saturday and Tuesday.*

Pri: *Oh, uau. So, he's serious about it.*

I leaned my back on the fence between two pens while Pedro examined the horse.

Me: *Serious about what?*

Pri: *About winning you back.*

Me: *What? No.*

But he had said so himself, hadn't he? Not with those exact words, but close.

Pri: *Lucia and I went to the mall last night and bumped into him and Jorge. We ended up going to dinner together and he kept talking about you, asking a lot of stuff.*

Me: *Why the hell is he doing this now? We've been apart for eighteen months.*

Pri: *He did try to get back with you before, remember? Now, he seems more serious about it. More determined.*

Me: *Introduce him to some other girls, see if he starts stalking them instead.*

Pri: *lol, right? As if you are that easy to forget.*

I smiled at my phone.

Me: *How do you know? You never slept with me. Or never kissed me.*

Pri: Querida, *I'm not into girls, but for you, I would make an exception.*

Me: *lol abobada*

Pri: *You know you love me, especially when I talk shit like that.*

Me: *True.*

Something poked me in my waist and I jumped forward with a yelp.

"Sorry," I told the man I almost bumped into. A couple of people stared at me as if I was nuts, but when I turned around to the fence, I saw what happened. "Hey, you." I approached the white horse inside the pen. I lifted my hand, and instantly, the horse pressed his muzzle against the fence bars and sniffed my hand. "Were you playing with me, uh?" I stretched my arm and rested my hand on top of his muzzle, and then I glanced at the horse's body. "Oh, you're a girl." I ran my hand under her chin. "Hi, pretty girl."

The mare snorted lightly. And I smiled.

"She's a pretty thing," a man said from my right. He was looking at the mare from over the fence. "Young, tall and strong, beautiful white coat."

"True," a second man said. He was beside the other one, his eyes on the plaque on the fence. "But I heard rumors she's a skittish little thing. Gets scared with everything. Even leaves falling."

"Yeah, that won't do at my ranch," the first man said, taking a large step back.

"Or on mine." The second one shook his head once before joining the other one and going to the next pen.

I glanced at the beautiful mare in front of me. "Don't listen to them. They have no idea what they are talking about." I scratched her neck and she seemed to stretch her head up, giving me more access. I chuckled. "You're perfect the way you are." And she was.

Tall, with strong legs, a lean neck, and a gray coat coming from her hooves to her knees.

"Gabi," Pedro called me from the other pen. "*Meu pai* asked us to meet him. I think he wants to show us a horse."

I scratched the mare's neck one more time before retreating. "Good luck," I told her and I could swear she lowered her head and her ears drooped, as if she didn't believe in luck.

WE WALKED around the place for almost two hours. There were vending carts spread on the perimeter of the preview area, but they were selling hot dogs and sandwiches and burgers.

This sale was nothing like the ones my father—and *tio* João Pedro, before moving to the U.S.—put together at our ranch in Brazil.

First, we had a preview area, but it was in a special place that looked like an open stable with pavement and waiters going around offering drinks. A couple of hours later, the guests were called to the main arena: a runway of sorts lined with tables and chairs—complete with tablecloths and plates and silverware and even elegant decorations. While watching as the horses were brought to the runway one by one, and a trained speaker read the horses' stats on a microphone, our guests had proper lunch with steak—from the prime cows raised at our ranch—and all sorts of side dishes. Plus, dessert and coffee. It was the finest auction I had ever seen, and one of the many things we did to secure the names Fernandes and Montenegro meant quality and excellence.

For this sale though, we were all called to an open arena where folding chairs had been placed. Pedro, Ri, *tio* João Pedro, and I took chairs, while Leo and Gui leaned against the arena's wooden fence behind us. Many people sat on the grass in front of the chairs.

This event could even be well organized, but it lacked style.

Finally, the show started almost half an hour late.

The horses were brought two by two. There was no one speaking; we had to find the horse's number on the sheet that was given to us upon our arrival to read the horse's stats. The only time one of the hosts stepped forward and spoke up was to start the bidding.

"This one," Pedro said as the light brown horse he had been looking at before was brought in before us. "What do you think, *pai*?" He glanced at his father. "Can I bid on him?"

Tio João Pedro narrowed his eyes at the horse, and then read the stats. "Go for it."

Pedro opened the bid with the minimum amount—two thousand dollars.

After a heated battled with three other men, Pedro won the horse for twelve thousand.

Half an hour into the auction—and another three buys from the guys—the white mare was brought in.

A smile spread through my lips, but then the crack of a loud whip came from the next stall, and she neighed loudly, stepping back.

Her handler tugged on her reins, hard, and finally made her stop right in front of us.

The mare's eyes were wide—in terror. She was scared and the guy handling her wasn't helping.

Mr. Goulding, one of the ranch owners, stepped forward. "Let's start the bidding on this lovely mare. Do I hear a thousand?"

Whispers filled the silence of the crowd. I heard the words scared and skittish and easily spooked one too many times. Poor girl. Wouldn't be bought because a bunch of men were afraid of training her properly? Most horses were afraid of something. You just had to have the patience to train them, to teach them there was nothing to be scared of.

"A thousand? No one?" Mr. Goulding sighed. "How about seven hundred and fifty dollars?"

Whoa! One thousand for such a magnificent horse was too low. She was worth five thousand minimum. Perhaps ... perhaps the owner was asking less because he knew the rumors had spread and no one would want to buy her now.

"She's pretty," Ri said from my side.

"But I heard she's too skittish," Leo said. "Hopefully, it's not true, though, because she's really a beauty."

That was it.

I raised my hand high. "Me! Seven hundred and fifty dollars."

"Gabi?" Gui hissed from behind me.

The host smiled at me. "Very well, young lady." He scanned the crowd. "Do I hear more? Seven hundred and fifty. Going once. Going twice." The man sighed. "Sold for seven hundred and fifty dollars to the Fernandes lady."

My heart soared. I wanted to jump up and go running to my mare, but I reined in my excitement and remained seated while they walked her out of the arena.

"Did you just buy a horse?" Pedro asked me.

I shrugged. "Why not? My dear Tostado is in *Brasil*. I might as well have one here too."

"Congratulations, Gabi," *tio* João Pedro said. "She's gorgeous."

I smiled at him. "Thanks."

THE GUYS STAYED at the auction, but I couldn't contain myself. I stood and went to find my new mare.

I tried not to think of Tostado too much, because I felt guilty. It wasn't as if I was replacing him; that would never happen. I was just adopting another child, in a manner of speaking. Didn't *tio* João Pedro and the guys have several horses each? And weren't they here buying more? Why couldn't I have more than one too? Even Bia had two horses.

I found the mare at the same pen she was in during the preview part of the event.

"Hey, girl," I said, sneaking my arm through the fence bars. The mare dragged her feet to me and immediately rested her muzzle on my hand. "Aren't you sweet?"

"She might be sweet, but she'll give you plenty of trouble."

I turned to the side and saw the same man from before, the one who had been looking at my mare with a friend, standing a few feet from me.

"I'll decide that for myself," I said, a little wary of him.

"If she wasn't so scared, I would have bought her. Heck, I would have paid a lot of money for her," the man said.

I frowned. "I'm glad she's so scared then, otherwise you would have bought her and I wouldn't have."

Something flashed in the man's gaze and I almost took a step back, afraid of the intense, hard glint in his dark eyes. "Are you trying to be a smart ass?"

"I'm just stating the facts."

Hissing, the man took a step toward me.

Then a young man appeared from the other side of the pen. "Here, Ms. Fernandes. The mare's documentation."

The man halted. "Not worth it," he hissed in a low voice, then stepped around me and walked away.

Unaware of the other man, the young boy jogged around the pen and handed a folder to me. "Check if everything is in order, then please come to the booth ..." He pointed to a small tent erected between the pens. "So we can finalize your purchase."

"Thanks." I took the folder from him. "I'll be right there."

He nodded before turning around and leaving for the tent.

I opened the folder and read the first line. "Your name is Eleanor?" I asked the mare, as if she could really understand me. "As much as I think Eleanor is a beautiful name, it's not a horse name." I tilted my head and tried to think of a trait or something that could give her a good nickname. The first thing that I had noticed was her smooth, shiny white coat. And an idea came to mind. Bia had a black mare called Preta, which meant black in Portuguese. I could play the same game with the word white ... "Branca. Your new name is Branca."

I reached inside the pen again and ran my hand over the mare's muzzle. "Do you like that, Branca?" The mare snorted as if amused and I chuckled. "That's a deal, then."

***

FINALLY, at noon the next day, I entered my apartment. Maybe because it was Saturday, I expected to see Tyler in the living room, or preparing himself some lunch in the kitchen, but the place was quiet. Lonely.

It had been almost midnight when we arrived back at *tio* João Pedro's ranch from the auction. We still had to unload the horses and settle them in their new stalls, make sure they had water and feed. *Tio* João Pedro and *tia* Agnes insisted we all slept at the ranch since we were all tired. We hadn't done much all day, but twelve hours in a car in one day was too much. I wanted to refuse, but at two in the morning and barely being able to walk anymore, I accepted. In bed, I pondered if I should send a text to Tyler about me staying at my uncle's place, so he wouldn't worry, but then I remembered he didn't actually care and stopped myself.

Now, walking around our apartment, I realized I also expected a note from him telling me where he had gone and when he would come back. Which was ridiculous. I hadn't warned him; why would he warn me? Besides our pretense, we didn't owe anything to each other.

Still, the apartment felt too cold and big without him here.

I shook those silly thoughts from my mind and busied myself. A warm shower, a nice homemade brunch, a nap—I was still tired, some TV time, reading, researching online about polo in the area —as if I hadn't found everything already. I also tried calling my parents online, but they still ignored me. This was getting old. What did they expect me to do? Hop on the first plane to Brazil and grovel on their doorstep? Keep dreaming ...

By four in the afternoon, I was bored out of my mind.

Giving up on being alone, I donned skinny jeans, a black blouse, black cowboy boots, and drove out to Hannah's ranch. By now, *tio* João Pedro should have taken Branca there, as we agreed, since Hannah would help me with Branca's fear and hopefully make her less jumpy.

But even if it didn't work, I already felt myself falling for the beautiful mare. A guilty pang ran through my chest, and as I parked in the ranch's parking lot, my thoughts turned to my dear Tostado. I missed that damn horse. I would have to arrange for him to be brought here soon.

"I thought you would come over at some point today," Hannah said as I walked in the stable. She was leaning over a stall, her hand over Branca's neck. When she saw me, Branca's ears perked up.

Smiling, I halted by Hannah's side. "And why is that?"

Hannah raised an eyebrow. "New toy?"

I laughed. "You're right." I faced my new horse and caressed her chin. "How are you doing, girl?"

Branca neighed lowly.

"She has been a very good girl, so far," Hannah said.

"Didn't she get spooked by anything?"

Hannah narrowed her eyes slightly. "When kids came in early this afternoon, right after your uncle dropped her off. They were screaming and running around. I think different place, loud kids ... it didn't help her. But she's fine now."

"She sure looks like it," I said in a low voice. Right now, Branca looked calm and strong. I ran my hand up and down her neck, then glanced around when a thought nagged at me. "Where is Leo?"

Hannah let out a loud sigh. "He and the guys went training."

"On a Saturday afternoon? That isn't like them ..."

"I know, but they have a tournament coming up next weekend."

"Oh, yeah, I had forgotten about that."

"They will probably train all day tomorrow through Wednesday, then they leave on Thursday."

"This one is in Miami, right?"

"That's right."

Miami was a big polo hub. I bet it would be easier to find a women's polo team there than here. I sighed. It didn't matter. I had come to the U.S. to stay with my family. Polo came in second.

Hannah glanced at the clock on the wall behind us. "I have a group coming in soon." She tilted her eyes, returning her eyes to me. "Say ... why don't you join us? This is a beginner group, so we'll go slow, and I'll be able to pay attention to her and see more of her behavior."

"I like that."

Hannah gestured to the door beside the clock. "That's the tack room. Feel free to get everything you need."

I dipped my chin once. "Thanks."

The sound of hooves and voices reached my ears. Hannah and I looked out the back gate.

"And I've got a group returning right now." She started toward the arena at the back. "Have to help them dismount and untack the horses."

"I can help."

She waved me off. "No need. Jimmy and Paul are outside. They can help me. Just enjoy Branca."

I smiled at my mare. "I plan to."

"Oh," Hannah said and I snapped my head back at hers. "Speaking of enjoying ... we haven't done a girls night out in a long time. As soon as I'm done with this group, I'm going to text all the girls and we're going out."

My eyes widened. "Out? When?"

Her smile widened and her eyes had a wicked glint. "Tonight!"

24

TYLER

New address. Same bills. How they found me this fast, only God knew.

I picked up the thick stack of letters from the mailbox and shuffled through them. As I suspected, ninety percent of them were for me, and from those, ninety percent were bills or late notices.

Shit.

Trying not to let the frustration and exhaustion get to me, I rushed to my apartment.

The day had been long. For some reason, every dog and cat and bird and horse in town had a crisis on the weekend, and Saturdays and Sundays were always busy days at the vet clinic. I left at seven something and still had to stop at the hospital to check on my dad. He was having one of his not-so-good days, which only brought me more anxiety and frustration. I hated that there was nothing I could do for him, other than spend the little free time I had by his side. I debated spending the night at the hospital, to stay longer with him, but I hadn't slept well the previous night. I needed my bed, so I went back to the apartment.

And, at ten something at night, found all the lights off. Gabi was out again.

I let out a long breath and marched to the kitchen, where I fixed myself a sandwich and ate it in two bites. Tired of my day and now of my night too, I pulled out a beer from the fridge. I deserved it.

I took two gulps in peace. Then, my thoughts assaulted me again.

Where the hell could Gabi be? She hadn't spent the previous night at home either. Was she still out? Had she come home and was out again? Ugh, why did it matter? She didn't owe me any explanation.

Still, I couldn't shake this ridiculous feeling growing inside my chest. I wouldn't name it because naming it would only give it power.

Tired but too wired to go to bed, I put on *Walking Dead* and watched two episodes before I started closing my eyes.

I should probably go to bed since I had to get up early to go to work tomorrow morning, but I needed a shower first.

After throwing away the untouched second half of my beer and shoving all the bills and letters addressed to me inside one of the drawers in my bedroom, I hopped in the shower. For the five minutes, I stood and washed under the warm water, I did my best to let my mind free and empty and, to my surprise, I was able to relax.

But the moment I stepped out of my bathroom into my bedroom and saw the open door to the hallway—and the darkness coming from there—I was reminded that Gabi was nowhere to be found and tension flowed into my muscles again.

I put on some shorts and grabbed my phone from my nightstand. Nothing. Not even a text. Curious, I opened my Facebook app, something I hadn't done in a long time. As I suspected, she had sent me a friend request. I accepted it and started browsing through her feed. Her last update was from last evening and it was linked to her Instagram. In the update, she had posted a pic of her posing beside a beautiful white horse. Half of her caption was written in English and the other half in Portuguese, and it read "Meet Branca, my new best friend." The first comment underneath her post caught my attention. It was from a girl called Priscila. I thought Gabi had mentioned her before. The comment was in Portuguese, but after hitting the translation button, I read it: "I've been already replaced?" Gabi had hit the laughing button on Priscila's comment.

I was about to close the damn app when a new post popped up. It was a post from Hannah and Gabi was tagged in it. A picture of them—Gabi, Bia, Hannah, and Hilary—squeezed together and smiling at the selfie. The caption read "Girls night out" followed by several hearts of different colors.

Groaning, I threw my phone on the bed and stormed into the kitchen. I could use another beer.

I twisted the cap, leaned my ass on the counter beside the fridge, and drank a big gulp. The cold liquid refreshed some of my tension. I hadn't gotten really drunk in years, but right at this moment, it seemed like a good way to erase all the problems from my mind and put myself to sleep.

I took another long gulp, intent in finishing this bottle in seconds, but the sound of jiggling keys froze me. I lowered my beer and stared at the door as the lock clicked and the knob twisted.

The door opened and Gabi walked in.

Well, wobbled in was more like it.

When turning to close the door, she almost tripped on her feet and kissed the wall. Instead, she was able to shoot out a hand and splay it on the door, steadying herself. Wasn't she twenty years old? Did she have a fake ID, or did she charm someone to buy booze for her?

Gabi closed and locked the door, then wobbled across the living room. She was halfway through when she finally lifted her face and saw me. Her eyes widened and her mouth made a little "oh" but, whatever that was, she recovered quickly. A little pink stained her cheeks as she smiled and resumed walking to the kitchen.

Even drunk, she was too pretty for her own good. She was wearing skinny jeans and black cowboy boots and a black blouse that hung low on her shoulders, not revealing too much, but enough to make one wonder about her creamy skin. Her long, dark hair fell in waves down her back and she even had a little makeup on. Yeah, no denying. She was beautiful. And I bet the men at whatever place she had been at had noticed that too.

"Hi, Tyler," she said. Her voice was steadier than I thought it would be. Perhaps she wasn't that drunk.

"Hey," I snapped back. Not sure why I felt on the defensive, but I didn't like this situation.

She reached a hand to the high counter and with her other, she took off her boots. "I just had a great night with my friends."

I know, I wanted to say. Instead, I muttered, "It seems like it."

She kicked her boots aside and lifted her chin, her eyes meeting mine again. "Bia is still upset with me, of course. I apologized five thousand times, but she's still being difficult." She shrugged. "I know she'll soften at some point, but this sucks, you know."

"Uh-huh," I said, just because I had no idea what else to say.

"Shame Iris is gone," she continued, oblivious to my lack of interest. "If she was still here, I bet Pedro and her would still be together and she would have gone out with us. She was a good friend."

"Uh-huh," I repeated.

She squinted her eyes at me. "What are you having? Can I have one too?" She reached for the fridge, but I stepped in the way and caught her wrist. She froze, her eyes big.

"Don't you think you already had enough?"

She shrugged, tugging on my arm. I let go of her, but didn't move from the front of the fridge. "What? Now you're acting like my brother ..." Not the best compliment I had heard from her. "I can hold my liquor, okay? Besides, I'm okay."

"It didn't seem so when you entered the apartment."

She let out a loud chuckle. "Well, I'm known for losing my balance after one glass of whiskey or a bottle of beer, so that's normal." She tapped her temple. "But I don't lose my wits."

"Right," I dragged out, not really believing it. She seemed more smiley and chattier than usual. If that wasn't the alcohol, I didn't know what it was.

She leaned her ass on the counter behind her. "Okay, then, if you're not gonna let me have a beer, hand me a damn soda."

With a sigh, I grabbed a soda can from the fridge and handed it to her, then I went back to my previous position, mirroring Gabi on the other side of the narrow kitchen.

She opened the can with a loud pop. "The night is young. We should put on some music and keep the party going. Or ..." She lifted her finger as if she had the best idea ever. "We could work on the questions for the interview."

I wasn't so sure that was a good idea. I didn't know about her, but when I was drunk, or even a little tipsy, my tongue got loose and I spoke things I didn't mean to say out loud. Everyone was like that, Gabi included, and right now, I didn't think hearing her drunken confessions would be for the best.

"Maybe tomorrow."

She tipped the can and took a long swallow. I watched as her long neck stretched. Too much creamy skin exposed. Too much temptation.

I shook my head and cleared my throat, pushing those thoughts away.

"Oh, come on, you're no fun." Gabi grabbed her phone and put on an upbeat country song, one of my favorites actually. "How can you listen to that and not want to dance?" She raised one arm over her head and moved it side to side along with her head and hips.

Goddamn it.

I groaned. "You should go to bed, Gabi."

She dropped the soda can on the counter and stepped toward me. "Don't be a party pooper." She grabbed my upper arms and tugged me forward. "Dance, *tche*."

"Gabi ..."

Her brows furrowed and her hands squeezed my biceps. She narrowed her eyes and started patting and groping my upper arms and shoulders, as if there was a mystery on them.

"Gabi ..." I groaned.

"Do you work out?" she asked, serious. "You have to, otherwise, how can you be this ripped?" Her hands slid down slowly to my chest. A spark of energy ran from her soft touch to my gut. "So hot?"

Groaning, I closed my hands around her wrists and pulled her hands away. "Gabriela, you're drunk." I released her. "You should go to bed."

Yawning, Gabi swayed to one side. My heart lurched and I reached for her, sure she would face-plant on the kitchen's floor. Instead, she twisted her legs and ended up gaining her balance back.

Laughter erupted from her throat. "I'm not sleepy. *Eu quero dançar.*"

I had no idea what she was saying. I just knew it couldn't be good.

Gabi shimmied her ass, and I averted my gaze. Shit, this wasn't going well at all. Then, she spun in place. Of course, in her state, she tripped—again. This time I reached for her at the same time she reached for me.

I encircled my arm around her waist and her hands smacked my chest, followed by her face. I froze as her warm lips brushed my skin, only for a second, but enough to twist my insides—and to send the spark of energy south. Startling me, Gabi laughed, her head falling back. Her neck was stretched right in front of me, so close to my lips. I felt myself giving in to this unwelcomed feeling assaulting me.

Shit, no.

Regaining my senses, I groaned and stepped back. After making sure she was steady on her feet, I let go of Gabi.

With a smile nothing short of dazzling, Gabi extended her hand toward me again. "*Meu Deus*, dance, *guri*."

That was it.

Without a word, I let her get closer, then I swooped her into my arms. She yelped before laughing again. "What are you doing?"

"Taking you to bed."

She yawned. "I'm not sleepy."

"The hell you aren't."

She closed her eyes. "No, I'm not."

Next, Gabi rested her head on my shoulder.

Counting my steps so I would focus on something else other than the beautiful girl in my arms, who was currently breathing down my neck and sending shivers down my spine, I took Gabi to her room. I deposited her in bed, and she turned to her side and kept on sleeping.

What the hell?

Well, I wasn't going to do anything else. If she wanted to change into something more comfortable, she would have to do that herself.

As if the place was catching on fire, I turned the lights off and rushed out of her room—making sure I closed the door.

I stopped in the middle of the hallway and ran a hand over my still damp hair.

Holy shit, so that was what I was supposed to live with? Temptation in the flesh? How would I keep up this pretense for two years when she was already dancing all over my personal space in less than a month?

Cursing under my breath, I went back to the kitchen to finish my beer, because I damn well needed it.

25

GABI

THE *MATE* WENT DOWN my throat burning, but it warmed my core and made my muddled mind less achy.

This morning, I had woken up late and with a nasty headache. *Droga.* I wasn't a lightweight and I knew I hadn't been that drunk last night, but headaches were a common visitor after a few drinks.

The worst part though wasn't the headache. *Não.* It was remembering what had happened last night after I had come home. *Puta merda.* I had been too happy and I practically kissed Tyler's chest. I sighed. Yes, he had a great, kissable chest, but he wasn't mine to take advantage of. Not really.

Only after taking a shower, putting on some clean clothes, and mustering a lot of courage, I braved coming out of my bedroom. And guess what? Of course, Tyler wasn't home. He had left for work.

At least, this time, he had left a note over the kitchen's counter.

WORK UNTIL LATE.

—Ty

Bom, it was a start. A start that brought a pang to my heart. Why the hell did I feel something just staring at the note? It was ridiculous.

After throwing his note in the trash, I rummaged the kitchen for breakfast, but nothing looked good to my queasy stomach. I didn't feel sick, but I felt that if I pushed, I would be. So, I settled for my beloved *mate*.

Determined to not waste my Sunday, I sat at the dinner table with my *mate* and laptop and started a new search. I had already researched polo clubs and horse ranches and all I could think of around the area, but there had to be more. I didn't want to accept that all my choices had been taken from me—other than waiting to talk with the polo director from the club here in Santa Barbara. I didn't want to get my hopes up, just to have him squash them like a fly on the wall.

So, I searched more. Tried new keywords. Increased my range. What if my commute got too far? At least I would be living the dream and loving it.

Thirty minutes later, I swallowed a scream of frustration. I had found a handful of ranches and places that taught polo for kids, but nothing looked promising. I added their names and phone numbers to the notes app on my phone, and set up an alarm. I would call them tomorrow, but I already knew the answers.

No, we don't play professionally.

No teams here.

This is just a school, nothing more.

No, we aren't interested in sponsoring a women's team.

Women's team? Is that a thing now?

I sighed.

Why was I setting up myself for failure? Wherever I looked, I couldn't see a light in this dark tunnel. There was no option here. I was stuck being a polo player wannabe and living forever in the shadows of my brother and cousins.

My phone rang, making me jump out of my seat. I had been so lost in my thoughts, even the song set up as my ringtone scared me.

The name "Hil" flashed on the screen.

A small smile tugged at my lips and I answered the call. "Hey, *guria. Tudo bem*?"

"*Oi*," she said, trying out Portuguese. All of the girls and even Garrett knew basic words and sentences. And curse words. Those they all knew. "Want to come over? I've been sketching the outfits for the fashion show and I got some fabric samples I would like to show you guys. I already called Hannah and Bia."

I scrunched. "What if I say I'm not coming?"

"Then we'll stay on the phone until you do."

"What if I hang up?"

She chuckled. "Then I'll call again."

"What if I don't pick up?"

"Then I'll go there and knock on your door until you open it for me."

This time, I chuckled. "Man, you're pushy."

"No, I'm just a great friend."

I glanced around my apartment. Tyler was gone, and my search was taking me nowhere. I had nothing better to do. Besides, spending time with my family and friends was always great.

"I'll be there in a few ..."

"Oh, this isn't a girls-only thing. The guys went practicing early morning and should be done at any moment. They will probably spend the afternoon playing video games."

"Ah ..." A heavy feeling dropped in my stomach. "Tyler is working today."

"On a Sunday?"

"Yeah, he usually works Saturdays and Sundays."

"That sucks."

I sighed. "It does." More than I wanted to admit. It was insane how lonely I felt whenever he wasn't here.

"Well, one more reason to come over. So you're not alone there, missing your honey."

I gasped, choking on air. "Your honey?"

She laughed out loud. "It's old-fashioned, but still applies!"

"*Meu Deus ...*"

"Okay, stop wasting my time. Just move your ass and come over!"

Amused, I shook my head, even though she couldn't see it. "*Sim, senhora.* Just ... let me finish some quick things over here and I'll be there soon."

"Good. See you soon, then."

"Tchau," I said, before turning off the phone.

I pushed out the chair and looked at the empty living room in front of me. I didn't feel as excited as I thought I ought for going to spend some quality time with my family, but it beat staying alone here, sorry for myself for not being able to do more and achieve my dreams.

Before leaving, I wrote a short note for Tyler.

ANOTHER WEEK FLEW BY. The guys left for a tournament on Thursday. They had played on Friday and won, as usual. They had invited me to go with them, but I thought seeing them in action would only make me more depressed. Instead, I told myself I would focus on researching more clubs and places, maybe even going to a few of them. Perhaps if I showed my face, it would give them a better impression?

I just didn't know anymore.

I had also talked to my mother. She told me my father was still pissed at me. She was too, but she was better at hiding it, and also at forgiving. She told me she had been able to calm him down enough not to run to the airport and get the first flight here. I was thankful for that, but she warned me she might not be able to hold him back forever.

"You should talk to him again, *filha*," she said.

I promised her I would, but I always chickened out.

Though I hadn't spoken to my father, I had talked to Priscila a lot. We texted a couple of times a day. She was curious about Tyler and often questioned my sanity.

"I just can't believe you're engaged," she kept repeating. "So sudden. It isn't like you."

She was right, but I couldn't simply tell her the truth. Could I? Maybe someday.

As for Tyler, I hadn't seen a lot of him the entire week. Only when he got home from work late at night. He usually ate something quick and went to bed. We hadn't started studying any of the interview questions, and that was making me worried.

Friday early afternoon, I was researching more clubs when Tyler walked up to me and stood right in front of my chair.

I set my laptop aside and looked up at him. "What's up?"

He wiped his hands on his jeans. "All right, so, I knew this day was coming, I just ..." He shut his mouth.

I straightened in my chair. "What is it?"

"The money from our deal, most of it is to pay bills. And most of the bills are from the hospital." He sighed and my heart lurched. Was he sick? "But it's not for me. It's for my father. He has cancer. Again. For the third time. And it's not getting better."

My chest deflated. "That's ... terrible."

He sat down on the coffee table. "He has been spending more and more time at the hospital now, but every now and then, he feels better and I like to bring him home. He's doing okay right now, and I wanted to go pick him up and bring him home this afternoon."

Oh, so he wasn't telling me this because he wanted to share something with me. He was letting me know his father would be coming home.

"Of course, you should bring him home when he's up to it." I stood. "I'll ... pack a bag and ..." And do what? I couldn't go to my brother's apartment or Bia's. They would all talk about it and think Tyler and I were having problems. Then, I should probably hide in a hotel. But for how long? Did it matter? It was for Tyler's father. If my father had cancer and wanted to spend some time at his place, then I would shoo out anyone in my way and—

Tyler caught my arm as I turned toward my room. I froze and he gently pulled me back. "Why would you pack a bag? You think I want you to leave?"

I took a step back. "*Sim* ..."

"I wasn't telling you this so you would leave. I was telling you all this so you would know what to expect when I bring him home this afternoon."

Oh. "And what did you tell him about me?"

He ran a hand through his hair. "Well, I thought about keeping up with the lie. We tell him you're my girlfriend." He grimaced.

Sure, downgrade me some more. From wife, to fiancée, to girlfriend. Soon, I would be roommate, then who knew. Maid? Secretary? Neighbor? An acquaintance?

Why did I care about this? It had been my idea. Now, I had to accept all the lies that came with it.

"Are you sure about that? I can just leave."

"I hope ... I hope my father will live for many more months. Years even. Hopefully, he'll feel well enough to come stay with me often, and I can't ask you to move out every time that happens." He paused. "Would you be okay with that?"

I offered him a reassuring smile. "Sure."

"Okay." He stepped back. "Then, I'm gonna take a shower and go to the hospital. The doctor was going to check up on him before he was allowed to leave, and I want to be there for that. Then, I'll bring him in."

"Wait, what about dinner? What does he like?"

"Don't worry about that. We can order something."

"Tyler, just tell me what he likes."

One corner of his lips tugged. "He loves breads and steak and potatoes and cheese. Just don't make anything too greasy or any heavy sauces or too much spice and it should be fine."

"I'll try."

He retreated to his bedroom but paused at the door. "Thanks."

"For?"

He shrugged. "For not looking at me with pity in your eyes. For not asking the five hundred questions everyone does when they find out someone has cancer. For not judging me for having so many bills. And ... for wanting to cook for my old man."

I smiled at him. "Anytime."

Me: *I know you're still pissed at me, but I need your help. Please, call me.*

I stared at my phone over an hour later, and Bia still hadn't replied. Or called me.

Merda.

I could make *pão de queijo* without her, but it was her thing. I wanted her to come over and help me with it. Besides, it would be a good excuse to have her alone with me and force her to face me and get over everything.

She couldn't stay mad at me forever, could she?

Another half an hour passed and I gave up. If I waited, there would be no *pão de queijo* and no dinner at this house.

I picked up the *polvilho* from the pantry and reached for the scissors in the knife set—then my phone rang. Relief coursed through me when I saw Bia's name blinking on the screen.

"*Oi, guria*, I thought you would keep ignoring me."

"I almost did." She paused. "But you said you needed my help. It better be for a good cause or I'm hanging up."

Ouch. "Hm, I'm meeting Tyler's father this evening, and I learned he likes bread and cheese, so I thought why not make some *pão de queijo* for appetizers. However, that's your specialty, not mine."

"Everyone can make *pão de queijo*. You just need to follow the recipe."

"Bia ..." I sighed. "Can we please just put that aside for the next couple of hours while you come over and help me with the *pão de queijo*? Besides, I still have to cook the rest of the dinner and I haven't even started it yet. I could use the help."

Though she remained silent for a long moment, I swore I could hear the grinding of her teeth on the other side of the phone. "Fine! But only if you have whiskey. I might need a dose of Jack and Coke to do this."

"First, ouch. I knew you were upset with me, but I didn't think you needed to drink to face me again. Second, yes, I do have whiskey. Come over and I'll have your Jack and Coke ready for you."

"Just text me the address."

I did and she replied saying she would be here in about thirty, forty minutes. Enough time for me to run to the flower shop two blocks from the apartment and buy some cute, small bouquets and some colorful candles and holders. I had finished spreading the bouquets and candles around the living room when Bia arrived.

I opened the door for her, unsure of what to do. Usually, we would hug, but with her being so mad at me, I thought it would be best if I stepped aside and gave her some space.

"Thanks for coming."

Bia stepped into the apartment and looked around. "Cute little apartment."

I shrugged. "It's cute, like you said."

I hadn't chosen a big apartment as I first wanted because I knew Tyler couldn't afford one on his own, and if someone in my family learned about his financial problems, they would think I was paying for everything and throw another fit.

She went straight to the open kitchen and found her glass of Jack and Coke on the counter. She took a long swallow and set it down again. "Let's get to work."

In an awkward silence, Bia made the *pão de queijo* while I worked on a bacon wrapped steak and potatoes au gratin—with lots of my own white sauce. It wasn't too heavy, but I kept a mental note to advise Tyler's father to eat just a little. And then was dessert—a Brazilian specialty. I hoped they'd like it.

"That smells good," she finally said, after almost thirty minutes navigating by my side in the kitchen. And after two glasses of Jack and Coke.

"Thanks. I hope he likes it."

"So, are you nervous?"

I spread the cooked potatoes into a glass pan. "A little, I guess." I poured the sauce over the potatoes. I glanced at her. "He has cancer."

"Oh, wow, that's …"

I added grated cheese on top and put it in the oven beside the steak. "Tyler seems worried about it, though he doesn't talk about it much." Not really a lie since Tyler never spoke about it to me before. "To be honest, I don't know the extent, only that it's the third time the cancer has come back and it's not looking good."

A knot adorned her forehead. "I can't imagine having to see your parent fade away from cancer." She paused, then continued. "I don't think Tyler knows I know this, but Garrett told me. Tyler's mother walked out on them a long, long time ago. He doesn't remember her much, but he does know she remarried and has other kids."

My heart sank as I poured myself a glass of Jack and Coke. Now that the food was practically done, I could use some alcohol in my veins to relax. "Wow, having his mother abandon him and now seeing his father getting sicker and sicker?" I shook my head. "It must hurt."

"*Bom*, for what is worth, now he has you." She glanced at me. "I mean ... I know it's fake but I know you. You care about others and now you care about his problems. I think."

"I do," I said, realizing it was true. And I didn't like the feelings it woke in me.

I averted my eyes before she saw a trace of these unwelcomed feelings in me. To busy myself while I waited for the food, I checked on the drinks in the fridge. We didn't have many options, but I hoped Tyler had bought whatever his father liked.

She put the *pão de queijo* in the oven, then turned to me. "Aren't you missing Brazil? Even a little bit?"

I glanced up at her. "A little. My parents, of course, even though they want to kill me."

"Imagine if they knew the truth."

I cringed. "Don't joke about that." I paused, thinking. "I miss Pri too. And the food."

"No one or nothing else?"

"Not me, but apparently Mateus has been missing me."

She cocked one of her brows. "Really?"

I told her about his texts and then Pri's texts, telling me he was asking about me, determined to win me back. I had no idea how because one, I didn't love him anymore. I just liked him as an acquaintance. And two, he was thousands of miles away. How would he win me back by not being here? He was nuts.

"Does Tyler know about him?"

I put the potatoes beside the *pão de queijo* in the oven, then faced my cousin. "About Mateus? Why would he?"

She shrugged. "*Não sei.* Just wondering. I hope Mateus doesn't show up here ..."

I knocked on the wood cabinet. "Don't joke about that either." I opened a cabinet door and picked up some plates. "Help me set up the table, please."

"Okay, then let's talk about something else." Bia picked up the forks and knives. "So, how is the search for a polo team going?"

Letting out a long breath, I grabbed glasses and took them to the table. "Not good. No club wants to sponsor a female team."

"Sexist pigs," she muttered.

I chuckled. "I don't think that's the main reason, but I appreciate the support."

Bia looked around the room. Her eyes locked on one of the small bouquet of flowers I had bought earlier. She grabbed it and placed it in the middle of the breakfast table.

"What do you think?"

I stepped back and looked at our handiwork. "It looks good. Cozy, quaint."

She sighed. "*Bom,* I think it's time for me to go."

"*Sim, claro.* I have to take a quick shower and be ready for when they get back." I walked to the door and paused, my hand on the knob. I stared at my cousin as she walked to me. "*Obrigada* for your help."

A small smile appeared on her lips. "*De nada.*"

"Does this mean you're not mad at me anymore?"

"*Não.* I'm still mad at you." Her smile widened. "But it means I might forgive you faster than I thought I would."

"I'll take that."

She took my hand and squeezed it. "Good luck tonight. I hope you charm the old man even more than you charmed Ty."

I snorted. "I didn't charm Tyler. You know we both are faking it."

"*Claro*. If you say so."

I put a hand on my waist. "What is that supposed to mean?" Chuckling, she opened the door and walked out. I stepped into the hallway. "Bia! Don't leave like that. What did you mean?"

But she didn't answer me. I would have gone after her, but I was running out of time. I still had to get ready myself. *Droga*.

26

TYLER

DAD WAS LOOKING MUCH BETTER than I expected, but I still had to help him with a lot of things.

"Wait up, Dad," I said, exiting my truck. I slammed the door shut and raced to the other side. The stubborn man had the door open and was already halfway out. "Dad!" I grabbed his arm for support. "Let me help you."

He tsked. "I still can do things, you know." He tried to sound angry, but it was just his way of joking and it only made me grin. "Or what's next? Are you going to be like the nurses that hold my hand while I go pee?"

I wrinkled my nose. "Shit, can we change the subject?" He laughed, but it turned into a cough. "Okay, take it easy."

He waved me off and tried to push me away, but I wasn't having it. I wouldn't take him to the bathroom, unless absolutely necessary, but I wouldn't let him walk across the parking lot with its rough concrete by himself. As far as I knew, his muscles and even his bones weren't the same anymore—hadn't been for a long time. He didn't have any strength left. What if his legs seized in the middle of a step and he fell face-first on the sidewalk? With his immune system affected by the chemotherapy and radiotherapy, he bruised easily and healed at a snail's pace. If it depended on me, he wouldn't get hurt on my watch.

Against his protest that he wasn't that old or that invalid, I hooked my arm on his and helped him as we entered the building and waited for the elevators.

"This place looks nice, but ..." He looked around at the lobby. "I thought our financial situation wasn't good. In fact, I thought it was terrible. How can you afford to pay rent at a place like this?"

"Our financial situation is much better than you think it is, and let me assure you, I can afford rent at a place like this." Especially because Gabi had paid the rent for a year in advance and didn't let me pay one cent for it. A fact that I still hated and tried to rectify, but Gabi plain refused any kind of help in that department.

At first, I felt guilty about that, but then I realized something. She never made me feel guilty. She never looked at me with pity, disgust, or mistrust. I felt guilty for liking that she was helping me.

So, I let that go. Now that she knew the real reason I was buried in debt and could barely pay for decent groceries the last couple of months, it filled me with relief.

I shook my head at my reflection in the elevator's mirrored wall. What did I care about what she thought? She was my business partner. I shouldn't give a damn about what she thought or didn't think.

That was the theory anyway.

At the apartment's door, I fished the keys from my pocket and paused. "Hm, there's something I didn't tell you."

My father turned to me. "What?"

"I've ... I've met someone. Her name is Gabriela, but she prefers Gabi. She's in here, preparing dinner for us."

His eyes widened. "You have a girlfriend?"

I tried not to wince. "Yes, I do. And ... one of the reasons I moved to another apartment is because we're living together now."

A big smile spread through his mouth, reaching his eyes. "That's wonderful. Open this door. I want to meet her."

I took a deep breath, unlocked the door, and pushed it open.

My breath caught.

The place was clean and organized. A couple of scented candles were on the corner table and the kitchen's high counter. There were small orange flower bouquets on the coffee table and the dinner table. The table was set with a red and orange tablecloth, elegant white plates, silver cutlery, and pretty goblets.

Beside the table, Gabi stood with a big smile, holding a tray of *pão de queijo*—I knew these because I had seen them at her brother's house before. Gabi looked beautiful in a dark blue dress with a wide, white belt, and white cowboy boots. Her hair was pulled into a tight ponytail and, even though I liked her hair down, this way I could see her pretty face. And she was ridiculously pretty.

"Wow," my father whispered beside me. "Are you sure she's your girlfriend? She's too pretty for you."

"Dad," I mock snarled.

We stepped into the apartment and Gabi met us halfway.

"Mr. Reid, it's a pleasure to meet you."

"Please, call me Charlie." He stared at her, visibly enchanted. "Oh my, oh my, you're such a precious thing, my dear. Beautiful and from the looks of it, gifted." He looked around. "This place looks and smells amazing."

"Thank you." Her cheeks gained a faint red tint, which made me smile.

"Let's sit down, Dad." I gently pushed him to the couch. He resisted me at first, but then Gabi dropped the tray on the coffee table and took my father's arm. He practically melted into her and let her guide him to the couch.

She sat right beside him and pulled the tray to her lap. "I heard you like bread and cheese, so I made these. Brazilian cheese bread. I hope you like it."

With a wide smile, my father grabbed one of the cheese breads and took a big bite. "Hm," he moaned. "These are amazing." He finished eating the first and reached for a second one. Then, he turned to me, smiling wide, like I hadn't seen in months. "Ty, I say she's a keeper."

Without meaning to, I glanced to Gabi and she glanced to me. She had a small smile on her lips and the red tint spread over her cheeks again. I smiled at her, feeling too happy for words. "I think she is, Dad."

DINNER WAS FUCKING INCREDIBLE. Dad would have eaten way more, but Gabi had warned us the white sauce on the potatoes could be heavy, so I had to take his plate away from him. Then, Gabi brought dessert to the table.

"This is called *brigadeirão*." She set a big, round plate over the table, with a chocolate pudding-looking dessert topped with granulated chocolate and sliced strawberry. "We usually make little balls of this and serve it at birthday parties. You know, bite size for kids. But someone had the great idea of make a big pudding out of it so we can have big slices instead." She cut out fat slices of the *brigadeirão*, placed them on small plates, and handed them to us.

My father took a big spoonful and moaned. "I always heard some women grab their men by the belly. Son, you better marry her."

Gabi coughed and I lost my smile.

Thankfully, Dad was so into the dessert, he didn't notice anything.

Gabi excused herself and went back to the kitchen. I watched her fumble with the coffee machine for a moment.

"This is the best dinner I've ever had," my father said. His voice was low, as if he couldn't bother speaking too loudly because he was too focused on eating more and more. "I mean it. From the appetizers to the dessert. I bet even the coffee will be spectacular." He shoved the last bit of *brigadeirão* in his mouth and moaned as he swallowed it. I rolled my eyes and he chuckled. "I'm serious, son. Look at this food. Look at her. Where in heaven did you find her?"

I looked at her, as if I needed to be told. It was impossible not to look at her when she was around. I knew she was gorgeous from the first moment I saw her and I knew she could cook; I just didn't know she could come up with a delicious banquet in the matter of three, maybe four hours—it had taken longer than I expected at the hospital. What still rendered me speechless was the way she made me speechless. She had this smile, this spirit, this presence that I couldn't explain other than it just felt like a magnet, pulling at me, forcing me to look at her, to pay attention to her.

Never in my life did I think I could look at a girl this way. That I could feel this disarmed and foolish around a girl. Now, seeing how she had prepared the entire apartment and made such an incredible feast just to receive my father ... what was I supposed to make of that? This girl was getting under my skin and I didn't like it. Still, I found myself standing up, picking up the plates, and taking them to the sink. Then, I leaned into the counter and crossed my arms.

"Is there something wrong?" she asked, pouring coffee into three small cups.

"Nope. In fact, everything is perfect."

She stopped and looked up at me. "Then, why do you sound so upset?"

"Because nobody does something nice for a stranger like that if they don't want something in return."

Her mouth fell open, but she quickly shut it. "Your father isn't a stranger. He's your father. You care about him and I'll not degrade that. We might not be involved, but right now, I care about your father too. But the thing that I really want you to learn is this: I am a nice person. A very nice one, actually. If you see me pissed or angry or being rude to someone, then know something is really wrong."

She placed the three cups and the coffee pot on another tray and took it to the table, leaving me alone in the kitchen.

That was the entire problem. She was too fucking nice, too fucking caring. If she was only a pretty airhead Barbie, I could deal with it. But pretty and smart and nice? How was I supposed to keep my distance from her?

With a sigh, I pushed away from the counter and joined them at the table.

I took the third coffee cup and sipped from it. My father was right. Even her coffee was better than the ones I always had. How was this possible? How was this girl so perfect?

My father took a sip of his coffee. "Now that I'm not busy savoring your delicious food, I can finally ask. How did you two meet?"

Gabi glanced at me with big eyes.

"Through Garrett," I said quickly. "You remember Garrett? From vet school?"

"Oh, yes," he answered with a frown.

"His girlfriend, Bia, is Gabi's cousin."

"That's good." He smiled to Gabi. "And what do you do, Gabi?"

Gabi offered him a tentative smile. "*Bom*, to be honest, nothing right now." She cleared her throat, obviously embarrassed about the topic. "I'm a polo player without a team, and right now, I'm looking for a sponsor to help me get a team together."

My father's eyebrows shot up. "Horse polo?"

"He loves horses," I told Gabi.

Her smile widened. "Yes, horse polo. My entire family is up to their necks in horse business."

"Gabi's brother and cousins are famous polo players," I explained to my father. "And her family has a big horse ranch in Brazil."

"That's really great," my father said. "Tyler also loves horses." He smiled. "It seems you two have a lot in common. I can see why you two get along so well."

He could? But Gabi and I had barely talked to each other since my father arrived, and we certainly hadn't touched or showed anything more intimate. My father was seeing things that weren't there.

The old man yawned.

"That's it." I stood and reached for him. "Time to go to bed."

I helped my father up, but instead of coming with me, he stepped toward Gabi. She was already up and getting all the cups and saucers back into the tray.

"Thank you for the amazing dinner, my dear." He pulled her into his arms and embraced her tight. From over his shoulder, Gabi looked at me. Her blue eyes glistened as she squeezed him back. My father kissed her cheek and pulled back. "I'm glad my son found you."

"Me too," she said with a firm voice, even though I could see her hands shaking slightly.

"All right, stop bothering her, old man." I grabbed his arm and veered him toward the guest bedroom. "Let's get you ready for bed."

"Good night, Gabi," my father called.

"Good night," she whispered back.

27

I PICKED up all the plates, trays, and cups and brought them to the kitchen, and then I took off my boots, put on an apron so as not to ruin my dress, and set to work.

My hands kept busy rinsing the plates before putting them into the dishwasher, and scooping the rest of the food in small containers and storing them in the fridge, but my mind was free and wild.

Charlie seemed like a great man, and despite his weak appearance, I was sure he had been a strong, robust man a few years ago. He had the same intense eyes as his son, and strong chin and jaw, and he had seemed pleased with the little production I had set up. For a moment, right before they arrived, I thought I had overdone it. After all, it wasn't anyone's birthday, graduation, or celebration. I was just going to meet the father of my not-so-fake husband—a man who was dying of cancer. Who, on their deathbed, wanted a party?

Yet, he had loved it. Or he had pretended he did.

"What is that pout for?"

I almost dropped the glass pan I was washing—it didn't fit in the dishwasher—at the sound of Tyler's voice behind me.

I glanced over my shoulder. "*Meu Deus*, you almost gave me a heart attack."

"Only because you were lost in thought." He grabbed a drying cloth and one of the bigger pots from the drying rack. "So, hm, the man didn't shut up about you until I left the bedroom, and even so, I thought he would get up from the bed just to tell me how wonderful you are one last time."

I smiled. "That's sweet."

He placed the pot in its place inside the cabinet then turned to me, his eyes serious. "Thank you. You certainly didn't have any obligation to do all this ..." He gestured to the kitchen and the living room. "But you did it anyway and everything was great. He loved it. Thank you."

"You're welcome," I whispered, returning my gaze to the sink before I sank into the depths of his warm eyes.

In silence, Tyler helped me organize the kitchen. We fell into an easy rhythm. I washed and he dried, and then put it away. After, he wiped the table, while I shook the tablecloth over the sink and folded it to be used tomorrow.

I washed the sink one last time and then reached behind me to untie the apron, but when I pulled on the ties, they got stuck. Biting my lower lip, I glanced to Tyler.

"Can you help me, please?"

Tyler, who had finished cleaning the table, and was now mindlessly looking out the window, glanced at my hands on my back.

"Sure."

I turned my back to him, holding up the ties. He stood behind me and his fingertips brushed mine when he took the ties from me. I pulled my hands away and folded them over my stomach. I could feel his tall, strong body behind me, so, so close. I felt it when he lowered his head to work on the knot, putting his face, his forehead, so close to my exposed neck. I suppressed a shiver.

After a quick tug, the apron loosened around me.

"Done," Tyler whispered, his breath tickling my neck.

This time, I did shiver.

I turned around and looked up at him. So, so close. "Thank you."

His eyes were fixed on mine. So, so close. "You're welcome."

Neither of us moved for another long second. Then finally, Tyler stepped back and went back to the window.

I let out a long breath, trying to calm my racing heart.

I had been nervous about meeting Tyler's father, but it had been a good night after all. And I deserved a little recompense. I found a bottle of my favorite wine in a corner of the pantry and opened it up.

"Want some?"

He shrugged. "Sure, why not?"

I poured a glass for me and one for him. "Here," I said, handing him a glass. Tired, I went to the couch where I sat down and lifted my feet on the coffee table.

Tyler leaned his back against the window and sipped from his wine. I tried thinking of something else, anything else, but with him standing there, turned to me, and with the intensity of the day, it was hard to come up with any other topic. Even though my curiosity was scratching at the surface, I wouldn't give in to it and ask the millions of questions in my mind. He had thanked me for that earlier and I wouldn't make him regret it.

Surprising me, Tyler spoke up.

"The first cancer appeared when I was seventeen. It was an early stage and small. The doctor removed it and did a few chemo sessions to make sure it hadn't spread. Soon after, the doctor said he was all clear. Two years later, during a check-up, the doctor found out the cancer was back, and it was a little bigger this time.

Dad was treated the same way. He had the tumor taken out and then did more chemo sessions. By then, he was already weak. It was hard to see him like that. Fortunately, a few months later, the doctor announced Dad was clear. However, I was more apprehensive this time. After all, he had said the same thing before and it didn't work. Dad had check-ups every three months after that, and not even two years later, it was back. And I had known it would come back. I just ... I can't explain it. I knew it would be back." He pushed off the window and halted behind the armchair beside the couch. He rested his free hand on the chair. "But this time the doctor said it was worse. It was bigger and the more aggressive kind. And from where it was located, he couldn't remove it all. He said that we wouldn't win this time. But I didn't lose faith. I still haven't. The doctor cut out part of the tumor and then Dad started aggressive chemotherapy and radiotherapy sessions. He has bad days and he has terrible days. That's why he spends so much time at the hospital, because he needs extra care from nurses and he needs IVs and such, which would be even more expensive if done at home."

He stopped talking and I swallowed the lump in my throat. "I can't process all of this," I confessed. If it was too much for me to assimilate, how could he live with it all?

"Well, at least now you know why the bills are so high. After battling this illness for so long, there was nothing we could do. I signed up for loan after loan to cover what insurance wouldn't and then we lost his insurance. I don't qualify for any more loans, and I just had to ignore the bills." He ran a hand through his hair. "The grace period of one loan had just expired when you made me the offer. That was the first one I paid off ... when you gave me the first third of the payment. Another one will expire soon."

"Do you need me to give you the second third sooner?"

He shook his head. "No, I can manage with what I still have from the first one. Thanks, though."

This was all just so terrible. Tyler had to deal with all of this alone. The emotional mixed with the financial weight had to be running him into the ground. How he was still going this strong was a mystery to me.

"I know ..." I started, but then shut my mouth. I drank the rest of my wine in one big gulp, hoping the alcohol would have an instant effect so I could say what I wanted to say. "I know we're in a pretend relationship, but since we're going to be spending a lot of time together, I would like to think of you as a friend and I want you to think of me as a friend too. Friends talk to each other and they lean on each other. So, when you need to talk or you need another pillar to help you keep standing, I'm here."

He stared at me for a long time, those intense eyes locked on mine. There was a new glint in them, something I couldn't quite make out. "Thank you," he finally said.

"*Bom*." I pushed off the couch and stood. "I should go to bed too." I walked to the hallway and turned into my bedroom.

"Wait," Tyler whispered, catching up with me. "I ... we ..." He ran a hand through his hair. "Dad won't buy it if we sleep in different rooms."

"Oh." My eyes widened. "Oh!" Heat crept over my face as his words sank in. "So, hm, you need to sleep in here." After all, his bedroom was a facade. I had known that when buying the apartment, I hadn't thought someone would be around to witness it.

"Yeah. Sorry."

"No, hm, it's okay."

"I'll grab some extra blankets and sleep on the floor."

My throat closed up. "Okay," I croaked. "I'll ..." I pointed toward the bathroom. "I'll go get changed in there."

"Sure, sure," he said. "I'm gonna go to my bedroom first, then come back with the blankets."

"Okay."

"Okay."

He retreated into the hallway and I let out a long breath.

My hands shook and my mind was a haze as I changed from my dress to the less skimpy pajama set I owned—shorts and a loose tee—brushed my teeth, and put on some face cream. When I came back to the bedroom, Tyler was—

His actions were completely erased from my mind as I took him in. Him. Without a shirt. Just some thin sleeping shorts. No shirt. A broad chest. Muscles. No shirt.

Meu Deus, he was ripped. I had seen it before, but it still boggled my mind how rock hard his abs and chest and shoulders and arms and—my mind became mush.

Tyler looked up and I averted my eyes. Swallowing hard, I thought back on what he was doing when I walked out of the bathroom. What was it? All I could remember was him and his naked chest. Oh, *sim*, he had been folding the blankets on the floor at the foot of the bed, making a bed for himself.

My heart squeezed. As much as I didn't like the idea of him sleeping on the floor, I also didn't like the idea of offering for him to share my bed with me. I took up a lot of space. What if I rolled in the middle of the night and landed on him? On that naked chest. No way.

But as I slipped under the covers in my bed, I couldn't help but ask, "Are you sure you're gonna be okay there?"

"Yeah, I'll be fine." He made sure the bedroom's door was closed, hit the light switch, and then lay in his makeshift bed. That wasn't probably too comfortable, poor guy. "Just for the record, I like the idea of having you as a friend too." A smile spread over my lips. In the dark, he cleared his throat. "Good night."

"Good night," I said, forcing my eyes closed before I spied on him.

28

TYLER

THE WEEKEND when my father was home, I didn't work at all. I stayed home with my father and Gabi. To say I was surprised by her was an understatement. Gabi was nothing more than kind to my father and helpful. She made plenty of food and even tried to adhere to my father's strict diet.

Her brother and cousins were still at the tournament, which I knew made her a little jealous. Though Hannah invited her and the other girls for a sleepover on Saturday, Gabi only went for dinner, saying she wanted to give my father and me some alone time. But she came back early, in case we needed her.

When Monday came, I had to go back to work. I hated leaving my father alone at home like that. Maybe I should have hired a nurse to stay with him. Or maybe I should have called the clinic and called out for the day.

I was messing with my phone, searching my contacts, when Gabi joined me in the kitchen. She halted by my side, a steaming cup of coffee in her hand.

"I know what's going on," she said, her voice low.

I glanced at her, then at my father, who was seated on the

couch, watching the news in the living room, not too far away from us.

"What do you mean?" I asked.

"You're worried about him." She turned to me. "I'll take care of him. You don't need to worry."

I gaped at her. "You don't need to do that."

"I don't need to do that," she said with one short nod. "I want to do that. Besides, the guys are still away, the girls are either in school or working, and I have no one else to bother."

"But ..."

Before I could say anything, Gabi walked away from me and sat down beside my father. I watched in awe as she talked to him about their day. A walk in the nearby park, maybe go see a movie —she had found a movie theater playing classics, then come back for a nap.

"—and if you want, we can go see Branca, my mare. Would you like that?"

"My dear, I would love that," my father said, his eyes shining with wonder. He was totally in love with her.

And I didn't know what to do about that.

She looked at me with a grin, then winked.

I swallowed the lump that lodged in my throat. Before I thought too much about it and lost my nerve, I agreed to it.

***

WEDNESDAY WAS my father's last day with us at the apartment. The next morning, he needed to go back to the hospital for his treatment. Because of that, Gabi had prepared another banquet, though everything had been a little modified to fit my father's diet.

Still, he had loved everything and couldn't stop complimenting her and her food and her smile and her kindness ... I had to grab his arm and take him to his bedroom, otherwise he would drool at her feet all night long.

After making sure he was okay and settled in bed, I went to Gabi's room. She was already in her pajamas—a loose shirt and mini shorts that showed way too much of her toned legs.

Suddenly, the room felt too warm.

"Everything okay?" Gabi asked as she slipped into her bed.

I sat down on my makeshift bed on the floor. It wasn't as bad as I thought it would be, but I wouldn't want to sleep here for another week, or more.

I let out a sigh. "Yeah, I think so." I opened my mouth to tell her how much I hated leaving my father at the hospital, but closed it again. I knew it was best for him there. I couldn't take care of him properly here.

Without asking, I scooted closer to the door and turned the lights off. I slipped into bed but didn't close my eyes. There was too much on my mind for comfort.

"I can hear your breathing," Gabi said, her voice low. "Are you sure you're okay?"

No, I wasn't sure. "How about those interview questions?" I asked, changing subjects. Working on those would definitely distract me. "Do you know those by heart, or do you need the lights?"

"Hm, I don't know them all by heart, but I do know there are a lot of questions about our childhood and growing up." She paused. "Like, what do you remember when you were a child? Where did you go to school? What was the name of your best friend? Things like that."

That was easy. I told her about my school, about my friends, about loving horses, about starting vet school, and about meeting Garrett. I also told her about how I had to drop school to work and pay the bills, which brought my mood down again.

But then Gabi told me about her tight family, polo, her family's ranch, the horses, the thousands of tournaments, the trips … Her life looked divine, directly from a movie. There had to be something wrong with her family. Such perfection wasn't true.

"Tell me something bad about your family," I prodded. Seriously, if there was nothing, I would go nuts right here, right now.

But then she told me a few things. About Leo's past with alcohol and his rehab time. About coming to the United States, and the mess with Hannah's ex-boyfriend, who had actually killed her grandmother, her horse, tried to kill her father, and more. About Ricardo's ex-girlfriend who sold the story of Leo's past to a reporter because Eric had assured her they would all go back to Brazil after that. How Ricardo hadn't dated since that betrayal. Then, she told me about Bia. I knew Bia had met Garrett in Colorado, but I had no idea she had walked away from their perfect family because of the pressure she felt at being a Fernandes. Next was Guilherme and Hilary's story with their own complications before they finally became a couple.

"And then there's Pedro," she said. "We thought he had met his soulmate when he started dating Iris, but a couple of months ago, she disappeared from our lives, and Pedro refuses to tell us what happened."

I stared at the darkness around me. Why was it a little satisfying to know they weren't that perfect after all? Though, of course I wouldn't wish that on anyone, not even them.

I cleared my throat. "What else? The questions, I mean. What else should we know for the interview?"

"Hm, let me think." She clicked her tongue. "Oh, about our parents. Did you get along with your parents? Did they get along with each other?"

Shit.

That topic had the same effect as talking about her family. It took my mind off my father's illness, but it went directly to another dark place. Though, this one used to make me mad when I was younger. Now it made me sad. "I don't know much about my mother. All I know is that she upped and left when I was four years old, and that now she's married and has more kids."

Gabi was quiet for a long time. "You never talked to her?"

"Nope." I sighed. "In all these years, I only saw her once from a distance, and she was with her two boys and one girl."

"*Droga.* I'm sorry I brought it up."

I shrugged, though she couldn't see it in the dark. "It's okay. I guess you would have found out someday, somehow." I pulled the thin blanket I had set beside me up to my chest. "Tell me about yours."

"My what? My mother?"

"Yes."

"*Bom* ... I don't know. I never had any problems with her, I guess. She was always there for me, and pushed me to be better, to do better. The only problem I have with my parents is polo." She paused. "And now you."

I chuckled. "Right. Me."

"Speaking of which," she continued, serious. "We should go to Brazil."

I became serious. She had talked about this before we had moved in together. "Oh-kay."

"I'm serious," she said. "I think it's better if we go and appease them there, then to have them come here to harass us."

I wanted to tell her that I wouldn't be going to Brazil, but that wouldn't be fair. After all she had done for my father these past few days, it was only right if I repaid the favor.

Shit. "All right, we can go. Just tell me what I need to do."

"All we need to do is choose a day and buy the plane tickets."

29

GABI

TYLER HAD SAID he was okay with going to Brazil, but I thought he would delay it as much as he could. He surprised me by saying we could go as soon as I wanted—or found available tickets. So, I purchased two first class tickets to Brazil for the weekend. Meanwhile, I visited Branca at Hannah's ranch. She was still scared and having some tantrums whenever a loud sound came near her. But Hannah assured me she was being well taken care of, and I believed her.

I had also visited Charlie at the hospital twice. When Tyler found out, he had asked me why.

"Because I want to," I told him, deadpan. And it was true. I had been home sulking about my failed polo dream, so why not go visit his father who was lonely at the hospital? Besides, he was sweet to me.

Then, it was time to go to Brazil. Gui insisted on taking us to the airport—Tyler and me both. This way, Tyler wouldn't need to leave his truck at the airport and pay the outrageous fees. My brother's words, not mine.

At first, Tyler refused, but then he relented.

Gui and Hilary drove us to the airport, and as I expected, the entire gang was there, waiting for us at the check-in area. I couldn't help the wide smile and the sense of love that filled my chest as I looked at each one of them. Bia, Garrett, Leo, Hannah, Ri, and Pedro.

"They always come when you leave?" Tyler asked as we loaded our bags on the conveyor belt that would take them away to the airplane.

"Yes, but usually I stay away for a few months. I don't know why they are here if they know I'll be back next week."

"Hm," was all he said before taking our tickets from the attendant and reading through them.

I turned to my family. "You guys know I'll be back in five days, right?"

"*Bem, sim ...*" Leo started.

I put a hand on my waist and narrowed my eyes at him. "Spill."

He looked at Hannah and she rolled her eyes. "The guys have sort of ... like a bet. Gui and Ri think your father will freak out."

"What does that mean?" I asked.

"That he'll send Tyler back and make you stay there," Ri explained.

I chuckled. "As if he could stop me."

"That's what I said," Leo said, his voice loud and proud.

I shook my head. "You guys are unbelievable."

"In any case," Hil started. "We came because we love you and we wanted to say goodbye and have a great trip, doesn't matter if it's only five months, five days, or five hours."

I smiled at her. "Thanks."

My brother embraced me. "I hope *pai* surprises me," he whispered in my ear. Me too. "See you in a few days."

I kissed his cheek. "*Tchau.*"

Tyler and I joined the long security line while my family stood at a distance, waving every few seconds and yelling, "we love you," "come back soon," "good luck," and "have a safe flight," in Portuguese.

It made me smile.

Beside me, Tyler shook his head.

"What?"

He glanced at me. "Your family."

"What about it?"

He shook his head once again. "Nothing."

"Oh no. Don't start talking about my family, then stop. Just spill."

"They are so fucking tight."

"What do you mean?"

"They seem to always be together and in each other's business. It would drive me crazy."

"You mean, it *will* drive you crazy, because, you know, we'll continue going to my brother's apartment and to my uncle's and aunt's ranch, and more."

He groaned. "God, I hope they leave me alone."

I frowned at him. "As far as I recall, the last couple of times we've been with them, you had a good time."

One corner of his lips tugged up. "I wouldn't say good time. But, yeah, it wasn't that bad."

I shook my head. I hoped he was joking about my family, because his previous statement didn't sit well with me. I respected Tyler's opinion. It seemed he wasn't a fan of a close family, but he didn't have to groan and complain about mine to my face. They were the most important thing in my life. It was them, with polo in a close second place. Without my family, I didn't know who I truly was. I was a part of them, and they were a part of me. That would never change.

Not sure what to say, I chose to stay quiet.

And, despite our new agreement to be friends, that was how

we remained for the next twenty-six hours—always side by side, but only talking to each other when necessary.

That all changed the moment we picked up our bags in the airport in Porto Alegre.

"We're here," I said, my back to the big glass wall separating the travelers from the people waiting outside. "My parents are probably somewhere behind that glass wall, watching us right now." I looked up at Tyler. "They will pay attention to how we act around each other, and if we want our plan to work, they have to believe we're in love."

A knot appeared on his forehead, but he nodded. "Just for five days, right?"

Hopefully, only for five days. "Right."

"Okay, then." He let out a long breath. "We start the show right now."

I gasped as Tyler stepped into my personal space, wrapped an arm around my shoulders, and pulled me to him. My face smacked into his chest, and my stunned hands landed on his hips. I pulled them back quickly. He leaned down and kissed my forehead, before turning to the cart with our bags.

"That was ..." I whispered, not sure what to say next.

I didn't think Tyler heard me because he smiled at me, a forced one, and said, "Lead the way."

I forced a smile too, but as soon as we started walking toward the exit doors, I caught sight of my parents and my smile turned into a real one. My steps sped up, and soon I was out the door and in my mother's arms.

"Gabi! It's so good to see you," she said, hugging me tight. "I missed you, *querida*."

"I missed you too, *mãe*." Then Dad was prying Mom from me only to replace her and squeeze me tight. I chuckled. "You want to break me?"

"Is it working?" Dad asked, laughing.

"He increased the weights of his workout a few days ago," my mom said, sounding not too amused. "Now he thinks he can do anything."

We laughed, but then both of them stiffened, their gaze falling behind me.

Clearing my throat, I stepped back, coming to stand beside Tyler. "*Mãe, pai*, this is Tyler. Tyler, this is Regina, my mom, and Luis Carlos, my father."

"Hello, Mr. Fernandes." He shook my father's hand, and then turned to my mother. "Nice to meet you, Mrs. Fernandes."

"Hello, Tyler," my mother said, her tone a little wary.

My father frowned. "So you're Tyler."

"*Pai* ..." I groaned.

"Yes, sir, I'm Tyler Reid."

My father hesitated. "Nice to meet you too."

I let out a relieved breath. "All right. Can we go now? I really want a shower, some food, and a nap. Not necessarily in that order."

My mother chuckled. "Of course." She took my hand in hers and pulled me toward the parking garage. "Maria is cooking your favorite."

Hm, my mouth watered. Right now, I was kind of glad I was home.

30

TYLER

PORTO ALEGRE WAS A BIG, chaotic city with too many cars and crazy motorcycle drivers. I was shocked to see the men, usually without a helmet, zipping between the cars.

On the ride out of the city, Regina—I started calling her Mrs. Fernandes, but she explained no one called each other by the last name here, unless it was friends using it as a nickname instead—told me they had a house in the city, but they spent ninety-nine percent of their time at their ranch about ninety minutes away.

I couldn't help but look around as the city was left behind. The road was narrow and only one lane in each direction for most of the drive. Sometimes, there wasn't even a shoulder lane. What were we supposed to do in case of emergency? Pull over in the grass? In the hill right off the road?

We passed three or four other smaller towns, and finally, the urban setting was replaced by farms with green lawns and plantations. Lots of cows and horses and sheep too.

Luis Carlos turned his big truck into a neatly paved road flanked by neatly cut grass and neatly shaped bushes and tall trees. Halfway down the road, a big wrought-iron gate with a fancy metal F stood between two tall stone pillars. Luis Carlos pressed the remote on his truck's dashboard and the gates opened.

I had never seen a ranch like this one.

The exterior of the house was brown bricks with brown wood accent. The windows were tall and wide, with brown shutters that actually opened and closed. As we parked and I gawked at the impressive house, Gabi told me it was made of brick, even the interior walls. There was no drywall here or wood framing. All the wood I saw was just decorative.

The front doors opened to a big living room, and beyond it, I saw the dining room.

"I know it's a little late for lunch, but I thought you two would be hungry." Regina showed us to the long wooden dining table. "Please, sit down."

Luis Carlos took the head of the table. Regina sat on his right, Gabi sat on his left, and I sat beside her.

"So, how was the trip?" Regina asked.

So far, Luis Carlos had spoken only a handful of times, but every time, his voice had been tight. However, besides the time on the road, his eyes never stirred away from me. He regarded me with hard eyes and furrowed brows.

"It was long, as it always is," Gabi answered. "I barely slept during the overnight flight, so I'm really tired."

Her mother nodded. "You never sleep during the flights."

"It's just so uncomfortable." Gabi glanced at me. "Didn't you think, Tyler?"

"Yeah, yeah," I said quickly. "Small space, the seat doesn't recline much ..."

Then a small woman with her short hair pulled tight behind her head and black pants and white shirt entered the dining room, bringing a tray with drinks.

"Gabriela," the woman exclaimed, her tone content as she set the things on the table. "*Que bom te ver, guria!*"

Gabi stood and embraced the woman. "*Tu também*, Maria. *Tudo bem por aqui?*"

I was lost as the two exchanged a few sentences in Portuguese. Until Gabi pointed at me. "*Este é* Tyler. Tyler—" She turned to me. "—this is Maria. She has been working for my family since I was a little girl."

"Hi, Maria," I said. "Pleasure to meet you."

Gabi translated and then said to me, "She said you too."

Maria nodded at me, and then said something else to Regina before leaving the room.

"All right, dig in," Regina announced.

I glanced at the pots and bowls in front of us. There was rice, black beans—which were fine—some weird green potato looking thing, some odd flour, and an alien-looking meat.

Gabi smiled at me. "I know it looks strange, but here. This—" She pointed to the green thing. "It's sweet potato. Our sweet potatoes here are green, not orange. But it's just as good. This is *farofa*, which is seasoned flour we eat with meat. And I know the steak looks weird with the bone in the middle, but it's actually juicy and tender. Brazilian steak cuts are different from Americans'. Try it. I promise you'll like it."

Well, she had handed me a few things before that looked odd and I ended up liking it. Besides, I was starving. I was sure I would eat almost anything that was placed in front of me.

Sure enough, I did like the green sweet potato, the *farofa* over the rice, the spicy black beans, and the alien steak.

"Glad you like it," Regina said, smiling.

"It's great. Thank you." I took another forkful. It was fucking three in the afternoon. I shouldn't eat too much, but it was just too good.

Gabi lifted her napkin to her mouth and Regina's eyes went wide. "That's … Gabriela, is that the ring?"

Oh, shit. I knew this subject was coming, I just hoped there would be an easier way to bring it up.

Gabi paled and glanced at me. "*Sim*, it's my engagement ring." She smiled, but it didn't reach her eyes.

Luis Carlos' face turned red. "Excuse me if that's too hard to take in."

"What he means ..." Regina put a hand over Luis Carlos' tense arm. "You two caught us by surprise."

"I told you almost a month ago."

Regina nodded. "It was a big surprise, *querida*. We'll need more time to get used to it."

"I don't get it," Luis Carlos hissed. "Why? Why would you get engaged so fast?"

Gabi lifted her chin. "Hm, I'm pretty sure you know the answer to why two people get engaged."

Luis Carlos slapped the table and Gabi flinched. "Don't be a smart ass with me, Gabriela."

Regina's hand tightened around Luis Carlos's arm. "What he means is that we didn't even know you were dating someone. Then, you announce an engagement even before you introduce us to your boyfriend."

"It was ... kinda fast," Gabi said, her voice low, unsure. "We started seeing each other over a year and—"

"It didn't look like it could work with her being away for so long," I cut in, trying to help her. I stared at Luis Carlos. Gabi could be afraid of him and worry about his opinion, but I couldn't care less. For her, though, I would try to be more civil. "But, every time she was gone, I counted the days until I got to see her again. And I knew she did the same. We missed each other." Playing my part, I reached over and entwined my fingers with hers over the table. "Then last month I realized that, with her starting college soon, she wouldn't come to visit her brother and cousins as often. I realized I didn't want to be away from her, so I told her my true feelings and proposed."

"And I accepted." She lifted our entwined hands, showing off her ring again.

Her father narrowed his eyes at her. "And you just threw away your entire life for him?"

"Luis Carlos," Regina whispered.

I could feel Gabi's hand and arm tensing. "I didn't throw away my life. I would have, if I had come back and started college. I never wanted to go to college, and you know that. You know what I always wanted to do, and you never supported me."

Luis Carlos let out a short, sarcastic chuckle. "Didn't support you? I did everything for you. Everything. I just encouraged you not to pursue a career in polo, because I knew polo for women is dead."

"Here. It's dead here."

He tilted his head at her. "And how is polo working out for you in the U.S.?"

Gabi pressed her lips tight. She didn't have an answer for that because it *wasn't* working that well either. I squeezed her hand in mine.

With a loud grunt, Luis Carlos pushed his chair back and marched out of the room.

With tears in her eyes, Regina stood. "I'm going to ..." She gestured after her husband, then she followed him.

Once we heard their heavy steps on the stairs, I let go of Gabi's hands. "That went well."

"Better than I expected."

"What did you expect?"

"I thought he would punch you once we approached the subject."

I gaped at her. "What?" She had mentioned her father

wouldn't be accepting of this, but to punch me? My imagination hadn't gone that far.

She shrugged. "I'm glad I was wrong."

"Well, I'm glad too."

We finished lunch and we took our plates to the kitchen, where Maria was mixing what looked like cake batter. She smiled at us.

Then, I followed Gabi upstairs and through a long corridor with too many doors.

At the end of the corridor, she stopped in front of a door and said, "This is your suite. The bed shoul—"

"We're sleeping in separate bedrooms?" That sounded odd. When my father stayed with us, we had to sleep in the same room for the sake of appearances.

"*Sim*. Probably a request from my father." She rolled her eyes. "Call him old-fashioned. If this was a real relationship and we got married—"

"We *are* married," I said in a low voice.

She stared at me. "But they don't know it. Anyway, the bed should be made, and there will be towels and toiletries in the bathroom. Do you need anything else?"

I shook my head. "Nope. I think I've got all I need."

She nodded. "I'm going to take a shower then nap for about an hour or so. I need to close my eyes for a minute or I won't last later tonight."

"Later tonight? Why don't you go to bed early tonight?"

"Oh, yeah, hm." She made a cute pout as if considering how to tell me. "Saturday night is family night."

"Oh-kay."

"Like ... not just my father, my mother, and me. My mother's family ... my grandparents and my aunt and my uncle and my little cousins will come over for dinner and they always stay until past midnight."

I just stared at her. More family? Who were these people and why the hell did they get together so often?

I groaned. "And you'll introduce me to all of them."

"Yup." She smacked her lips. Then grinned. "Sorry."

I sighed. "It's okay. I guess."

"Okay, hm, this is my bedroom." She pointed to the door across the hallway and few feet to the left. "Call me if you need anything."

"Will do," I said as she retreated.

She entered her room and closed the door.

I entered my bedroom, and once more wondered what the hell I was doing. Then, I repeated my mantra.

Debt free, debt free.

31

I ENDED up napping for over one and a half hours. But at least now, after eating, showering, and sleeping, I felt human again. These trips ... I wouldn't stop doing them, but they were terrible. Twenty plus hours between two or three flights and layovers and not sleeping well. Just terrible.

I put on some jean shorts and a tee and cowboy boots, pulled my hair into a ponytail, and left my room. I paused when I saw Tyler's bedroom door was open.

Meu Deus, where could he have gone? I hoped he hadn't bumped into my father. *Meu Deus*, my father would skin him alive if—

Loud voices rang through the corridor and, my heart accelerating, I ran toward the stairs, but then saw the TV room with the door open—and the voices coming from there. I spied inside. Tyler was seated on the wide suede sofa, his feet propped up on the ottoman, and the TV on an action movie.

"Oh, hey." He pointed the remote to the TV and turned down the volume. "Did I wake you?"

"No. I woke up by myself. Did you sleep?"

He shook his head. "I lay down but couldn't sleep."

I glanced at the TV. "I see you already got the hang of the TV."

"Your mother showed me how the remote controls worked. Netflix here is a little different, but I managed to find something."

"Good, good. Hm, have you seen my father?"

"Seen, no, but I heard your parents talking downstairs, in Portuguese, a little while ago."

"I'll go talk to him. Better to clear the air now than to endure his glares when my family arrives later."

"Do you want me to come with you?"

"No, I think I should talk to him alone. At least once."

He nodded. "Good luck."

"Thanks."

I went down the stairs and found my mother in the kitchen, as always. I often teased her that she should open a bakery, because she loved cooking and everything she cooked was so good. At least the ranch employees were always pampered with lots of goodies.

She looked up from the table where she was mixing some batter and smiled at me. "Hi, sweetheart. Were you able to rest?"

"Not as much as I wanted, but I'll survive." I looked around. "Have you seen *pai*?"

Her smile faded. "He's at the main stable."

As I suspected. When wasn't he around his precious horses?

My mother let go of the bowl she was stirring, turned to the oven, checked whatever was in there, then spied on a pan on the range, and came back to the bowl. "Do you need help? I can help you—"

"Don't be silly. You know I can handle the kitchen all by myself."

"I know, but it's nice to help and be helped sometimes."

Her kind eyes met mine. "I appreciate the offer, but I would rather you go talk to your father and make amends first. Then, when you two have solved everything, come back and help me. Deal?"

I smiled at her. "Deal."

My father was in his second office, as I called it—a room in the stable with a desk and chairs, a computer, and some shelves with files. His office inside the house was much fancier.

Joaquim, a stable boy, was with him, talking about some buyers interested in coming over to look at the horses. My father saw me at the door and stopped talking for a moment, then he finished quickly and dismissed Joaquim. The boy scurried out the office as if it were on fire, though he took a second to stop and greet me.

"Can we talk?" I asked, still from the door. I was going to try and be as respectful and mindful as I could.

He shrugged and looked down at the papers in front of him. "Sure."

Sighing, I took a chair across from his desk. I went directly to the point. "What can I do so you won't be mad at me?"

He looked up at me. "Break the engagement, send the guy away, and stay here."

"*Pai*, be reasonable. You know that's not happening."

He clicked his tongue. "What can I do, Gabi? You're practically an adult—"

"I *am* an adult."

"—you've got your own money, you've got your own life. It's not like I can control you. But that doesn't mean I'm happy. This decision ... it took us by surprise. An engagement? Where did that come from?"

"I already told you, *pai*. We didn't expect this to happen either, but our feelings spoke louder." I paused. "I'm sorry I sprang this on you like that."

He let out a long breath. "I'll need some time to adjust."

"I understand. Just please ... try not to be too rude to Tyler, okay?"

He didn't answer right away. "I can't promise anything."

At least that was a start.

32

I WASN'T ready to meet more of Gabi's family, but they started arriving around six in the evening, despite my wish to just watch a movie and go to bed early.

Gabi took me outside to a large back patio with a pergola, where there was a long table with two benches, and a wide brick pillar with a hole in the middle. Gabi explained to me that it was called *churrasqueira,* and that they made Brazilian-style *churrasco* with it. Luis Carlos put pieces of steak through long metal spear things and placed them on the *churrasqueira.*

"That's called *espeto,*" Regina said, handing me a cold glass with beer.

"I think his head is going to be a huge knot soon, for learning so many new words so fast," Gabi said with a smile.

"*Trying* to learn, you mean," I said. "It's too many. I'll have forgotten half by the time I go to bed."

Regina chuckled, but she didn't quit. She passed a full plate to me, introducing me to more Brazilian cuisine. *Polenta frita, salsichão* with *farofa,* chicken hearts ... All the food had been great so far, but I was getting overwhelmed with all the new flavors.

The guests arrived soon after, and I was introduced to her grandmother and grandfather, and Regina's middle sister, Rosane, and her husband, Bruno, and their two kids, André and Luciana, who were eleven and eight, and Felipe, Regina's younger brother.

"He's thirty-four, a lot younger than my mother, and he never married," Gabi whispered to me. "And he never had a serious girlfriend either. My mother says he'll die alone."

I frowned.

Gabi had a big and tight family on both sides—her father and her mother. Meanwhile, I had no one. My mother disappeared, my father was dying. Soon, I would be left alone.

A sudden pain cut through my chest and I had to inhale deeply, calming my emotions. This wasn't the time and place to get all sappy.

The grandparents didn't speak English. Rosane and Bruno could speak it, but they weren't too great at it, and the kids were just learning. The only one who could carry on a good conversation was Felipe, but ten minutes into a conversation with the guy and I was already convinced I didn't like him.

"Last winter, I went to Greece. It was crazy, man. I went on a cruise in the Greek Islands with some of my friends, and I gotta tell you, I never partied so hard."

He was the first member of Gabi's family who didn't speak or seemed to live around horses, but he did speak a lot about his playboy lifestyle. About his expensive and frequent trips, the many, many parties he went to, and the flock of girls who kissed the ground he walked on.

And, to be honest, the guy's looks weren't anything out of the ordinary. The Fernandes bloodline came from Gabi's father, so this guy wasn't anything like Gabi's brother or cousins. He was okay, though. He wasn't too tall, but seemed to work out a lot. He had black hair and big brown eyes. But nothing special.

The guy was getting on my nerves. Gabi, on the other hand, seemed to know exactly how to navigate around him. Sometimes, she added fuel to the flame in a teasing way and he didn't even notice, and sometimes she cut him off completely. And all the while he thought she was his fan.

Poor guy.

"Let's eat! *Tá na mesa!*" Luis Carlos said, taking a big wooden tray full of steak to the table.

In a flash, everyone squeezed into the benches around the long table. I sat between Gabi and Rosane, my hips pressing on both of theirs. I knew this was normal for them, but it was uncomfortable to me. I scooted as close to Gabi as I could without pulling her to my lap, but that only made Rosane get closer and squeeze me more.

Around the table, people passed food around, talked, and laughed.

I pushed aside my jealousy for Gabi having such a tight family, and for a moment tricked myself and pretended I was really a part of all of this. I was part of this family now, and if I needed them, they would help me.

With that thought pulsing inside my head, I smiled and tried enjoying the night.

33

GABI

"I'M SORRY ABOUT THIS," I said as I drove us back to Porto Alegre. Both of us were dressed up—Tyler in dark jeans and a dark gray shirt with the sleeves rolled to his elbows. His hair had a little more shine than usual, which led me to believe he had applied some kind of gel or mousse. But just enough so the strands didn't fall into his eyes all the time.

As for me, I had opted for a tight black dress and black high heel sandals. The nightlife in Porto Alegre was a lively one and people dressed like models. It began late and ended early in the morning.

"It's okay," he said, looking out the window. "I get it that they expect you to introduce me to your friends and go out like a normal couple."

I flinched.

A normal couple. Worse than those words were when husband and wife crossed my mind.

"*Sim*, but we don't need to go."

He glanced at me. "What do you mean?"

"We can simply go to our townhouse in the city, order some

food, and go to sleep. My parents will never know we didn't meet my friends and go clubbing. Not unless we tell them about it."

He stayed silent for a long while and I was about to say his name when he finally said, "No. It's fine. Let's go meet your friends. At least time will pass faster."

Or it could be incredibly awkward and slow. I groaned. I had hoped he would agree to skipping the club and holing up inside my family's house. At the club, I would have to face my friends. The girls would ask me three thousand questions about Tyler and me, and I knew they would be watching us closely. I already had lied to too many people. If I could avoid lying to more, I would.

On the other hand, this would be my last opportunity to see my friends before moving to the U.S. for real. I had been so worried about my polo career and being close to Gui and Bia and Leo and Ri and Pedro that I hadn't thought about the rest. I was about to leave my friends behind, and it hadn't hit me how much I would miss them until now.

My throat closed and I had to take a deep breath before a tear escaped.

In the city, I drove us to one of the best neighborhoods and stopped my car in front of a fancy building's closed gate. One of the security men from the front entrance approached me.

"*Boa noite, senhorita Gabriela.*"

"*Oi, Raul,*" I said in Portuguese. After a few more exchanged words, the gate opened and I drove my car down the ramp to the parking garage underneath the building.

"What's this place?" Tyler asked as I parked my car beside a white Mercedes.

"This is my best friend Priscila's place."

"I thought we were going clubbing."

"We are, but clubbing starts late here. Like, after midnight. So, people here get together somewhere before going clubbing."

He shook his head. "That makes no sense."

"I know."

We stepped out of the car and went to the elevators.

Inside, I turned to him. "Are you ready?"

His jaw popped. "Will I ever be?"

I let out a hollow chuckle, not sure how to answer that. Would he ever be? Would I ever be? The more time this went on, the more time we spent together, I wondered if this was a mistake.

This wasn't the time and place to worry about that.

I sucked in a sharp breath and rang the bell.

The door opened wide not five seconds later.

"There you are!" Priscila yelled in English. She had short blond hair, bright hazel eyes, and was taller than me. She was pretty, especially when she was smiling so widely at Tyler. "Hi, I'm Priscila Casagrande, Gabi's best friend." She shook his hand. "Nice to meet you."

"You too, Priscila," Tyler said.

"Please, call me Pri. That's what my friends call me." Priscila stepped aside. "Come in."

And into the lion's den we went.

34

TYLER

I DIDN'T KNOW what to expect this evening.

When Gabi had told me we were going out, I had thought she would take me into a little town for a traditional Brazilian dinner or something. I hadn't expected her to tell me we were going clubbing in the city with her Brazilian friends.

Just what I wanted.

My mind had been swirling in worry about my father, but it was hard to think about that when Gabi wore a little black dress that hugged her curves so well. I wasn't blind. Besides beautiful, she was hot. My fingers itched to touch her, to feel her. Not just pretending, but for real.

I bet she was delicious.

No, I couldn't think about that.

Priscila led us through a wide foyer to a big, open living room and dining room where some other people our age were hanging around. They all had drinks in their hands, and there was plenty of finger food on the low tables in the center and corners of the room.

I was introduced to Adriana, Lucia, Natalia, Rodrigo, and

Diego. From what they told me, most of them had gone to high school together and tried to stay in touch now, even though they all went to separate colleges.

"Can I get you anything to drink?" Priscila asked.

"A beer is fine," I said.

"Okay." Then, she looked at Gabi. "The usual?"

"*Sim, por favor.*"

Priscila disappearing into a hallway I guessed led to the kitchen.

I turned to Gabi. "Everyone in Brazil speaks English?"

"No, but more and more do." She looked down at her feet and then said, "Especially wealthier people. Almost every rich kid takes English lessons at private English schools these days."

Of course. Rich people. She was one of them. Sometimes it was so easy to forget that she had had a gilded crib and more money in her bank account that I could even imagine.

"Here you go." Priscila handed me my beer and a glass with what I thought was Coke and whiskey to Gabi. "You get a free pass with the first drink, but if you guys want more, please, feel at home and go get it yourself." She winked at Gabi. "Especially you."

I didn't know what I was expecting, but the party flowed in a normal way. Music played from speakers somewhere, drinks and finger food were spread on the low table in the middle of the living room, and people gathered in small groups chatting.

At some point, Gabi turned to Priscila and the two of them whispered. Suddenly, Gabi said something to Priscila that made the girl gasp. Shushing her, Gabi pulled Pri away from the group, and the two of them continue talking in hushed tones.

What the hell was that about?

Just then, Rodrigo and Diego asked me about what I did in the United States, and a conversation started. I told them the usual stuff—I went to vet school, but didn't finish yet, and I was working at a vet clinic. When they asked how I met Gabi, I told them what we had been telling others, that we had met through Garrett, which wasn't really a lie.

When the topic shifted to something else, some gossip about someone I didn't know, I excused myself and went looking for a restroom. I found one in a hallway leading to several doors. After I was done, I took my time coming back to the living room.

I started looking at the paintings on the hallway walls—beautiful landscapes, most of them of green pastures. Some depicted horses. The hallway abruptly opened to a large room, a mix of an office and library. I didn't intend to enter it but something caught my attention. A giant horse painting behind the desk. It was impressive and lifelike. Then, I noticed the entire place was horse-themed. There were little horseshoe and horses statuettes all over the office—on the desk, the side table, the shelves. Even four bookends atop the shelves were of horses.

The bookshelf was divided into five large sections that ran along the entire wall and the middle shelf was sans books. It had portraits though, and to my surprise, there were several picturing Gabi with Priscila. In one, they were probably twelve years old, smiling, in front of a big pool. In another, they were inside a stall, embracing the same horse. In a third one, they were dressed in graduation gowns and caps, probably their high school graduation. And in a fourth one, they were atop beautiful horses, wearing helmets and high boots and mallets, ready to play polo.

"There you are."

I glanced over my shoulder and saw Gabi under the big archway.

"Sorry. I didn't mean to snoop, but the place sort of called me."

Her heels clicked on the hardwood floor as she approached me. She halted before me and smiled at the pictures. "She was always there for me when it came to polo."

"I thought your family supported that idea."

"They do, but they don't." She shrugged. "I guess they never thought I would leave the country and they knew there was no future in it here. I had thought about dedicating my life to it, being some kind of pioneer, but then, who would I get to play? I would probably fight for it all my life and die old without having played. But the few times I tried to get a team together, Priscila was always there. If it had worked, I know she would have been on my team no matter what."

That was cool. I hadn't had a friend like that in … I didn't even know how long. Since pre-vet school? It had been years.

Gabi seemed to have it all, though. Good friends, great family—on both sides. She was beautiful, and she was rich. And still, she didn't seem happy. How did that happen?

Before I could formulate something to say, she crouched down and picked up a portrait on a lower part of the shelf. "Look at this." She chuckled. "Damn, I was so awkward."

In the picture, two little girls around seven or eight held a pony's reins. If she hadn't told me it was her, with her hair a little darker and somehow curlier, I wouldn't have known. The other girl I was guessing was Priscila.

Despite the long, thin limbs, she didn't look awkward. She looked pretty for a little girl. Pretty and happy with a big smile and some crooked teeth.

I opened my mouth—to say what, I wasn't sure—when Priscila showed up at the door. "Hey, lovebirds, we are almost ready to go."

"Oh, good," Gabi said, turning to her friend. She quickly slid her hand in mine, as if that was the most natural thing in the world, then tugged on my arm. "Let's go."

"Sure," I said, letting her pull me out of the office.

Priscila smiled at me as we walked past her. "Get ready for the best night ever."

Her statement instilled me with both curiosity and apprehension.

35

GABI

THE DRIVE to the club took about twenty minutes. We all left our cars at a parking garage across the street and went together to the club.

On the way, Priscila kept stealing glances at Tyler and me—because I had told her the truth. I tried keeping it from her, but I couldn't. She was my best friend, and I had never kept anything from her before. I couldn't start now. She had gasped, startling everyone, so I pulled her to a corner and told her. At first, she was shocked, but then she thought it was an adventure and told me I was about to fall in love. I laughed in her face. If only ...

The club was a simple dark blue building with a big neon sign. Nothing more. There was a short line in front of the main doors, but the line was moving, as if everyone was getting in.

"You know how at American clubs the bouncer is told to let in a certain number of people and sometimes they are picky about appearances?" I asked and Tyler nodded. "*Bom*, here that's not a thing. While the club still has space inside and they are over eighteen, the bouncer will allow them to enter, regardless."

"Interesting," was all he said.

Priscila presented our VIP tickets to the bouncer and we slipped inside.

The place wasn't anything out of the extraordinary. Other than having three different rooms playing three different types of music —pop, rock, and electro—the place was like most clubs anywhere. Large dance floor, a few tables and chairs and sofas, bar along an entire wall, and upstairs VIP rooms.

We took the stairs and went to our designated VIP room over the pop music area. A black suede sofa marked the perimeter of the room with low tables in the corners and an empty space in the middle so people could dance. Right away, a waiter showed up and took our orders.

"Can you order a beer for me, please?" Tyler asked, probably guessing the waiter didn't speak English. He sat down on one of the couches with a table right beside it.

"Sure." I also ordered a Jack with Coke for me and loaded fries, then sat beside him.

Priscila plopped down beside me, caught my elbow, leaned into me, and whispered in my ear, "Mateus is here."

"*O quê?*"

"I just saw him at the bar. He waved at Adriana and I think he's coming this way."

My eyes bulged. "*Não.*"

"*Sim*. Sorry. Do you want me to stop him? Tell him something …"

Droga, this wasn't good. "What can you possibly say to make him turn around and go away?"

"I don't know. I'm just trying to help."

"I know, sorry." I sighed. "There's nothing we can do, I think. Just … let him come."

She nodded. "Okay, but if you need anything, let me know."

I showed her a small smile. "*Obrigada.*"

"Anything for my best friend." She winked me and returned to her drink.

I turned to Tyler, and holding my breath, slid my arm around his and leaned into him. He stiffened for a brief second, before taking my hand in his and looking at me.

"Everything all right?" he asked in a low voice.

I smiled at him. "Yup."

He cocked an eyebrow at me, as if noticing my lie, but he didn't call me on it. Instead, he kissed my forehead—tingles spread through my face—and then he raised both our hands and planted a soft kiss on top of mine. The shiver that ran up my arm was—

"Gabi, *oi.*"

His voice twisted my gut, but I forced myself to keep smiling as I turned to him. "*Oi,* Mateus. *Tudo bem?*"

I couldn't lie—Mateus was handsome. I wouldn't have dated him if I didn't think that, but for some reason seeing him now didn't bring the tingles I had always felt when I was younger. No. Right now, he felt like a regular guy I had no interest in.

"I'm ... doing okay, I guess." His eyes shifted to the man by my side. "Hi, I'm Mateus." He extended his hand to Tyler.

Tyler took Mateus hand and shook it firmly. "Hey. Tyler."

Mateus's smile lost one watt of its brightness as his gaze settled on the ring on my finger. When he looked back at me, his eyes were wide. "So, it really is true."

"What is true?" I asked, feigning ignorance.

"You're engaged to this guy." His voice gained a darker tone.

Tyler's body went rigid.

I squeezed his hand. "You knew that."

"I thought it was a sick joke." He leaned over the table and hissed, "You don't think I see what's happening here? I know you want to move there. I know you would do almost anything to live there." He turned to Tyler. "How much is she paying you, pal?"

Tyler rose but I held his arm. "Who the hell are you?"

"I'm her boyfriend!"

I gasped. "Ex-boyfriend, Mateus. We ended everything over eighteen months ago."

He stared at me. "I came back. I looked for you. You know I don't want it to be over."

I rolled my eyes. "And I made it clear I'm not getting back together with you." I lifted my hand and wiggled my fingers at him, showing off the ring. "Besides, I have someone now and I'm happy."

"*Mentira*," Mateus hissed. "I know you're only marrying him for the green card." He turned to Tyler again. "And you're getting what? Money? Someone in your bed every night?"

This time when Tyler stood, I couldn't hold him back. He slipped from my hold as if I was holding an ocean wave—strong and unrelenting.

As Tyler rose to his full height, towering over Mateus by at least four inches and a lot of muscle, Mateus gulped but held his ground.

Afraid he would lunge at Mateus and end up killing him, I stood and held Tyler's arm back, as if I could hold him.

"Think or say whatever shit you want. Your opinion doesn't matter to me or to Gabi," I heard him say, his voice a low growl almost lost among the loud music, but with enough bite to carry through. "Now if you'll excuse me ..." He reached for me and wrapped his arm around my waist, pulling me into him. "I have to take my *fiancée* to the dance floor."

Tyler emphasized the word fiancée and Mateus sneered.

Then, he stared Mateus down for another five tense seconds before pulling me to the dance floor. He halted right at the edge, where we could be easily seen from the table, and turned to me. Looking into my eyes, he put his hand on my hips and tugged me closer.

"What are you doing?" I asked in a low voice, though there was no one near to hear us.

"Pretending," he said, his tone still harsh and cold.

A pop song blasted through the dance floor with loud beats that, in any other situation, would have me dancing in no time. But right now, I was frozen in place. I swallowed hard as I took in Tyler's big hands on my hips, the warmth radiating from them, his long, hard body a few inches from mine, and his handsome face, his big hazel eyes fixed on mine. I knew the place was packed and dancing people surrounded us, even bumped into us every few seconds, but it was like Tyler and I were in a bubble—just him and me.

He leaned in closer and whispered in my ear, "Dance." His hot breath on my neck was enough to make me shiver from head to toe. Slowly, he pulled back and started moving his hips. I swallowed hard again. *Meu Deus* ...

His woodsy and manly scent filled my nostrils, more intoxicating than any alcohol I could drink. I felt incredibly tipsy.

His big hands squeezed my hips. "Right. Dance," I said, snapping out of the daze.

I started swaying side to side with the beat, utterly aware of our brushing legs and the little space between our bodies. The place had been warm before, but it was nothing compared to what it was now. It was so hot in here, it was hard to breathe. At least, that was what I told myself, because the other option ... it wasn't an option.

After two songs, I finally relaxed and was able to convince myself I was just dancing with a friend. *Sim*, a friend, even if Tyler wasn't really a friend.

Then, he had to shatter that image.

Without warning, Tyler stepped right to me, his chest glued to mine. One of his arms snaked around my waist, while his other hand cupped my nape. And then his mouth was on mine. I gasped in surprise, but there was only so much I could do. My lips parted and his tongue didn't waste time. It teased mine, eliciting more gasps from my throat. His lips were soft and demanding and simply delicious. Maybe it was all the alcohol I had consumed, but I simply melted. I melted into the kiss; I melted into him. I wound my arms around his neck and held him tight, making sure my body was pressed against his everywhere.

His hand curled on my back, digging into my skin, and I gasped into the kiss.

Tyler pulled back and relaxed his arms. "Sorry," he said, a different gleam in his eyes. He kept his arms by my side, but he barely touched me. "Everyone was looking. All your friends. And that ..." He sucked in a sharp breath. "Mateus was watching too. I thought we should give them something."

My hand rose of its own accord, but I stopped it before it could reach my swollen lips. *Credo*, that had been one hell of a kiss. And his body? So hard and long and—

"Gabi?"

"Hm, *sim*. Yeah." I shook my head to clear my thoughts. So ... he hadn't done that in the spur of the moment. No, he had calculated it. Had he calculated how affected I would be? I filled my lungs with the stuffy club air and almost coughed. "Good thinking."

He glanced over my head, toward the general direction of our table. "They are still watching."

"Maybe we should give them something else to talk about," I suggested, eager to leave this place.

"What do you mean?"

Leaning into him, I rose on my tiptoes, as much as my already high heels allowed, and put my mouth on his ear. "Let them think we're leaving early for certain reasons." I stayed with my mouth hovering over his neck, so my friends would think I was whispering indecent things in his ear. Or that I was licking his neck. It didn't matter.

Tyler inhaled a sharp breath and I could swear he fought against a shiver, but that was probably my super active imagination. Or the alcohol in my veins seeing things that weren't there.

"Yeah, that sounds like a good plan."

"All right. Let's go home."

"And sleep."

I pulled back and looked up at him. "Of course *and sleep*."

What? Did he think I was really making a move on him? Not that it hadn't crossed my mind, but I wasn't like that. I wouldn't expose myself like that.

Hand in hand, we went back to the table. As we approached, Mateus scoffed and walked away. Good riddance.

I halted beside Pri and she immediately leaned into me. "Are you sure you guys are just pretending?"

"I'm sure."

"And how can you kiss him like that and just pretend?"

I shrugged. "Eyes on the prize. He's just a means to an end. And that end is polo."

"Can't you have fun on the way?"

I gaped. "Pri!"

"I'm just saying. You two will be married for the next two years. Why the hell not enjoy it? Who knows? Maybe you guys will realize you are meant for each other anyway."

I snorted. "One, find a random guy and then realize he's the one. That's a fairy tale. And two, you know me. I'm not that kind of girl."

"I know, I know, but, come on. He's hot. And you're married."

"It's a fake marriage, remember?"

She sighed, eyeing Tyler. "If it were me, I would have a hard time remembering it."

I chuckled. "Only you could make me laugh about this situation."

She shot me one of her dazzling smiles. "That's what best friends are for."

I embraced her. "I'll miss you so damn much."

"I'll miss you too. But I'll come visit you. Now I'll have an excuse to go to California all the time."

Chuckling, I pulled back and looked at her. "Come visit me before I go back."

"Will do."

Tyler tugged my hand. "Aren't we leaving?"

I smiled at him. "Oh, we sure are." I winked at Pri and she winked back at me. Then, I waved bye to the rest of our friends. Lucia wiggled her eyebrows at me, knowing exactly what we would do as soon we were out of here. At least, what we wanted her to think. I squeezed Tyler's hand. "Let's go."

36

TYLER

GABI'S PARENTS had gone to bed already, but she was outside, seated on the back porch with a mug of tea in her hands and watching the dark starry night.

Last night, we had left the club and went to her family's townhouse in the city. When they had mentioned a townhouse, I had imagined a narrow, small house in a nice neighborhood. I should have known by now that the Fernandeses went all big all the time—and they still managed to look and act simple and nice. The townhouse was a huge three-story home inside a fancy gated community in an equally fancy neighborhood. The house had been prepared for us and the guest bedroom was all set. Without exchanging words, we both went to bed in our own bedrooms.

This morning, we had a hearty breakfast, and then Gabi took me around the city. She had to stop by the university to cancel her classes, then she took me to her favorite restaurant—a beautiful Italian place inside a mall, then she drove around showing me museums and parks and other important places. Later that afternoon, we came back to the ranch and had dinner with her parents.

Thankfully, her father didn't seem to want to kill me anymore, but he still wasn't pleasant.

Later, Regina and Luis Carlos got a glass of wine and retreated to their bedroom. Gabi had mentioned they did that almost every night. They sat down in the armchairs beside their bed and watched a random movie from Netflix while sipping their wine. Then, they went to bed.

Gabi made tea for herself and went to the porch.

I spied her profile through the kitchen window. She had on jean shorts and a thin tank top, but now she had some kind of thin wool shawl wrapped around her arms. Her beautiful legs were folded between the bench and her ass, and her long hair was loose on her back. My gaze fixed on her pretty face, on her cute nose, and on her full lips. Those lips that had been on mine last night.

Damn, last night.

That punk Mateus had messed with my head. I would like to think I would have defended any woman from his insults, and I was doing my duty as a gentleman. I had to stand up to him— what I hadn't expected was the sudden will to break his nose. Really, really bad. Instead, I pulled Gabi to the dance floor almost without thinking. No, I wasn't thinking. I was just feeling.

And then I had to kiss her. I had to pull her body against mine and feel all her perfect curves and her sweet lips. I had gotten a hard-on from that. Thankfully, she hadn't noticed. Fuck, what the hell had I done?

Thankfully, she hadn't mentioned any of it today, but to be honest we had barely talked to each other all day long, other than her mini tour of the city, and we had spent almost every hour together.

Several times, I had wanted to break the tension and start some random conversation, but what was there to say? Besides, I was afraid that if I tried to say anything, I would ask if I could kiss her again.

Fuck. What the hell was wrong with me?

Outside, Gabi rolled her neck and then stretched her arms high above her head. The shawl fell from her arms, and my eyes caught as her shirt rode up enough to show a thin strip of smooth skin over her flat stomach. Looking at her now, at her toned arms and legs, I wondered ... she was a polo player, did she have a six pack too? A girl with a six pack ... that I hadn't seen with my own eyes yet.

She dropped her arms and leaned back on the bench, wrapping the shawl around herself again.

I should know better; I should do better. I should have turned around and gone to my bedroom to sleep.

Instead, I walked out and sat in the chair beside the bench. "Hey."

She looked at me with a small smile. "*Oi.*"

A heavy silence fell around us, but I was tired of this constant tension. "So, what are you doing out here?"

She looked out at the horizon. "I usually just sit here at night and enjoy."

"Enjoy ... what?"

"The quiet, the calm, nature ... life."

I glanced out, to the back garden, the pool, the stables beyond. "Will you miss it?"

She didn't answer right away. "*Sim.* I hadn't realized I would miss this place until we got here and I thought about leaving it all behind."

"Do you regret it?"

"What?"

"The deal."

"No, no, I don't. It's just ... choices, you know. We can't have it all. I'm leaving this place and my parents and my best friend behind so I can chase my dream."

Her dream ... "You haven't told me how things are going in that area. Any luck finding a sponsor or at least team players?"

She pouted. "Nope."

"What's your next step?"

"I'm not sure yet. I have a meeting scheduled with the polo director at the club in Santa Barbara. I'll try to convince him to sponsor an all-female team."

I nodded. "Sounds like a good plan."

"It probably won't work."

"Why not?"

She shrugged. "I don't know. It just seems too simple. Too easy."

"I hear you. Nothing in life is easy, huh?"

She glanced at me, her head slightly cocked to the side. "Are you talking from experience?"

I snorted. "Who isn't? Everyone has their hardships through life. You know mine."

She frowned. "I know. Sorry. I was so deep in mine, I forgot about yours."

"It's okay," I said, my voice low. "It's still new to you, and, well, it's my problem not yours."

She stared at me, her blue eyes darkening. "Right. It's none of my business."

"Right." I had planned on just stating it, but that single word came out with more bite than I intended.

"Right," she repeated. Taking her empty mug from an end table, Gabi rose to her feet. "I'm ... going to bed. Good night."

I didn't have time to recover and bid her good night. Like a scared cat, she scurried into the house, shoved her mug inside the dishwasher, and rushed up the stairs before I could blink.

Sighing, I buried my head in my hands.

What the hell was I doing?

Debt free. Debt free.

This debt free thing better erase all this drama from my life after it was all said and done, otherwise I might question if it was worth it.

I COULDN'T DEFINE if our last day in Brazil was good or bad. It was good in the sense that we relaxed most of the day. Gabi rode Tostado and I rode one of their prized horses and explored the ranch. Then, we had another dinner with her family. I was getting used to this.

But it had been bad because Gabi had been tense around me all day. I hadn't meant to snap at her last night, and now I didn't know how to fix it.

Hey, sorry I was a jerk. You have done so much for my father and eased so much of my problems, I should treat you better.

But every time I tried opening my mouth and uttering those words, a lump of cotton got stuck in my throat. And so the hours passed, and nothing got solved.

Because of that, the trip back to the U.S. was just as tense and quiet as the trip to Brazil. On the ride back to the apartment, I rehearsed in my head what to say to her once we were safe and alone inside our place again, but Gabi didn't give me the chance. She stepped into the apartment, dropped her bags right beside the door, and rushed to her bedroom.

And instead of going after her and breaking the tension, I placed her bags beside her bedroom's door and went to mine. Like a damn coward.

37

———

GABI

With my *mate* in my hand, I sat down on a kitchen stool and stared at the fridge.

We had been back from Brazil for a handful of days now, and Tyler and I had barely spoken since he snapped at me, saying his problems were none of my business.

I pushed thoughts of Tyler from my mind and focused on my problems.

I didn't know what else I could do about polo. I had looked online for nearby clubs and schools. Only a handful of clubs sponsored a women's team and only two of them were looking to add to their roster, but one club was in Texas and the other was in Florida.

I had contacted a few schools and asked about female players; there weren't many and the ones I found didn't want to play as a career or didn't think they were good enough for it.

I had just moved to Santa Barbara. I wouldn't move to Texas or Florida now, especially because I knew Tyler wouldn't come with me, and trying to have a pretend marriage while living in different states wouldn't be agreeable with the immigration office, and because both clubs said they couldn't ask for a visa for me right now.

So, I was stuck in Santa Barbara, without a team, and for a few days, without a family too. The guys were gone for the weekend for a big game in Colorado. Hannah and Hilary would stay because of the ranch and classes, and Bia didn't follow them around anymore since she had her own classes and Garrett.

I was super jealous because I wanted to go with the guys.

However, mostly, I wished I were going so I could play with them.

I sighed and drank from my *mate*.

The front door opened then slammed with a loud bang.

A big frown between his brows and his lips turned upside down, Tyler marched to his bedroom without acknowledging me.

"*Oi* to you too," I muttered.

After a few moments, he appeared into the kitchen—without his shoes and with upper buttons of his shirt undone. His golden skin peeked from underneath along with a hint of his muscles.

My belly turned to mush and I forced my eyes up to his face. Which didn't really help, because, even though he looked angry, he was too handsome for his own good.

Giving up on this ridiculous fight, I asked, "Want to talk about it?"

"Talk about what?" he snapped, reaching for a beer inside the fridge.

"Whatever set you off."

"Nothing set me off," he barked. I flinched. "Damn, sorry." He took a long sip, and then let out a long sigh. "Crappy day, that's all."

"Okay." I retreated from the stool before he decided he wanted to throw the beer bottle at me or something. Holding my *mate*, I sat down on the couch in the living room.

"Sorry," Tyler mumbled. He hadn't moved from his spot on the kitchen island.

I shrugged. What did he want me to say?

I swiped the remote control from the coffee table and turned on the TV. I flipped to *The Bachelor* and clicked on any episode.

A minute later, Tyler sat down on the armchair beside the couch. "What the hell is that?"

I chuckled. "*The Bachelor.*"

"So, that's *The Bachelor*. I've heard of it, though I've never seen it before." Two girls started arguing in loud shrieks and their hands flailed as though they were trying not to drown. Tyler's jaw hit the floor. "That's ridiculous. How can you watch this shit?"

"It's fun," I simply said. "They are all miserable people who try to find love in a reality TV show, knowing millions of people are watching, and most of the time, rooting for them to fail. Makes me feel less miserable about my love life." I slapped my hand over my mouth, not believing what I had said. Tyler arched one eyebrow at me. "I mean ..." I started to say, but shook my head. "Forget I said anything."

"Speaking of love life, we haven't studied those damn questions for the interview."

"*Droga*, you're right." I picked up my phone to look for the questions, but then I saw the time. "How about I cook us dinner, then we can get some drinks and work on those."

He leaned back in the armchair and plopped his feet up. "Sounds like a plan." He snatched the remote from me. "But I have one condition. Let's change this shit to something decent."

With a smile, I stood and went to the kitchen.

<h1 style="text-align:center">38</h1>

TYLER

I ASKED if Gabi needed any help at least three times, and she turned me down. So, I went to my bedroom and took a quick shower. I put on some sweatpants and a T-shirt and went back to the living room.

I glanced at the TV—I had paused on an episode of *The Walking Dead*—then to Gabi—she was checking something in the oven. My eyes flickered between the TV and Gabi again. I turned off the TV and sat on a stool at the kitchen counter. It seemed that even though I hadn't apologized for being a jerk and snapping at her—more than once—the tension was gone and she had somehow forgiven me. If she hadn't forgiven me, then she was at least enduring me, which was already more than I deserved.

"I'm here and I can help," I told her again. "Just let me know what to do."

"Since you insist, set the table, please."

I obliged and we fell into an easy rhythm. She cooked and I navigated around her to get the plates, glasses, forks, knifes, and napkins, and anything else that was needed. The moment struck me as odd and amusing—this was what real couples did. They cooked and set tables together and talked about their days.

The only difference was that the real couples stole kisses here and there, and maybe the guy squeezed the woman's ass, while the woman elbowed him in the ribs. One corner of my lips tugged up.

Perhaps that would have been fun, were this real.

Still, as I put down the plates and forks and glasses, I looked up at Gabi, so focused, manning the stove and the oven, then dipping her finger in the pot and tasting whatever it was and smiling at it. I felt my mouth stretching into a bigger smile.

She was beautiful and caring and emotional and kind.

Sometimes I wondered ... how would it be if this relationship weren't fake?

I shook my head and went to the fridge to get water. It didn't matter how it would be because it wouldn't happen. This was temporary. Just a deal.

Or so I told myself.

"Dinner is ready," she announced, bringing a pan to the table.

I lifted the cover and spied inside. "What is it?"

"That's black beans, Brazilian style." She went back to the kitchen and brought a plateful of some thick yellow sticks. "These are called *pastel*. It's a parcel of crisp pastry filled with cheese—" She pointed to the ones on the right. "—and ground beef." She pointed to the ones on the left. She put the plate on the table and went back for yet another pan. "And this is simply white rice." She sat down. "I hope you like it."

"It smells good."

I followed her cues about putting the beans on top of the rice, and how to cut the *pastel*. And, once she even brought the cinnamon from the pantry and dumped a lot inside her minced beef filled *pastel*. As usual, she urged me to taste it. I didn't want to, but since I had yet to try one of the Brazilian food she cooked and not like it, I surrendered. And it was too freaking good.

She chuckled. "You always looked so scared of the food I make, and then you always like it."

"What can I do? I have no idea what to expect. Though, I admit, I'm yet to be disappointed."

She smiled and I was entranced. Damn, how hadn't I realized it could be so easy to fall for her? That was a lie. I had realized that; I was just deluding myself.

"So." I stood after we finished. "You cooked, now I clean." I brought the plates to the sink, but she followed me with the glasses.

"I'll take that, but just because I'm gonna do something else." She picked up a clean pan from the cabinets and started some other food.

"Do you want to fatten me up?" I asked, eyeing the dark gooey-ness in the pan.

She chuckled. "*Meu Deus*, no!"

The chocolate smell coming from whatever she was doing set my mouth watering.

After I was done putting the dirty dishes in the dishwasher and washing the ones that didn't fit, I poured a glass of wine for each of us and we sat on the floor of the living room, one on each side of the coffee table, with the drinks and the *negrinho* still in the hot pan in the middle.

"Usually, we roll them in little balls and decorate them with chocolate sprinkles, but my friends and I always did this way." She handed me a spoon. "Dig in." She grabbed a spoonful of *negrinho* and popped into her mouth. "This is so good," she said, her mouth full.

I chuckled and delved my spoon in the pan. This time, I wasn't hesitant; after all, it was made with chocolate. I moaned as the goodness teased my taste buds. "Holy shit, this is good."

"Told you."

Again, that smile. Her smile and her big, blue eyes. They caught me every time.

I cleared my throat. "So, the questions."

"*Sim*, right." She pulled out her phone and opened a webpage with a list of questions. "So, here are a few questions: When and where did you two meet for the first time? Could you describe the first meeting? When did you meet next? Where were you living at the time? Where was your spouse living? What did you two have in common? Where did you go on dates? When did the relationship become romantic? Who proposed to whom? Why did you have a lo—?"

"Wait, wait," I interrupted her. "That's enough. Slow down."

"Sorry. But, hm, that's not even five percent of the list."

"Shit." I took a sip of my wine. "Just pick a random one and ask."

"Who proposed to whom?"

I snorted. "You did."

"You can't say that!"

"Why not? It's the truth. And it's the twenty-first century. Women can propose."

"I know that, but we already came up with a story for my family. We have to stick with that."

"Right, right. Okay. Next."

"Did your parents approve of the match? Why and why not?"

"My father did, but your parents don't."

She stared at me with wide eyes. "Your father approves of me?"

"My father is in love with you. If he could, *he* would marry you."

The smile that sprouted on her lips ... it was the brightest thing I had ever seen. "That's so sweet."

"That's gross. But, well, it's better than your parents and their opinion about me."

She lost her pretty smile. "I know you think they hate you, but they don't."

"Right."

"I'm serious. I think they don't like the situation, that I decided to move away, that it was so sudden, but they certainly don't hate you."

"Next," I said, my voice harsh.

She pressed her lips into a thin line as she scanned her phone's screen. "Hm, does your spouse drink coffee in the morning?"

"No, she drinks *mate*," I answered. "Then, she drinks a cup of milk with a little coffee, and she eats some bread like thing, like bagels or biscuits or donuts. Whatever is handy."

One corner of her lips tugged up. "It seems you've been paying more attention to me than I thought."

I shrugged. "I'm observant." I leaned forward and crossed my arms over the table. "Now you. Tell me something you noticed about me or something I usually do."

She tapped her finger onto her chin, considering. "You run your hand through your hair a lot when you're stressed."

I frowned. "I do?" She nodded. "Well, it seems you've been paying attention too."

She shrugged then she scanned the list again. She chuckled. "There are some questions in here ..."

"Like?"

"Like, what size is your bed? How many windows are there in your bedroom? What color are your spouse's pajamas? Who sleeps on each side of the bed? What form of contraception do you use?" Her cheeks gained a red tint. "When was your wife's last menstrual per—" She cut herself off and cleared her throat. "Yeah, those are quite embarrassing. Oh, oh, but this one: Have you ever had an argument that resulted in one of you sleeping in another room? Who, and which room?" She chuckled. "Like, every night?"

"We can't tell them that, though."

"I know, I'm just …" She dropped the phone and took another spoonful of *negrinho*.

"And what about past relationships? Are there questions about that?"

She glanced at her phone's screen. "Doesn't look like it. This isn't a full list, though. We should check some others. However, I don't see why they would ask us about past relationships. It has nothing to do with our relationship now. Don't you think?"

I clenched my hands into fists. "It might, when someone's ex keeps sending messages or calling, even though the girl already made it clear she moved on." Her eyes went wide. "Someday he might even show up here."

"How do you know …?"

"You tell Bia, Bia tells Garrett, and Garrett tells me." I had known for a while, but after meeting the ass in Brazil, I felt like he didn't deserve Gabi at all.

She swallowed hard. "Don't worry. I won't let him ruin our deal."

"Hm, so, that means what? You want to get back with him, but now you can't?"

"That's not it!" Her cheeks reddened. "I broke up with him over eighteen months ago, and I haven't really considered making up. I wouldn't, even if we didn't have a deal."

"Right," I said, my chest suddenly tight with jealousy. Which was ridiculous. Like she said, she didn't plan on going back to him, and this was a fake marriage.

I had to repeat that in my head: *fake marriage.*

There. Maybe now it would stick.

"What about you?" she asked, her eyes narrowed. "Any exes I should worry about?"

I almost spat out the wine I was drinking. "To be honest, no, I don't think so. I haven't been in a serious relationship in so long." I stared at my glass. "I didn't have time to pay attention to anyone while I was trying to work my ass off to pay for my father's medical bills."

"Sorry I asked," she whispered, her shoulder drooping.

"Gabi, no, look ..." I let out a long sigh and finally said what I should have many days ago. "I'm sorry about what I said before. I don't want you getting deeply involved in my problems not because of you, but because you don't deserve to carry their weight. I appreciate everything you've done for me, and what you still do for me. Really." I paused and she slowly lifted those blue eyes until they met mine. "Thank you, and I'm sorry."

She stared at me in silence for a full minute. I thought she would either throw her wine in my face or simply shoot up and walk away, but she surprised me by nodded, one corner of her lips tugging up.

"It's okay," she said. "I understand why you were on the defensive. I guess in your shoes, I would be too." Smile gone, she pointed a finger at me. "Just don't be such a jerk, or I'll start kicking your ass."

I chuckled. "That's a deal." I sipped from my wine and waved a hand at the list. "Go on. What else should we know?"

She cleared her throat and stared at the list. "Hm, let's see ..."

We continued studying for a few more minutes, until most of the questions led to more information and conversation, and we simply gave up on them. In the end, we put on a random movie and watched it together.

Almost like a real couple.

39

GABI

THE DAYS WERE TICKING by and it was making me frustrated. I hadn't heard from the immigration lawyer about my green card process, though she had sent me an email telling me sometimes these things can take months. And I was going nowhere with my dream of playing polo professionally.

In need of burning off pent-up energy, I decided to accept the guys' invitation to practice with them.

"I didn't think you would show up," my brother said, sliding out of his Jeep.

I crossed my arms and leaned against my car. "Why not?"

He shrugged. "I don't know. Too early?"

"It's almost nine in the morning. What do I think I do all day?"

"Sleep?" he teased.

I smacked his shoulder and walked to the back of my car. Gui picked up his bag from the Jeep's backseat, while I opened the trunk of my SUV and grabbed my bag.

"Thanks for inviting me," I said.

"My pleasure."

Together, we walked from the club's parking lot to the training field in the back. There, *tio* João Pedro looked over his tablet while Leo and Ri finished lacing up their shoes.

"Oh, look who is here," Leo said with a smile. "Came to get your ass kicked?"

I snorted. "I want to see you try."

I set my bag on the bench behind him and changed from my boots to my tennis shoes. First, we stretched then exercised. Only after one or two hours of intense exercise, did we pull out the horses and practice.

"I'm here, I'm here," Pedro shouted as he ran down the path to where we were grouped.

"And why are you late?" *tio* João Pedro asked.

Pedro dropped his bag and looked up at his father. "I overslept, sorry."

"And I even knocked on your door before leaving and you told me you were up, *idiota*," Gui said.

"Yeah, I lied. *Desculpa*." Pedro quickly slipped his sneakers on. "But I'm ready now."

Ri, Pedro, Leo, Gui, and I stood side by side facing *tio* João Pedro. "Okay, *guris*, I want you to be careful with Gabi."

"Hey," I protested. "I can keep up with them."

"I know you can. If you were a boy, I confess I would have considered adding you as a fifth to our team and rotate you all between games." That was actually a nice thing to hear—if I could get over the if-you-were-a-boy part. "But *os guris* can be tough when playing and I don't want to see you hurt."

I shook my head. "And I don't want to be treated differently because I'm a girl." I looked to my brother and cousins. "Let them come. I'll give it as tough as they come."

Gui grinned at me. "That's my girl."

"I'm not your girl," I muttered.

He winked at me. "You kinda are."

I blew a raspberry at him.

"Okay, stop playing around," *tio* João Pedro said loud and clear. "Let's start. Five laps around the field. Go."

We set off running. The guys started nicely, maintaining a good pace, until the last lap. Then, they sprinted down the course.

"*Filho duma …*" I pressed my mouth shut and pushed my feet, running after them. Oh, I wouldn't stay behind. Grinding my teeth, I pushed my legs as I never had before and, halfway through the last lap, I caught up with Pedro.

"Hey!" he complained, as if I wasn't allowed to be a fast runner too.

But that wasn't the end of it.

The muscles in my legs burned, but I pushed even harder and soon passed Pedro and Ri. There was only Gui and Leo in front of me. I could barely breathe as I pumped my arms and pushed my legs. Faster, faster, faster.

Gui crossed the pretend finish line first, by a couple of paces, then Leo was next, and I was third—just two paces behind Leo. Ri and Pedro caught up with us only three seconds later.

"Wow," Pedro said, breathing hard. "I had forgotten how fast you can run."

I chuckled, but had to stop to breathe. My lungs were killing me too. "I haven't trained with you guys in what? A couple of months? Prepare to be amazed!"

Next, *tio* João Pedro walked us through a long series of stretches, and then we did some cardio and strengthening workouts. Jump rope, jumps, and run practice on the agility ladder, a series of push-ups, sit-ups, and jumping jacks, touch-sprints, and a lot of squats and lunges. I noticed the guys kept tabs on me, to make sure if I was doing everything right, if I could keep up, or if I could do better it than them, I didn't know. However, I was determined to prove to them that I was as good as they all were.

We had a ten-minute break while the horses were brought out to the field.

Typically, in polo, a team went through a lot of horses during practice and games because the animals got too hot and tired too fast. The guys had twenty horses—one for each chukka per player, and four extra just in case. During practice, they rotated the order of the horses so they all would get the same amount of training.

This time, I would use the extra set of four horses.

"I'll go with her," Gui said, mounting his first horse.

"But that's still three against two," Ri said. "Call Malcolm or Thomas or anyone from the Knight House. See if one of them is holed up here at the club and wants to lend us a hand."

"That's a good idea," Leo said, picking up his phone. "Except the guy wouldn't have stretched and be ready to play."

"Then we give him fifteen minutes to stretch while we play the field," Pedro said. "Call them."

In the end, Leo called Malcolm, while Ri called Thomas, Pedro called Reese, and Gui called Justin. To our surprise, Malcolm was at the club and Justin had just arrived. Their own practice started in a couple of hours, but for some reason, these two decided to come over early.

"Malcolm offered to help," Leo said.

"Justin too," Gui said.

"*Bom*, we can use both, if they want, just not at the same time," Pedro suggested.

"Fine by me," Ri said.

While waiting for Malcolm and Justin to get to the field, the guys and I took the horses for an easy gallop around the field—we didn't want to tire them before the game even started. When we saw them both nearing the field, we took the horses back to where *tio* João Pedro was perched with his tablet.

"So, what are we doing exactly?" Malcolm asked.

"We're gonna divide into two teams of three and play," Leo said.

"And you guys can take turns," Ri explained.

"And who is that?" Justin asked, gesturing to me. "I don't think we've got to meet another Fernandes wonder. How many polo guys did your family produce?" He chuckled at his amusing joke.

Then, I unstrapped my helmet and took off my goggles. My braid, which had been strapped to the helmet, fell over my shoulder.

"How about a polo girl?" I asked, defying them with my high chin.

Malcolm's jaw hit the ground. "Gabriela?"

"You guys want to play with a girl?" Justin asked, his tone a little elevated.

"Hey, this is my sister, you idiot," Gui snapped.

Justin narrowed his eyes. "I know she's your sister, but you want us to play with her?"

Tio João Pedro stepped forward and looked up at the guys from the other team. "If you have a problem with that, then leave right now. Just be warned, I bet she can kick both of your asses." He turned around and walked to the bench at the edge of the field as if nothing had happened.

Justin raised his hands. "Sorry, but I'm out." He walked away.

"Malcolm?" Gui asked.

Malcolm snapped his jaw shut. "I'm a little shocked, but, hm, hey, why not? Give me a few minutes to change and stretch."

The guys agreed, and he left the field in the direction of the lockers.

Gui glanced at me. "Are you okay?"

I nodded, though my insides were seething. "I'll be okay."

Not ten minutes later, Malcolm was mounted on his first horse, and with his mallet in hand. He steered his horse to stand beside Gui and me.

"This won't be easy," he said. "Leo is the best and—"

"I'm the second best," Gui added.

"I know, but all of your family is good."

Gui jerked his chin to me. "She is too."

"Relax," I said. "This is just a fun practice, nothing more."

He took a deep breath. "All right. Here goes nothing."

The game started and as Malcolm predicted, it wasn't easy. But it was so much fun. We played two entire chukkas, scoring no goals whatsoever. The game was too equally matched.

On the interval between the third and fourth chukkas, Gui pulled his horse to my side. "Have you noticed the crowd?"

I tried not glancing around again. "It's not a crowd."

"It's at least twenty people. And I see more coming."

"All club workers, probably."

"Not all, but I do see the secretary of the polo manager."

I straightened my back and widened my eyes at him. "You're kidding?"

"Why would I kid?" He smiled at me. "Come on, *mana*, let's show them how a girl plays."

I smiled back at him. "Hy-ah!" I yelled to my horse.

I kept my horse close to Leo, pushing him, and making him irritated. It didn't take long for him to make a tiny mistake. When he was passing the ball to Pedro, I brought my horse across Leo's and I stole the ball. I maneuvered around him and raced to the end of the court.

And scored a goal!

"*Gol*!" I yelled.

"And she wins!" *tio* João Pedro shouted from the sideline.

Gui rode to me. "Beautiful game, *mana*."

I smiled. "Thanks."

"Wow," Leo said, approaching. "You really turned into a great player these past three years. Keep training and you'll soon take my ranking."

I rolled my eyes at him.

We brought the horses back to where the staff was waiting to take them away, and dismounted.

"I have to apologize," Justin said, walking up to us. "I wasn't going to watch the game, but as I was walking by, you guys caught my attention and then I couldn't stop looking. Gabriela, I'm sorry for what I said earlier. You play as well as any of these guys. Congratulations."

My smile only widened. "Thanks."

"That really was a great game," a woman said. Beside me, Gui stiffened. The woman extended her hand to me. "Hi, I'm Brittany Morrow, the polo manager's secretary."

I shook her hand. "Hi. I'm—"

"Gabriela Fernandes," she finished for me. "One more Fernandes playing polo, and to my surprise, it's a she, not a he."

I sighed. "Yes, I get that a lot."

She crossed her arms. "So, what do you do? Just play for fun?"

Gui gently elbowed my back. "Actually, I want to play professionally, like my brother and my cousins."

"Women's polo isn't as popular as men's." She narrowed her eyes. "But, if we could get some other girls who could play as well as you do ..."

My heart skipped a beat. "What are you saying?"

"I can't speak for my boss, but if I were him, I would be interested in putting together a women's team, starting with you." *Meu Deus.* She pulled out a card from her purse. "Here. Give me a call. Mr. Helms is out of town this week, but we can try to schedule a meeting with him soon and talk about this. What do you think?"

"What do I think?" I chuckled. Then, I cleared my throat and said, "Actually, I already went to his office and spoke to another woman, a receptionist, I think." This felt redundant, but she had to know about it. "I have an appointment scheduled with Mr. Helms in a few days."

Brittany frowned as she pulled out her phone and checked on something. "You must have spoken with Ellen. Between us, she's new and bossy. And she must have done something wrong because there's no appointment with your name on it."

My stomach dropped. "W-what?"

"It's okay," Brittany said, her composure intact. "Even if your appointment was canceled by mistake, I'll find a way to squeeze you in his schedule. Is that okay?"

I swallowed, getting excited again. "It's more than okay. It's a great idea."

She smiled. "Great. I look forward to hearing from you." She waved before turning and walking away.

"*Meu Deus*," I said once she was gone.

Gui pulled me into a big hug, and the guys all cheered and patted my back and kissed my cheek.

They let me go when *tio* João Pedro stepped in the circle and grinned at me. "I'm proud of you, *guria*. You'll do great." He patted my cheek.

"This is amazing," Gui said. "We're going to celebrate tonight. My place." He looked at tio. "You too, *tio*. Come with *tia* Agnes."

He chuckled. "No, no, we're too old for your parties, but I'll be thinking of you." He glanced at me again. "Good luck."

My heart swelled. "Thanks."

40

TYLER

Work had been shitty. I got a call from the nurse saying my father had a bad time after chemo, and now Gabi texted me saying we had to go to her brother's place for a party.

Fuck my life. I didn't want to go.

One, I wasn't in the mood for parties. Two, her family was chipper and cute. I couldn't deal with that. Not with everything else going on.

"Can't you tell them I'm working third shift or something?" I asked her once I got to our apartment. She was almost ready, wearing a short jean skirt, a blouse with lace details that revealed too much skin, and dark blue cowboy boots. She had her long hair loose and the dark strands contrasted with her fair skin and bright blue eyes.

She was too fucking pretty for her own good.

"I can ..." she said, her voice low. She disappeared into her bedroom and I could hear the opening and closing of drawers and some tapping on her cell phone, then she emerged from the room, her purse in her hands. Without looking at me, she walked to the door. "*Tchau*," she said as she unlocked the door and stepped out.

Fuck.

"Wait," I called out without really thinking about it. Shit. "Give me ten minutes to shower and change. I'm coming with you."

The smile that sprouted on her lips ... I didn't want to think about it.

Instead, I shook my head and took a lukewarm shower—much colder than my usual scalding water. Then, I dressed in my best dark jeans and one of my not-too-crappy plaid red shirts. Last, I shoved my brown cowboy boots on. Her entire family was about horses. She was all about horses. If wearing cowboy boots more often would get me more points, great.

What the hell? What did I care about points with her family? They were none of my business. I just had to spend some time with them, pretend our relationship was real, and be done with it. I had done it a few times already. I could do it a few times more.

Though Gabi had her SUV's keys in her hands, I insisted we go in my truck, beat up the way it was. She didn't argue or complain, which rubbed me the wrong way. Why wasn't she arguing or complaining?

"What is this party about anyway?" I asked as I drove us toward her brother's place.

She smiled at me. "I went to practice with the guys today. The secretary of the polo manager saw me playing and said she wants to schedule a meeting for me with her boss to discuss the possibility of the club sponsoring an all-female team."

I frowned. "I thought you already had a meeting with him."

Her smile faded. "Me too. Apparently, it was erased from the system, or never entered."

I inhaled deeply, trying to push my bad mood down. Gabi didn't deserve it. "I'm sorry about that, but I'm glad you have a second chance."

She glanced at me, a new shine in her pretty blue eyes. "Me too."

I felt much better by the time we parked my truck in front of her brother's building. Inside the elevator, I slipped my hand into hers, startling her.

"We're pretending, remember?" I told her, but truth be told, I was telling myself that. Because even with my bad mood, even when I was a jerk to her without meaning to, she had become someone I imagined always there, a new support, a good friend.

And I couldn't imagine her leaving.

41

GABI

IT HAD BEEN a week since Brittany Morrow saw me playing with the guys, and so far, I hadn't received word from her. I had practiced with the guys twice more since then, and even though our games always gathered a small crowd, Ms. Morrow or Mr. Helms, or anyone who mattered in the polo world, hadn't shown up again.

I tried keeping my hopes up, and I even researched local female polo players—there weren't many.

I paced the living room, bored with being home all day. However, there weren't a lot of places I could go. Gui and the guys were at a practice game against a team from Los Angeles, Hil and Bia and Garrett were at their classes, Hannah was working at her ranch, and no one knew about Iris—could I even consider her part of our group? I wasn't so sure anymore.

And, as for my dear husband, he was at work too.

Seriously, once I had my green card in my hands and I still hadn't found a team for me, I would have to find a part-time job to keep me busy.

To distract myself, I put out my workout clothes and set out for a run, but before I could leave the apartment, my phone rang.

I frowned at the unknown number. "Hello?" I answered.

"Gabriela? Hi, this is Brittany Morrow."

My heart jolted. "Oh, hi. How is it going?"

"Good, good." Her voice was tight, which didn't sound too good. "Listen, I spoke with Mr. Helms, and even though I insisted he had to see you play before he made a decision, he said he's not looking to sponsor a women's team right now."

My chest deflated. "Oh."

"I'm so sorry."

"No," I whispered. "It's okay."

"Though I'm just his secretary, I think the club would benefit a lot from having a women's team. Can you imagine what our female members would think? They would love it." She paused. "I can't guarantee anything, but I'm going try to change his mind. It might take time, though, so don't hold on to this."

"Thank you," I said, though my heart was already broken.

"I have lots of connections in the polo world. When I have free time, I'm going to send you a list of names and phone numbers. Maybe you can find some other club that wants to sponsor a female team. Or, if you're lucky, you'll find one that already has a women's team and is looking for another member."

"That would be great."

"It's the least I could do. Again, I'm sorry. Good luck."

She ended the call and I stared at my phone, as if it had just played a joke on me. Because, really? After all the hoping, screaming, and celebration? This was how it was going to end?

Running wouldn't do it for me anymore. I had to go for a ride.

So, I switched from my workout clothes to jeans, a plaid shirt, and cowboy boots, and left the apartment. Thirty minutes later, I parked my car in the parking lot at Hannah's ranch. Besides hers, there were seven cars here, which meant there was a class or a riding group in progress.

I stepped out of my car and took a lungful of fresh air. Nothing like the smell of the trees and the flowers and even of the horse's stink coming from the stable to make me feel better. Soon, I would feel even better.

Jimmy was inside the stable, brushing Preta, one of Bia's horses.

"Miss Gabi." He smiled at me. "How are you?"

I shrugged. "I can't complain." Which was the truth. Things weren't exactly going my way, but I had a loving family, good friends, food on my table, clothes to keep me warm. I tried to remember that many people would give their left hand to have things I took for granted. "But it'll be better soon. How's Branca doing?"

"She's good," he said, stepping out of Preta's stall. "She's been a little quiet and she gets a little spooked with certain sounds, especially when there are too many kids around. All the yelling? Yeah, she doesn't seem to like that. But she's still young. All she needs now is time to get used to it all."

"*Sim*, that makes sense." As if sensing we were talking about her, Branca peeked her head over her stall's door. I smiled. "There you are." I approached her and ran my hand over her head. I could swear she leaned into my touch. "How are you, girl? Do you like it here?"

She snorted, as if trying to tell me something, and I chuckled.

"She seems to like you," Jimmy said. I glanced over my shoulder and found him opening Minuano's stall, a smile on his lips.

"She better since she and I will spend a lot of time together from now on." I scratched under her chin and she shook her head, as if that tickled her. "Can I take her out for a ride, or should I wait until the next riding group is back, or something?"

"No need to wait," Jimmy said, now brushing Minuano's coat. "Do you want help tackling her?"

I chuckled. "Do I look like I need help?"

"No, but I try to be a gentleman, Miss Gabriela."

I grabbed the saddle and reins from the tack room, and quickly saddled up my beautiful mare. Five minutes later, I was on top of her and we rode into one of the trails along the property.

I HEARD some low screeching noise. Branca's ear prickled and her steps slowed.

I ran a hand over her neck. "It's okay, girl. It's probably just a squirrel."

Not ten feet from us, a small squirrel jumped from a low branch to another.

Branca neighed and reared up. I tightened my grip on the reins and was able not to fall, but then Branca went crazy. Amused or curious, the squirrel stayed on the branch, watching my mare while she threw her hind legs second after second.

"Whoa, Branca, calm down." I tried reaching for her again, to try to touch her and calm her down, but the moment I let go of the reins, I slipped. "Shh, girl, it's all right."

Like a mini tornado, Branca turned around without direction, kicking her legs high. Then, with a high pitch, she tripped over a low stump and fell to the side. I yelped as I braced myself and rolled to the side before she could fall on me.

Instantly, Branca tried getting up, still neighing like a crazy animal, but her leg gave and she fell on the ground again.

"Shhh," I said, approaching her, arms out. "You're fine, girl. I'm here." I splayed my hands over her neck and pushed her down against the ground. "You're fine," I repeated, hoping I could calm her.

She only resisted me for a minute or so, but she kept twitching. While running my hands over her soft coat, I examined her. Her left front fetlock looked twisted the wrong way. My stomach sank.

Oh, she was hurt. That was why she couldn't get up when she tried a few moments ago.

Careful with my movements, I fished my cell phone from my pocket and called Hannah.

"Gabi, hi," she answered.

"You're out with a group, right?"

"Yes, why?"

"I'm here. At your ranch. I took Branca for a ride, but she got spooked by a damn squirrel and I think she twisted her ankle."

"Oh no," she said, her voice sorrowful. "I can call my vet right now. If he can't come, I know he'll send someone right away. Okay?"

"*Sim.*"

"And tell me where you are. While I call my vet, I'll drop this group off and then I'm coming to meet you."

I told her which trail I had taken and how far I thought I was, then hung up.

Branca's breathing was fast and her eyes were wide. She kept staring at the trees as if waiting for the squirrel to come jump on her. Damn squirrel. If he showed up again, I would hunt him down and skin him alive.

While waiting for Hannah, Branca tried moving again. As much as I wished I could have held her down, I couldn't control a thousand pound animal by myself. Her breathing accelerated and her muscles straining, she pushed on her hind legs and tried standing. Only to let out a cry and fall on her knees again.

"It's fine, girl," I repeated, running my hands over her neck and flanks. "You'll be fine."

She was probably in terrible pain and I could do nothing to help her. My new, pretty, young horse, and she already had gotten injured. I only prayed it wasn't as bad as it looked.

I didn't know how long it took Hannah to arrive, but I was thankful she was mindful. She hopped down from Argus at least thirty yards back and tied his reins to a low branch before approaching us slowly.

"How's she doing?" Hannah asked, her voice low and gentle. Her hands showing in front of her, she knelt beside me. Branca twitched. "It's okay, girl. I'm not gonna hurt you." Still, she scooted about three feet back, to ease Branca's apprehension.

I looked back at Hannah, my vision a little hazy from all the unshed tears in my eyes. "She tried getting up again and couldn't."

Her sympathetic look almost broke me. "My vet is the best. He'll be able to get her up and running in no time. You'll see."

I nodded. "So you called him?"

"Yes, and he was in the middle of a surgery. His secretary told me his assistant would be coming over, and when Dr. Bohm was free, he would head over."

Dr. Bohm ... why was that name familiar?

Before I could mull it over, Jimmy and a horse appeared on the trail, followed by a beat-up truck I knew well. My throat closed.

Branca neighed and jerked with the sound of approaching hooves and wheels.

"Shhh." I pressed her to the ground. Hannah moved closer and helped me by holding her quarter down.

Jimmy halted, lifting his closed fist, and two seconds later, Tyler killed the engine of his truck.

Tyler hopped out of his truck. He wore an unbuttoned white lab coat and he held something similar to a doctor's bag. With sure but slow steps, he moved toward us. His eyes met mine and the compassion and the intensity in them nearly killed me.

He knelt beside my mare's head and dropped his bag behind him. He showed off his empty hands. "Hey, Branca. What happened here, pretty girl?" His gaze slid over her.

"There." I pointed to her twisted fetlock.

He locked eyes with me. "What happened?"

I wiped some of my unshed tears. "*Uma porcaria dum esquilo!*" I hissed.

Calm as ever, Tyler reached over and grabbed my hand. "In English, Gabi."

"Sorry ..." I took a long breath. "A squirrel jumped from one tree to the other, right above her head. She freaked out. Like ... I've never seen a horse go this nuts in my life." And I had practically been born and raised among horses. "She started spinning, until she tripped on that stump." I gestured toward the broken tree stump.

Tyler looked over me. "You're hurt."

"What?"

He cupped my elbow. "You haven't seen this?"

I gawked at my scrapped and bleeding elbow. "No."

He frowned, looking all over me. "Did she fall on you?"

"No, no. I rolled off right before we hit the ground."

He twisted my torso around. "Your shirt is ripped here." He pulled on the fabric, just on the back of my shoulder, and sucked in a deep breath. "It's purple." He pressed two fingers around the wound. "Does it hurt?"

I swallowed a cry. "Yes." Now that he had pointed out my injuries, they started throbbing. Nevertheless, I slapped his hands away from me. "Enough about me. Take a look at her!"

His frown deepened, but he let go of me and turned back to my mare.

"I think we'll need a trailer to bring her out," Hannah whispered. "So, I'm going to go back with Jimmy so we can leave the horses in the stable, then I'm going to come back with the trailer. Is that okay?"

I nodded and barely heard as Hannah walked away, hopped on her horse, and left with Jimmy. My eyes and my mind were on Tyler as he reached for a syringe inside his bag and filled it with some clear liquid.

"Sedative?"

"Not exactly. More like something to help her relax before she decides she won't let us touch her anymore and ends up hurting herself more." He pointed to two places along her neck—right under her chin and near her shoulder. "Hold here and here, please. And press her down tight. She might fight me once the needle goes in." I nodded. He lifted the syringe. "Ready?" I nodded again. He placed a hand in the middle of her neck and injected Branca with the medicine.

She jerked once, twice, three times. Then, it was like she decided it was better to just lay back and relax.

"That was quick."

"It's almost instant," Tyler said, putting the used syringe into a disposable bag. He sat back, his eyes focused, and I watched him and his hands as he slid them over my mare's body, trying to find any other injury.

"So?" I asked after a few minutes.

He clicked his tongue. "She has a few scrapes from falling on the ground, nothing much, but the serious issue here is her fetlock. We need to see how bad it is."

"You mean take an x-ray?" I asked, and he nodded. "Do you have the x-ray machine with you?"

"It's in the truck with the ultrasound machine." He splayed his hand over Branca's neck and leaned down on her. "You'll be fine, okay, girl? I promise." He kissed her neck.

My heart swelled. A tear escaped, but I wiped it away. I wiped them all before more could fall.

He turned to me and stared into my eyes. "She'll be fine."

New tears sprung to my eyes. "You can't promise that."

"Well, then I can promise that I'll do everything I can and more to make her well again."

I nodded.

A tear rolled down my cheek.

I gasped when Tyler's reached over and wiped the tear from my face. His hand lingered against my cheek, his eyes boring holes into mine.

Something vibrated. "Shit," he hissed as he reached for his phone before it set my mare off. His hand left my face, and I almost leaned forward, not wanting the connection to break.

Then, he answered the phone.

42

TYLER

"Hɪ, Dʀ. Bᴏʜᴍ," I answered, careful to keep my voice low.

"Are you at Miss Hannah's ranch?" he asked, his tone all business-like.

"Yes."

"How's the horse?"

"I don't know for sure yet, sir. We're going to move the mare in a few, and I'll take a few x-rays. Once I know if it's just a sprain or if it's worse, I'll let you know."

"Good. Call me once you have the results, and let me know if I need to go out there."

"Yes, I'll call right away. Thanks." I put my phone away and sat back on the ground.

Gabi stayed on her knees and hovered over her mare. "Pretty, pretty girl," she whispered, running her hand over Branca's shiny white coat.

"Didn't you buy her a few weeks ago?"

"*Sim.*" She glanced at him over her shoulder. "Why?"

I shrugged. "I haven't had a horse, any pet actually, in many, many years. I guess I forgot how easy it is to get attached to them."

I scanned the length of the mare. I didn't think she had grown to her full size yet, but her thighs were thick and strong and her mane looked soft and cared for. "She really is a beauty."

"She is. But she's skittish. The seller warned me she got spooked by anything, but I thought, nah, I've seen horses get spooked at flapping flags and rolling soccer balls and even a plastic bag floating in the wind. I know how to deal with those. Ugh. I was careful with all of that, but a damn squirrel?" She fisted her hands.

"That happens," I assured her. "I once saw a horse who was scared of rabbits, and another who went crazy when the owner's puppy got too close."

"If only I had been more careful."

I scooted closer to her. "There was nothing you could have done, Gabi. Stop putting this on your shoulders. Besides, we don't really know how she is yet. She might just have a mild twist. With a little physical therapy, she should be brand new."

She turned those huge, worried blue eyes at me. "But what if it's broken?"

I inhaled a sharp breath. It was a possibility but one I didn't want to consider yet. If it was broken, if the ligaments were ruptured, we would have to talk about surgery, or depending on the severity, putting the mare to sleep, and looking at how Gabi was emotional now, I didn't want to be the one talking to her about that. Hopefully, I wouldn't have to. Hopefully, Branca just needs some medicine to help her heal and a little rest.

"Will you let me look at your injuries now?" She grunted, but sat back on the ground, putting her back right in front of me. From the rip in her shirt, I saw she was wearing a black tank top underneath. "Can you take the shirt off, please?" She looked back, an eyebrow cocked. An urge to roll my eyes hit me. "So I can look at the injury better without having to rip your shirt more."

"It's already ruined." She started shrugging off the shirt but winced, hissed, and stopped. "*Merda.*"

"Hurts too much?"

"A little." By the way her nose was scrunched and her lips pressed into a thin line, I knew she was lying. "I hadn't even noticed it until you pointed them out."

I pushed the shirt down her shoulders for her. "You were too worried about Branca to notice anything else."

She pulled the shirt to her lap and looked down at it. "So, how bad is it?"

It didn't look good. The area behind her shoulder was darkening, but thankfully, it looked like she had only bruised the muscle and besides feeling sore for a few days, it should be fine. Next, I slid my hand down to her elbow. The bleeding from the small scrapes had stopped, but I wanted to apply some antiseptic on it just to make sure all impurities and bacteria stayed out. Although, I didn't have any with me right now. "You'll survive," was all I said.

"Haha, very funny."

"Just apply some antiseptic on your elbow and take something for muscle pain when we get home. You'll be fine." I let go of her arm.

She tried rolling her shoulder but hissed again. "*Filho duma ...*"

I had no idea what she had said, but it did sound like a curse. Or the beginning of one.

I shot up at the sound of a truck approaching—Jimmy's truck with the trailer attached to its bed. After a few maneuvers, Hannah turned the truck around and backed it until the trailer was close. If I hadn't given Branca that sedative, she would be kicking and jerking right now. But as it had taken her over, she just blinked, really out of it.

Another man was with them.

"This is Paul, a riding instructor," Hannah said. "He's going to help us."

I quickly shook his hand. "Good."

With a lot of effort and grunting, the five of us were able to slip the stretcher under Branca, then pull her into the back of the trailer.

Gabi entered the trailer too. "I'm going with her."

I opened my mouth to protest, but the glare she shot me told me I shouldn't argue. So, I closed the trailer's door with a sigh and ran to my truck.

At the stable, we all grunted again to put Branca in her stall.

A new class started arriving at the same time as us, so as soon as they helped us with Branca, Paul and Jimmy guided the students to the arena outside.

"I'll be right back," Hannah said, going to help them set up the class.

Gabi still hovered over a half-sleeping Branca while I went to my truck and picked up the x-ray machine and other equipment.

"Can you help me?" I asked, dropping the x-ray machine on the ground.

"Of course," Gabi said, snapping out of her daze. She turned to me all business-like. "What can I do?"

"I'll bring over the ultrasound machine too, and the laptop. We'll hook up everything and—" I stopped. "I'll show you once I have everything set up."

I went back to the truck and reached for the ultrasound machine in the back. Gabi appeared by my side and got the laptop. "Anything else?"

"Those cables." I jerked my chin toward a roll of cables on the other side of the truck bed.

She swiped those up, and we went back to Branca's stall. Gabi watched Branca while I connected the cables and turned on the laptop and the machines. I stood and handed her a flat panel.

With a little knot between her brows, she took it. "What now?"

"Now, you come here." I knelt beside Branca's hurt leg and

tried to straighten it as much as I could without bothering her too much. The small dose of sedative wouldn't last long and we had to work fast before she started panicking again. I lifted Branca's leg. "Place the flat panel underneath." She did and I lowered Branca's leg over it. "Just make sure it stays in place and that Branca doesn't move."

Next, I picked up the portable, but not too light x-ray machine and aligned with the flat panel. When the light blinked indicating it was straight, I pressed the button and the x-ray appeared on the laptop's screen.

I dropped the machine and turned to the laptop.

"What does it show?" Gabi asked, still holding on to the flat panel.

"Oh, sorry." I scooted to her and helped her take the flat panel from underneath the mare.

Then, we both looked at the screen.

"Not that I'm an expert in reading x-rays, but I don't see anything wrong."

"There's nothing wrong with the bone, but see here." I pointed to the ligaments disappearing behind the bone. "These don't look right."

I picked up the ultrasound machine, which looked like a thick laptop with an attached mouse, and leaned over Branca. Careful, I slid the probe over the mare's fetlock and cannon. The image appeared on the machine's screen.

"And ..."

"Here." I pointed to the ligaments, appearing much clearer now. "They don't look ruptured or cracked. But they are swollen." I looked up at Gabi and her big, anxious eyes. "I have to show these images to Dr. Bohm before making a final diagnosis, but between us, it seems it was just a mild sprain. With the right care, she'll be good as new in no time."

Gabi squealed and threw her arms around me. I barely had

time to push my arm back before the two of us went barreling to the ground, but I caught her with my other arm. To my own surprise, I held her as tightly as she held me.

"Thank you, thank you, thank you," she whispered near my ear over and over again.

I chuckled, trying not to inhale her sweet scent and let it go to my head. "I didn't do anything."

She shrugged, her shoulders brushing against mine. "You were here, enduring my heart attack."

I felt her heartbeat through her chest, and it wasn't fast enough for a heart attack. Though, with her body practically on my lap and her legs tangled in mine, my own heart started speeding up.

I pulled back and looked into her eyes. "It's actually pretty cute seeing you caring for Branca so much in so little time."

Her smile faded away and those eyes became two blue, round marbles. Her gaze flicked to my lips and lingered there for a second too long.

An urge, a desire rushed through me. I cupped her neck and leaned—

"I brought coffee," Hannah announced from somewhere in the stable.

Gabi and I sprang apart. She stood and went to the stall door while I sent the images to Dr. Bohm, then picked up the equipment and placed it neatly into a corner.

"Thanks," Gabi said, taking a big mug from the tray Hannah was holding outside the stall.

"Want some?" she offered me.

I nodded and picked a mug too. "Thanks."

"So?" she asked, looking from me to Gabi and back to me.

"I just emailed the images for Dr. Bohm to check, but I would say it's just a mild sprain."

Hannah smiled wide at Gabi. "That's wonderful news. We'll

get you the best equine physical therapist around, and she'll be new in no time."

"Do you know many equine physical therapists?" Gabi asked.

"Well, actually, no." Hannah placed the tray over a bench. "But give me until tomorrow at noon. I'll find out plenty."

"Actually." I ran a hand over my hair. "Equine physical therapy isn't a certified profession yet. Most people who work with that are vets or regular physical therapists who took a workshop on it and then learn on the job."

"Oh ... that's not really good news, is it?" Gabi said with a pout.

"There's more," I said. "I didn't finish vet school, yet, but I had the chance to take two of those workshops before I had to quit."

Gabi's eyes widened. "You did? So ... you can do it? Wait, no, you have work and stuff."

I shook my head. "I've been working less, so I think I can spare some of my free time for Branca."

"Are you sure?"

Fuck, she sounded so hopeful, and even the light in her face, showing me how much she liked this idea, was too much for me.

I smiled at her. "Yeah, I'm sure."

She squealed again, but this time, instead of throwing herself at me, she punched my shoulder lightly.

"Ouch," I said, faking a hurt pout, since I had barely felt it.

"That's great," Hannah said, smiling at us. "You can come over anytime. If I'm not here, Jimmy or Paul are. If you need any of us. If you don't, then feel free to walk in when you can."

"Thanks." A whimper-like neigh came from the stall. I glanced at the stall as Branca tried to stretch her leg. "She's almost back. I should wrap her fetlock with a temporary cast and give her something for pain before she's fully normal again."

I walked into the stall while the two girls stayed outside in the stable hall, drinking coffee and talking more about Branca, and the accident, and the therapy. I did my best to ignore them and focus on my job, but when Gabi laughed or smiled wide and her beautiful eyes twinkled, it was hard to.

Dr. Bohm called me while I wrapped Branca's fetlock and gave her a shot for pain. She would need several of those for the next few days. As I thought, Dr. Bohn had looked at the images from the x-ray and the ultrasound and arrived at the same conclusion I had. Though, I didn't tell him I was volunteering to be Branca's physical therapist, because honestly, besides those workshops, I hadn't worked on this for the longest time. I had never used it in practice. I just hoped I didn't mess Branca up.

Well, I would never put Branca's healing in danger. If I thought it wasn't working or I had no idea what I was doing, I would admit it to Gabi and help her hire someone with more experience.

But this new thing actually filled me with something I hadn't felt in a long time: purpose. While in vet school, I had always wanted to know more about physical therapy, but that was one area that was lacking. Which only interested me more. Right now, I wanted to help Branca. I needed to. For her, and for myself.

I finished up and left to the stall. Gabi and Hannah stood outside, watching as Branca returned to herself.

"I'm all done here," I said, picking up the x-ray machine from the ground. "I should go back to the clinic now."

Gabi grabbed the ultrasound machine. "I'll walk you out." Walking side by side, she glanced at me. "Thanks."

"You're welcome."

She bit her lower lip. "I want to pay you for the therapy sessions," she said as if she had been afraid of saying that at all.

I almost tripped on my feet. "No way. I won't accept that."

She sighed. "But this isn't your main job. I'll be taking more of your time."

"And this is what people in a relationship do for one another, isn't it?" I dropped everything in my truck's bed.

She scrunched her nose. "But we're not in a relationship and no one needs to know about the payment part. Please? It just feels right."

I glared at her. "It doesn't feel right to me." I finished attaching everything on the back so it wouldn't move while I was driving.

She sighed. "I'm sorry. I didn't mean to make you mad."

"I'm not mad, I'm just ... frustrated."

"Sorry," she mumbled again. Then, she glanced over my shoulder and her eyes widened. "*Droga*. Hannah is spying on us."

I stiffened. "Why?"

Gabi shrugged. "I don't know. But ..." Red spread over her cheeks. "We can't part without being like real fiancés."

I sucked in a sharp breath. "You mean with a kiss?"

She nodded. "*Sim*, but from this angle, I'm sure you can just kiss my cheek and she would never—"

I shut her up by cupping her face with my hand and pressing my lips to hers.

Damn it. Most of the time she was okay, great even, but sometimes I just wanted her to shut up. And, nothing better than to do what we should be doing. For pretense only, of course.

Enjoying this pretense too much, I stepped into her personal space, brushing my body on hers. Gabi gasped—her mouth parted and I couldn't stop myself. I snaked my tongue inside her mouth and deepened the kiss.

Her hands clutched my shoulders, her nails biting my skin through my shirt, and then her lips moved with mine—the same rhythm and, if I wasn't mistaken, the same hunger.

The few times we had kissed, the few times we had touched or moved into each other, I was always stunned by how good it felt. By how *right* it was.

But no, this wasn't right.

Schooling my expression to a neutral one—and not the scowl that wanted to burst through—I stepped away. "Bye."

"*Tchau*," Gabi whispered, her dazed eyes on me.

The scowl faded and one corner of my lips curled up as I hopped into my truck and drove away. It was good to know I could render her that dazed.

Now if I could only control myself, then she wouldn't have to be dazed, and things would flow smoothly.

43

GABI

A WEEK PASSED since Branca's accident and I spent most of my spare time with her—meaning, all of my time, since I had nothing to do. I even declined the invitation to join the guys for more practices because I wanted to make sure Branca was all right.

Tyler had come to see her twice since then. His therapy was slow going for my taste, but truth be told, I would think anything was slow going at this point. All I wanted was for Branca to be healed as soon as possible.

I was walking Branca around the arena, slowly so as not to irritate her fetlock, when I got a call from Brittany asking me to meet her at the club.

That made me super wary, but curious too.

"Were you able to set up a meeting with Mr. Helms for me?" was the first thing I asked her.

"No, but I think I'll be able to help you somehow," she told me.

Without hesitating, I took Branca back to her stall, made sure she had everything she needed, and drove to the club.

There were only a few members around, but save for the ones

who were playing tennis or polo, everyone was impeccably dressed—the men in dress slacks and shirts, and the women in dresses and high heels. I was sure I would be kicked out of the club for wearing such casual clothes. *Bom*, if I was kicked out, then the guys had to be too, because they all didn't dress as they should, as the club rules stated.

And that was why I didn't worry. They wouldn't kick the guys out, and they wouldn't kick me out.

Brittany was waiting for me at one of the outside tables of the main dining room.

"Ms. Fernandes, it's so good to see you." She stood and shook my hand. Again, I noticed her clothes. Black slacks, a blouse, fancy pumps, and makeup on her face. All business-like.

"It's good to see you too," I said, trying to sound pleasant.

"Please, sit down." She gestured to the chair across the table. We both sat down and I felt like jumping in my own chair. "I'm sure you're curious why I called you here."

"You're right," I said.

A waiter walked by our table and Brittany called him. "Can you bring me a cup of coffee, please?"

"Of course, Ms. Morrow." He glanced at me. "Can I bring you anything, Ms. Fernandes?"

I had no idea of this guy's name, but he seemed to know who I was. "Hm, just some water, please."

He nodded and disappeared into the building.

"Sorry about that," Brittany said, dragging it on. "I'm moved by coffee. This will be my fourth cup today." And it was only ten in the morning.

"Americans do drink a lot of coffee," I added, trying to sound interested in whatever nonsense she was talking.

"All right, let's jump right in." She sat straighter and looked up at me, a slight smile on her lips. "I think I found a girl to play polo with you."

My mouth fell open. What did she mean? "But ... one girl? No team? No club?"

"Well, yes." She flipped her ponytail to the side. "I know one girl isn't much, but I thought it could be a start. You two can join forces and go after two other girls and a sponsor together. Wouldn't that be great?"

Bom, when she put it like that ... "*Sim*, yes, it would." I frowned. "But who is she?"

"She'll be here in a few minutes," was all she said.

Promptly, the waiter came back with her coffee and my water. "Anything else?" he asked. We both answered that we were good. "I'll be around if you need anything." He stepped back and retreated to the wall.

Meanwhile, Brittany sipped from her coffee, watching the club with a pleased gaze. And I simply sat there, counting the seconds until said girl, who I didn't even know, appeared.

"Ah, there she is," Brittany stood again and smiled to someone behind me.

I glanced over my shoulder. A beautiful, tall Black girl with long and thick black hair approached us with a smile of her own. Like everyone else, she was dressed up in fancy pants, a dress blouse, and sandals.

"Sorry I'm late," the girl said.

"It's okay," Brittany said. She looked at me. "Gabriela, this is Kelsey Murray. Kelsey, this is Gabriela Fernandes."

We shook hands.

"Please, call me Gabi," I said.

Brittany smiled at us. "I know you two have a lot to talk about, so I'll leave you to it, but don't hesitate to call me if you need anything, okay?"

"Thanks," Kelsey said, still smiling.

I nodded. "*Sim*, thanks."

Brittany walked away and Kelsey took a chair for her. "So,

you're the girl Brittany told me about."

Frowning, I sat back in my chair. "What did she tell you?"

"She told me you play as well as your cousins and brother."

"You know my cousins and brother?"

"I do play polo, and everyone who plays polo knows who the best in the world are."

"I guess that's true." Hope tickled my gut, but I pushed it down. This was too good to be true. My path hadn't been easy so far, and it wouldn't start being easy now. "So, you play polo. Where? And for how long?"

"I always loved horses and, thankfully, my parents were able to afford lessons for me since I was about eight years old. I learned about polo soon after, but, like you know, it's hard to find a female team, and they don't let you play on the male teams, so I quickly let that go. However, we were living in Canada during my high school years, and some girls from my high school played polo for fun. So I joined them. But we moved back to this area before I graduated high school and I was never able to find another girls' team around here. I still ride, but to be honest, I haven't played polo in two years."

The hope faded from my gut. Two years? That was a long time. If she was a prodigy like Leo, then I believed she was still good at it, no matter what, but what if she was like the rest of us? What if she was average? Then two years without playing was a long, long time. If she was good at it before, it was probable she wasn't good at it anymore.

"Oh," I finally said, trying to erase my shock. "Hm, that's great. That you still ride and that you still like polo, but ..."

"You're worried I can't play anymore, right?" The question caught me by surprise and the words didn't come. "I get it, believe me. You're probably a great player and you want to put together a great team. I get it. But I was a good player and I like polo way too much. Please, give me a chance. Play with me a couple of times, let me shake the rust off, then you decide if we can start our own team or not."

"That sounds ... fair, I guess." And it brought hope back to me. I had a big love and hate relationship with hope. "All right, we can schedule a few practice games to see how you are doing."

"That's great!"

I tilted my head. "What do you say about meeting me here tomorrow morning at eight thirty?"

As AGREED, Kelsey met me at the club at eight thirty sharp. We trudged to the field and started stretching.

"So, they will get here and you'll just tell them I'm practicing with you all?"

I nodded once. "*Sim.*"

"What if they say no?"

I rolled my eyes. "They won't say no. I bet they will be happy for me, for us, and they will like having you around. Besides, this makes the game even. Three to each side."

She smiled wide, her nervousness showing through her slightly shaking hands. "That sounds great."

"They will be here around nine, so I thought we could get ahead of them in some stretches and exercises."

"Good idea."

As we stretched and worked out, Kelsey told me a little about herself. She was twenty like me and lived with her mother. Her parents divorced when she was starting her senior year of high school. That was why she moved back from Canada—her father still lived there. Her mother was originally from Los Angeles, but

Kelsey had moved to Toronto when her mom came back from Canada. Kelsey was attending college for pre-med because that was what her mother expected of her. Though she wanted to work with horses. If she had a choice, she would be a riding instructor on a small ranch, earning a miserable salary, just enough to pay cheap bills, as long as it meant she was doing what made her happy.

That made me even more hopeful. She loved horses, like I did, and she needed the money. It would be awesome if she played really well, and we could put a good team together, find a sponsor, and get more than a miserable salary for her.

It was eight-fifty when *tio* João Pedro arrived.

"*Bom dia,*" he said, his *mate* in his hand and his bag slung over his shoulder.

"*Oi, tio.*" I smiled at him, barely containing my excitement. "*Tio*, this is Kelsey Murray. She used to play polo. I invited her to practice with us today. I hope you don't mind."

Tio João Pedro turned to Kelsey. "*Oi*, Kelsey, nice to meet you. I'm João Pedro, Montenegro's coach. Glad to have you for practice today."

Kelsey beamed. "Thank you, sir. I'm the one glad to be here."

We got ready to play and while we warmed up, a new idea came to my mind. I needed to research how it would work if I wanted to sponsor a team. All businesses started with a little investment. Maybe I could invest in my own polo team.

I would be the first player, and Kelsey could be the second.

THE COFFEE MACHINE BEEPED. With my eyes still on the laptop's screen, I stood and reached to the counter behind me, grabbing a clean mug from the drying rack.

"What are you doing?"

I yelped and almost dropped the mug. "*Credo* ..."

"Sorry," Tyler said as he stepped into the kitchen. He glanced to the laptop and the mug in my hand. "What are you doing?"

"Hm, I was gonna get some coffee and continue my research."

He grabbed a clean mug for himself. "Researching?"

I poured myself some coffee and sat back on the stool with a sigh. "Colleges that offer polo as one of their sports." I had called colleges before to see if any players wanted to join a team, but I hadn't thought about applying to them as a student and getting to play.

He got some coffee and stood behind me, watching the screen. "And?"

"First, it's hard to look for the word polo and college because most of the stuff that pops up is water polo. Second, the few colleges I found are too far away. Like, across the country far away."

"I see." He grabbed a glass from a cabinet and filled it with cold water.

I didn't know what else to do. I had given it more thought since meeting Kelsey and first coming up with the idea of sponsoring our own team. I had researched even, and it was no good. At least not yet. I still didn't have a green card, and to have my own business, or team, I had to wait for my green card.

At least that was moving. Earlier this week, I had received a letter from the government with a time and date for my interview. Tyler and I still had some time to nail down every little detail about our fake relationship.

"Ugh." Frustrated, I opened my social media app and started scrolling down my feed.

Hilary had posted a pic of Gui and her during the weekend, Ri had posted a picture of a glass full of whiskey, and Leo had posted a picture of Hannah riding Argus at the ranch. Pedro had posted a picture of him during yesterday's practice, and Bia posted a pic of Garrett and her on date night—at a Brazilian restaurant in L.A.

Besides that, my feed was full of pictures of my friends from Brazil. At parties, weddings, get-togethers, girls' nights out. Always having fun and smiling and kissing their partners.

Speaking of pictures and partners ...

"Ty, come here."

He glanced at me. "What?"

"Just come here, please."

Frowning, he walked up to my side. "What?"

"Look at this." I pointed to some small text on the screen. He bent on the waist and leaned forward, getting closer to the screen. And to me. Quickly, I pulled up my cell phone and kissed his cheek—while snapping a selfie.

Tyler pulled back, his eyes wide. "What was that for?"

I shrugged. "*Bom* ... I was looking at my social media feeds and everyone was posting pictures with their boyfriends and husbands, and I thought, why not post one too?" My cheeks flamed. "I mean, they do think we're together, right? And we haven't taken as many photos as we should, and posted them online, in case the immigration office decides to investigate us."

The frown was back. "In that case ..." He settled down his mug. "Let me see that picture."

"You're going to erase it."

"Why would I do that?" Wary, I handed him my phone. "It's blurry. We should try it again."

I reached for my phone. "Let me see."

"I'll take the picture. Ready?" He leaned over like before without waiting for my answer. I stared at his profile, still wary of whatever was going on. "Any day now."

I rolled my eyes but conceded. I leaned into him, and closing my eyes, puckered my lips to kiss his cheek. Then, his lips pressed against mine. Before I could process what was happening, his hand cupped my face and his lips moved. A zap of desire surged through me and I started melting into him, rejoicing in the pressure of his lips on mine.

I snapped out of it and pulled back. I opened my mouth but nothing came out.

"I think this picture is better, don't you think? Here you go." He handed me my phone.

I stared at the phone, our picture taking over the screen. A picture of his lips on mine. Slowly, I reached over and took the phone from him. "Hm, yeah, thanks." I cleared my throat and lifted my gaze to his. "For the picture." My cheeks flamed.

One corner of his lips tugged up. "You're welcome."

His cell phone rang, cutting through whatever spell had bewitched the entire kitchen.

He glanced to his phone and the frown settled between his brows. "It's from the hospital," he whispered, straightening. "Hello?" he answered. I could hear a woman's voice from the other side, but couldn't make out the actual words. But whatever she was saying couldn't be good as Tyler's shoulders tensed and his jaw popped. "I'm on my way."

I stood. "What is it?"

His eyes met mine and I saw pure anguish in there. "He's not doing well." He ran a hand through his hair. "I need to go." He walked past me like a robot on a mission—all action and no thought.

"Wait." I slammed my laptop shut and went after him. "I'll drive you."

He shook his head. "No need. There's nothing to be done th—"

I caught his arm and squeezed gently. "Tyler, I want to go with you."

He stared at me for a moment, as if searching for an answer in my eyes. However, what was the question? Finally, he let out a loud sigh and nodded. "Fine," he grumbled.

I rushed to my room, where I grabbed my purse and a jacket and slipped on my boots, and met Tyler at the front door.

I unlocked the door and glanced at him. "Everything will be fine. You know that, right?"

44

TYLER

Gabi knew my father was dying, that any moment now could be his last, so why would she say something like that to me? I sighed and tried to relax in the passenger seat of her Grand Cherokee.

With everything going on in my life? It wasn't easy to relax.

I glanced at the girl by my side. Her hands were tight against the wheel and her eyes fixed on the road. She looked beautiful, as she always did. Damn, I had no idea what had come over me and why the hell I had kissed her like I had earlier. I just knew that, if she hadn't pulled away, I would have kept kissing her. I would have pressed my mouth on hers, until she parted her lips and I could deepen the kiss.

I shook my head and glanced out of the window.

What the hell was I doing?

This was a damn deal. In less than two years, she would be gone from my life. I spied at her again. Or would she? Did I want her to be? What if ... what if this could actually work? What if I showed her how much she enticed me, how much I thought of her and wondered how our relationship would be if we actually stopped pretended and surrendered to our feelings—to my feelings. I had no idea if she felt the same or not, though there were times when I thought she did.

The car stopped and I shook my head, surprised we were already in the hospital parking lot.

Gabi glanced at me. "Are you okay?"

I looked at her and started to nod, then gave one short shake of my head. "I don't know," I confessed.

Gabi reached across the seats and took my hand in hers. She squeezed it gently. "I'm here for you, okay. Anything you need." Her eyes, her beautiful blue eyes, showed me she was sincere, and it made me even more emotional.

"Thanks," I muttered.

She offered me a tight smile, then pulled her hand back, and hopped out of the car.

Gabi and I entered his private room—perks of finally having some cash and paying out some of the fifty thousand bills I had—and found him sleeping. He had monitors hooked up on him, and in my non-medical opinion, his heart seemed a little too slow for my taste.

He looked even more like a mummy than his usual self. White, pasty skin, sunken eyes, and too fucking thin. A jolt cut through my chest and it was suddenly too hard to breathe.

Gabi stepped into me. She wrapped an arm around my back and rested her temple on my shoulder. "I wish there was more we could do for him."

Deflated, I leaned into her. "Me too."

She stood on tiptoes and kissed my cheek. "Can I do something for you?"

I glanced at her, at those big eyes fixed on me. Could she do something for me? More than she had already done?

A knock echoed from the door and I took a step back, as if it had been wrong to be standing so close to my fiancée—to my wife.

It was just pretend.

The door opened a sliver and nurse Annie peeked in. "I thought I saw you arriving." She stepped in and closed the door.

"How is he doing now?" I asked, focusing back on the man lying in the bed.

She sighed. "He's stable. We were able to get his blood pressure back to a more acceptable reading, but ... he's too weak. The doctor will come in later and talk to you about it."

My insides chilled. "What do you mean?"

She shook her head once. "Dr. Hansen is with a patient now and it might take a while. You should get comfortable. He'll stop by when he can."

She left the room without further explanation, and I stared at the door as if it was a joke. She was coming back and telling me more, right?

"Ty?" Gabi's soft whisper jolted me and I turned to her. "Do you want to talk?"

I moved past her and leaned my ass against the closed window, on the other side of the room. "No. I'm fine."

She stared at me with those knowing eyes. Damn it. Those eyes. I had a fucked-up love and hate relationship with them.

She stood there, in the middle of the room, for a long time, staring between my father and me. What did she want me to do? To tell her that I was scared? That I wasn't ready? That I didn't think I would ever be? This man raised me alone. He had been the best father a boy could have. And for reasons I still didn't understand, he was being taken from me too soon. Too fucking soon.

I glanced out the window, lest Gabi saw the tears welling in my eyes.

"I'm gonna ..." she started, but she didn't finish. Moments later, I heard the soft click of the door closing.

With a sigh, I plopped down in the nearest chair and let one single tear fall. Just one. I wasn't ready for more. Not yet.

I HATED hospitals with all my heart and soul. Though I understood that hospitals saved lives, all I could think about was the many people who came here to die.

Trying not to look much around the corridors or at the patients and family and friends waiting to hear about their loved ones, I took the elevator back to the first floor where I found the cafeteria. I bought a coffee to-go cup, but ended up sitting down at one of the tables overlooking a courtyard in the middle of the hospital.

I had done all I could, right? I mean, not directly, but I had made the deal with Tyler. I had already given him one third of the cash I promised him. With that, he had paid the most important bills and was now paying for a treatment for his father. But money wasn't everything. Even with all the money in the world and all the treatments, some illnesses couldn't be cured.

Why then did I feel so guilty? So useless? Even when I tried helping him, tried comforting him and talking to him, Tyler shut me down.

Because I was nothing to him, that was why. I might be his wife on paper, but that was it. Just on paper. I bet he hated sharing all of this with me. I bet that if he could, he wouldn't have told me about his father and the reason he wanted so much money.

I was halfway through my coffee when my phone vibrated in my pocket, and I rushed to pick it up, thinking that it could be Tyler and he wanted me to go back to the room so he wouldn't be alone.

Silly me.

Kelsey's name flashed on the screen.

With a frown, I answered the call. "Hey, Kelsey, I wasn't expecting your call. How are you?"

"I'm good. I'm great, actually. I'm at the club right now."

"Oh."

"I found a third girl."

"What? No way!"

"Yes, way!"

"*Meu Deus*, that is great. Who is she? When can I meet her?"

"Her name is Melissa Page and you can meet her right now. She's here at the club with me and she wants to meet you too."

My heart wilted. "No ... I can't come now. Can't you schedule something with her later?"

"She's from Florida and she needs to go back this evening. According to what she just told me, she's in negotiations with a club from England. She doesn't want to leave the United States, but since she has no other options, she'll take their offer. Unless we can offer something better."

I cursed under my breath. Did this really have to happen now? I glanced at the courtyard. This was fate being cruel. As much I wanted to tell her to stay put with her until I got there, I couldn't just leave Tyler here, not when the nurse looked like the doctor had really bad news for him. He might not want my shoulder, but I suspected he soon would take any shoulder available. And I wanted to be there for him.

I couldn't abandon him now, even for my career. For my dreams.

"I can't go," I said, my voice almost breaking.

"What? You have to come. This is the opportunity we were waiting for."

"I know, believe me, I know, but I can't go." I took a deep breath. "Tell her I'm so sorry. I want to meet her and play with her and see if we are a good fit, but unfortunately, I'm in the middle of something and I can't leave." The line went silent. "Hello?"

"I'm here. I'm just ... I can't believe you're letting this go."

"I can't either," I muttered. "Thanks for letting me know."

I turned off the call and gave myself one minute to stare at my phone, wishing things were different. Then, I pulled myself together, ordered two cups of coffee, and since I wasn't sure what Tyler liked, a huge box with assorted donuts and croissants and scones and other pastries, and marched back upstairs.

46

TYLER

THE ENTIRE TIME Gabi was gone, I kept wishing she would come back. I heard footsteps on the other side of the door and stared at it, thinking it was her who would come in at any moment. I was scared and even though I was relieved when she left, I realized I didn't want to be alone when the doctor came in to talk to me. I had no idea what the hell that meant, and I wouldn't take the time to think about it now. Right now, I needed to breathe in and out. Breathe in and out. And wait.

Then, finally, the door opened and Gabi stepped in, balancing a huge box and two cups in her arms. I rushed to her and took the box before she dropped everything on the floor.

"I thought you might be hungry and since we don't know how long we'll be here ..." She jerked her chin to the box. I peeked under the flap and saw at least a dozen random pastries. The sweet aroma filled my nostrils and I felt my stomach tightening with hunger.

"That's ... thank you." I walked back to the corner of the room and settled the box on a small, round table.

"Here." Gabi placed a to-go cup beside the box. "Coffee. Cream, no sugar, right?"

I almost smiled at her as I sat down. "Right."

She took the other chair across the table. "I didn't know your favorite ..." She pointed to the box again. And again, I fought the urge to smile. Why was she being this considerate?

I picked up what looked like my favorite. "I think this is raspberry muffin."

"It is."

"This is my favorite. And blueberry muffins too. And raspberry and blueberry donuts too."

Her lips stretched into a thin smile. "So, basically anything raspberry or blueberry?"

This time I did smile. "Basically."

"Good to know." She picked up a butter croissant from the box. "Is that your favorite?"

"Hm, my favorite is anything pumpkin, but since it isn't fall yet." She shrugged.

"Good to know," I repeated her words.

We ate in silence for five minutes—time in which I ate two muffins and one donut. I guess I was hungrier than I thought. Or it was because it was so normal to stay by her side, that it made me uncomfortable. And, before I spewed some blasphemy from my mouth, I filled it up with food instead.

She sipped from her cup and glanced at my sleeping father. A pain cut through my chest. She looked at him with so much interest, as if she really cared about him. And she barely knew him.

I opened my mouth to say something—I didn't even know what—when the sound of a knock startled me and the door opened.

I stood as Dr. Hansen walked in.

"Mr. Reid." The doctor took my hand. "How is it going?"

"I'm fine," I said, my voice harsher than I intended. "I want to know about him." I gestured to my father.

The doctor nodded once. "Well, he's ... doing okay, for now."

I crossed my arms. "What does that mean?"

"We always talked about this, Mr. Reid. Unfortunately, there's nothing we can do for your father but try to delay the inevitable. However, I concluded the last few sessions of chemo haven't been effective, and in fact, have made your father weaker and more ill. He can't keep food down and he won't unless we stop chemo."

My stomach dropped. "You're suggesting we ..." I couldn't say it.

"It's your choice. I'm just giving you the options."

I closed my eyes. How could I choose? I couldn't even say it out loud.

I felt Gabi's body pressing to my side, her hand on mine, her fingers entwining with mine. "What are the options?" she asked, her voice firmer than usual. She was trying. She was putting on a brave face for me.

"You should talk to your father when he's awake, but the options are to still take a few sessions of chemo and maybe radio and hope it'll make a difference, enough to delay the outcome a little more, or ... you can stop it now and just make him comfortable until the end."

"Until the end," she repeated as if she too needed him to confirm what that meant.

"Yes, until he passes away," the doctor finally said.

I squeezed Gabi's hand.

"When do we need to decide?" she asked.

The doctor shook his head. "Whenever you want. Until then, we'll keep with the original plan. Chemo treatment every other day."

"All right," Gabi said. She had taken charge of this situation.

"Thanks, doctor. We'll talk about it and let you know as soon as we can."

"I'm sorry," the doctor said.

"Thanks," she whispered.

The doctor left the room and my knees wobbled. I retreated to my father's bed, knelt on the floor, and rested my forehead on the mattress. No, no, no, this couldn't be happening. When the cancer came back a third time, the doctor had warned us it would take a miracle to save my father, but until now, I believed in miracles.

Gabi's hand weighed on my shoulder. "I'm so sorry ..."

I jerked away from her sympathetic touch. Anger and despair boiled in my veins. I stood up and went to the window on the other side of the room. I placed an open hand on the cool glass, trying to contain my rage, because all I wanted to do was to punch the damn glass.

"Ty," she whispered from somewhere behind me. "Talk to me."

"Talk?" I turned to her. I suddenly wanted to yell at her. At the world. "Talk? My father is dying and there is nothing I can do and you want to talk?"

She flinched. "I ..." She swallowed hard. "I want to help you, but I don't know what I can do. Please, tell me what I can do."

"For starters, you can stop pretending to care and just leave."

She flinched again. Her eyes glistened, and I averted my gaze because I couldn't deal if she started to cry right now.

"I don't think you mean that," she said, her voice breaking.

"Please, go away. Go home. Whatever. Just ... leave me alone."

She opened her mouth, then closed it again. Slowly, she retreated to the chair where she had left her purse, picked up, and after a kind glance at my sleeping father, she left the room.

And I punched the wall right beside the window.

47

GABI

I didn't want to, but I left because Tyler asked me to. Wiping my tears, I walked down the corridor to the elevator and spotted Dr. Hansen talking to a nurse close by. I veered from my original destination and marched to him. I halted a safe distance from them, so I couldn't eavesdrop on their conversation, but close enough for them to know I was waiting to talk to one of them.

The doctor saw me, said something else to the nurse, she wrote something down in a chart, then left.

"Ms. ...?" he started.

"Gabi Fernandes." I extended my hand to him. "I'm engaged to Tyler."

He took my hand and shook it. "Yes, I've seen you around a few times."

"Doctor, I know some kind of cancers are too aggressive and there isn't much to be done, but ... if money wasn't the question, was there something we could do for Charlie?"

"Ms. Fernandes, there are always experimental drugs and treatments on testing, but that's what it is, experimental. You never know how and if they will actually work."

"Do you know of any new, testing treatments around?"

He frowned, examining me as if I was one of his patients. "I do."

"Do I need to schedule an appointment, or can you send me all the info through email?"

His frown deepened. "I can ask my assistant to send you an email with the packet."

I picked up the small notebook on my purse, scribbled my email on a blank page, ripped the page, and gave it to him. "Please, do so."

"I will, but ... Ms. Fernandes, just so you know, even if these treatments are revolutionary and prove to be efficient at some level, I'm afraid they won't cure Mr. Reid. Unfortunately, his cancer is too advanced. All you'll do is delay the inevitable."

My heart squeezed. "I understand. Even so, I would like to have the information."

He nodded. "Yes, Ms. Fernandes. My assistant should send it to you tomorrow."

"Thanks."

New threads of hope coursed through me, though I pushed them away. This was the first step of three hundred. Maybe Tyler wouldn't want to hear about it, maybe his father wouldn't be eligible ... there were so many variables.

As I exited the building, I picked up my phone and called Kelsey.

"Is she gone?"

"Oh, yes, she left over an hour ago." A pause. "Are you going to tell me why you couldn't make it? I thought this was all that mattered to you."

It was.

Until now.

I couldn't be so blind to it anymore. Tyler and his welfare and the welfare of his loved ones mattered to me, which could only mean one thing. I liked him more than I should.

"Unfortunately, things don't always go according to plan," I said, referring to more than one thing in my life.

"You sound like you could use a drink. Want to come over?"

I sighed. "No, I just need a good night sleep. Thanks, though."

"Call me if you need anything, okay?"

I smiled to the phone. "Thanks."

I turned off the call, halted beside my car, and glanced back at the hospital, looking up as if I could see Tyler standing by a window. He was hurting and I wished, I hoped, that was something I could do to help him. But right now, all I could do was give him space, time to process it all.

Tomorrow though, tomorrow I would take care of him.

I DIDN'T SLEEP WELL and I woke up early, waiting for a miracle. Tyler could come home or the doctor could have sent me the information packet already, but at six in the morning? I was dreaming.

Since it was too early to do anything, I put on some workout clothes and went running around the neighborhood—it would be good to pass the time and clear my mind.

I ran for over an hour, then came back home and took a long shower.

I put on a long T-shirt, and with my hairbrush in hand, I walked out of the bathroom. I lifted my arms high to brush my hair when I heard something crashing. I yelped and turned around, seeing my bedroom door wide open and Tyler, with a small box at his feet. However, his intense gaze was on my legs.

Ah, *droga*. I quickly lowered my arms as heat spread through my cheeks. "Are you all right?"

His gaze slid up my body until it locked on mine. "It's fine." He finally unglued his eyes from me and crouched down to pick up the box.

I tried to swallow the question, but I couldn't. "How are you?"

He glanced at me again, his eyes pained. "I'm ... fine." He turned his back to me and I took that as a dismissal. Fighting tears, I closed my bedroom's door and changed from that oversized T-shirt into a tee and jeans shorts. If I had known he would be home so early, I wouldn't have even thought about putting on something so comfy. So intimate.

I was kinda glad I did, though, because now there was no denying. Even if he never admitted anything or never acted on it, I knew he liked what he saw. And that was enough for now.

I finished dressing and brushing my hair then left my bedroom.

I made into the kitchen and put the kettle on the range to heat up water for my *chimarrão*. A minute later, Tyler joined me. He started the coffee machine, but when he reached for the mug, his hand slapped it instead, and it tumbling to the ground.

He cursed out loud.

"Careful." I raised my hands. "Stay where you are." Barefooted, I jumped out of the range of the broken mug pieces—there weren't many and most were big pieces—grabbed the broom behind the pantry door, and pushed them aside. I glanced over Tyler, who closed and opened his hand, looking ready to punch someone. "Are you okay?"

He let out a long breath between his teeth and rolled his shoulder. "Define okay."

It pained me to see him like this. Even with the money from our deal, his biggest problem could never be solved. I couldn't heal his father because I had money. There wasn't anything any of us could do.

I did the only thing I knew. I let go of the broom, stepped into him, and wrapped my arms around his shoulders. I pulled a frozen Tyler into me and patted his back.

Slowly, he relaxed into my arms, and wound his arms around my waist, holding me tight.

After a long time, he whispered, "Sorry if I'm always a jerk."

"It's okay," I said. "You've been on your own for so long, you don't know how to share your feelings and worries with me, but I do care. I'll bother you until you do."

He snorted, but only held on to me tighter. "I would like that."

I would really like that too.

I SPENT the next morning practicing with Kelsey and the guys. I was amazed about how well Kelsey still played after so long, and how well we played together. After practice, even *tio* João Pedro said so.

In the afternoon, I went to check on Branca and was surprised to find Tyler there. He had taken her out to the arena and was walking with her. At some point, she stopped and nickered, tugging on the reins. With a half-grin, Tyler turned to her, and smoothed his hand down her long neck. He said something, then stepped into her and embraced her. She lowered his head on his shoulders, as if embracing him back.

My heart squeezed.

When they turned around and Tyler spotted me, I approached them.

"Hey," he said. His expression was neutral, if not almost happy, with the corner of his lips tugged up. I preferred him this way.

"I didn't expect to see you here," I said, stopping right beside them. I leaned into Branca and smoothed my hand down her side. "Hi, pretty girl."

"Dr. Bohm asked me to check on her, so I took advantage of

that to work on her some more." He tapped her head. "She's doing well. Soon, she'll be able to gallop."

"If another squirrel doesn't scare her, you mean," I said in a low voice.

Tyler's brow curled down. "I was thinking about that. I know Hannah is working on Branca's fear, but I was wondering if you would let me work with her too. Probably alongside Hannah. I think we can help each other and make progress faster."

Warmth spread through my chest. "I would like that."

Branca tugged on her reins and shook her head, pulling Tyler off-balance. He had to take a step forward so as not to fall, and I instantly reached for him, to try and keep him from kissing the ground. Chances were, I would have gone with him, but it had been instinct.

Then we straightened, my hands on his forearms, and the toes of our feet touching, our gazes meeting, and only a foot between us. His eyes searched mine, as if looking for a secret or something even I didn't know what it was, but that wreaked havoc inside me.

"Branca is lucky to have found you," he said, his voice hoarse.

"I was the lucky one," I said, my voice low.

"No." Tyler shook his head, but his eyes never left mine. "She is. And I am too." He paused, then pulled his arm back so my hand slid down to his hand. He held on to me. "I am lucky to have found you," he whispered.

He leaned into me.

Drawn to him in a way words couldn't describe, I rose on my tiptoes, and—

Branca nickered and stepped back, tugging on the reins again. Tyler jerked to the side.

"Holy shit," he barked, quickly recovering his footing.

I pressed my hands on my flaming face. *Meu Deus*, what had just happened? Forcing myself to remain cool, I lowered my hands and turned to Tyler. "Are you okay?"

"Yeah, I am." He shot a fake glare at Branca. "But someone here must want more exercise."

I reached for the reins. "If you want, I can take over from here."

Tyler shook his head. "Why don't we both work on her until I have to go back to the clinic."

I smiled at him. "I would like that."

48

GABI

THAT WAS IT. I wasn't having it anymore.

I was tired of this hot and cold thing. Of laughing together one night, to his barking the next. And what was up with all the times we had almost kissed? Or the times we had kissed, even if it had been just for show? Those happened, right? And they had been as hot as hell. I wasn't imagining them all, was I?

I hoped I wasn't or I would just embarrass myself.

Half an hour before Tyler's usual time to arrive home, I drank two glasses of wine to help me loosen up a little. Then, I took a quick shower, let my damp hair loosen, and put on just a big-sized gray T-shirt—it was off-shoulder, with long-sleeves, and it went down to my thighs, barely covering my ass.

He got home almost fifteen minutes later than usual and I was already nursing my third glass of wine, afraid the first two would fade from my system if he took longer to arrive.

I was seated on one of the stools in front of the kitchen's counter when he opened the door. The lights were dimmed and he didn't see me there until he was halfway through the living room and turning into the bedroom's hallway.

Eyes wide, Tyler skidded to a stop. "What the ...?"

I glanced at him as if I hadn't seen him entering. "Oh, hi." I returned my attention to the book I had placed in front of me. Just something to help out with my acting.

He didn't move a muscle. "What are you doing?"

I crossed my legs, exposing more of my skin, and pointed to the book. "I'm reading."

He took two steps toward the kitchen, then stopped again. "Gabriela, what's going on?"

I feigned innocence. "What do you mean?"

His jaw popped. "Usually, you're out with your family or you're preparing dinner. In normal clothes and with the house's lights turned on."

"I ate earlier with Bia," I lied. "So I just decided to take a nice shower, put on some comfortable clothes, and read a book while drinking my fav wine before going to bed."

He swallowed hard. His eyes fell to my legs. "Couldn't you do that in your room?"

"I could, but I wanted to wait for you and ask you how your day was."

He crossed his arms. "Oh, did you?"

The sharpness in his words, the coldness in his eyes. *Meu Deus,* I had been mistaken. He didn't want anything with me. He hated me. Mortification rolled up like a lead ball and dropped into my stomach. I pushed the book and the wine glass aside and hopped off the stool.

"I just thought ..." I mumbled, looking down at the floor. I shook my head once. "I'm sorry." Then, I raced toward my bedroom.

But, as I ran past Tyler, his hand shot out and closed around my wrist. He yanked me back, toward him, making me gasp, then held me close, his hands on my upper arms.

"What is your game?"

I felt like crying. "T-there's no game."

He pushed me back until my back was against the wall. "Then what is it? There has to be an end game here. Otherwise, why would you be wearing this? What do you want from me?"

"*Pelo amor the Deus*, because I thought you wanted me as much as I want you," I shouted and immediately slapped a hand over my mouth. His eyes widened, matching mine.

Taking advantage of his shock, I pushed him back and stepped away from his grasp, intent on burying myself in my bedroom and never coming back.

"Wait." He reached for me again. "I'm just ... I had a bad day and—" He clamped his mouth shut. Instead of words, he used his body. He pushed me back against the wall and didn't stop there. He leaned down, his hips pushing into mine, his hard-on evident. "I do want you," he whispered before his lips crashed on mine. "I want you way too much," he said as his lips moved along mine.

Tyler slipped his hands around my thighs and brought my legs up, pressing his hard, hot body against mine. With a gasp, I wrapped my legs around him. Desire rolled in waves over my body, and I gasped again when Tyler pressed his hips against mine.

He kissed me as if I was his last breath and I melted in his arms. Without warning, he broke the kiss, stepped half a foot back, making me drop my legs, and knelt in front of me.

I frowned at him. "What are you do—*oh!*"

Tyler pulled my panties down, then brought one of my legs around his shoulder, and buried his face in my center. My knees buckled and I cried in surprise and pleasure when his tongue reached my clit. Then, he slipped a finger inside and I spread my hands wide, trying to hold on before I melted to the floor.

Meu Deus, this was too much.

I hadn't had sex in ... I didn't even know when because it had been the last time. For sure over a year, maybe almost two years?

Still, I didn't remember feeling this energy, this pleasure, this heat spreading through me, turning my legs into jelly, and making me feel like I would explode into a thousand pieces.

Tyler's tongue didn't stop. The opposite. Its onslaught sped up. He slipped a second finger inside me of me and started pumping faster and harder. My belly hardened as I tried to prolong it, but I could nothing. I was a goner.

A second later, I moaned again and the climax took me.

While I trembled in pleasure, Tyler scooped me up in his arms and took me to my bedroom. He deposited me in bed, and with his eyes on me, he undressed.

I bit my lower lip and admired as he bared himself. *Meu Deus*, he was beautiful. I had already drooled over his sculpted chest and abdomen, and arms and shoulders, but the rest of him was equally ripped and taut.

Naked, he crawled over me, a small square foil in his hands. Where the hell had he taken that from?

Before I could ask, he tugged at my shirt and asked, "How about we lose this?"

With a soft chuckle, I pulled it over my head. I still had it in my arms when he leaned into me and closed his mouth on my breast. I sucked in a sharp breath. *Meu Deus!* He played with my breasts, licking, sucking, smoothing them with his hands, driving me crazy with each millisecond. But I needed more ...

"*Droga*, can you please just get inside me?"

Tyler pulled back and cocked an eyebrow at me. "The pleasure is all mine." He opened the foil package and rolled the condom over his hard-on. Then, he settled back over me, and looking into my eyes, he slipped inside me.

My hands closed around his upper arms, I held my breath, totally surprised and in paradise. *Meu Deus*, I had forgotten how this could feel, how good sex could be.

Still holding my gaze, Tyler began moving. In and out, in and out. Slow at first, but with each thrust, he moved harder and faster.

All right, I was wrong. Sex had never been this amazing, this great before. I wound my legs around Tyler's hips, wanting more, needing more.

"More," I whispered.

"I can't ..." Tyler slowed down a little. "Gabi, I haven't done this in a while. I won't be able to hold on for long."

For some reason, that confession only made me happy. I hadn't done this in a while too. Did this mean we were both waiting for the other?

"It's okay," I told him. "Just keep going."

One corner of his lips turned up. "Yes, ma'am."

He lowered his mouth to mine and kissed me, his lips moving against mine with urgency and passion. Then he sped up, thrusting inside me harder and faster, just the way I wanted. I held on to him, not breaking the kiss, as I felt the heat build.

I cried out as I climaxed again, and a moment later, Tyler stilled inside me. He groaned, finally breaking the kiss, and his body trembled over mine. He lowered his head to my shoulder and held me tight as he rode down the climax.

After a moment, Tyler rolled to my side and looked at me. "If you had told me yesterday that this would happen today, I would have thought you were out of your mind."

"To be honest, me too." I stared into his eyes. "But I'm glad it did."

He entwined his fingers with mine. "Me too." He leaned into me and pressed his lips on mine in a soft kiss. "Give me a few minutes and we can go again."

I chuckled, but oh man, I was so into that idea.

I DIDN'T EXPECT to wake up alone, but here I was, alone in my bed. Sadness filled my chest and tears brimmed my eyes. *Que porcaria!* I thought we had finally crossed a line last night. A line we both wanted to cross before but were too afraid to.

The only thing I could think of was that he had regretted it. He hadn't liked having sex with me, or he realized he really didn't like *me* after the sex part. Which only made this entire deal worse. How was I going to face him for the next twenty some months?

A sob rose to my throat, but I swallowed it. I wouldn't cry for Tyler.

A loud bang and a ringing noise came from somewhere in the apartment. Frowning, I slid out of my bed, slipped into the same shirt I had on last night, and quietly opened my door. I heard rustling and another bang, but not as loud this time, followed by a hissed curse.

My heart squeezed. What the hell was Tyler up to?

I shut my bedroom door and rested my head on the cool wood. It didn't matter what he was up to. I was determined not to leave this room until he had to leave for work, which should be in ... I glanced at my phone—another forty minutes or so.

I groaned.

All right, what could I do in meanwhile? Take a shower and wash his scent from my body. A shiver rolled down my spine at the thought of his body on mine. Of his weight over me. Of his breath on my skin. Of his mouth in mine ...

Meu Deus, it had felt amazing. Perfect even. It hurt that he hadn't felt the same.

I wiped at the tears forming in my eyes and focused on what I would do to pass the next forty minutes. Besides taking a shower, I could take off my bedding to wash it later. Because I also needed to get rid of his scent in my bed, otherwise I wouldn't be able to sleep another night there.

I sighed.

Another ringing sound came from behind the door and I frowned at it. What the hell? Was he intent on making my life miserable from now on?

Despite my good sense, I opened the door again and spied out. From here, I couldn't see more than the short hallway where the bedrooms were located and a corner of the living room, but now I could hear it better. The mixer was on.

The mixer was on? Why?

Curiosity won and I tiptoed out into the hallway and spied around the corner, into the kitchen.

Tyler, with disheveled hair and wearing nothing but his boxers, was mixing something in a big bowl. Behind him, the coffee machine was on, and there was bacon and eggs in a skillet on the range. On the other side of the kitchen's counter, the table was set with two cups, two glasses, two plates, two sets of silverware ...

What was going on?

He glanced over his shoulder and his eyes widened at me. "Hey." He stopped the mixer. "Did I wake you up?"

I shook my head. "No," I said meekly. "What are you doing?"

I wasn't blind. I could see what he was doing. I just needed him to confirm it, to say it out loud.

"I'm making us breakfast."

Us.

He was making *us* breakfast. A dam broke in my chest and I smiled—feeling relieved and silly and happy in an instant.

Slowly, I walked to the kitchen, but stayed on the other side of the counter. "For a moment there, I thought ..." I shook my head as heat spread over my cheeks.

"Thought what?" Tyler took the bowl to the range.

"It doesn't matter."

With a ladle, he dropped a little of the batter in a skillet—he was making pancakes.

He glanced at me. "Tell me."

"It's silly," I whispered.

He checked on the bacon and the eggs, then turned to me. His eyes wandered over my face, lingering for a moment on my cheeks. "Oh, you woke up and I wasn't there. You thought ... you thought I had left."

I averted my eyes, feeling sillier by the second. "*Bom, sim.* What else was I supposed to think?"

One corner of his lips tugged up. "I wouldn't do that."

"That's the thing. How would I know you wouldn't do that? You could have realized you're disgusted by me and all you could think of was running away." His smile widened. "Are you laughing at me?"

"Not at you, but at your silliness." He went back to the range. He quickly turned off the heat and put all the food on big plates. Instead of taking the plates to the table, he placed them on the counter and looked at me. He was serious again. "I woke up early and decided to cook a nice American breakfast for you. You're always cooking Brazilian stuff for us. I just wanted to repay you."

"Just to repay it?"

He ran a hand over his head. "And it gave me time to think."

"About?"

"Us," he said firmly.

I took a defensive step back, suddenly afraid of what he would say. I might have misinterpreted this entire breakfast thing. Maybe this was his way of saying, "Hey, I had a good time, but I think we should just continue being business partners slash almost friends."

My throat seized.

He reached for my hand and tugged me closer, erasing the distance I had just put between us. "I like you, and after last night, I think you like me too." He placed my hand on his hard, warm chest, then slid his hand down my back, pulling me even closer. He leaned into me. "I want us to give it a try."

"Us?" I croaked, lost into his hazel eyes.

"Yes. Us. For real. Like a real couple."

Then, his lips were on mine and a relieved sigh escaped my throat. I wound my arms around his neck and down his shoulders, feeling the hard muscles underneath his skin.

If it depended on me, breakfast be damned, but ...

"Sorry." I pulled back. "I know you have to go to work. We should have breakfast so you can go."

He groaned, brushing his lips on mine. "I should feel guilty about it, but I honestly don't. Today, I'm going to be late for work."

His hand clasped my nape as his mouth claimed mine. Without breaking the kiss, Tyler pushed me back, slow step by slow step, until we were back in my bedroom and on my bed.

49

TYLER

I COULD HAVE STAYED in bed with her all day and I was sure I wouldn't get bored. Maybe tired, but I could do tired with her. I just needed to lie down beside her, hold her tight, and sleep with her skin pressed to mine.

Heaven.

But I was also a responsible guy and I was already thirty minutes late.

Under the table, Gabi's toes grazed my calf. "Thanks for breakfast."

I shrugged. "It's not like the *carreteiro* and the *pastel* and all the other amazing things you make."

She grinned at me. "It was great."

I stared at her pretty face, at her wide smile. She was my wife. My fucking wife! This gorgeous, insanely hot woman was my wife. Damn. We had come back from the bedroom not ten minutes ago and I was already hard again and thinking of the next time I would be able to take her to bed.

Shit.

"You're welcome." I took a long breath. "But now I really need to go." I stood and took a few plates to the sink. I started organizing it all, but Gabi appeared by my side and took them from me.

"I can do this. Go get ready."

"Are you sure? I don't mind." She waved me off. I leaned into her and placed a quick peck on her soft lips. "Thanks."

I took a quick shower, all the while wishing Gabi was under the warm water with me. I would love to press her against the tiles and take her right here.

Whoa, what the hell was I thinking? I was more than up for giving us a try, but there was no reason to go fast. I had to tell my mind to slow down. But my body didn't listen. Just thinking about Gabi being in the shower with me had given me a massive hard-on. Holy shit, if I really didn't have to go to work now, I would have walked out this shower dripping wet and found her.

It was okay, though. Hadn't we just agreed to become a real couple? Tonight I could have her again. I would have her again. To hell with going slow. I wanted her and I wanted it fast.

When I finished my shower, the kitchen was organized and clean, and Gabi had put on jeans.

I pouted. "I like you without the pants better."

Red spread through her cheeks. "I'm sure you do." I walked to her and placed my hands on her waist. "I'll stop by the hospital after work, but I should be back around six. Call me if you need anything."

She glanced at me from under those long lashes. "Are you planning on taking a lunch break?"

"Yes. Why?"

"I haven't much going on, unfortunately, and I was wondering if you wanted me to—"

I shut her up by brushing my lips on hers. It was hard staying away from her. "I would really like that."

She smiled at me. "Text me when you're free. I'll meet up with you."

"Will do." Then, I wrapped my arms around her and pulled her into me, pressing her body against mine, wishing I had more time so I could enjoy more of her. But I was contented with kissing her. "I'll see you later," I said.

I forced my feet to move and rushed out of the apartment before I didn't leave at all. On the way to the clinic, I called the hospital to check on Dad. Everything was normal—he was tired and weak, but hanging on. And at work, I lied that I had gotten a flat on the way. I felt guilty about the lie, but not much. It had been worth it.

"What are you smiling about?" Lena asked.

I lifted my head from the paperwork I was doing. "What?"

"You're smiling. You rarely smile and certainly not when doing paperwork. What's up?"

I forced my lips to relax, though I still felt like smiling. "It's nothing."

She harrumphed, and after a I-know-you're-lying glare, she walked out of the room.

I exhaled loudly and checked my phone. There were no texts from Gabi. She never texted me before, outside of important stuff, why would she start now? Besides, I would be the one texting her soon to arrange for our lunch date.

A lunch date.

I was going on a freaking lunch date with my wife, and for some reason that made me incredibly pleased.

If only all things in my life were this easy and felt this good.

IN THE MIDDLE of the week, I went to check on Branca. I had texted Gabi, letting her know I was coming, in case she could too, but she had gone to a practice with her brother and cousins, and Kelsey, the girl she hoped to play with in the future.

I really hoped things worked out for Gabi. I hoped she found two other girls and they found a sponsor, and they won tournaments. Seeing her happy would make me happy too.

Happier.

I hadn't felt this content and satisfied in a long time. The only thing that could make this all better was if my father suddenly healed and his cancer was gone. But I knew that even a miracle couldn't save him now. All I wanted was for him to hang on for as long as he could.

At the ranch, Hannah was getting a group ready for a trail ride, as usual. She waved at me from a distance and I waved back. She was cool, just like the rest of Gabi's family. I had resisted in the beginning, but there was no denying. They were all good people and cared about each other. It was great seeing them all together, and even if I wasn't too sure of what was really happening yet, Gabi and I were a real couple now. I was part of this family too.

With a small grin on my lips, I walked into the stables and went directly to Branca's stall. She saw me coming and came to the door.

I stopped in front of her and caressed under her chin. "Hey, girl. Ready to exercise a little?"

She nodded her head up and down and I laughed, as if she had really answered at me. I grabbed reins from the tack room and placed them over her head. I opened the stall door and pulled her out. "Let's go have some fun."

50

GABI

THE FIRST WEEK of being a real couple had been awkward, and great, and it had flown by too fast. Before I had cooked because I needed to. I mean, we had to eat, right? But now I cooked because I wanted to please him. Like this evening. Tyler had already left the clinic and had gone to visit his father at the hospital, but when he got home, dinner would be ready.

I smiled at the sauce as I stirred the pot with a wooden spoon.

My phone rang. I grabbed from the counter and, without looking at the caller ID, answered it.

"Hello."

"Gabi, hey, it's Melissa. How are you?"

I frowned. Melissa? It took me three seconds to remember her. The girl from Florida who was being scouted by a club in England. How did she get my number? "Oh, hey. I'm ... doing fine. Surprise by your call, though. How are you?"

"I'm great and I have great news."

I stopped stirring the sauce pot and focused on the call. "Hm, what do you mean?"

"Kelsey told you I don't want to move to England, right? There are a couple of clubs that have a women's team here in Florida, but they don't want any other teams, but well, I've been practically harassing a few clubs that don't have teams and I might have found one to sponsor a new team!"

I leaned on the counter. "What? That's great!" That meant she wouldn't have to go to England.

"Yeah, it is. The only thing that is bothering me right now is that they don't want just four girls. They want six to eight, so they can rotate between them. But my idea is to accept their offer, and with time, convince them to separate the eight girls into two teams."

"That sounds like a great idea. I'm glad for you." I barely knew her and she was calling me to let me know she had found a club? Good for her. But I was a little jealous.

She chuckled. "Girl, I'm calling you because I told them about you. They want you on their team."

My knees wobbled. "W-what?"

"Yes!" She chuckled some more. "The director said he still wants to see you play but by the sound of it, only if you mess up really bad would they withdraw the offer."

My chest felt like it would burst with excitement. "*Meu Deus*, that's ... incredible!"

"Right? I'm gonna give him your number, okay? He's going to call you with all the details and the offer and such."

"*Sim*, yes, please do."

"Awesome. Expect a call from him tomorrow, then. I told him about Kelsey too and I think he's going to call her too." She let out something that sounded like a squeal. "Can you imagine, girl? Our own polo team? What a dream come true!"

"It is."

"Well, I have to go now. Call me tomorrow after the director, John Cross, calls you. I want to know all the details."

"Will do."

"I can't wait for you to move down here and for our team to start winning all the tournaments. Talk to you tomorrow."

"*Tchau*," I whispered on the phone as reality set in.

Meu Deus. Move to Florida?

I couldn't. For many reasons. One, I had moved to the U.S. not only to play polo but also to be near my family who lived in California. Two, what about Tyler? With his father here, sick and tied to the hospital, he would never move down there with me, and because of the green card, I had to stay close to him. Our interview with the immigration office was scheduled for next week. As far as we knew, they would keep monitoring us during the next two years. If they found out I was living away from my husband, chances were they would pick up it was a fake marriage and deport me.

Even though it wasn't a fake marriage anymore.

The sound of keys jingling broke my daze, and I turned to the door in time to see Tyler opening and entering the apartment.

"Hey, you," he said, locking the door again. He walked up to me and only stopped when he was glued to me. He pressed his lips on mine in a soft kiss. "How was your day?"

"It was okay," I said, trying to think this thought. Should I tell him about Florida? I probably should. But then what? It wouldn't matter now, would it? My mind was a knot of thoughts.

"Mine was okay too," he said. "Though my father wasn't doing too well this evening."

"Oh no."

And just like that, I pushed all thoughts of Florida out of my mind. Right now, Tyler and his father were more important. Telling him about it could wait.

I served dinner and we ate while we talked, then after we cleaned the kitchen, we snuggled on the couch to watch a movie, me with a glass of wine and him with a beer.

But we didn't make it halfway through the movie. I think we got to twenty minutes before our clothes were all spread around the living room and we turned the TV off.

"I DIDN'T SEE any pictures of you two together before your wedding," officer Brody said. He was seated across the table from Gabi and me, with our thick file folder open in front of him. He didn't look all that impressed with us.

"It's because we didn't take many pictures before," Gabi said, her voice even and calm. We had talked about this many times already. Even if we started faking this marriage, it wasn't fake anymore. We had nothing to hide, nothing to fear. "We were hiding our relationship from my family because I didn't think they would understand. That's the only reason we haven't taken many pictures and why we didn't post any online either."

He leveled a look at her. "And why were you hiding your relationship from your family?"

"Because ... we didn't think it was serious. Not in the beginning. I didn't want them asking me about that guy from the pictures when, in truth, I didn't know if I would ever see him again." She glanced at me. "But I saw him again. Several times. And things got serious pretty fast."

I reached across our chairs with my open hand. With a smile, Gabi entwined her fingers on mine. I squeezed tight.

From there, the interview was easy. Officer Brody asked her only a handful of questions we had studied before. Where we lived, for how long, who cooked, who cleaned, who liked what kind of movies, what was our favorite color, and other silly stuff.

He hadn't given us an answer, but we didn't get bad vibes from the man, so we thought Gabi had passed the interview. We decided to go out for lunch at our favorite local diner to celebrate before I had to go back to work.

After ordering our food, we talked.

"I'm going to stop at the hospital before going home," I reminded her. My father wasn't doing well and I wanted to spend every spare second I had with him.

"I know. Text me when you're leaving the hospital. I'll get dinner ready."

I lifted our entwined hands and kissed her palm. "You're too good to me."

Her cheeks gained a rosy tint. "You're biased."

The waitress brought out our huge burgers and fries.

After a few bites, I noticed Gabi could barely chew because she was smiling.

"Happy?" I asked.

"Very." She looked at me from under her eyelashes. "And you?"

"Me too." I narrowed my eyes at her. "You aren't planning on divorcing me after the two years, right?"

"Maybe." She smiled. "I'll see if how you treat me."

"I plan on treating you right. Actually, better than right."

"I like that plan."

As we were leaving the restaurant, my phone rang. Absent-mindedly, I picked it up and glanced at the screen. And halted.

"It's from the hospital," I told Gabi. She squeezed my other hand. "Hello?" I answered.

"Tyler, it's nurse Annie." Her voice was cold. Tired. "You should come over."

I swallowed hard and kept the worries locked in my chest. There was only one reason for her to be calling me. "I'll be right there."

52

"How is he doing?" Gui asked.

I glanced to the armchair Tyler had been seated in since we came back from the funeral. He hadn't moved an inch since. In fact, he had barely moved at all since getting the call from nurse Annie two days ago.

We had immediately left for the hospital—I drove because Tyler was nervous. We got there and the doctor was waiting for us.

"He only has a few hours left," he said, his tone solemn, dejected.

Thankfully, Charlie woke up long enough to say goodbye to his son. But Tyler's world blew up after that. The doctor assured us he wasn't in any pain, but the sixteen hours we spent at the hospital were painful to Tyler. And to me. I hated seeing him suffering like that. I hated not being able to do something to help.

His father died in the middle of the night, while Tyler watched over him like a hawk. Tyler went into a stasis mode and I took over everything—I talked to the doctors and nurses, I called the funeral place and arranged everything, I called my family and let them know about the funeral details.

There were only a few people at the funeral. My guess was that either word hadn't spread that Charlie had died, or he didn't have many friends later in his life.

After, my family and a few friends of Charlie and Tyler came back to the apartment with us. And since then, Tyler looked like a statue dressed in all black and seated in the armchair.

"Not good," I said, my voice barely above a whisper. "He hasn't said much since we went to the hospital. I know he hasn't slept yet and he barely ate."

Bia wrapped her arm around my shoulders. "And how are you?"

I offered her a tight-lip smile, showing her I appreciated the concern. "I spent a lot of time at Charlie's bedside these past few months, but I didn't really know him." I sighed. "But I'm hurting for Tyler." I glanced at him again. Still in the same position, staring at the same blank spot on the wall. "He knew this would happen eventually, but I guess one is never really prepared for it."

"We're here if you need us, you know that, right?" Hannah said.

I nodded. "I know. *Obrigada.*"

Ri leaned closer and whispered, "You haven't told him about Florida yet, have you?"

Florida.

I hadn't told Tyler about it, but I had told my family about it, because I wanted some guidance. Who was best to help with polo things than the guys?

As agreed, I had spoken on the phone with John Cross, the polo director of the club in Florida, and his offer was pretty great. We did talk about having two teams in the future, which made me feel better about this whole thing, but in the end, I told him I had to think about it. He sounded a little upset about it, but agreed to it. He said he would call me again in two weeks to find out my answer.

I already knew my answer, but I guess I was still hoping for a miracle.

"No," I finally answered. "I guess I won't."

"Why?" Pedro asked. "I don't want to sound like a jerk, but you said he wouldn't move with you because of his father. Well, now he can."

I knew that but ... "That's asking too much. His father just died. He needs time to process, to adjust. I can't invite him to move with me to another state."

"I know, I know," Pedro said. "It's just ... we know how much you were waiting for an opportunity like that."

"True, but one of the reasons I moved here was to stay close to you guys. Living in Florida would be like living in Brazil. I would be able to see you guys only a few times per year."

"But you'll be living your dream," Leo said.

I sneaked another peek at Tyler. Was my dream of playing professional polo more important than him? Was my dream more important than being with him and giving him strength during this difficult phase? I didn't think so.

I gasped, realizing something too important to ignore. My chest hurt with the clarity and certainty of it.

I loved Tyler. I loved Tyler way more than I loved polo and that was big. Huge.

"But the man she loves will stay behind," Hilary said. I stared at her, my eyes wide. She smiled at me. "It's written all over your face."

My cheeks heated and I was sure I was a deep shade of red. "*Bom*, it's true and that settles it. I ... I love Tyler—" It was a relief to say it and finally meant it. "—and he needs me now more than ever. I won't be going to Florida."

"I understand," Ri said.

And that was the end of that conversation.

The other people left soon after, and then my family left too.

I cleaned up a little of the mess in the kitchen, prepared a sandwich, grabbed a drink, and placed it on the coffee table in the living room. I sat on the arm of Tyler's chair and gently touched his arm.

"Ty?" I called. He didn't move. He didn't blink. "Tyler?" I asked louder.

He snapped his head at me and stared at me as if seeing me for the first time in a long time. "Hey," he said, his voice rough.

I pointed to the tray on the coffee table. "I've brought you something to eat."

"I'm not hungry."

I sighed. "Then let's go to bed."

He didn't say anything. I stood and took his hands in mine. Thankfully, he didn't fight me, and when I tugged, he rose. Hand in hand, I guided him to our bedroom. I pulled off his jacket, then he helped me with his shirt and pants. I handed him his pajamas and he put them on while I changed from my dress to my pajamas.

Together, we crawled into bed. I lay on my back and he wrapped his arms around me, his head resting on my chest, as if he needed to hear my heartbeat. My eyes filled with tears again as I wound my arms around him and pulled him tight against me.

We didn't say anything else and soon, I felt his breathing slow down. Only then, I let the tears I had been holding in the entire day fall.

53

TYLER

I DIDN'T WANT to go, but Gabi insisted. As usual.

It had been only one week since my father had died, and I still felt like a zombie walking around. I was scheduled to go back to work in a couple more days, but I was thinking about coming up with some other excuse to miss another week. I didn't feel ready for anything.

"It's just dinner," Gabi said. "Like they always do. We haven't gone to one in ages. Besides, it would be good to get out of the apartment a little."

I groaned, knowing this battle was lost.

So, I showered and got dressed and let her drive us to her brother's apartment.

In the car, I glanced at her.

Damn, she had been the epitome of kindness and patience this past week. Even when I was acting like a jerk and didn't deserve it. She stayed with me, she calmed me down, she cooked for me, she massaged my back out of nowhere, she hugged me tight many, many times per day, she forced to go on a short walk with her every day so I wouldn't be stuck in the apartment, rotting away. She always had nice words and small smiles and gentle hands.

I had no idea what I had done to deserve all of that, but I was glad she was here with me. I couldn't imagine not having her in my life anymore. She was now everything to me. Everything.

Holy shit, I was really falling for her.

I knew this could happen. I knew this would happen. I just thought it would take more time. But really, with the way she was, the way she looked, how she acted, how she took care of me, how she had taken care of my father, her plans and ideas and principles ... I was surprised it took this long. Actually, it took me this long to *realize* I was falling for her. Deep down, I had known for quite some time.

Luck and circumstance might have brought us together, but our relationship evolved quickly, and right now, I was sure Gabi was the one.

For some reason, a deep fear of losing her filled my chest, and it was suddenly too hard to breathe. I had just lost someone I loved; I couldn't bear the thought of losing her too.

Needing to touch her, I reached across the seats and placed my hand on her thigh.

She looked at me. "Are you okay?"

I forced a small smile. "I'm with you, so yeah, I'm okay."

Her lips curled up in a grin and my heart squeezed. Yup, I wasn't falling for her. I had already fallen.

At her brother's apartment, everyone was so nice, it almost made me sick. I wanted to shrink into myself, to turn back and go back to my bed with Gabi in my arms, where I could hide from the world and pretend everything was all right.

But for Gabi, I greeted them all as best as I could, and I was introduced to three new guys I didn't know, or couldn't remember. Malcolm, Justin, and Reese were players of the Knight House, one of Montenegro's biggest competitors.

"What are they doing here?" Gabi asked in a whisper.

Hannah rolled her eyes. "Apparently, they are Ri's new party buddies."

"You know, they are all single like him," Hil added.

I glanced at the living room. Ricardo, Malcolm, Reese, and Justin were standing behind the couch, with drinks in their hands, and absently watching the TV while talking.

"It's just so odd to see them here," Gabi said.

The girls continued talking about how the three guys had just been automatically added to the group by Ri and they really didn't like it. I wasn't in the mood to listen to that, so I made my way to the living room.

"Want something to drink?" Garrett asked as I sank down on the couch. Pedro and Leo already had the joysticks in their hands and resumed their game.

"Yes, hm, beer will be fine," I said.

He brought me a beer and plopped down beside me. "Next one, you go get it. You're practically family now."

Family. Gabi was my only family right now. And these people were her family. It would be nice to actually belong to their family. To have more people to care about. And despite everything, I could easily see me having a good time with the guys and video games, and the horses, and the monster truck races they always talked so much about.

I looked over my shoulder. Gabi was in the kitchen with Bia, Hannah, and Hilary. She smiled at something Bia said, then drank a sip of her Jack and Coke.

My heart squeezed.

This beautiful, caring woman was my wife.

Tears burned behind my throat and I swallowed them. What the fuck? I was like a sappy romantic movie right now. Too emotional, too raw, too wounded. I knew it was all because I had lost someone important to me and my emotions were all screwed.

I sighed. This phase would pass, but I knew the love I felt for Gabi would stay there, stronger than ever. She was my anchor now, the only thing I had left.

"Your turn." Leo shoved the joystick on my hand. I started passing it back to him but stopped. What the hell. This was my family now, right? And they were trying to distract me, to make me feel a little better. Well, I would take advantage of that.

I grabbed the remote with both hands and scooted closer to the middle of the couch. "Great."

The time flew while I played with the guys.

Later, Leo found a polo ball beside the couch, and he started dribbling it like he was playing soccer. Then Gabi came from the kitchen with the broom and easily took the ball from him. She dribbled past him as the others cheered, and she sent the ball under a sofa table along the wall, as if she had made a goal.

The guys cheered and the girls laughed.

And I smiled for the first time in days.

"You're just too good," Ri said with a smile.

"Dude, you're a natural," Garrett said. "It's a shame you won't accept Florida's offer."

My smile faded. I frowned at him. "Offer from Florida? What are you talking about?" The room went quiet, the paused video game music the only sound in the entire apartment. I twisted around and glanced at Gabi over the couch. "What is he talking about?"

She shot a glare to Garrett, then looked at me. "It's nothing. You shouldn't worry about it."

"Why shouldn't I worry about something that will kill your dreams?"

She sighed. "I got an offer from a club in Florida. But I knew you wouldn't move there with me, especially now, so ... I declined."

I rose to my feet and faced her. She got an offer from a club and didn't tell me? Worse, she had considered moving to Florida. The question was, did she consider moving down there without me? A deep pain like I had never felt cut through my chest. It was a deeper pain than losing my father. Different. Like the hurt of being betrayed. Or being pushed aside.

"You just forgot about it, because giving up on your dreams or the possibility of moving down to Florida isn't something worth telling your husband, is it?"

"Tyler, I—"

"Husband?" Gui interrupted her, his voice a gasp of surprise. "Did you just say husband?"

Gabi looked down at her feet.

I was already feeling betrayed. Why not add fuel to the flames? "Yes, husband. Gabi and I were never engaged. We never even dated. She made me a deal and I accepted. We got married so she could get a green card."

There was a loud collective gasp.

"I knew it," Gui hissed. "I knew it. My gut told me so. But Gabi insisted it wasn't and ..." He tilted his head, looking from me to Gabi and back at me. "I thought you two really liked each other, so I forgot about that."

"We do like each other," Gabi said. "We didn't plan on it, but it happened."

I was swimming in anger and frustration. Did we really like each other? Did she really like me?

"And what did you get out of it?" Gui asked in a bark.

"Money. I got a lot of money. With all my father's treatments, I was drowning in debt, still am."

Gui cursed. "You son of a bitch." He turned on Gabi. "I can't believe you did this."

"Gui, shut up." She waved her brother off and turned to me. "Ty ... your father wasn't doing well, and I knew you wouldn't go with me. I didn't want you to worry. That's why I never said anything."

"But you're giving up on your dream, for what?"

She stared at me. "I thought that was obvious." I snorted. She was taking care of me, stupid me, while she could be living her dream of playing professional polo. I bet that if my father hadn't been sick, if I hadn't been vulnerable, she would have left. "Besides, we had to make it look like our marriage was real. Is real. I couldn't live away from my husband. The immigration office would find out and take back my green card."

That was the nail on the coffin. She had blatantly admitted she stayed because she wanted her green card. It wasn't because of me. It wasn't because she liked me.

Without a word, I whirled around and marched out the door.

54

Tyler ran out the apartment and I ran after him.

Until Gui grabbed me by my wrist and pulled me back.

"Gabi, wait," he said, his voice none too gentle.

I jerked my arm back. "Let me go."

"Husband? Really?"

I groaned. "That's not important right now." The anger in his eyes told me otherwise. For the first time, I looked at the expressions of my family and noted all of them looked a little surprised, except for Bia and Garrett who knew the truth. *Merda.* I sighed. I didn't have time for this. "I'm sorry we lied to you."

Gui pointed to the door. "You gave money to that guy!"

"That guy was practically your friend five minutes ago. He hasn't changed, Gui. He was in a bad place when we met. His father was dying and he was buried in bills. He had a crappy apartment and didn't have a decent meal or a decent night sleep in too long. I offered him the only thing I had. Money to cover his debts. Money that he didn't get because we divided into three parts." I clenched my hands, the rage growing inside me. "Tyler is a great guy with a kind heart. He didn't use me. For all accounts, I used him. Until we actually let down our guards and realized we liked each other." I gulped "I love him, Gui, for real, and right now, I'm going after him to try to fix this mess."

Stunned, my brother let go of my arm and I scurried out of the apartment.

When I got to the sidewalk, Tyler was already half a block ahead of me.

I ran after him. "Tyler, wait."

He glanced over his shoulder. "What do you want?"

I halted in front of him, causing him to stop. "I want to talk to you. I want to explain."

He crossed his arms. "It's okay, Gabriela." I flinched from the use of my full name. "You don't owe me any explanation. This is a fake marriage after all, isn't it?"

"No, it's not, not anymore, and you know that." I edged closer to him. "I don't get why you're so upset about this. I'm not going to Florida."

"Because of your precious green card."

"No, *droga*. Because of you. I don't want to leave."

"Right, because that's what you said upstairs."

"What?"

"Before I left." He jerked his chin to the building behind us. "You said you knew I wouldn't want to go, and you couldn't go without me otherwise you would lose your green card."

I gaped at him. *Droga*, I had said that, but it wasn't only that. That wasn't the main reason at all. "Tyler, I—"

"Enough, Gabriela." He took one large step back. "I don't want to hear any more of it. Ever." He strutted past me.

"Where are you going?"

"I don't know," he said, walking away.

I watched as he practically ran from me.

When I couldn't see him anymore, I walked back to my car and went back to our apartment. Alone.

I DIDN'T SLEEP WELL, and when I got up, I felt worse. Tyler wasn't in my bed with me, or in his previous bedroom, or anywhere else in the apartment.

Where could he be? Where had he slept? Had he slept at all?

I tried to rein in all my worry. It was okay. Tyler was an adult and he probably just needed some time to cool off.

Instead of biting my nails off, I decided to make breakfast and start my day. Hopefully, Tyler would walk in soon, we would make up, and everything would be all right.

But as the hours went by, nothing happened. I paced the apartment, staring at the door, waiting for him. And he never came. I grabbed my phone and almost called him, but always gave up. He needed time. I had to give him time. He would come home soon.

Though I had no news of Tyler, I had gotten several texts from Garrett, apologizing for letting the Florida thing slip. He didn't know that Tyler didn't know. Bia also texted, asking me to forgive Garrett. I texted them both back, letting them know I wasn't mad. It was okay. It wasn't Garrett's fault. It was mine. I should have told Tyler sooner, even if it was just to let him know about it, so there were no secrets between us.

The guilt inside me and my anxiety wasn't helping.

So, instead of waiting for Tyler at the apartment, I wrote a quick note for him and left it in the kitchen counter, and went to Hannah's ranch.

It was almost noon when I got there and Hannah was finishing up with a riding group.

"Hey, you," she said as I entered the stable. "Came to see Branca?"

"*Sim*. I'm gonna take her for a ride. Is that okay?"

"Sure. There are no groups out right now, so you can choose any trail."

I stopped by Branca's stall. The mare saw me and her ears perked up. She came to me and pushed her muzzle into my belly.

I smiled and ran my hands under her chin. "At least someone is happy to see me."

Hannah glanced at me. "That doesn't sound good. How is Tyler?"

I shrugged. "I don't know. I was able to catch him after I left Gui's place, but he just walked away and I haven't seen him since."

She frowned. "Have you called him?"

"Not yet. I'm trying to give him some space." I ran my hand along Branca's neck. "How was Gui after I left?"

"Upset. But we talked to him. He was mostly upset about the money, more than the lie. But he'll be okay. Like Tyler, he just needs a little time to process it all. I'm sure he'll understand."

"Do you understand?"

She paused. "I think I do. Leo and I talked about it on our way back here last night, and we both concluded that we would have probably done the same in your shoes. What you did was nothing wrong. However, that doesn't mean you didn't lie to your family. And that's gonna take a while to fix."

I sighed. "I know."

She patted my arm. "It'll all be okay, though. I'm sure of it."

Unfortunately, I wasn't so sure.

Hannah stayed with me while I tacked Branca, giving me an update on her progress.

"She's doing pretty good," she said. "It has been a while since Tyler has been here to work on her, with his father's death and all, but Jimmy and I have been giving her some special attention. I can't say it's as effective as Tyler's therapy, but at least she was moving a little and putting that foot to good use."

"That's nice of you. Thanks."

She smiled at me. "My pleasure." She handed me some reins.

"Here. I've gotta make a phone call, then check on the horses in the other stable. I'll check on you and Branca later."

I nodded. "Thanks."

She walked out the stable. I slid some reins over Branca's head and gently pulled her out in the arena. For the next half hour, I walked around the arena beside Branca, gently exercising her and strengthening her hurt leg while my mind took off.

I thought about everything and anything.

I thought about Branca and her leg. I thought about Tyler and his therapy. I thought about Gui being mad at me again. About the offer from the Florida club. He would call again soon and I had to tell him my answer. It hadn't changed since the argument last night.

I thought about Tyler and our situation the most.

He hadn't showed up at home all night and morning. I had no idea where he was, and even though I knew it was crazy, I couldn't stop my brain from imagining him getting wasted in some bar and then ending up in some random girl's bed. My stomach turned each time that thought crossed my mind.

I knew he wouldn't go to Florida with me, but now I wasn't even sure he wanted to see me ever again. Apparently not, otherwise he would have come home again, wouldn't he? But what did that mean? Our relationship was over? Did he regret it? Our marriage was fake again?

It was too much, too confusing.

I wanted to fight for him but I needed a signal first. I wouldn't lay my heart open only to have him stomp all over it. If there was no sign ... then, all I wanted to do was run away. I wanted to give up on everything. If he decided the deal was over, then I had no choice but to give up on everything.

And why the hell did I care about this deal so much? The deal wasn't more important than he was. What did I have to do to prove that to him?

As if sensing my unease, Branca nudged my shoulder with her muzzle.

"Hey, pretty girl." I reached up and caressed her forehead. "How are you doing? Feeling better? I hope so. I can't wait to see you galloping again."

She shook her head, as if saying she wasn't in any hurry to gallop again. I chuckled.

I took her for one more lap, then hosed her off, put her in her stall, made sure she had plenty of water and food, and left while Hannah was talking to some of her clients who had just arrived. Not feeling like chatting, I just waved at her and she waved back at me.

My heart was in my throat the entire drive home. It sank to my stomach when I parked my car into my parking space and Tyler's beat-up truck wasn't beside it.

Droga.

It was late afternoon. Where could he be? He couldn't avoid me forever, could he?

I dragged my feet into the apartment and gave in. I pulled out my phone and finally called Tyler. It rang several times, but he didn't pick up. I sat down on a stool in front of the kitchen counter and watched the clock on the microwave. Once ten minutes had passed, I called again. And again it rang, but no one picked up. I repeated the process three more times.

Disappointment mixed with anger and worry. I didn't know what was worse ... to imagine that something had happened to him or to let it sink in that he really was avoiding me.

I was about to call him a sixth time when my phone rang. My heart deflated when I saw it wasn't his numbers—it was from Florida.

Frowning, I answered. "Hello?"

"Miss Fernandes? This is John Cross. How are you?"

The polo director of the club in Florida. Perfect timing. I inhaled deeply. "I'm good," I lied. "How about you?"

"I'm doing great." He paused. "Sorry for going directly at it, but I've been pretty busy lately. My to-do list is miles long. So, do I get a yes on my offer?"

Droga. I wanted to say yes, but I couldn't. I didn't expect Tyler to change his mind, forgive me, and decide to move to Florida with me. And going without him wasn't an option. I would lose my green card and would have to leave the country.

"I'm sorry, Mr. Cross, but I can't accept it. I want to, but I can't go right now."

Silence. "I was hoping you would say yes." His tone changed from cheery to cold in one breath.

"I'm really sorry."

"No, it's fine. We have plenty of girls around here who want to play professional polo. I'm sure I can find a good one to fill the spot I was holding for you."

I flinched with the venom in his words. "That's great," I forced myself to say. "Good luck with everything."

I hung up before he could say anything else that made me want to cry.

Too many things made me want to cry in the past few days. I didn't know how much longer I could keep holding on.

55

WHENEVER MY PHONE RANG, I thought it was Gabi. Several times, it was, but sometimes it was just people and companies asking me to pay my bills. Unfortunately, most of the first installment of the deal was gone and I still had too many bills to pay.

Shit.

"You don't look too good," Lena said.

I ignored her. She had been on my case since she got at the vet clinic early this morning and found me sleeping on the couch in the backroom. I still had a few days off, but I had given up on them now.

Lena had said I looked like shit, and I bet I smelled like it too, so I went to the nearest Walmart, bought the cheapest jeans and T-shirt and underwear they had in my size, came back to the clinic, and took a quick shower in the bathroom in the backroom.

I poured more coffee into my mug.

She halted by my side and reached for the coffeepot. "You know, running away from your problems won't make them disappear."

I glared at her. "It seems to be working so far."

"I'm just saying." She shrugged. "Everybody has trouble in paradise, Tyler. Don't think it's always perfect."

"I didn't ask for your opinion."

She leveled a hard look at me. "I'm trying to be nice. To be helpful. But apparently, you're back to your pre-Gabriela angry phase. Let me tell you a secret: everyone liked you better during your Gabriela phase."

She strutted out of the backroom.

Shit. Even I liked myself better during my Gabriela phase.

Was that phase over? I glanced at my phone. I didn't know.

I didn't even know why I was so mad at her. She said she wouldn't go, but until when? Until the two-year period was over? Then, she could divorce me and go to Florida and play polo? What if she got an offer from another country? That was a possibility. She had come to the U.S. to play polo, so that was what she would do. That was her priority. Not me. Not our marriage.

I didn't want to fall even more for her and have my heart broken. It was already breaking with the idea of losing her, of letting her go. But my mind kept telling me to avoid getting even more hurt, I should let her go now.

But if I let her go, she would lose her beloved green card. Maybe ... maybe we could rent another apartment in the same building, a one-bedroom one, under some alias name. I could move into this apartment and then we could pretend we lived together, but hopefully we would barely bump into each other in the hallway.

Damn it. It all sounded so fucking insane.

My mind hurt and my emotions swirled inside me, making me confused. I didn't know what to think, I didn't know what to do.

And that was the reason that when she called again later that night, I ignored it again. I just didn't know what to say to her right now.

So, as the night went by and the clinic was filled with only our patients' sounds, I settled back into the worn couch in the back-room, knowing I would barely sleep, and if I slept, I would wake up with a pain in my neck, but I didn't have it in me to do anything else right now.

I was hurt from losing my father, and I had just lost someone else I cared about too much. The only other person I thought could be my everything.

I felt stupid.

It was better if I stayed away, and worked every waking hour I could to keep my mind busy, otherwise I would sink into a dark world I wasn't prepared to face yet.

56

GABI

FOURTH DAY WAKING up with no Tyler in sight. I checked my phone. No calls, no messages.

I forced myself to get up from bed, to make breakfast and eat something, to shower and put on some real clothes. Then I waited.

Should I call him again? What if something had really happened to him? Worry won out and I decided on a new approach. At this time, he should be at the vet clinic, so, instead of calling him again, I called the clinic.

"B+D veterinary clinic. This is Lena. How may I help you?"

"Hi, hm, is Tyler Reid there?"

There was three seconds of silence. "Is this Gabriela?"

"Hm, yes."

The woman sighed. "Yes, he is here."

I let out a long breath. "So, he's okay."

"If brooding and driving everyone crazy is your definition of fine, then yes, he is." I almost felt sorry for her. "Want me to transfer the call to him?"

He hadn't been answering any of my calls before, why would

he answer me now? "No, it's okay. I just wanted to know if he was okay. Thanks."

I hung up and stared at my phone.

So. Tyler was fine. He was at the vet clinic. Only God knew where he had spent the previous four nights—I flinched, thinking of the possibilities—but at least he wasn't hurt and forgotten at some hospital.

Tears sprung to my eyes.

He really was avoiding me. He hated me and wanted to be away from me.

Polo and green card weren't worth it anymore.

Never had imagined I would care for someone so much that I put them before polo. I knew that maybe it would happen someday, when I was older and ready to settle down, when my polo career was already solid and successful.

All of this had started as a sham, so I never considered I would push polo to second on my priority's list before I even had a chance on it.

But I couldn't fight the feelings in my heart.

I picked up my phone again and called the immigration lawyer. She wasn't available, so I left a message for her, asking her to call me later, but I asked the secretary for another kind of lawyer. She gave me a name and address and I didn't waste time.

I called the lawyer's office and offered an insane amount of money to be squeezed into the lawyer's tight schedule. The secretary didn't sound happy to put me in an appointment for tomorrow morning.

With nothing else to do, I did two things: I went online and bought an expensive airplane ticket to Brazil for tomorrow night, and I started packing.

I was breaking down in a million pieces, my heart was breaking, but I had to be practical here. I had given Tyler time to find me and he didn't.

When I entered the lawyer's office the next morning, he didn't seem happier than his secretary, but I didn't care about his opinion as long as he did his job.

"Are you sure about this?" he asked before taking my documents.

"Yes," I said loud and clear. "I want to file for divorce."

TYLER

I IMMERSED myself in work and the days flew by.

The clinic had closed so I went to check on two dogs who were spending the night with us. Me. Because I was planning on sleeping here again. This would be the fifth night. Damn, I would have to go to Walmart again and buy more underwear. And maybe another T-shirt.

Lena appeared at the door. "So what? Are you living here now?"

I groaned. "Can't you leave me alone?"

"I wasn't going to tell you, but I think that if it was me, I would have liked to know." I glanced at her over my shoulder, wondering what the hell was she talking about. "Gabriela called yesterday morning. She wanted to know if you were okay." She shook her head. "I don't know what the hell happened, but it seems you two aren't in a good place, which means you two were in a good place when together. So fix it."

She whirled around and left the room. Moments later, I heard the front door closing and the lock turning.

Shit.

I hadn't thought Gabi would call the clinic. Not that I cared. I mean, I wasn't hiding from her, I just didn't want to talk to her, not yet.

I grabbed a cup of coffee and sat down on the couch that had become my bed.

What the hell was I doing? Avoiding the woman I liked—hell, *loved*—because I was too hurt? I sighed, wishing my father was still alive, so I could go to the hospital instead and stay there with him, so I could talk to him and hear his advice. Maybe he would have been able to undo the tangle in my mind, in my emotions, and see a clear path.

"Marry her," he had said so many times. He was in love with her, probably as much as I was. Damn, how I wished I had told him I'd already married her.

And I was now losing her.

I was avoiding her, and as consequence, pushing her away. Who knew what was going on in her mind? What she had decided?

Holy shit, what if she had accepted the offer from the club in Florida?

A painful pang cut through my heart.

I reached for my phone, thinking about calling her. But I stopped myself. No, I wouldn't call her. I would go home. I was still upset, I was still pissed and hurt and many other things, but I had to talk to her. I had to tell her I didn't want her to go to Florida. Not without me. And I had to do all that face-to-face.

I checked on the dogs and cats, and called the intern who should be arriving for the night shift in a few minutes. He said he was on his way, so I picked up my things and waited for him to arrive in the parking lot. Once he parked his car and greeted me, I drove home.

To my surprise, Gabi's SUV wasn't in its parking space.

I raced to the apartment and unlocked the door. It was dark inside.

I switched the lights on. "Gabi?" I called, already knowing she wasn't here, but hoping she was.

I went to her—our—bedroom, pushed the door open, and turned the light on.

And gasped. Her things—her hairbrush, her phone's charger, her portraits—were all gone. Even her closet was open and the clothes were gone.

My heart dropped.

On the bed, I saw a stack of papers and, on top, a note.

With trembling hands, I picked it up.

Tyler

I'M REALLY sorry for everything I've done to upset you. Know that it was never my intention.

Though I'm breaking this deal off, you'll find the check with the rest of the money to pay your debts. Think of it as my gift to your father. He would like to see his son free of any bills and enjoying life.

You're a good man and deserve the best.

The divorce papers are under the note.

TAKE CARE,

Gabi

I DROPPED the note as if it had burned me.

Breaking the deal? Divorce papers? What the hell?

My hands still shook as I grabbed my phone and called her. It went to the voice mail. I tried again and again, and every time the voice mail greeted me. Her phone was turned off.

I paced the room and ran a hand through my hair, thinking about what I could do, what I should do. Where could she be? Who should I call?

I called Garrett.

The phone rang once, then the call was turned off. What the hell?

I was about to call him again when I got a text from him.

Garrett: *I'm in class. Will call later.*

Damn it.

All right. Where could she be? There was only one obvious place. Her brother's apartment. I almost called Gui, but decided he was probably still pissed at me for marrying his little sister behind his back, so I drove there. He wouldn't slam the door on my face, would he?

Thankfully, the doorman already knew me, so he didn't even announce my arrival to the Fernandeses. I rang the doorbell and Pedro opened the door for me, surprise all over his expression.

"Hm, Tyler, *oi.*"

"Where's Gabi?" I asked, pushing my way inside the apartment.

Gui, who was at the kitchen getting a drink, put his glass down and glared at me. "What are you doing here?"

I held my chin high. "I'm here looking for my wife."

"Wife," Gui hissed. "Your wife? You left her alone for five days. You didn't even return her calls. Where the hell were you?"

"Gui, I don't want to argue with you, okay? Not now. Just let me talk to Gabi." I walked toward the hallway leading to the bedrooms.

Gui stepped in my way, his hands clenched into tight fists. "Gabi is gone."

That didn't process. "What?"

"I came back from the airport an hour ago. She's already flying over Nevada or Texas or whatever, on her way to Brazil."

My knees weakened. "W-what? No."

"Why do you care? From what I understand, she gave you all the money you needed to pay your debts. Even though she's walking away from this without anything but hurt."

I grabbed the check from my pocket, lifted it in between us, and ripped it in several pieces. "I don't care about the money. I care about her." The pieces fell on the floor as Gui watched with wide eyes. "I *love* her." I took a deep breath, trying to calm down my racing, hurt heart. "I just lost my father and I was so scared of losing her too. I was hurt and didn't handle this situation well." I ran a hand through my hair, thinking. "But I'll fix this."

Gui crossed his arms, a frown in between his brows. "And how the hell are you going to do that?"

I glanced around, looking for a laptop. "I'm going to buy the first airplane ticket to Brazil and I'm going to bring my wife home."

58

GABI

ONE OF THE things that hurt the most was to see how happy my parents were when they picked me up at the airport the next morning. All I wanted to do was cry, but they kept talking about how it all would work out, and how I could finally go to college, and maybe someday run the ranch with my father.

It all just made me feel more broken.

This time, I had gotten home in time for lunch. Even Maria was happy to see me.

"*Desculpa*, but I'm not hungry," I said, retreating to my bedroom.

I lay down on my bed and tried to sleep. Despite the exhaustion from the trip and all the emotional problems from the last three days, I couldn't close my eyes. My mind kept reliving everything, trying to think of what I could have done differently, what should I have done, but in the end I concluded my only error was to have come up with this deal in the first place. I should have stayed in Brazil and gone to college and let go of everything else.

A couple hours later, my mother came to check on me. She brought me some cake and *mate*, but I pretended I was asleep. At night, I went down for dinner, but only answered the essentials. When my parents started talking too much, I excused myself and went back to my bedroom.

Again, I barely slept all night. To be honest, I had barely slept since the last time I slept in Tyler's arms six nights ago.

I waited until it was past nine—when I knew my father went off to manage the ranch—to come down and have breakfast.

"*Eu fiz o seu preferido*," Maria said in Portuguese, showing me a plate of one of my favorite dishes—*nhoque de batata*, or potato gnocchi.

I tried to smile, but I was sure it looked more like a grimace. "*Obrigada*, but I'm not hungry," I told her in Portuguese. I made myself a black coffee and went out to the back porch. I sat on a bench and looked out at the stables.

My mother showed up from inside the house. "There you are. I thought I was going to have to drag you off your bed."

"No need for such drastic measures."

She sat down beside me. "I'm worried about you, honey. You don't look well. Want to talk about it?"

I shook my head. "No, I'm fine. I'll be fine. Just ... give me some space and I'll be fine."

She patted my knee. "Just know that I'm here, okay? If you need to talk. No judgment, no motherly advice ... just talk, like two friends."

"Thanks."

She patted my knee again and then went back inside the house.

I stared at the stable in the distance. I should go see Tostado. I missed him and I had to tell him that soon Branca would be coming and she would be keeping him company. I hoped they became good friends.

Speaking of friends, I should probably talk to Pri, let her know I was back. She would probably want to come over, but hopefully she had classes all day. We could schedule something for the weekend—it would give me more time to stop moping.

Me: *I'm back.*

Pri: Oi, guria. *What do you mean?*

Me: *I'm at the ranch with my parents.*

Pri: O quê? *Why?*

Me: *Long story.*

Pri: I'm gonna skip classes. Be there in a couple of hours.

Me: Não, *Pri. Go to your classes. I need time to think. Come over this weekend.*

Pri: *Are you sure?*

Me: *I'm sure.*

Pri: *If you need anything, I'm here, okay?*

Me: *Obrigada.*

I smiled at the phone. Hopefully, I would be feeling a little better during the weekend and Pri was sure to make me feel even better.

With a sigh, I stood and went back to my bedroom. I took a long, warm bath in my big bathtub—I probably soaked in there for almost an hour. Then, I got out and blew my hair dry. It was getting colder here and if I went out with damp hair, I would get a cold in no time. Since I would go out later, I put on jeans, a long sleeved tee and a thin cardigan, and cowboy boots.

Then, I unpacked my bags—the ones I was able to bring. I had left a couple at Gui's apartment. Some other time he would bring it or send it to me.

I wasn't looking forward to it, but my clothes wouldn't go back into my closet by themselves. And the sooner everything was in its right place, the better it would be. Though, the last piece of clothing stared at me from the end of my last suitcase. I let out a long breath and, with shaking hands, picked it up. I unzipped the cover and peeked under. My pretty wedding dress, the one that for some inexplicable reason, I had bought. The one that now held too many memories I wanted to forget. I gently placed it in the back of my closet, where it was mostly hidden by my thick coats and jackets.

At noon, my mother called me for lunch. Thankfully, my father was at a business meeting and couldn't be with us. Fine by me. I loved him, but right now, I needed to avoid his criticism.

"Any plans for the afternoon?" my mother asked as we took the plates back to the kitchen. Maria shot me a glare, telling me she could do that, but I ignored her and continued helping.

"Not really. Just to spend some time with Tostado."

"That's good, honey." She smiled at me. "Come back for a snack by three, please. Maria made another one of your favorites."

I rolled my eyes. If I didn't go back to working out soon, Maria would fatten me up really quick.

I waved them bye and left for the stables.

Tostado was in his stall. Joaquim, a stable boy, was opening his stall, a brush in his hand.

"Gabi," he said, surprised.

In Portuguese, I told him to give me the brush and go do some other chore. He seemed glad to do so.

"Hey, pretty boy," I said, entering Tostado's stall. He neighed and met me halfway, pressing his muzzle on my side. I chuckled and embraced him. "I missed you too." I dropped my head over him and sighed. "How about I brush you really good, then we go for a slow ride? Just to get the rust off my bones, hm?"

He snorted, as if saying yes, and I chuckled again. Only horses could make me smile and feel better when in truth all I wanted was to crawl in my bed, curl into myself, and cry.

In the tack room, I grabbed reins, a saddle, a thick blanket, and stirrups. I was placing everything carefully over Tostado's stall wall when I heard.

"*Oi.*"

With a gasp, I dropped the saddle on the ground. I turned toward the voice. "Mateus. What are you doing here?"

"I came to see you."

"But how ..." I stopped myself. I knew how. "Pri told you."

"Not her exactly. She told Adriana, who told Jorge, who told me."

I groaned on the inside and picked up the saddle. "Don't you have classes too?"

"I do, but I thought seeing you was more important than my classes."

Too cheesy. "Mateus, I appreciate the visit, but I'm not really in the mood to talk."

"Then I won't talk. We can just go for a quiet ride." He smiled at me. "It has been a long time since we rode together, huh?"

I did all I could not to glare at him. "I really don't want to be rude, but I want you to leave, Mateus."

He took three steps toward me. My instinct told me to retreat but I held my ground. "*Por favor*, Gabi, give me a chance. Even if it's only to be your friend for now." He reached for my hand. "I miss you."

"I can't believe what I'm seeing."

The new voice in stables made me freeze. For about two seconds. Then, my heart kicked into overdrive and I glanced over Mateus' shoulder, to the open gates, where Tyler stood.

"Tyler," I whispered in awe. *Meu Deus*, it was Tyler. He was here. In Brazil, at my family's stable. I rushed to him, but stopped after four steps, too afraid of getting burned again. "You're here."

He glared from Mateus to me. "Yeah, but I'm starting to regret it."

59

I HAD COME with one small duffel bag and my passport. Nothing else. At the airport, I rented a car and followed the GPS directions to the Fernandeses ranch.

With a look of surprise, Regina received me at the house's front porch and then told me Gabi was in the stable. She told me which path to follow to get there and I practically ran all the way.

Just to find Mateus and Gabi together.

I narrowed my eyes at the punk making a pass at my wife. "Yeah, but I'm starting to regret it."

Gabi stared at me, dumbfounded. "What?"

"So, what is this? We didn't even break up properly and you're already with this guy?"

"No, it's not—"

"There's nothing for you here, pal," Mateus said, interrupting Gabi. "Go back to the hole you came from."

Shit. My anger escalated and I gritted my teeth. It was the only thing I could do not to jump on the punk and land my fist on his pampered face.

"Mateus, stop it," Gabi said.

"If she wanted something with you, she wouldn't have left. But she's here now and I'm here now." The guy placed his arm around Gabi's shoulders and she stepped to the side.

"Stop it," she repeated.

He turned to her. "But Gabi, you did come back for me." He grabbed her wrists and she jerked back, but he didn't let go. "You know we belong together."

Oh, that was it. Red covered my eyesight. I lunged for the punk. He saw me coming and finally let go of Gabi.

"No!" she yelled right before I clipped his face and landed a pretty nasty punch on his cheek.

He stumbled back and whimpered, his hand over his face.

My fingers hurt, but I welcomed the pain. It grounded me.

"What the hell, Tyler?" Gabi asked, her eyes wide.

Shit.

I had tried to defend her and ended up acting like an ape.

Gabi turned to Mateus. "Are you okay?"

And now she would take care of him.

Damn it.

I just couldn't win.

Defeated and feeling like my anger would explode out of me at any moment, I marched out of the stable. I was halfway back to the rental car when I heard footsteps and then her voice.

"Tyler, wait." Like she had done the other day, she planted herself in my way, forcing me to stop.

"Not now," I growled.

She put my hands on my waist. "Not now? You came all the way from the U.S., took three flights to get here, and now you're telling me no? The hell with it. We're gonna talk. Right now."

"Not sure right now is a good time." I huffed, my hands closed in fists.

"Talk to me. That's the only thing you need to do." Her face … her expression … I couldn't read it. It was a mix of surprise and happiness and hope. But that was probably my hope and anger talking. Slowly, she reached for me. "I can't believe you're here."

The image of her staying behind to check on Mateus filled my mind and I took a step back. "I'm an idiot. I thought …" I shook my head. "I should have known he would be waiting for you. And now you probably think even worse of me for hitting him."

"I'm certainly surprised by that punch, but I'm even more surprised that you came to Brazil." One corner of her lips tugged up. "And, the only explanation I can come up with is that you came because of me."

I shrugged. "Yeah, and then I caught you with him."

She glared at me. "Stop being an idiot. He found out I was here and came alone. I didn't invite him here and I didn't want him here. And I just told him to get the hell out of this place."

I didn't know what to say to that. Again, my chest was a tangle of emotions I didn't know how to deal with. I thought … I thought I just had to come here, tell her I loved her, and ask her to come back home with me.

But then I saw that jerk with her and … ugh, the anger was still strong.

I took a long breath, trying to expel the anger from my system. "I was hurt," I started. We needed to clear the air from our previous argument before starting another. "I had just lost my father and I suddenly realized my new biggest fear was losing you. And then I learned about Florida and I realized I really could lose you. At any moment. After all, you had gone to the U.S. to play polo, not to find a husband. And one day, you would walk away and go play polo. Maybe it would be tomorrow, maybe it would be once the two years were up, I didn't know. I just knew that the fear of losing you was too great and I let it take over me. I kept myself away before you pushed me away. But I wasn't handling the situation right. I was just avoiding it."

"I should have told you the moment I got the offer," she said. "I should have told you about it and also told you I wasn't going to accept it."

"I know, you couldn't accept it because you would lose your green card."

"No, you idiot. I wasn't going to accept it because I knew you wouldn't come with me and I didn't want to leave you. It was you, Tyler. I didn't want to go because of *you*."

I stared at her. I really stared at her. At the beautiful woman in front of me. At the girl who had stolen my heart without even trying. At the girl who had left because she thought it was the best for me. At the girl who gave up on our deal, but wanted to pay all my debts anyway. At the girl who was the most kind, the gentlest, the most deserving woman I had met. At the wife I loved more than anything in the entire world.

"Yeah, I'm an idiot," I said. She chuckled. "But this idiot knows what he wants and he wants his wife back."

She took a step closer and cupped my face with her hand. "I love you, you idiot. And I'm so happy you came for me." Her eyes filled with tears.

I wrapped my arms around her waist and pulled her to me. Looking into her eyes, I said, "I love you too."

Then I kissed her.

I molded my mouth to hers, moving my lips in a desperate way, trying to show her how much I needed her, how much I wanted her, how much she meant to me.

I was breathless when I finally pulled back and said, "I love you and I would do anything for you. If you want to move to Florida to play polo, let's do it. I bet they have plenty of vet clinics and vet schools around there."

Her smile was the most beautiful thing. It lit up her entire face and made me want to kiss her away. "We can talk more about it later, but I just want to let you know that I love you for considering it."

Then, she pressed her lips on mine and I forgot about the rest of the world.

SIX MONTHS LATER
GABI

I ROLLED MY SHOULDERS, the nerves getting to me.

"Relax," Kelsey said from my side.

I glanced at her and scoffed. "Look who is talking." Her entire body was visibly tense.

She offered me a shy smile. "Well, when the captain is nervous, I get nervous too, so relax, and I'll relax too."

I rolled my eyes at her.

My eyes on the field in front of us, I caught my foot on my hand and stretched my quad. I tried focusing on the empty field, but I couldn't help noticing the crowd around it.

It seemed *everyone* was here. Across the field, I could see Tyler standing with Gui, Leo, Ri, Pedro, *tio* João Pedro, and my father. To the side, Bia, Hannah, Hil, *tia* Agnes, and my mother were seated and chatting. Even Priscila was here—she had come with my parents to see me.

To see my first official game as the captain of the newly formed team, New Reign, the first all-women team of the Santa Barbara club. We had chosen this name because we were women, delicate and strong, just like a rose and its thorns. It was appropriate.

After Tyler and I had made up in Brazil, we had come back and moved to Florida so I could accept the offer from the club there. In the end, Melissa had moved there too and we started playing together.

During our first tournament in Europe, we met Caroline, who was an American living in London. She was from California and had made it clear she would love to come back to the U.S. someday.

It didn't take long for my team to win several tournaments and gather the attention of not only the Santa Barbara club, but several others. We ended up receiving about six offers in total. Plus the counteroffer of the Florida club, who didn't want to lose Melissa and me.

The offer from the Santa Barbara club hadn't been the best, but it was where Melissa and I wanted to move. And it was where Kelsey was living, and where Caroline wanted to be.

So we formed a new team and accepted the offer.

Then Tyler and I moved back to Santa Barbara.

I glanced at him across the field. As if feeling it, he looked at me, his eyes locked on mine. Even from here, the intensity of his gaze scorched my skin.

"They're at it again," Melissa said from somewhere behind me. She was checking on the horses again, as she did three hundred times before any game.

"I know, I can see," Caroline said from my left. She was stretching too.

I groaned. "Can you guys stop?"

"You have to stop," Melissa said with a laugh. "Every time he comes to watch our practice, it's almost like you guys are undressing each other with your eyes. You don't need that right before an important game!" she teased.

Warmth spread over my cheeks. She was right, though. Tyler's gaze was intense, and our passion hadn't lessened yet, even after almost six months together, and I didn't think it would, even if we spent another six, sixteen, or sixty years together.

After the outburst at my brother's apartment, and everyone finding out we were already married, we came clean with the rest of the family. As expected, my father and mother didn't take it well at first. I didn't think they accepted it fully yet, but Tyler and I would prove to them that we were meant to be.

That he made me happy and I made him happy.

Even though we were six months into our marriage, my green card had been finally issued, and I had paid all of his debt. He had complained, saying that wasn't the agreement, but I reminded him we were married for real now, so the deal didn't matter anymore.

I knew the topic of money bothered him a little—the effects of having so little and struggling for so long. But we were a couple now. My money was his money, end of story.

Though, he had insisted on working, even if part time, so he could pay for tuition and finish vet school. Garrett, Bia, and he talked about opening a vet clinic specializing in horses—including physical therapy. And if the horses needed some help with their psychological side, they would call on Hannah and Leo.

It was actually pretty amazing and I truly hoped it worked out for them.

Across the field, Tyler said something to the guys, then stepped away from them. I followed him with my eyes and when he turned a left at the corner of the field, I realized he was coming this way.

"Oh, here he comes," Kelsey teased. "I knew this would happen someday. He'll come, push you down to the ground, and you'll have sex right here." She gestured to the grass in between us. "In front of everyone."

I scrunched my nose. "Just shut up."

The other girls laughed, but they retreated a few steps when Tyler approached us. He had already greeted them earlier, but he waved at them again. Turning to me, he stepped right into my personal space and placed a heavy hand on my waist.

"Are you okay?" he asked, his hazel eyes locked on mine.

"*Sim, porquê?*"

"I don't know." He ran his other hand through his hair. "I guess I would be really nervous right now, so I wanted to check on you."

"I am nervous, but I'm also excited." I smiled at him. "This is all I ever wanted. I'm here in the United States with my family. I'm playing polo with the best team in the world, and I even got a bonus out of all that."

He cocked one eyebrow. "Oh, and what is that?" The curve of his lips told me he knew exactly what I was talking about.

I rose on tiptoes and whispered, "You, silly." I pressed my lips on his. I began lowering the balls of my feet, but he wrapped his arms around my waist and pulled me to him. He pressed his mouth to mine again and moved his lips with such softness that took my breath away.

He pulled just one inch back and look into my eyes. "No, I'm the one who got all the bonuses." He squeezed me a little more. "Go out there and show them what you're made of."

"That's what I'm planning."

He gave me another peck. "I love you."

"I love you too," I said, before kissing him again.

Around us, the girls groaned.

"Get a room," one of them whispered, probably so the rest of the club wouldn't hear it.

Tyler and I chuckled. He dropped his arms from around me, stepped back, kissed my hand, and turned to go back to the other side of the field. And I stared at him, wondering how the hell I got so lucky.

It didn't matter how I became so lucky, what mattered was that I would do all I could to keep things the way they were.

I grabbed my helmet from my bag and turned to the girls. "Let's go kick some ass!"

They cheered and I smiled, never feeling happier in my entire life.

THANK YOU

THANK you for reading *Breaking Down*!

Reviews are very important for authors. If you liked my book, please consider leaving a review on your favorite online retailer and/or on goodreads, please!

DID YOU LIKE THIS BOOK, then check my other books here: http://www.julianahaygert.com/books/

DON'T FORGET to sign up for my Newsletter to find out about new releases, cover reveals, giveaways, and more!

If you want to see exclusive teasers, help me decide on covers, read excerpts, talk about books, etc, join my reader group on Facebook: Juliana's Club!

ABOUT THE AUTHOR

While USA Today Bestselling Author Juliana Haygert dreams of being Wonder Woman, Buffy, or a blood elf shadow priest, she settles for the less exciting—but equally gratifying—life as a wife, a mother, and an author. She resides in North Carolina and spends her days writing about kick-ass heroines and the heroes who drive them crazy.

Subscribe to her mailing list to receive emails of announcement, events, and other fun stuff related to her writing and her books: www.bit.ly/JuHNL

For more information:
www.julianahaygert.com

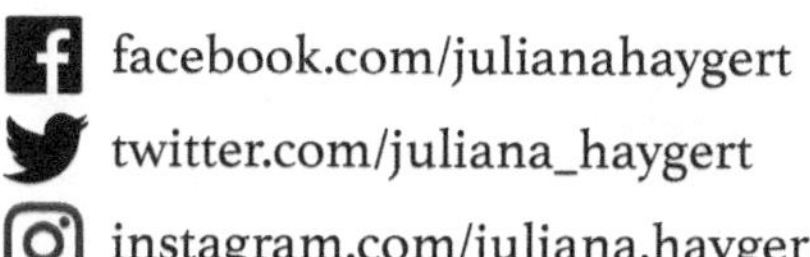

ALSO BY JULIANA HAYGERT

To find links and more info, go to:

www.julianahaygert.com/books/

Shorts

Into the Darkest Fire

Tested

Rite World: Blackthorn Hunters Academy

The Demon Kiss (Book 1)

The Hunter Secret (Book 2)

The Soul Bond (Book 3)

The Shadow Trials (Book 4)

The Infernal Curse (Book 5)

Rite World

The Vampire Heir (Book 1)

The Witch Queen (Book 2)

The Immortal Vow (Book 3)

The Warlock Lord (Book 4)

The Wolf Consort (Book 5)

The Crystal Rose (Book 6)

The Wolf Forsaken (Book 7)

The Fae Bound (Book 8)

The Blood Pact (Book 9)

The Wyth Courts

Winter King (Book 1)

Spring Warrior (Book 2)

Summer Prince (Book 3)

The Fire Heart Chronicles

Heart Seeker (Book 1)

Flame Caster (Book 2)

Sorrow Bringer (Book 3)

Earth Shaker (Novella)

Soul Wanderer (Book 4)

Fate Summoner (Book 5)

War Maiden (Book 6)

The Everlast Series

Destiny Gift (Book 1)

Soul Oath (Book 2)

Cup of Life (Book 3)

Everlasting Circle (Book 4)

Willow Harbor Series

Hunter's Revenge (Book 3)

Siren's Song (Book 5)

Breaking Series

Breaking Free (Book 1)

Breaking Away (Book 2)

Breaking Through (Book 3)

Breaking Down (Book 4)

<u>*Standalones*</u>

Daughter of Darkness